A Step into Darkscape

The Assassin Princess Novels, Volume 2

Blake Rivers

Published by AIL - An Infinite Legacy, 2023.

A STEP INTO DARKSCAPE

First edition. September 7, 2023.

Copyright © 2023 Blake Rivers.

ISBN: 979-8223149828

Written by Blake Rivers.

For Emi, always for you x

Part One: Darkscape

*the old man's yellowed eyes lingered for a moment before turning back to the game,
his dark weathered brow furrowing.
the chequered board was set, the gold and silver pieces in play.*

Chapter One

Ami looked up from the page and out to a sky scored with lines of orange and yellow, where a dying sun danced behind buildings, towers and trees, throwing shadows like warriors against the windows. The gentle *shookedy-shook* of the wheels on the tracks made a sleepy sound through the car, allowing Ami to work in a lucid state beneath a din of crying children and scorning mothers, her pencil sketching her thoughts, dreams and memories into characters and scenes; a rough draft of a graphic novel yet to be born.

Her eyes passed over the page, yet in her head a war was being fought in a darkened wood with swords, light and magic; creatures of the night, men of the day, heroes and villains on each and every side.

Time passed.

Yet as each stop came and went, as passengers took their seats and rose to leave, Ami continued to work, lost in memory and fantasy.

It'd been a lonely trip so far, but if she'd have stayed in the city—alone with her thoughts—there would have been only the one tumbling through them.

Hero. Her beloved Hero.

But then she'd found the advert. It'd been hidden in the back of a magazine she'd found lying on a park bench, squeezed between an article on breast feeding and a jumble of celebrity pictures. She'd almost missed it amongst the garish colours and distasteful comments—but there it was: a small quarter in black and white with an image of an old house off to the side.

Ami had put down her Chai Latte and read the sparse words over.

Need to get away? City getting you down? Need to work on that novel?
CURRINGTON HOUSE
Country Getaway

SHE'D STARED AT THE advert, envisioning the buildings around her being swept away into the distance, leaving only the green of nature's original plan.

A few days later and Ami was on a train, heading for the deep middle of nowhere, fully aware that she was running away from herself, running away from Hero, running away from life.

It'd been six months since she'd found she had powers that her peers would never have, that she belonged truly to a world a veil beyond her own, and that magic existed, both light and dark.

Ami had experienced them both, and her adventures in Legacy had left her heart and mind troubled, especially when her heart continued to yearn for her hooded, mysterious man.

Hero had been a revelation, an Indian summer when there should've been only fall, an ending to an ordeal that gave her hope and a little light when dealing with the dark. But what future was there for them? She a princess with powers beyond anyone's understanding—especially her own—and he, a Guard of the land of Legacy, with responsibilities to their kingdom? But even more than that, their feelings were a distraction to the normality of life she had to return to.

She couldn't keep living in two worlds. She had to choose.

After leaving him, Ami had wandered alone in the Solancra Forest, the tangled and magical realm of the unicorns, and there sought out the one who'd helped them all so much, who'd sacrificed and lost so much.

As it turned out, Talos found her instead, appearing one night from the shadows as she took respite within a copse of trees. She greeted him with a hug, burying her face into his mane, the stump where his horn had once been pulsing in a gentle white light as he nuzzled against her.

Ami had stayed with him for a few days after that, strolling through the glades with him in conversation, laying down upon the meadow to watch the little ones prance, dance and play beneath the blessed sun; and in those dusky evenings, Talos had taken it upon himself to teach her a little of the power she possessed. Mostly she'd just watched in awe as he showed her secrets and trained her to harness the power. She'd been especially fascinated by the ability to change one's body into a pure ghostly form, to pass easily through walls and trees.

"You can change and you can focus, defy most natural laws," he'd told her. "You can be all, be anything, be power, be pure."

She'd tried to follow his examples, but in the end had not quite gotten the hang of it, and with her heart heavy with Hero, her confidence had failed her.

If she were truly honest with herself, the power scared her, and when she'd eventually left, saying goodbye to the unicorns and the memory of Legacy, and had returned to life as she'd once known it, she found that the simple was now much more complicated; that being *normal* was so very difficult. For now she *knew*. She *knew* she was powerful and could do magical things with her hands and her mind, but she had to resist or else risk being caught—the burden and consequences were severe. So much had happened in such a small amount of time; her world had been ripped apart and remade. She'd killed, had almost been killed, had been used by and infected with the darkest of magic, reborn again to win the day ... but at a price.

She looked back out of the window now as the train began to slow, the last of the towns gone, green shadows where there'd once been life. Hills crested and rolled away, bringing memories of the Planrus Lands, of the mountains of Edorus.

A long, low platform appeared, empty and dead, a sign coming too quickly, the second slower, the third stopping at her window. Currington.

She gathered her papers and pushed them into her bag, giving only a casual glance at the scrawl she'd scribbled.

THE DOORS UNLOCKED with a click.

THE TRAIN LEFT THE station at an almost hurried pace and Ami was left standing alone, the only passenger to have departed. All was silent. A dog barked once from far away and a breeze lifted across her skin, but there were no lights but for the misted moon, and no sign of life.

Walking to the end of the platform, Ami descended the concrete steps to the gravel path below.

From memory, she knew roughly where to go—a mile east along a stretch of road that would take her past a single farm, and then, a little further along, down a sloping driveway to the large, old country estate.

Cheap and picturesque, she was to rent one of the cabins at the back of the property. It was perfect and just the isolation she needed.

Here she was truly out in the sticks, and with nothing but those sticks she would build a life, a wondrous and *normal* life.

Up above, the black clouds cupped the moon, the silver light weeping onto the fields in tears, running in streams and shadow. Before Legacy she'd have been terrified of a night such as this and would never have made the journey, but she was no longer the same Ami. She was the Assassin Princess, Princess of Legacy. She could take her pencil from her pocket and command it to transform into the sword of her forebears, a magical unicorn horn made steel ... She was no longer afraid of the dark.

After a while she reached the farmhouse on her left, set far back from the road. It was surrounded by a multitude of hulking metal machines, silent monsters, skeletons of tractors, diggers—a harvester perhaps—that peered out from the undergrowth; and up ahead, where the land sloped, was a cluster of trees and a gate that barred her entry. A small post was stabbed into the ground a few feet in, leaning over into a nest of brambles. Currington House.

Ami wrapped her hands through the rusted bars and pushed, the gate opening with a screech and a whine. The hinges were old and hardly ever used, and when she pushed it back into place, it gave an old groan that sounded almost grateful and relieved. She walked on, eying the shadows and following the sloped driveway round to the right, the house itself coming suddenly into frame. A looming block of black, its many windows looked like closed eyes in a dark face, lifeless and empty, its short wings stumps where perhaps arms were meant to be.

The driveway straightened and narrowed into a grass path that led across the front of the house where an old wooden porch fronted the building. A single lamp hung naked above, rocking soundlessly from side to side.

"Who goes there?" a voice called from behind the lamp. It was shrill and cracked, and made Ami jump out of her skin.

A long stick rose in silhouette and pointed.

Ami reached for her pencil, but stopped as the stick hit the light and lowered a shade, the glare lessening, revealing the outline of a frail figure, a woman, seated in a rocker. A blanket was pulled over her shoulders against the chill, her face all wrinkles and bristles, her eyes deep empty tunnels.

"I said who goes there?" she snapped.

"Hi," Ami said, turning fully to the porch. "I'm a little later than expected but—"

"Expected? Who expected you?" The woman shuffled forward, her dress crepe paper thin. "Why are you here?" The stick tapped loud on the wooden floor.

"I'm Ami Rose? I was meant to—"

"Ah," the old woman sighed and shuffled back into the rocker. "You shouldn't be out this late, Miss Rose. My brother is asleep now and nothing in heaven or on earth will wake him, so you go on back around the house. Cabin thirteen will be yours and it will be open. You just go back there and he'll take your details in the morning." *She's blind,* Ami thought as she watched her mouth pucker, the wrinkles around her lips stretching and collapsing over her ruined gums. "You can call me Grammy if you want, though we ain't kin."

The old woman began to rock then—*shookedy-shook, shookedy-shook*—and raised her stick to knock the shade back up. Ami squinted as the light hit her. The conversation was over. Giving her one last look, feeling more than a little spooked, Ami strode away, rounding the dark house to a path that led her through a cluster of low wooden cabins, each numbered, though in no particular order.

Ami found thirteen hiding in the far corner, the windows dark and the door ajar, and once inside she wasted no time in looking around her new digs.

The living space was cosy, with a small kitchen off in one corner, a separate bathroom and bedroom, all fully stocked for her needs. The bed looked warm, and putting her bag upon the floor, Ami decided that perhaps she would try it out first before anything else.

She pulled off her clothes and slipped beneath the duvet, falling asleep within minutes.

SHE DREAMED OF LEGACY, of stepping into the castle and standing at the foot of a table. Seated at the head of it was her Hero. He beckoned her over, smiling as he did. She came, her steps slow, graceful, her white dress billowing freely around her.

"Another one!" Hero shouted.

"Benjamin, calm down."

"Another one—another two!"

"Benjamin, you know I can't keep up with you when you behave so."

Ami opened her eyes and stared at the blank wooden wall. The voices were close and unknown, and for a moment she couldn't possibly imagine what was going on, or where she was. These were not the walls of her bedroom, or voices she knew.

"We can't go on like this. We just can't," the man's voice broke.

"I know, I know, but what can we do?"

Ami shuffled across the bed and dropped to her feet, grabbing her bag and fumbling around for a fresh set of clothes. Listening still, she made her way into the bathroom and soon emerged dressed and curious.

The voices were coming from just outside, and slipping her pencil into her jeans, Ami opened the door.

It was early morning and the world outside seemed too bright and fresh, the lush green grass bearing the weight of a misty dew, while in the skies and the nearby wood, birds trilled and chirped, heralding in the miracle of a new day.

An old couple stood but a few yards away examining a cabin close to her own. She recognised Grammy from the night before, skinny and sharp in grey, her stick gripped tight. Her blind eyes seemed to locate her easily, and placing her hand on the old man, she turned him to face her.

"We have one guest left," Grammy crooned. "I forgot to say."

The man turned to her, a salesman's smile brightening his features from coronary to only weather-worn. He sauntered over, his hand held out.

"Hello. I'm sorry, we must have woken you. I'm Ben Manning, owner of Currington House."

Ami stepped from the doorway with a smile. "Ami Rose." She shook his hand, firm and sure. *A man's grip,* her father would have said, *never leave it sloppy. Untrustworthy.* "Everything okay?"

"Oh, sure, just some wayward guests, a moonlight flit or some other darn thing. Left their dog though, poor thing."

"It'll be okay," Grammy said from far away.

"It's okay for you," he snapped, looking back at her. "You can't see a damned thing!" He turned back to Ami, his smile returning. "I hope you enjoy your stay here, and please, do pay up before you leave. It would be appreciated."

She could think of nothing else to say, and so nodded, leaving the man to walk away, leading the old woman by the arm.

Shaking her head, Ami took a moment to look around, seeing the place for the first time in daylight.

It was so very beautiful.

The old house stood a silent sentry to her left—handsome, if not a little ragged—while opposite, up a slight slope, was a thick wood where trees swayed gently, leaves rustling in the breeze. Someway beyond the cabins there were green and yellow fields stretching for many miles without a grey building in sight.

She took a deep breath, inhaling each flowering scent and earthy smell, before ducking back inside and closing the door.

AMI CLEARED THE BUREAU, smoothing her hands over the wood, and lay her papers down. With her sketchbook open she sat back in the chair to draw, and within no time at all had created two new characters, both elderly and one blind; she would give them powers to see through time, or … something. She'd work it out later.

Soon sketched lines became faces in graphite strokes and scenes were taking shape before her, but as time went on she found herself looking out of the window and into the thick woodland more and more. It was a muse for her creativity and a temptation she was finding hard to fight, the lure of adventure tick-tocking away with the wane of the day, the sun of early morning already too low in the sky. *Had she been working for that long?* The dark greens of the clustered leaves shimmered gold as if on fire, moving constantly above shadowed trunks. Power tingled at the back of her neck.

Dangerous.

Is something out there?

She ignored the feeling as best she could, but her eyes strayed back to the window regardless, only to see—framed perfectly by the centre pane—a small dog upon the grass, apparently looking directly at her. Its pink tongue was stuck out and lolled up and down, its brown and white patched body heaving with each pant.

"Cute doggy," she murmured. It barked at her, its eyes never leaving her. Sighing, she finally gave in.

Well, all work and no play, and all that.

Closing her sketchbook, she got up and left the cabin.

The air had grown so very warm, and the sky had turned a beautiful deep blue with only the smallest puffs of white cloud hanging magically above her like funny shaped ornaments, heavenly decorations. Gone were the cars and horns of the cities and towns; no chattering, tightly squeezed, busy people. Ami breathed it all in.

The dog watched her.

"Here boy," she called, looking around to see if the old couple were about, but she saw no one. "Come here, here boy." She put her hand out, but still no takers.

She took a few steps toward the animal.

He took a couple of steps back.

Ami took a few more steps, and the dog countered again.

"Oh, we're playing a game are we?" Ami looked around again, but she was alone. "I know a little thing that might get you moving." Lowering herself slowly to the ground she got on all fours and threw her arms out in front of her, the universal gesture of play. But it didn't work. Instead the patchwork pup turned tail and trotted off toward the wood. It stopped at the edge of a pathway that cut through the trees, barely seen except for a small green sign. *Public Footpath.*

Curious, Ami followed, first starting on all fours and then rising slowly to her feet. The dog looked back.

Is he wanting me to follow?

Dangerous.

She felt for the pencil she'd slipped into her pocket, gripping it.

The dog waited patiently until she'd caught up, the path before them a narrow dirt track that cut between the trees.

Memories of the Mortrus Lands filled her with an exhilarating fear, the deep, dark and mystical forest where both her natural and hidden powers had been put to the test, her very claim to her individuality challenged—but here at least, they were only trees, only woods.

The dog moved on, his small head swinging back constantly to check on her.

"It's okay," she said, "I'm coming, Pepper." She didn't know his name, but it seemed to fit, and he seemed happy with it, trotting a little faster.

A feeling of unease grew inside her though as they continued on, close knit trees becoming less dense, shadowed spaces becoming larger. It was a familiar feeling, all mixed up inside. She thought of her brother Adam's tainted voice touching her name as if a fractured crystal, precious but sharp ...

Dangerous.

But Adam was gone.

Sunlight broke behind branches and became a white fire behind shadow. It shifted and moved across the path, touching her booted feet with flickering fingers. Flowers bloomed here and there, and all the beauty she'd seen, heard and smelt intensified.

Butterflies swooped low, high, circled and darted; insects hovered and then disappeared above and below; all the while the small dog trotted on.

Ami's senses sharpened as he came to a dead stop in the middle of the track, as still and immovable as a stone.

She almost tripped over him.

Perhaps she'd been lured into the woods as a ruse so that an army of Jack Russells could pounce on her, attacking from each side of the track? Amusing, but unlikely. Suppressing the thought, she gripped the pencil and stepped past the small dog.

Immediately on her left, the woodland thinned to reveal a broken wooden shack. Desolate and clearly abandoned, it sat bleached and battered in the embrace of the many limbs that held it.

The dog growled and Ami followed his stare to the empty doorway that rose above a rickety porch, lifting and breathing with the breeze. There was a whisper in her mind that sharpened its tongue, and quite suddenly she knew that whatever this place was, it'd known *power*.

"What is it, boy, what do you sense?" But he wasn't talking. Ami bent down to him again, but he growled at her touch and urinated where he stood.

"This is too weird," she whispered, withdrawing the pencil and looking around. Alone. "I'm going in, Pep, you coming?" The dog stood immobile. The pencil shimmered a violet-jade and lengthened in her hand. The hilt and blade took shape, marbled and licked in green flame.

She brought it up to her face, looking at her reflection in the polished surface, the symbol for infinity clearly etched into the hilt.

The breeze lifted her hair and Ami listened for a time to the creaking of the branches, to the old wood of the shack lifting in their grasp. It sounded like voices, though light and far away.

Dangerous. Again.

Her palms filled with a fire that seeped beneath her skin as quickly as it'd arrived. It felt good.

Stepping forward into the long grass, Ami placed one foot upon the step and stared into the dark doorway.

Her second step creaked, the old wood beneath bending a little too far for comfort. She looked down to it, and from the corner of her eye caught the figure of a man on the porch, his arm raised—but when she looked up there was no one. The dog whimpered, yet had joined her, reluctantly recruited, and followed her as she climbed the remaining steps onto the porch.

A chill swept her body as if a winter wind beneath her clothes. It caressed her neck as she raised the sword higher, looking to her left where she'd seen the man. Nothing.

Eyes forward, she ventured on.

Inside, the shadows swallowed her and there was a musty smell like a neglected tree house, a place children played long ago, but not in a long, long while. The rooms to her left and right weren't fit for people, big or small; an animal, much like a squirrel, scurried across the floorboards and jumped to climb the branch of a protruding tree, disappearing.

The whole place creaked, almost swayed, anchored precariously as if in danger at any moment of launching into the sky. *Dorothy's house,* she thought. *Follow the yellow brick road.* An eerie chill solidified in her mind, and she knew beyond doubt then, that she wasn't alone ...

Pepper had gone quiet, and turning to look for him she saw the man again, as before, *definite* and *there.* He was old, very old, dark skinned with white hair just covering his scalp; perched on a chair that hadn't been there, he was bent over a small table on the porch. His arm was outstretched, his fingers clutching a small, golden chess piece.

Ami shook her head, but the man remained. He'd stopped in mid-move, his head cocked as if listening for something. Listening for her.

He knew she was there, too.

Dangerous.

Ami raised her sword, pivoting slowly on the spot to face the door once more—but then he was gone. Simply wasn't there, as if he'd never been.

A growl of uncertainty came from the pup and he ran from the house and back out into the sunlight. Wary but curious, Ami turned back into the shack, feeling *Dangerous. Dangerous,* yes, her Shadow Princess left deep within the Mortrus Lands. Forever there, forever with her.

Her sword burst into coloured light, chasing the shadows.

Ahead of her was a staircase, stunted and broken, and from the light of her blade she could see the fallen balusters, coloured a pale blue, preserved in the gloom. But there was something else, something reflecting within the rotted dust that would otherwise have been lost to darkness.

Checking the rooms to her left and right, Ami moved down toward it, keeping the blade raised, tilted toward the object. It was buried side on, and as her fingers stroked downward, brushing the debris aside, it revealed a shape she'd seen only moments ago. The gold glinted, looking gothic and sinister, flickering purple and green and gold.

Pepper barked, but Ami ignored him, her eyes fixed upon the chess piece, a rook, the tiny battlements of the castle clear.

She touched it and the world suddenly spun out of control.

Tornado, she thought. *Auntie Em?*

But it wasn't a tornado, and in that fraction of a second she lost all sense of time and place—and then hit the floor, her sword falling from her hand.

Pepper barked furiously behind her, the noise thumping through her head.

"Pepper," she managed, "be quiet will you?"

The dog relented, resorting to an unsettled growl instead.

Ami pulled herself up and grabbed the sword, pointing it down at the piece; it hadn't moved, but it *had* moved *her.*

"What *are* you?" she whispered, studying it without touching it. She felt the presence again, the sense of another on the decrepit porch behind her, but she ignored it, pointing the sharp tip of her sword at the golden rook. They touched.

A flash of white light spun her, spun the shack, spun the world, landing her back on the floor in a daze.

"Shit," she murmured, stunned and sluggish. "What *is* that?"

She wasted no more time in getting to her feet, but instead held her sword tightly in one hand and snatched the rook up in the other.

The white light struck again behind her eyes, and the world spun as the cool metal dug into her palm, her blade bursting into green and white flame. She felt sick, but was determined to hold on until the change fluttered to a steady roar, then a hum, a thrum that danced to the rhythm of the world around it; *but which world?* she wondered.

She opened her eyes to walls that were no longer wooden but stone, cold and grey with masoned steps rising up to the second floor, complete and solid. Her sword was still within her grasp as was the totem, and though it all looked *almost* the same, she was definitely somewhere else.

Through the narrow doorway Ami saw a slice of the outside world, where great rounded stones littered a grassy plot that was filled with flowers of reds and blues and purples and yellows, some winding up the trunk of a nearby tree, others shooting wild, drooping and hanging over a cliff edge. *The sea. I can smell it, hear it.* Beyond and to the ends of the earth was the blue-grey ocean, bringing to mind memories of lazy days at the beach, adventures at the coast, of fun and happiness ... Someone was coming.

Ami pulled herself to her feet as faint voices floated over the crash of waves from somewhere nearby. She couldn't be found here, but the rooms that lay open to each side of the hall were empty and held no place to hide.

"... waking him, I'm sure. But why?"

"It is not ours to question why. You know this."

Ami looked to the golden chess piece in her palm, and then back to the doorway where shadows now approached and overlapped, footsteps grinding dry mud and gravel. She turned and touched the rook instinctively down upon the first stone step, and in a sickening spin and a white flash of power, the walls around her morphed back into wood, the air becoming dry and hot, scented with green and growth. She fell to the ground, her empty stomach wanting to heave.

The dog barked out a warning and Ami jumped up, pivoting up on to her toes, stopping short of the blade trained on her heart.

Chapter Two

The sun had risen over the eastern hills, a sight that Hero had seen many times before, from the city walls, from turrets and towers, and now from the high up windows of Legacy's castle keep, the ancestral home of the Lord of Legacy that was now—temporarily—under his stewardship.

He brooded on the sight, thinking of all that his city had suffered over the years without a ruler, and how despite these woes, he'd seen true strength in his people as they rebuilt their homes and lives in the wake of disaster; each and every person held Princess Ami as a guiding light in their hearts.

But Ami had returned to her own layer, leaving the survivors of Adam's wrath ultimately on their own, and although it'd been agreed upon and accepted, Hero regretted letting her go so easily.

And now this.

A fear passed once more like a shiver through the land, plucking the skin of the weary, the war-torn, the ones who'd once fought each nightly riot and claimed to know death by sight, by smell. This tremor had travelled far across the mountains and through the Commune Valley, where traders and traffickers had brought warnings from the East. Then others had whispered of the stirrings up river, the strange happenings at the mouth of the Mortrus Lands, the mystical forest revealed as the origins of power.

What the disturbance was, was unclear. Some spoke of a fog that hung from the dense and blackened trees; others whispered of dark beasts, red eyes, and hidden rasping breaths. The ground was said to shake, to crack.

Hero meditated on these things long and hard, for rumour could damage, yet deliberate inaction could destroy. It was time for the Guard to find out the truth.

He turned his back on the view and eyed his lieutenants, Raven and Florence. They had fought beside him now in peace and war, each proving themselves capable and vital. They would be Legacy's envoys.

"We hold this land together on the promise that Ami will return as princess when she is needed, on the hope that with her we will always be strong. In her absence, we must find out all we can to keep us safe. Any disturbance from the Mortrus Lands is of concern, and so I ask that you, Florence, ride to the spring of the river and report back what you find. Your power and swift gallop shall come into its own should you need to flee quickly."

"Of course, Hero, I shall leave immediately." The girl gave a half bow and left the room.

"Raven, I have a special task for you." He stepped forward and placed his hand on his shoulder. "Set a fire and seek conference with the Shadow Princess. I believe the *stranger-girl* will answer our call should we need her. Perhaps she will know of these things. If Ami is needed, she will be able to call to her."

"But Hero, it would be better if you—"

"I'd like you to do it in my stead, Raven."

"Okay, anything." Raven nodded, turned and headed out of the room in Florence's wake.

It was of personal shame that Hero himself shunned this task, for who better to visit the Shadow Princess of Ami than he? Yet it felt necessary. With Lady Grace gone, the lands were his responsibility in Ami's absence; it would do no good to endanger his people should he be distracted ... but that of course was a truth wrapped in a lie, for the real reason was that his heart ached for Ami, but no matter how long he'd waited, and no matter her last words to him, she'd not returned. He was bruised, pure and simple.

"Oh, Ami," he breathed, and turned back to the window to watch the morning come.

RAVEN STEPPED OUT OF the stairwell onto the roof of the keep, his thoughts on Hero. For the life of him he couldn't understand why he avoided Ami, or even the shadow of her. There'd been affection there by the end, from both sides, but now he found that Hero mentioned Ami less and less, and his captain's mood had certainly darkened—not least due to the rumours of trouble to come that had unsettled them all.

Reaching out to Ami was the right thing to do. Raven could only hope that her double was substitute enough.

Pushing his thoughts aside, he strode to the edge of the castle walls, the battlements of grey rock and flint rough beneath his palms, and looked out over the landscape of the world. It was a breath-taking view, and he was now the highest point in all the lands. His eyes passed over each of them, far away yet easily definable. Planrus, the rolling green hills of the horizon, leading to the unicorn valley of Solancra; the mountains of Edorus; the sea beyond the southern Madorus Lands, and finally to the north, the Mortrus Lands.

Somewhere in the last was the Shadow Princess, the dark version of Ami, ripped from her within the deathly woods, forever to reside there, young and powerful, and seemingly all knowing. An oracle of sorts, the Shadow Princess knew everything Ami had ever known, had ever done, and everything she would soon do—her past, present and future. To reach her, he would kindle the fire that Hero would not.

He gathered the wood together—old crates, discarded pallets, all left to weather and rot—and built a pyre, a beacon he hoped she'd see from her lost realm in that magical place.

Tinderbox in hand, he set the wood alight.

It took only a few moments for the pile to blaze, and Raven sunk to his knees in front of it, closing his eyes, feeling the immense heat that threatened the hair upon his chin.

"Shadow Ami, from deep within the Mortrus Lands, I call to you," Raven whispered. He waited, hearing the wood crackle and burn behind closed lids. He welcomed the calm, lapsing into a gentle meditation that each Guard learned, keeping them rational, clear of head and pure of heart. He pictured the blue sky above him, the clouds sailing past too fast, the flames before him heating stone and twisting high in rings of infinite orange and red. Soon the world began to change and the flames flew high and wide, scorching him and pushing him backward. Burnt embers shot into darkness while above him shadowed trees swayed uneasy in their sentry duty. The fire spat and sputtered as it lowered, sealing him within a tight, warm circle of light.

The girl sat beyond the flames, her dark hair full and dripping with pearls of violet, her eyes jewels of malevolent green; and then settling, the colours waned to their natural tones, each flecked with fire.

"Greetings, Raven of the Guard. It has been too long already." There was a tune to her voice, a song behind her words, so soft. He wanted to join the melody.

"This is the place that you'd meet Hero?"

"It is. It is an in-between place, neither truly here nor there, but a creation to bond the two. I know why you have come, for I feel a change in the land, a shift in the power."

"Do you know what it is, what is happening?"

"I do not, though I see much. I see Ami and what she has discovered. You should go to her. She needs your help."

"I shall report back to Hero at once—"

"Not Hero's help, but yours, Raven of the Guard."

A sudden wind tugged at his robes, and the flames reached for him, bending and coiling.

"Go to her now. Trust in her judgement, her curiosity and instinct. With Ami, you will find the cause." Raven dodged the curling flame but was soon caught and lashed by another that wrapped an arm of golden white around his wrist. It burned, yet gave no true pain, and began slowly pulling him into the fire.

His screams were silent and without breath, his fall an endless tunnel of hell's tongues that licked and flayed, eventually cooling and leaving him shivering and weak in the dark.

The smell of earth, wood and moss flushed the smoke and char from his nose, for now there was no longer a fire, nor a mountain peak wind, but instead a peace that Raven had only ever found in the Planrus Lands with the orchards and streams and rolling sweet meadows.

His hand grasped for his sword.

Trees, to the left, to the right, behind and in front, a wood so green and the sun so low, giving deep dying tones to a strange and unknown place.

His face was smattered with cold, wet earth, and wiping at it idly he moved forward, squinting to see.

In a perpetual gloom, hidden from colour, stood a wooden shack, and sounding from within he heard a thump and a scuffle.

Sword in hand Raven moved to face it.

THE FIGURE SPUN, A shadow unfolding and unfolding until a blade was revealed, flicking and cutting his hand. The shadow's hair

23

framed a beautiful face and deep brown eyes, glittering a galaxy of green-purple stars.

He dropped his guard and his sword, stepping back from her with his hands raised. "I surrender."

"Raven?" Ami lowered her blade and grabbed his hand, dragging him from the shack and down the steps to the grass. She glanced all around, frantic for a moment. "It's good to see you, Raven." She smiled and gave him a small hug. "But what are you doing here?"

Licking his small wound, Raven looked back to the shack. "My sword—"

"No, don't," she said, stopping him. "There's something wrong here."

"That's why I've come, Princess." He frowned, feeling torn from his blade. "There are some strange goings on in Legacy. The land is unsettled, and it needs its princess. Rumours of dark things ... The Shadow Princess—the other you—sent me to find you." He filled her in on the last few moments with her counterpart. Ami stared at the porch as he spoke, her gaze far away.

"Ami?" Raven touched her shoulder. "What is it?"

"In there," she said, pointing into the shack. "There is a portal of sorts, a gateway. I found another place. What is wrong in Legacy? Tell me."

"We hear tell of smoke rising from the ground at the river, cracked and scorched earth where the Mortrus Lands lay. Some have told of animals or creatures ... the land has shaken."

"An earthquake?"

"A quake of the earth, yes—small and never lasting—Legacy has never experienced any such thing before. What is this place you found?"

"I don't know." She took Raven's hand, inspecting the scratch. Giving small pressure from her thumb, the wound soon healed with not a mark left.

"Thank you."

"I'm sorry. Reflexes, you know?" She let go of his hand. "But you did take me by surprise."

"I was hoping to find you—your Shadow Princess sent me here, after all—but I could not be sure that it was you scurrying within that old musty shed."

Ami laughed, and looked back at the porch. "A musty old shed that holds secrets. What did my other self say exactly?"

"That I was to help you." Raven stepped one foot upon the wooden step, the creak from it a stranger within a world of creaks. Somehow it didn't sound right. "That I was to trust you and your curiosity, and that together we would find the cause."

"Is only Legacy affected? Something from the Mortrus Lands?"

"Perhaps." He climbed the rest of the steps up to the porch, reaching inside for his blade. As he did, a chill crept his spine. "Perhaps there is more to it."

"Strange things have been happening here, though no beasts, cracks or smoke. There was an old man on the porch ..." She pointed but Raven saw no one. "I then found a piece within, a golden rook from a chess set. When I grasped it—I somehow entered another place."

"If only Hero were here," Raven muttered. "He would know what to do."

"Where is he? He didn't come with you?"

There was a hurt beneath her words he chose to ignore. "He is overseeing Legacy, awaiting word from Florence who's scouting the validity of the rumours. He may yet join us, if there is anything to join."

"There is something to join. There is a power here, a portal to another layer. Could it be one the Sentries left? Could this be another place like the Mortrus Lands?" She started once more up the steps, her sword held before her. Reaching the doorway, Ami stepped inside with Raven behind her.

"Are you sure we want to go wherever it takes us?"

"Is a Guard of Legacy scared of the unknown?"

"No, Princess," Raven said, affronted, "of course not."

They stopped at the fallen stairs, and Ami pointed to the shining, golden rook. It looked harmless, yet very much out of place. Raven felt a cold hand slink around the base of his neck. He pivoted and pointed his sword back out of the door.

"What is it?"

"I—I see a man ..."

Ami took his hand in hers and reached down with her sword hand to snag the golden totem. She grasped it tight, and the world slipped from beneath them. Raven gagged as reality moved and he was thrown to the ground, his hands and face meeting cold stone that spun to a sudden sickening stop.

There, towering over them, were three robed figures.

"What have we here?" asked one, his voice high and cracked. "Visitors? Plunderers? Heretics?"

A black cloth descended over Raven's eyes and all went dark.

FLORINA HAD GALLOPED hard and fast, determined to find answers to Hero's cause. She was a member of Legacy now, as both Florence the woman, and Florina the unicorn. She had the best of both worlds, enjoying the pleasures of banquets with her fellow Guards, and of running free and swift across the many far away hills. Even her mate, Talos, could never truly appreciate the change within her. She'd gained a new sense of duty to those she'd fought with, but still treasured the power and freedom of her birthright, and it was with this unity of loyalty that she now entered the Planrus Forest, slowing to a canter to investigate rumour and fear.

What manner of beasts she'd heard tell of ... Black, shapeless menaces, shadow-shifters with red eyes crawling from the ground. Fear held people like smoke, drifting above the city on a breeze; it was the smog they waded through to reach the end of each and every day. Oppressive and suffocating.

She broke through the last of the trees and stopped, hiding her crystal horn beneath drooping branches.

In the fast flowing ebbs of the river was a beast, wading to the other side. Its fur was as black as onyx, matted with dead leaves and twigs. She watched its hide sway in step and was sure that no such creature hailed from these lands.

It crawled up the bank and moved into the Solancra Forest, now hidden from view. She listened for a moment as the trunks bent, allowing its passage, branches tearing as it went, its black back a mountain in shadow.

This is not right. What if there are more? She headed north to the flow, and toward the Mortrus Lands.

Chapter Three

Thin hands gripped tightly beneath her arms as Ami was lifted none to gently from the ground in a shuffle and sweep of robes, the cloth across her eyes blinding, the unknown magic around her binding.

"They are not from here," a voice croaked.

"That much is obvious. They appear willingly by the sacred well. They are for *her*, for *him*."

"But they are not the same. We cannot assume."

"I see no difference. She'll not wish to be disturbed. Let's be done with them."

With a swift tug of her arms, Ami was unceremoniously hauled across the floor, yet as much as she struggled against the clasps of her captors, her body refused to move, and even her power seemed to have been muted. Paralysed and unable to speak, yell or cry out, she could only listen to the old voices whispering and sniping beneath the folding waves of the sea. Salt air stung her nose, her blind eyes watering beneath the veil.

"Stop," a voice cried, and Ami heard a familiar sing of steel. Forward motion ceased. "This is different. Can you not feel it? Have your senses dulled with age?"

"I feel ... So you shall inform her? Is it wise to be so bold?"

"Let us keep them as always, and take only this. She'll want to see this."

Then she was moving again, sliding from cold stone to gravel as the air changed and freshened, the roiling waters much closer. Her fear and anger were coiled with curiosity, for though she was powerless for now, there was something vital in the loose tongues of these men. They were taking her somewhere, evidently to leave her while stealing her sword for another to study. Dangerous as that was, had she not crossed the layers to seek out those dangers that threatened them all? The power had led them here, and Ami was inclined to trust its instincts.

With a soft thump, Ami was hit from the side and knocked off balance, Raven's stiff body tumbling against hers as their captors struggled to pull them both up a short rise. Tight claws grappled and set her right again and they were heaved over the zenith together.

"She'll be pleased with us."

"With you, Jonus, if the find is worthy of her time," another panted.

"Is it so important, you think? Will she think it so?"

"Oh yes. I sense the utmost importance. Perhaps I'm gaining wisdom through proximity."

"Do not blaspheme, Jonus."

There was a sudden turn and their path descended, the air becoming old, stale and musty with a tang and taste of roots and dirt.

They came to a halt and Ami felt herself being pushed up against a moist earthen wall, her arms raised, her wrists and ankles shackled.

With a flourish, the veil was lifted, and Ami looked out across a barely lit hollow. Three dark walls of rock and soil faced them with a slope off to the left, while to the right, a small doorway had been fashioned, its wooden entry closed and barred with three worn steps leading up to it.

Raven was beside her, chained and captive also, while opposite them stood three old men. Their white beards were long, almost to their feet, and each wore a hooded cloak.

One of them held her sword, and she looked at it longingly. *If they find out what it can do,* she thought, *then nothing but mayhem can ensue.* And more corpses could end up scattered at her feet.

Reluctantly, Ami let her gaze slip from the blade to the face of the man who held it. "Who are you?"

"Oh, we may ask the same of you," said the keeper of her sword, "yet it isn't ours to ask. Come." He turned to the door and lifted the barring beam effortlessly before disappearing through. The others followed just as swiftly, the door closing behind them.

Ami looked to Raven.

"Are you okay?"

"Yes, I believe so. And you?"

She nodded, chains clinking as she did. The only light came from the tunnel to the left, wan and murky grey, illuminating nothing insightful or helpful; no magic key, no Lassie to run for help. They were alone.

"What the heck happened?" Raven whispered, his voice much like the sea, barely heard, quiet even against the dripping of water somewhere near or far. He pulled against his chains and twisted as a worm worked its way across his shoulder and kissed at his cheek. With a small yelp he shook it off and watched it drop to the ground. "This wasn't exactly the day I had planned."

"Me either ..." She thought of the golden rook that was no longer in her hand. *Damn it.* "Did you hear them talking? They think they've found a prize, a prize for someone they revere."

"Yeah, and they have your sword. And mine, for that matter. Who are they going to give it to?"

"I don't intend to wait around to find out." Ami closed her eyes and felt out for *Dangerous*. She saw beyond the dark cave, the sodden walls of a strange land, and let her mind focus on the dewy grass, the tall columns and arches, incomplete as they were. She looked down to her hands which now pulsed in green flame, folded in shade and colour that sank beneath her skin.

"Oh my." Raven's voice was far away as he pulled at his chains, backing up from the fire that was now Ami. She was consumed, the light throwing shape and shadow across the mud and stone, her body its own furnace, leaping colours of bright green and purple, violent licks of white splaying and burning the root-riddled ceiling. Her clothes burned from her body, her naked skin rewrapped in the familiar dress of tight fabric and dangerous curves.

She pulled from the manacles as the fire winked out, the darkness refilling the silent tomb.

"That was something," Raven sighed. "Oh, Princess, if only I could do that."

"Relax, Raven. Every superhero needs a sidekick." She inspected her dress. It stopped just above the knee, her black boots just below. *Perfect.* She smoothed her hands over the magical material, her mind on Hero. *He should be here.*

"Superhero?"

"Never mind." She smiled and reached up to break his bonds, snapping the metal from his wrists and then his ankles.

"How did they capture us so easily?"

"Magic," she said, disturbed by the idea. In her layer, magic was a concept of myth and legend, yet in others it seemed more than common. "And with the sword, they'll have access to even more."

"Were they wizards? Priests? They all dressed the same, the beards, how they talked. Some kind of cult?"

"Perhaps." Ami walked the small chamber. "We should really go that way," she said, pointing to the door the men had gone through, "but something tells me we'll only find trouble that way."

"I'd like to avoid trouble."

Ami nodded. "Then back the way we came then. We better hurry."

THEY ROSE FROM THE earthen tunnel to a sky filled with gold-flecked clouds, embers of lands beyond layers that patterned the earth in shaft and shadow. It was such a beautiful sight that for a moment, Raven became lost in it. To his left the hill sloped away to the very edge of the cliff that sharpened to a point; and there, as a monument or temple, stood a lonely stone tower, most likely the place of their kidnap. A dirt track led from it to where they now stood.

The blue-grey sea surrounded all, continuing unimpeded to the empty horizon where the gold met silver and faded and blurred.

"So now we know where we came from," Ami said, turning to look up the hill. "Let's see where we're going."

Setting off again, they soon crested the summit of the slope and hunkered down to survey the land beyond.

A slope rolled down the other side into a scoop of a valley that was mostly taken by wild woodland, yet rising like a monolith, and cutting into the wood, was a tall grey wall that dwarfed all else before it. It seemed the frontier of some kind of fortification, rising high up above the tallest of the trees.

Turreted and crenelated, the *chemin de ronde* was guarded by small specks of men that patrolled above a hidden entrance.

Ami smiled and turned to him, her eyes a burst of jade and emerald. "This will be easy. I've done this before." She sniffed the air, as a predator might. "Hold on to me."

Raven was unsure. The woodland before them was smaller than some but looked dense and dark. Without a sure path it would be easy to lose one's way, and once through they'd be searching for entry under the very noses of the guards—plus, the glow in Ami's eyes made him feel uneasy. Despite these feelings, he trusted in his princess and so grasped her hand once more. To his surprise, instead of descending the slope he was lifted into the air, pulled to his feet as if by a giant bird.

From his minute height, Raven was able to see an entire town contained within the fortified walls; streets and houses, so many buildings, a river and something larger beyond—but the fall was short and the landing swift, a cut through treetops, leaves flying, branches whipping and snapping.

They landed with a thump between two tall elms, shaded under a luminescent green. Breathless and dizzy, Raven collapsed to his side while Ami bent low to the ground, silent in stealth. For the first time in a long time, she was the Assassin Princess.

"We're alone," she said finally, standing up straight. "For now at least, and the trees will give us a little time to gather our wits without fear of being seen."

"You are impressive," he said, shaking away his awe. Above, a perfect tunnel had been cut through hundreds of branches. Blue and pale white peered back at him, a bird shooting across and bridging the gap. "And you've certainly hidden us in the thicket. What are we to do?"

"I need to get my sword back. So much damage could be done, and they already know power, somehow, from somewhere ... the power is here. I felt it from the first moment I found that shack."

Raven pulled his hood down and ruffled his hair. She watched him.

"There are certain things I can remember from when I joined with the Sentries in the Mortrus Lands," she continued. "A lot I have forgotten, but I do know that the Mortrus Lands were only one of a network of portals. They all joined, through space and time. The shack opened up to the tower." She opened and closed her hands, rubbing her palms. "And I dropped the chess piece."

Raven stepped past her and peered through the trunks. If there was a path through, and he guessed there was, they were well hidden from it. He saw and heard nothing but woodland animals, birds and perhaps squirrels or other such creatures. "So they have the sword, and they may have an idea of what it can do."

"And that is very dangerous, but if we're to figure out what's going on, that very danger might lead us to the source."

"Should we not go back into the tunnel? We're not captives any longer, and neither are we helpless—"

"Yet they throw a cloth over our faces and we fall down." Ami shook her head, inspecting one of the trunks. "No, we need to find out who they are, where they reside and who they're taking the sword to. We need to be able to sneak in and sneak out. I can do so much, but I was just as paralysed as you."

"So on to the wall then, through the—" He broke off as Ami disappeared up the tree trunk, an animal scurrying quickly out of sight. A few leaves fell, skimming his face, and when he shielded his eyes he could just about see her, a dark shape too high, a shadow amongst shadows slinking between branches. He waited and watched. After a time she scrambled down the same way she'd gone up, and landed deftly in front of him.

"We're near enough, and the trees are climbable—"

"For you maybe—"

"But from up there I can see others walking a path not half a mile away," she pointed over his shoulder, "so I think you should cling to my back as I take you up."

"And then we swing through the trees like monkeys?" He laughed, imagining the sight.

"Yes, exactly. Me Tarzan, you Jane."

Raven shook off the phrase, not understanding, and peered up to the trees. "Then what?"

"Then we jump for the top of the wall and take out the guards, then into whatever is beyond."

"That simple? Do you have to kill?"

Ami frowned and tilted her head, her eyes flaming green. The sight of it sent shivers down Raven's back. Did she actually have to reason it out, to think about the value of life and whether it was worth destroying?

She broke into a smile and laughed.

"I guess not. We could knock them out from as far away as the trees I reckon, so we aren't seen."

Thunder rumbled far off and Raven felt the ground give a little beneath them, though his concern was more for the danger in those jaded eyes. The Assassin Princess killed, had killed for fun, for no reason. Had she changed, or would she just break, maim and murder?

"Come on, time to get a wriggle on." Ami's body sheened in a glow of green and violet, and Raven felt the spark of her touch on his arm. She leant against a tree trunk and squatted, allowing him his own purchase upon her back before lifting him up. Soon they were flying up the trees, the woodland blurring around them.

JONUS LED THE WAY THROUGH the dark corridor, jumping steps two at a time, his brothers struggling to keep pace behind him. The narrow earthen walls soon merged with cobbled flint and stone, the steps rising steeper still and opening out onto a large torch-lit hall. It was dark in its disuse, shadows scurrying the edges where a dank smell of rot rose from wooden benches that might have been of some other place and use once. It was known only as the Western Hall, and as far as Jonus knew, had never had another name. He strode across it, his eyes fixed on the door opposite that led to the Court.

This find, this event, was disturbing and exciting and *she* would certainly want to know of it immediately. He was certain. The blade was heavy and unyielding in his grasp, the power running through it obvious and immense. His brothers felt it too, being of The Order, but this was not for he or they. It was for *she*, and *she* would decide the fate of the strangers. He strode on ahead, swinging open the heavy door that hit its frame with a hollow crack.

The Court was as shadowed as the Western Hall had been, though lit with wall mounted torches. It was the biggest room within the palace with only three doors running to it, one from the south and one each for east and west. Around the edges were wooden benches and carved statues glaring from the walls, the floor a mix of stone and marble flags, white and red, chequered as a chess board. At the northern point sat the throne, ornate in wood, silver and gold.

She was not upon it.

Jonus turned to each side, searching the shadows. "Where is she?"

"Do not be impatient," warned Sanus, grasping his arm. "She is pious, she will do as she pleases and be where she wishes."

Jonus shrugged him off. "Of course she will, but this is important, Brother, this is—" A shudder from beneath stopped him, the very ground moving. "She is in the Solar Room." He rushed to the eastern door and burst through it with as much gusto as the first. The eastern stairs spiralled up before him, carpeted in a fiery red and gold. He took to the stairs as a man half his age and flew upon them, separating from his brothers below. Small windows against the wall shed daylight upon his flight, glimpses of sky and cloud as he hit the landing of the upper floors at a run, stopping only to catch his breath before entering the double doors directly above the throne.

And there she stood, her back to him, her skin glorious, soft and bronzed. Her arms were raised to the air, to the wide open gallery, to the very world, light shimmering up her body as sun-touched ripples, sparking from the tips of her fingers to fall upon the town. Another rumble ensued, and Jonus felt the whole world tilt somewhere deep in its bowels. *It's him.*

"Madam Romany." He swallowed audibly and stepped forward. "Madam Romany, I have—"

"Be quiet." A simple whisper, nothing more, but Jonus no longer felt his tongue. He bit it hard as he tried to address her again, but his mouth was useless. He tasted blood as it seeped into the back of his throat. Panic rose in him and he stepped closer, wielding the sword before him.

"Don't move." The sword dropped to the floor with a clang, yet still she did not turn, her naked arms raised high into the air, the day's light nothing compared to her radiance; even though he could not move, speak, could hardly breathe, his heart pounding his old chest, he still worshipped her as his beautiful goddess.

Her simple dress of white shifted as she finally turned, the garment a radiant armour across her chest, her midriff embellished with a small green jewel at her navel. If he could have, Jonus would have bowed to the ground and shuddered in her presence, for she was most beautiful, and most terrible.

Her face loomed over him now, her eyes a fiery red, her dark hair falling down her shoulders in streams. Upon her head was a tiara, sparkling silver, around her arm a golden serpent armlet.

"You dare to interrupt me here," she whispered.

Jonus looked away, looked around the room from his stationary stance, anywhere but into those blood-red eyes. It was a simple room, furnished with nothing more than the carpet beneath him and the bare stone walls around him. Four pillars stood outside of the walls and held the canopy of the gallery up, the opening itself four windows long, one whole side of the room itself. Out there, the town sprawled upon the hill beyond the courtyard.

She took his face in her hand and stared at him until his eyes rolled back to hers. They were on fire now, burning him. He would've screamed if he could. His face contorted with the agony of the punishment. Each vein, each artery, each ligament and muscle felt aflame, yet he could not move, could not cry out.

Finally she let him go, slowly moving her attention to the fallen sword. "For what trinket did you disturb me?"

She reached to lift the sword, but stopped before her hand touched the hilt. Jonus watched her closely as her face smoothened, becoming ageless—then her eyes were on him once more. Jonus knew this a façade. She was truly a dangerous goddess.

"Where did you get this? Speak."

He could move again and immediately fell to the floor, the agony from moments ago burning a trail under his skin. He moaned, pulling himself up onto his knees, turning his head to her with effort. "A girl, a girl had it in her ... possession. We found her ... the temple, in the temple." He coughed and closed his eyes tightly, fighting off the coming of a complete blackout.

He shivered as her hand smoothed over his skin, caressing his cheek. "A girl? And you stole this sword from her?"

"We captured her. She is below, held below with another."

"Now there are two? Are you sure you are telling me everything?" Her voice was slick silver and he didn't trust it's sincerity. At any moment she would snap him, and he would gladly die in her service, but he would prefer to live. He opened his eyes once more and faced her. She looked so curious, innocent and so beautiful. *My goddess.*

"We chained them and I took the sword, for I felt power within it. Power that I have only ever known from—"

"A power to equal me?" She tut-tutted and pushed him to his back. "Nothing is equal to me. You have brought me an interesting trinket, nothing more. You interrupted me, now leave before more punishment is given."

Jonus scrambled backward, pulling himself to his feet. "And the girl, Madam?"

"Keep her below. I may wish to question her."

Jonus backed out from the room, taking hold of the double doors, pulling them closed. As he did, a tiny sliver of light remained.

He spied her hunched over the sword, staring down at it. She raised her eyes to him, and Jonus fled.

Too flippant, he thought as he descended the stairs slower than he'd ascended them; *too flippant, and she is lying.* Whatever they'd found, it was meaningful to her, and she didn't want him to know it. He would do her bidding, of course, and keep the strangers below, for what did it mean if she meant to keep her secrets to herself? She was a goddess and he her slave.

Jonus met his brothers at the bottom and told them all that had happened, all except his doubts. Those he pushed firmly from his mind. *She's lying. She's worried.*

Chapter Four

Their flight through the trees was nothing to her, as easy and as quick as stepping across a bridge or climbing a stair, yet Raven clung to her with all his strength, one arm around her waist, the other around her neck. The ground was far below, a green and brown blur, and if his grip were to loosen, his fall would be terminal—yet she sensed a deeper worry in his grasp than that.

Did she have to kill?

Of course she didn't, though the nagging need to take life from another, to feed upon them as a vampire drinks blood, had been an evil temptation—Adam's influence—his influx of death within her veins. But she couldn't blame him entirely. There was something within her that wished to destroy just as much as the artist that wished to create. With the power she possessed, Ami was able to do both at the same time. *Did she have to kill?* No, but part of her *wanted* to. She was tempered by her own power—that which was hers alone—the Shadow Princess, *Dangerous*, the girl within that gave her strength. She thought she'd beaten the darkness, thought she'd recovered from it, but it remained, lying in wait just beneath the surface. Raven saw it in her. If Hero had come instead, could she have trusted herself in his arms?

Up ahead she spied the grey flint of the wall through the thinning thicket of trees, and with one final fantastic leap soared upward, bridging the gap between.

They landed amid the battlements, Ami crouching low and immediately scouting the area. Two soldiers approached from the left, precariously close and deep in discussion.

Leaving Raven between the crenulations, she dropped down into the narrow walkway and sunk low to her knees. It took only a moment for the soldiers to notice her, but before they could raise an alarm, she launched at them, taking the sword of one and aiming it at the other, hitting him pommel first between the eyes. He fell to the ground with a solid *thump,* while the second soldier backed away, his hands raised.

"Now, don't you do anything stupid you'll regr—" but he never got to finish as Ami whacked him round the side of the head, felling him the same as his friend.

"No," she whispered, chucking the sword to the side and looking down upon her unfortunate victims. "No regrets."

Raven jumped down from the wall's edge and joined her, stepping over the bodies, looking all around.

"There's only these two," she assured him. "Let's tie them up."

"Huh," he said, bending down over one and digging his fingers into his neck. "Still alive."

"Of course they are," she said. "You said we don't have to kill them. You were right. Now, help me tie them up."

"What with?" he asked, looking around.

Ami picked up the first soldier and dragged him forward, laying him upon the other. "By the belt. I just need them trussed so they don't separate."

"Separate?"

"You'll see."

Raven pulled the second man up so the bodies were together, and once back to back, Ami unbuckled one of the belts and threaded it through both.

"What are you planning? That won't hold them, they will just unbuckle—"

"Not planning on holding them."

"Don't kill them."

Ami tightened the belt and pulled, levering and lifting them both into the air. She swung them out toward the wood and let go, the two men sailing high, disappearing into the trees.

Raven ran to the wall and looked out, shading his eyes to see.

She listened for a heartbeat, hearing the faint *bum-te-boom-te-bum.* "They're alive."

"How can you tell?"

"I just can," she said, smiling, turning from the wood to look out across the opposing vista.

Nestled within the four tall walls was a sprawling town upon a hill, a colourful and shaded mix of streets and houses hemmed in by delicious forestry and wild flora. The land without was an untamed mess of nature with no further sign of occupation, but within Ami saw life that walked and talked and lived as she did. Houses butted against narrow streets, and while some leaned this way, and others leaned that way, all were oddly shaped and painted gaudy colours of pinks and blues and reds. From this height, she thought it almost looked a zoo for her perusal, the tiny people a game to be observed.

Looking down a particular street, she saw that all doors were ajar and all windows were flung open, and what looked like the entire populous of the row were up and about, washing windows, stacking crates, walking from tavern to tailor in their faded cloths and leathers. Some drove carts or rode horse-drawn carriages, while others simply walked on foot, dragging large bundles onward and upward, deeper into town.

In the distance many townsfolk gathered, swarming a market square, the stalls and people alive and brazen with the shouts of: *"Lovely apples!"* and *"... pears for a bale!"*

They were all crystal clear and small, like pastel coloured ants, going about their business.

Over the crescendo, lines of chimney smoke and smog scored and dispersed, a grey haze painting the clear canvas of blue.

Ami sniffed the air, tasting a coming storm.

"Stranger and stranger still. Are we going down?" Raven asked, pulling his hood taut.

"Yes, we have to." She considered him for a moment, and then looked back to the sky, feeling a buzz in the air, static raising the hair on her arms. "I already feel so far away from home. I once thought all this a dream, you know?"

Raven placed his hand on hers. "It's an adventure." His smile brought a tune to her mind that she hadn't felt on her lips since her time in Legacy. She hummed it now as she took Raven's hand and hopped the wall to the street below.

THERE WERE NONE TO challenge them as they entered the town, and for that Raven was glad. Without a sword he felt naked and unprotected, and he hadn't the power Ami had, wasn't bred among the elite of Legacy. In the Guard he'd always been a protector, a soldier, a man of action with a blade in his hand. He reached for it now, but his scabbard was empty, useless.

Ami had crouched low to the ground, her eyes that of a predator scouring the shadows. She'd changed in ways that he doubted she'd even noticed. It was natural for her after all, a simple extension of herself, where one moment she was as any woman, no matter how strange of manner, and then the next was a finely tuned weapon, honing in on danger and attacking. He felt safe with her, and yet unsafe. She was their leader, their rightful ruler, and he would honour her and follow her always, but he knew it was dangerous, *she* was dangerous—the hair-trigger of a taut crossbow, her aim unknown, her range unimaginable.

Raven joined her now and together they walked up the side of the thoroughfare, their eyes everywhere.

"So what next, Princess?"

"We walk, observe." She looked back at him and smiled, laughing a little under her breath. "Honestly, I'm not sure. This is all new to me."

They followed the street round to the left as it curved a little with the line of jaunty houses. Low windows looked in upon families sitting and rising; kitchens in which pans steamed and bubbled over open fires, large tables spread with plates and littered goblets. Raven passed one doorway that had swung wide open into a darkened hallway stacked on either side with piles of clothes. It smelt funky in passing, and he was glad to have moved on.

Up ahead the street was partially blocked by a wooden cart, fully laden with its tailgate open. In the back were four people, two women and two children, a girl and a boy, sat around the edges while men on the ground loaded up the middle section with crates and roped together belongings.

"Easy, Toby, you're gonna hit the little ones," the elder woman said, her grubby face looking down at one of the men with scorn. He'd thrown a rather large sack quite close to the children, though they were too busy slapping each other's hands in some kind of game to notice.

"You're such a stick, Martha."

"You mind I don't beat you with it too, Toby Martin!"

"Yes, Mrs Martin." Toby rolled his eyes at Raven as they passed, laughing in jest. "Ah, the Missus. Barrel of laughs."

Raven nodded and smiled politely and moved on, aware that the children had stopped to watch them. Ami had turned round to watch them back, but he took her arm and pulled her swiftly along with him.

"Best keep our eyes to ourselves, Princess. They'll be eyeing us and lynching us next."

"Them? They seem jolly enough?" Ami looked over her shoulder but soon turned back again. "True enough. They're all frowning after us now. Every one of them."

"We stand out. We're strangers." Raven was glad when the street curved again, this time to the right. The people they passed were in their own worlds and gave little comment, and if anything only a brief stare. But it was obvious they didn't belong. He kept his head down. "We could do with somewhere to hide out."

Ami shook her head. "We're here to find out what's going on, where these men are. We can't hide."

"Just for a little while, Princess, while we gather ourselves. How about there?" He pointed across the street to a row of buildings with open doorways and faded signage. Beside one darkened door, the sign read simply 'Books'.

"Looking for a book on sword-stealing, bearded old men?"

"What—? No. But it could be useful to have a little local knowledge." He cleared his throat. "In the Guard, we're trained not only to be stealthy and lethal, but to blend. I suggest blending. Perhaps books can give us an idea ... perhaps the man ...?" A figure moved within. He seemed to hover in the shadows.

Ami considered this, her gaze wandering to an approaching coach. It was horse-drawn, the hooves clip-clopping harsh upon the cobbles. The driver looked at them, a frown creasing his brow. Raven followed his gaze back to Ami.

"Ah, your dress. That's what drew his attention. Those we've seen are in pale, drab clothing. Hardly any colour, like the streets. You're conspicuous in your beauty."

Ami's cheeks rouged as she looked down on herself. "You're sweet and right. It's a lovely dress but ..."

Raven jumped back as green fire swirled from her feet and up her body. It engulfed her completely, the flames hot and deadly. As soon as they appeared, they left, leaving her dressed in a grey robe not unlike Raven's own. Her hair was covered by a hood, her empty scabbard hidden within.

"This would be better."

Raven turned to the bookshop, but the man had gone.

"Sorry," Ami said. "I guess that was quite conspicuous too. I have the instinct kinda built in, but I'm lacking in the experience."

"It's okay," he said, seeing her falter and hating it. "No one saw. Let's go." He took her hand and felt the power beneath her skin, her eyes flashing violet for a moment as they walked across the street.

The inside looked dark and murky, the smell of old printed pages seeping out into the street, while above the clouds hung heavy once again, the first patters of rain tapping upon the sign. A far thunder rumbled and the ground gave a shiver.

AMI CLOSED HER EYES before crossing the threshold, stretching the moment out, the smell of the old books close yet caught in stasis as she searched for *Dangerous*. She saw the rain in her mind, in that *other* place, saw it hit the perfumed grass and explode before the white steps that led to the platform beneath the arches.

There was the rosebush to her left, forever in bloom, forever growing against the stone walkway; and standing against it was her shadow-self, caught in the shower and looking radiant and forever young, forever her double.

She reached out to take herself in hand, but instead felt Raven's large, roughened fingers coaxing her forward, the moment snapping, her eyes opening.

Ami could smell the roses still, even as she followed his lead and entered the shop.

And just in time, as the few drops were joined by many, quickly becoming a torrent, falling hard, heavy and fast. Thunder grumbled of the promised storm and made good on that promise, rocking the sky.

Quite suddenly, Ami was hustled aside by a small, mousy man who skipped out into the rain to grab the sign. He pulled it awkwardly into the shop, pushing away Raven's help, and swung the door closed with a bang that was lost in a volley of thunder.

Again, the earth gave a small quake.

"I wish she wouldn't ..." he whispered, turning full circle before finding the perfect spot to store the sign. He dragged and whooshed against the floor in long, brown robes, his shaven face a healthy pink, his eyes small and dark, buried deep. "I'm sorry," he said, looking up at them, "I cannot have the shop getting wet, not even a little. The books, you see ...?" His voice drifted off as he swept his arm back at the shelves. "They are old, some of them, and very precious. Delicate. You're not from around here."

"How can you tell?" Raven asked, with a wry smile.

"It's obvious. I've never seen you. No one comes here, no one new. Visitors aren't permitted, which makes you two very out of place indeed." He clasped his hands and shuffled further into the shop. "That's dangerous for you, dangerous for me, and dangerous for anyone else who you approach, hm?"

"We're sorry," Raven said, "perhaps we should go."

"Go? In this weather? Out of the question." A smile broke across his face as he stepped behind a large desk and moved books from one pile to another, making it so tall only his eyes could be seen peering over the top. "No, it would be an even more dangerous thing for you to go out when she is ... well, when it is storming."

Ami approached the desk. "She?"

"Oh, you caught that, huh? Well, it's no secret. The weather, the storms? She creates them. She, who owns this land, rules it—though it wasn't always so." The man retreated again into the back of the shop, disappearing behind a dark curtain drawn half across the room.

Ami and Raven exchanged glances. So there it was, the one the old men had talked of. *She.*

Around them books were piled on almost every surface, stacked six and seven high, leather bound, dusty and moulded. Some weren't too shabby, kept behind wood and glass toward the back of the shop, kept in such shadow that Ami couldn't read any titles clearly, though she doubted they'd mean anything to her if she could. Raven was also browsing, perusing the books on the desk.

The man reappeared with a tray, a metal teapot, and three goblets.

"Ah, yes, you are still here. I thought you would be. Here, have some tea." He placed the tray on the desk and stepped away, looking at it. There was a long pause as they watched the man watch the tea. A subtle quake grumbled beneath them, and the stacks and piles of books shifted from side to side, the windows rattling—and then it stopped. The man smiled. "Now I can pour."

He grasped the teapot in one hand and each of the goblets in turn. Soon Ami and Raven were sipping the hot, bitter liquid. It was not the tea Ami was used to, far from it, but it had a certain charm and she drank it down quickly. Outside the rain lashed the window panes and the world grew darker still.

"It will last a while," the man said, and put his goblet aside, raising his hand. "The name is Britanus, and I own the only bookshop in the whole town. Now, you could say that I am very rich, or you could say that I am very poor. I would go with very poor, as there is a reason there be only one shop. Most cannot read."

"You know we are not from here, yet you haven't asked us where we're from," she said. "Are you not curious?"

"Curious?" he mused. "Perhaps a little, but I am thinking you will only lie. Strangers in a strange place, now told how dangerous that truly is, and you would divulge where you are from? Not terribly astute."

"Okay, so we don't tell you where we're from. Seeing as you know us to be strangers, perhaps it's not too much to ask you where we are?"

"Truly lost, aren't you? The town is named Darkscape." He then turned and busied himself with some books, giving short, sharp glances back at the windows. "Are you here to buy any books? I have quite a selection you may well be interested in." He frowned and turned from them to a shelf behind. Reaching up, his fingers barely grazed the upper most volumes. After a few seconds of struggle, he released a frustrated sigh and looked to Raven. "Would you be so kind as to help me, sir?"

"No problem," Raven said, stepping to his side. The man pointed to the book in question and Raven grasped it, pulling it down and setting it on the table.

"What is it? Why would I be interested in this?" Ami asked.

"Why indeed?" Britanus whispered, saying no more. He brought a lit candle from across the room and placed it at a safe distance, close enough to see the book clearly.

The volume itself was leather, large, the width of a hand double-spanned. She wiped the dust from the cover. There was no inscription, but a symbol only, the same symbol that was on her blade.

∞

"Familiar, yes?" Britanus gripped the cover between his fingers and threw it open, flicking through the pages apparently at random before coming to a text scripted on yellowed, age-spotted paper.

All three leant over the book to read the small words.

T'was the beginning of time, before time were noted, before th' world was sliced, many times unfolded. When knowledge and wisdom were that of the Being, and other creatures grew up from crea-tion.

"This talks of the beginning of the world," Ami said.

"Does it? Oh ..." Britanus turned back to his desk and began sorting through more books. Ami continued to read.

Guardians of life, when life was worth living, shepherded herds with hearts full of giving. Yet came a time when Being became, too large and power, too much to sustain. The world cracked and life all but shattered, the shell contained, broke pieces unnumbered.

"The Sentries," Raven murmured.

"Yes, it's talking of the moment the world divided into layers, but this is only an introduction." She flicked through the pages with her thumb, seeing pictures and drawings and words side by side. "It would take a whole year to read through all of this."

"Two, if you study it," the man said, coming back to them, "but it is not a book of leisure, more of reference. You riffle the pages, randomly, like so, and ah!" He'd taken the book in hand and flicked his thumb through, turning the page open to a drawing of a girl, so elegantly designed, so perfect in line and form. It was her. "You find something of interest." Britanus turned again and scurried busily to the back of the shop. From the full flowing locks of dark hair laying across her shoulders, to the black dress that clung to each curve, a sword in her grip and eyes tipped with green ink. It was her.

"The Assassin Princess," she whispered, tracing the lines of fading ink with her fingertips. "How am I in this book, Raven?"

"I don't know. It's a very old volume, so very old," he sniffed the pages, "musty and dry."

"It's my face." She looked to the back of the shop for answers, but the man had disappeared in shadow. Outside the full storm was upon them, the wind a gale that could lift the roof. *We're off to see the wizard ...*

The Assassin Princess shall be the culmination of power within one girl. She shall be the closest facsimile to the Sentry, and the means to bring all layers together. It will be her fate.

Ami stepped back from the book and looked from the page to Raven. "Who wrote this? How could they know about me, hundreds or whatnot years before?"

"Perhaps ..." Raven shook his head.

"Go on."

"I don't know how it could be possible, but, you know yourself that some layers of this world move at a different time and speed to others. Perhaps, to us, this was not written too long ago. Perhaps the author is from Legacy. In this layer, the text has been here for many tens, hundreds of years."

It was possible. She'd learned this fact from Talos of the unicorns who'd been captured by her twisted brother and tortured by him over hundreds of years—though in Legacy, only thirty had passed. If someone had witnessed the events of only months ago, was it possible that a record of it could be sitting in another layer? The proof was in her hands.

She looked at it again, riffling through the pages a little more, letting the book open where it would. The page that opened before them was titled *The Mortrus Lands*. Below it, a rough sketch of a black forest.

Here'th lay a most darkened secret, a forest that is camouflage for its true nature. Broken and fractured, a sorrowful monument to the Being. Once part of the whole, then a gateway between layers, tunnels of portals, and now only a mystic horror.

"This is so strange." Ami brought the book to a close and slid through the first couple of pages. Only the symbol was inked, no author listed. She closed the cover and Britanus returned.

"Well, I hope you found it instructive, or at least of interest." There was a glint in his eye that Ami wasn't sure she liked—the familiarity of him was somehow obscene, coming from the small, unassuming man. Had he recognised her from the book? He must have. "Would you like to purchase?"

Ami stared at him, transfixed.

"Why does the earth shake?" Raven asked, breaking her trance.

"The book is something truly unique, just like yourselves. It could teach you much."

"That's not what I asked," he said, crossing his arms.

"And yet, that is what I have said. Think on it."

Ami shook her head. "We have no means to pay, and no means to carry such a large tome through your streets."

"Then perhaps you should make it smaller." His smile did not falter, his eyes on hers. Beyond the leaded panes the storm was finally lessening, the patter upon the glass calming, merging with passing hooves, cart wheels trundling. The shop filled with a welcome amber light.

"And maybe the sunshine is payment enough." Britanus turned back to his desk and fumbled behind his books before rising from them with a torn piece of paper. He handed it to Ami. Upon it was written: *Receipt – 1x Book – One ray of sunshine, paid.*

The man smiled once more, showing his uneven rows of greying teeth.

"Thank you," she said, gripping the large volume beneath her arm.

"Are you sure you can carry that where we're going?" Raven asked, but Ami only nodded.

"Where would that be then?" Britanus asked. "Maybe you came to visit the great palace by the river that cuts through the valley? Perhaps that is where you are going? Or perhaps you'd leave the town, having seen all you want to of this place?" His smile dropped and Ami felt the warning behind the words.

"Thank you," she said again, "for all of your help, and the book, of course."

Taking Raven's arm she turned on her heel and headed for the door. Britanus reached it first however, and opened it, swinging his sign outside once more.

"You are most welcome. Please call again, should you need any other reading materials."

They nodded and stepped out into the street, the cobbles wet with so many shining rivulets of gold and trickling silver.

Once out of sight, Raven turned to her and gestured to the book. "How are we to carry such a monster without drawing attention?"

"Somehow, he knew. He knew a lot." Taking the book in both hands and holding it at arm's length, Ami pondered the volume. "Somehow he knew. Make it smaller." Pulses of coloured power swept from her palms and swam across the surface of the book. It began to shrink, down, down, further down until it was no bigger than a playing card. She handed it to Raven. "Keep a hold of this."

"Surely it should be yours to hold, were we separated—"

Ami shrugged, grinned and pulled at her grey robes. "No pockets."

HERO SAT WITH FLORENCE within the magically restored library at Legacy's castle keep, waiting for her to speak and relay everything she'd done and seen. It was difficult for her; he'd never seen her shaken before, always the brave and fearless Guard, the brave and fearless unicorn. He'd placed a goblet of wine by her hand, but so far it remained untouched. Hero had finished his and now craved another.

"Hero, these were not creatures from this world. I am fearless when it comes to fighting, defending, yet I couldn't stay there any longer. The things I saw." She stopped, her eyes filling with tears that she refused to spill. "The things I saw. They were dark. Dark monsters with teeth, rows of teeth, sharper and finer than any sword of steel. Their eyes were a glowing red. I watched them from the Planrus Forest, I watched them rise from the ground, as all the rumours say. The river no longer has only one spring, but many where the earth has broken and steams. Soon the forests on both sides will flood because of it. And there were noises, Hero, noises of men with wicked voices, calling up from the earth as if from the depths of some hell. I dared walk only a few paces when flames shot up between my legs. I ran. I ran for my sanity and—"

"It's okay," Hero said, reaching across to hold her hand. "You're safe now."

"None of us are safe, Hero. It's spreading. Whatever it is, its spreading, and soon it will reach our lands. The quakes we feel? It's the land ripping itself apart beneath us."

Hero leant back in his chair and looked up to the ceiling, far, far above. It was a painted picture of beasts and men, a depiction of an old seafaring tale he'd once heard when he was younger.

"We need help, Hero. We need Ami."

"Raven has been sent to seek out Princess Ami."

"He has not returned. Perhaps he will not. We need to see your guide, the other Ami. The Shadow Princess."

Hero nodded in agreement and hoped he wasn't too late. He couldn't lose Legacy, and he couldn't bear to lose *her*. "Let's set the fire."

Chapter Five

The heavy rainfall had flooded the earthen cavern, reawakening the stench of the long dead. It made him feel sick and woozy, but Jonus breathed it in all the same. After all, how many had they left to perish here against the sodden walls over the years? He'd never kept count and yet remembered each and every sunken corpse he'd unchained and dragged away. In fact, if he closed his eyes he could still recall their final screams in echoed memory.

All for her.

But there would be no screams now.

The manacles were empty.

"They weren't released," he said finally, turning to his brothers with fiery torch in hand. "The iron is broken."

"Perhaps an accomplice?" Sanus suggested. "Someone who came to their rescue?" Murmurs of agreement rose in response, but Jonus shook his head.

"No. It's the girl. I thought just the sword, but … *She—*"

"Be careful of your words," Franus warned, but Jonus took no heed, his fingers stroking down his beard.

"My words are always carefully spoken, I assure you, yet a mystery remains. We cannot question the strangers if they are not here, and if they are not here, then they deserve more consideration than we're giving them. The sword is powerful, but we found more than a sword; we found the girl who held it." He sighed, the glossy looks reflecting none of his thoughts, only the fire in his hands. "Madam Romany will not be pleased if we do not recapture this girl."

"And her companion?" asked Laous.

"He can die. His sword was little more than tin." Jonus turned then and led them back through the doorway, along the passageway and up into the palace. He stamped his feet with each step, scraping his sandals along the ground. He detested the mud, the dank, the dark, the rain—oh, how he hated the rain. It was a relief to step into the warmth of the hall, with its high ceiling and wide open space. He breathed it in, continuing to his left with his brothers following; through a further doorway they entered a room that ran the back of the Court and sat directly below the Solar Room.

This was the Lunar Room, the double of the Solar, featuring a large gallery that opened above the courtyard, a massive four-walled enclosure of brick and stone. All was deserted, the courtyard and room alike, the recent rainfall giving rise to tendrils of vapour, a light mist that reached to touch and caress, to chill.

In contrast to its twin though, the Lunar was lavish and beautiful, mosaics covering the entire floor with pictures and symbols, the walls adorned with blue, red and gold pigment and paint, murals bleeding—a woman depicted, a goddess.

Six white moons circled a larger seventh in the centre of the room, while opposite each was a drape of soft sapphire, hung to hide the alcoves beyond.

Jonus slipped the now extinguished torch into its bracket as the six took their appointed places.

"Are we all ready?" Jonus asked, looking to each of them in turn, each brother standing within their mosaic moon. They nodded, and at once the moons began to glow and pulse, lines of light shooting to the central lunar that flared and roiled with pure white flame; the surface bubbled and rose up into a sphere of power that shone brighter than any star in the sky.

They were as one now, and Jonus ceased to be alone in his thoughts, images of the captured girl fluttered through their communal mind, their sights set, the sphere infused and ready.

The girl, their thoughts sang, *seek her out. Bring her.*

The sphere hovered for a moment and then left through the gallery, up and out into the sky above the hillside town.

IT SEEMED THAT THE townsfolk had run for cover with the arrival of the storm, abandoning their horses and carts, leaving the market square stalls unmanned and open to all manner of scavengers. A flock of birds had landed upon one stand to peck at the fruit, sorting and choosing, throwing what they didn't like to the ground, while stalking the many fish stands, alley cats skulked; skanky, mangy, they teased and pawed fat fish that'd already met their fate by the blade. The flies of course had joined in, and Ami was able to hear their foul buzzing upon almost every stall—yet all was not yet lost, for though it appeared but an empty stage set, its actors reluctant to appear, there seemed some stirring from the wings ...

At the very edge of the thoroughfare, outside a florist's humble stand, Ami and Raven watched as the first doors swung open, and men, women and children emerged, looking to the skies and giving great sighs. The grubby and shaken walked amongst the well-dressed and well-to-do, their voices a hushed din that grew from a whisper to be heard above the gusting wind. Traders took their places, calling out for buyers to sample their wares, to the hungry and the poor, to the wealthy and weary. Drivers mounted carts and carriages and whipped their horses' reins as cartwheels rattled and rolled, clattering hard upon the cobbles.

Ami motioned for Raven to follow as they began to explore the sudden rejuvenation, passing through the bodies and dodging cantering horses, making their way from stall to stall and always, looking out for the bearded old men.

Trimmed green cloth displayed apples, oranges, bananas and pears, cherries of red and blue, and even potted jellies and jams, while other nearby arcades traded in belts and buckles, leather jerkins and boots—anything leather, it seemed—tanned and tailored; one stall over from there, a dark haired man lined up bottles of liquids and lotions, claiming to a couple of elixirs and potions, and everywhere calls and cries of wares and produce—a crowd drawing a crowd from a reticent people who all held the ghost of a singular shared expression. Ami noticed it and pointed it out to Raven, noting the similarity in each who looked otherwise so different: their expressions of fear and relief.

Yet still the people returned: the cobbler, the tailor, the small apprentice boys at the anvils, fires roaring, bellows *huffing*. Children resumed games of chase while their parents traded and bought, the set alive and vivid, the actors in character, playing out their appointed parts with feigned zeal.

Ami observed, her eyes cutting the jagged line of the surrounding rooftops, the simple homes and uneven pavement, the drab and dirty pastel of jackets and cloth pants, skirts, worn out sandals stepping and slipping in horse dung and fallen straw—and then to the faces. Fear and relief. It was all around her. *This is normal for them,* she realised, *this is how they live. In fear and relief.*

She grabbed Raven and pulled him further into the crowd before taking a tight side street, no more than a dirt trail between houses that opened to a wilderness of green behind. Birdsong, twitter and tweet ruled here, overlapping with the sounds of the market's hushed calls of *tomatoes and apples and pears.* They were alone in the midst of a sprawling town. Dense trees rolled down the far slope of the hill behind them, parallel to the thoroughfare, and beyond where the town could not reach was a vast forest. The outer wall continued below them and out of sight, hemming them in, only a few arms of lanes and roads stemming from the main sprawl.

"They were all hiding," Ami whispered, looking around her. "They were scared of the storm. Perhaps they've reason to be."

"The book man, Britanus—what did he know?"

Ami's power prickled as she looked down the slope, and focussing in, saw a cut in the land where a dark river wound its way through. She pointed through the trees where there looked to be a well-trodden path that ran the edge of the town. "There's a river, he said. It's down there. He also said that there was a palace."

"I can't see a palace, Princess." Raven shook his head, his eyes rimmed red, alert but tired. Ami wondered, not for the first time, what it would have been like to be trained by the Guard, trained under Hero's watchful gaze. Would he have given her special treatment as their princess? Or perhaps been harder on her knowing what she was capable of? She missed him. There was a savage and selfish sting in her heart that it was Raven that stood before her and not Hero.

She took his arm, glancing once more toward the faint sounds and jeers of the now bustling market square. All that had happened, all that was still happening, weighed heavy on her. The shack of power, a step into another layer, the quakes and the loss of her sword, the *she,* the enigma as of yet unseen. She'd ignored her duty for half a year, avoided it all as she arranged a life for herself away from the madness of layers and magic—but this was what she was meant to do, to seek out each layer and explore. Perhaps if she'd have done so sooner, she'd have already solved the mystery. Danger lurked at every turn and it was her job and duty to find it and confront it.

"Come on, let's get going."

They walked to the path beneath the shade of the trees.

THE TRAIL SLOPED DOWN and away, leading them through a stone archway built into the town's outer wall. Unmanned, unguarded, the way was overgrown with wild brambles coiling for grasp, clinging to the once grey stone, now green and yellow with moss and algae. Raven touched the wall as he passed, wondering how long it had been there and who'd built such a structure? Either way, it marked the edge of civility, where beyond, the wiles of nature ruled the untamed valley.

Ami forged a way for them through the jungle, a lost land where even the sun could not penetrate the darker shades of green and shadow; creatures stirred and burrowed in the dark, eyes peering, watching them—he grabbed for his sword—but there was nothing there, and he withdrew his hand from his empty scabbard and continued on.

Soon there appeared a wide black ribbon up ahead that snaked across their path, cutting the land in two. Its surface reflected the sky a dull grey, flawed with thick, slow ripples, where insects danced like skaters on tar, and birds strutted back and forth.

"Not so close," Ami said, holding Raven back and pointing further upstream. "Look there."

Turning to look, Raven's senses were suddenly overwhelmed, for upon the banks of the low down valley there rose a colossal structure that had, until now, remained hidden behind the hill. Its four square, turreted walls were a courtyard of red and white stone, hosting a single rising tower to dominate all, its crenelated tip level with the crest of the hill. A bridge connected the two banks, arching over the black cut and between the outer walls.

"The palace?"

"That would be my bet," she said. "Couldn't possibly be anything else."

It was magnificent, and yet seemed strange, the sight of the single monolithic tower filling Raven with a kind of dread. "And this is where we must go?"

Ami nodded. "The book man suggested it, and it seems likely that any *she* who was able to shake the world would reside in such a place."

They stepped together to the water's edge, the grass giving way to black sludge and stone.

"What do you suppose this is?" Raven asked, looking down at the thick, black water. A faint odour of rot came off it in waves, offending his senses and churning his stomach over. He looked to Ami for her thoughts, but something else had caught her attention.

"Princess?"

"Shh. Listen. Can you hear that?" she asked, her head tilted to the side.

Raven listened, hearing only the buzz and drone of the nearby insects, the sound of rustling leaves.

She pointed down the river. "There."

Hovering just over the bridge was a tiny ball of light. It looked to be a miniature sun or star, stuck in mid-air as if waiting for something. A moment later it moved of its own accord, switching banks in a blur, then switching again, then again, slowly working its way closer. It was pulsing, searching ... and then quite suddenly, racing toward them.

"It's coming for us," she said, groping for his arm. "We gotta go. Now."

"Princess, I—" Raven's arm was almost yanked from its socket as Ami pulled him back up the bank and sped them back through the wooded jungle, up and away from the river. The sounds and smells of the surrounding flora mingled and mixed into a toxic drone that joined the other and followed them at a pace.

"It's right behind us," he shouted, feeling his skin prickle, not daring to look up, knowing it was above and closing fast.

Their retreat was swift, and making it through the brambles beneath the arch, Ami pushed him aside and turned to face their pursuer.

It descended a screaming star-shot, landing in front of them and taking shape in white fire, shooting burning flares over their heads. One scored Raven's cheek, and Ami in turn raised her hands, her palms filling with ripples of coloured light, striking the now furious sphere. Stray sparks spun to form the legs, arms, and body of a warrior-woman, her light-sword presented, while the opposing fire created a matching adversary, a warrior-man, swinging a burning blade.

Raven's eyes were drawn to the fight, but before the first blow could fall, Ami was leading him back the way they'd come, along the narrow backstreet and into the market square.

"I don't know how long I can hold it off," she breathed, visibly weakened by whatever had just begun behind them.

Raven took her weight and steered them to the edge of the bazaar, away from the main throng of people. He rested her against the wall of a tavern, ignoring looks and stares from the passing trade. Her eyes flashed the colours of the fight unseen.

"It's draining me."

"Can you walk?" he asked, worried for the pallor of her skin and the waxy sheen it'd taken.

"I'll be okay. We need to get away."

Nodding, Raven took her weight again and gently led her into the crowd, dodging carts, cattle and people alike that cut across their path. If others took notice, Raven took none of them, concentrating instead on keeping his balance and holding Ami upright, her weakening body becoming heavier and heavier.

Then behind them, screams broke out.

A sudden rush of people overtook them and carried them, thrusting them into a stall of meat and fish that fell to the floor with dead, wet splats, the air filling with the deadly drone once more. The townsfolk scampered and their way became clear, but Raven came to a halt at the centre of the square, the noise entering his head and singing there. His ears rang, the single note bounding and rebounding inside his skull, buzzing for release.

It was above him.

It blotted out the sun.

It was a fallen star hurtling to earth, and raising his arm to block out the sight, he stumbled and lost his balance, spilling them both to the ground.

"No!" Ami shouted, and thrusting her hand up to the light watched a burst of green flame fly from her fingers into the sphere.

With a gnarled, dry scream the ball of light shot skyward, swirling in white and green until it disappeared from view.

The sound left Raven's head, leaving his ears ringing as he helped Ami up.

She was deathly pale.

Stumbling and unsteady on his feet, Raven navigated the rest of the way across the square, taking a small side street that seemed appropriately out of the way and out of the light.

Here the houses were so close together he could span the street with arms outstretched, and carrying Ami as best he could he leant against a doorway, pinning her there.

A door opened a few houses away and a face appeared, an arm beckoning.

"In here, quick. Don't hang around, come on."

Ami nodded her consent, and together they ducked into the open doorway, slamming the door behind them.

To Raven's surprise, the sphere of light did not return, even though he kept expecting it to break through the door at any moment, to fly through the shuttered window—but all was calm, and soon even the townsfolk quietened their furore, the shock and excitement dying down as life resumed.

They were led to a table, and lowering Ami to one of the available chairs, Raven slumped into another, looking up into the face of their host for the first time.

It was a girl, a young woman, her dark brown eyes almost black in the tired gloom of the room. Her hair was long, dark also, lavishly spread across her shoulders and down her chest; her bare arms were delicate, a gentle coffee-coloured exposure at odds with her simple woollen dress. But it was her face that took him in that moment, her soft features, full lips, her expression of deep concern.

"Please," she said, her accent tinted, "what can I get you? What do you need? You are hurt?"

"No," he said, shaking his head. "I am, but my ankle needs nothing but rest. Ami?"

Ami smiled and sat up. "Rest only, yes, though I am thirsty." A pause as she peered up into the girl's face. "Thank you."

"Yes, thank you. You have given us safe harbour, and it seems whatever pursued us hasn't tracked us here."

The girl smiled. "You're very welcome." She took two wooden goblets from the table. "Water, yes? I can get you some. Hold on."

Raven watched her as she moved quickly into the back room and pulled the lever of a pump. Water sloshed and she returned with the goblets. He accepted his with a smile, and Ami took hers with thanks.

"I'm glad to have helped. You seem terribly lost." The girl remained standing, her dark eyes flicking from one to the other of them. "I hope you are not trouble-makers."

"No," Ami said, "at least, I hope not. We are from ... elsewhere though."

"Yes, this is, I'm sorry to say, obvious." She smiled. "You need rest. You can stay here, for a time. Please, relax, you are safe."

"What was that thing?" Ami asked, already looking better, her strength returning.

"A great magic," the girl said with a solemn nod. "A magic that only The Order would have cast." She reached across and Raven felt her hand on his. "But you are safe. This house, this house is protected with charms. They cannot find you here."

Smiling still she withdrew her hand, Raven feeling the absence as keen as a burn. And then she was gone again, into the darkened kitchen beyond.

"Who are The Order?" Ami asked.

"Ah," the girl's voice came, deep from the shadows. "Of course, you may not know. The elders form an order of priests who have been given small magics, a little each, so that they may do the bidding of *she* in the palace, and praise *her* name. Apart, each elder can only perform small deeds, but together they can conjure great and powerful things—though, not as great as *she*."

Her voice filled the house, not quite an echo, but equally as eerie. Raven was glad when she reappeared, carrying a loaf of bread and some dried meat.

"Here, some sustenance. Please, take what you need. You must have had a long journey. This place is ... isolated."

Raven nodded. "We have travelled far."

"Where abouts are you from?" Her accent gave Raven a shiver.

"An island, far away," Ami said. "I don't think any here would know it. We were wrecked and managed to climb the cliffs to land, and found your town."

"Ah, I see," she said, smiling. "Forgive. I am curious only, though you have no reason to tell. Please, take the food, the drink—is plenty of."

Ami nodded and Raven followed her lead as they reached for the bread and meat, and after a few bites, and several clean, crisp swallows of water to wash it down, felt the better for it. The girl took a seat next to Raven, having brought a bowl of small red berries. She offered them and took one for herself.

"I'm Sofia-Maria," she said. "I'm happy to meet you."

"Ami, and this is Raven."

"Good. Happy to know you."

Raven was sure he saw a glint in her eye as she looked at him. "Happy to know you, too," he said.

THE PAIN HIT HIM WITH a slap and Mattus fell, cracking his head on the floor.

The circle was broken, and though a few of the others stepped to his aid, he noticed that Jonus did not.

"What is it, Brother? What happened? Why did you break the circle?"

Mattus stared up at the images upon the ceiling above, his head turned this way and that in aged, old hands as they checked him over.

"It was the girl," he managed, though it was hard to speak. His head hurt, feeling as if he'd been stabbed over and over. "The curse she threw."

"We all felt it," Jonus said, "but why did you fall?"

"Did it cause none of you pain?" He was pulled up against his will; the cold mosaic floor held little relief, but much more than Jonus's accusing eyes.

"No," Laous said, a sentiment echoed by the others.

"Harsh, yes," Jonus said, "and it broke our bond, but not the circle. Why did you break the circle?"

"The pain, it was like—" the girl's face came again as he—they—looked down upon her; she looked up at him. "Her face." He paused, running his fingers over his own cragged wrinkles, his sallow skin leading to a beard he'd had for an eternity. "Her face. It—"

"When Madam Romany hears of this ..." Jonus broke off and left the room.

He pulled himself together with little help from his brothers, and contemplated the girl. *Her face. So familiar.*

GOLDEN LINES OF LIGHT fell from the shutters, cutting the floor into sections and segments like a dusty old cake; and there the fairies danced, twirling and flying, here and about.

Ami watched them for a while. The girl had disappeared into the shadows once more leaving the room silent in her absence, and Raven said nothing but gave only an occasional sigh that sent the dust-fairies into a frenzy of fun. Oh how lovely it must be, she thought, to be a fairy, cheerful just to be, alive in a single moment, in a single shaft of light. Stories, fantasies, the young girl within still dreaming away ...

Turning from their magical show, she looked over the rest of the room, seeing cupboards and shelves that held a few items only: a figurine of a girl made from varnished clay, a few scrolls of paper, held loosely with string. There was also a portrait about the size of her hand, a painting of three figures, expertly depicted in fine lines: a man and his wife, a blond-haired boy.

Behind her were more shelves, the highest holding a row of plates, carefully placed and positioned, the second holding books, bound by hand and loved and worn. Ami read the spines easily, though the words were faded: *Cooks Diary*, *Food Far & Wide;* an impression was building that she didn't much like.

The last shelf held a mismatch of objects: wooden and metal toys mostly, all standing in lines. Little soldiers, some fallen. She touched one, its small sword blunted. Boy's toys.

"This—"

"Ah, the sun is setting low in the sky," the girl said as she returned and leant against the doorway. "You are more than welcome to stay. There are plenty of beds."

"This is not your house?" Ami asked, knowing already that it couldn't be so.

"I am housesitting, for a friend," the girl replied.

Ami said nothing more, but only watched as the girl touched her hands to the table and turned her eyes on Raven.

"Would you like to see the rest of the house? I can give you a tour."

She felt it now. Danger here, hidden within the walls, hidden within the girl. Running her hand through her hair, she nodded and feigned a yawn. "I think we'd like that. Perhaps we could stay the evening, if it is little trouble? Then we'll be on our way first light."

The girl shrugged, her hair shifting across her bare shoulders. "Sure. This way." She looked back at Raven, obvious and suggestive, and then led them into the darkness of the house, taking first a candle from a hidden nook and lighting it with a tinderbox.

The flame pulsed and swayed as they followed her, Ami keeping herself between Raven and the girl.

"Kitchen," she said, pointing without looking, "and bathroom. Here is cellar and stairs to bedrooms." With this she turned and looked to Raven, the flame held beneath her cherub face.

Her eyes glistened and Ami felt Raven shift behind her.

"Thank you."

The girl gave way, passing her the candle.

"Straight up, you will see. Don't get lost." Then she was gone to the shadow once more, soft footsteps marking her departure.

Ami signalled for them to be cautious, and led them on and up the stairs.

Old yet sturdy, the steps ended at an open landing and sleeping area that evidentially served the family who lived there. To the left was a large bunk, a straw filled mattress and off-white sheets. To the right was a smaller bunk, a child's bed. There were toys close by, small wooden blocks, a rocking horse.

She pulled Raven close and whispered in his ear. "She isn't housesitting. There's something wrong."

Raven swapped positions. "What do you think is wrong?"

"Everything. I sense it, I feel it, I—"

The girl appeared at the top of the stair. "You can sleep here safely. The window is covered, but you can tug the cord and release it." She took Raven's hand and led him to the large bunk gesturing to the cord, stroking his arm.

Ami bit her tongue. Sofia-Maria wasn't who she claimed.

"Thank you," Raven said as he was pushed gently to sit upon the bed. "Are you sure the owners won't be back to find me within their sheets?"

"No," she whispered. "They've gone for a while."

An icy finger of fear trailed the nape of Ami's neck, and she backed up to the stairs, the sudden certainty of what had happened a solid stone in the pit of her stomach.

"I'm going to use the bathroom," she said, and leaving Raven with the girl, quickly turned back down the stairs into the shifting light and shadow, the sun turning around the house unseen.

Instead of the bathroom though, Ami approached the doorway to the cellar, the simple slats of wood nothing to break open. A little pressure at the lock and it gave with a click. She slunk in behind it and refastened the catch.

There were no steps, only a slope into the earth, and issuing from the dark below was a pungent smell she recognised from a different place. It opened memories of a dark, wet cave where she'd found men chained and forever rotting, forever mad. She recalled how she'd sliced them through relentlessly with her blade, ending their immortality with her twisted and dark power. The smell of blood and death was unforgiving and unmistakable. And it was here with her.

She turned a corner, her hand dragging the wall, stone and putrid muck.

Another corner and it was confirmed. With her eyes now aflame with power, she saw the bodies of the three. The parents, the child—not that anyone would recognise the massacre in front of her as human. They'd been here a while, and by the spatter of blood on the walls, they'd been killed here too.

"Found them?" The voice filled her with dread as she looked up into the girl's radiant face.

"Yes, I have."

"Then you are the one, that's a certainty, as if your eyes of burning fire weren't already giving you away." She came a step closer, sauntering, oozing confidence.

Ami held her ground, readying herself for a fight, her mind focussing, the power, both good and bad swelling inside, coiled tight and ready to spring.

"Who are you?"

"Who am I?" The girl laughed, a bright sound that echoed unnaturally. "I am *she*."

"What have you done with Raven?" A few steps closer now, too fluid, too light, too easy in the face of destruction—the girl should fear her awesome wrath—couldn't she feel it?

She shouldn't have left Raven with her.

"He sleeps."

"What do you want with us?"

"What do I want? I don't want anything. You see, Ami, may I call you Ami?" She paused. "Or Assassin Princess? Oh, I have waited a long time to meet you. I thought you only a story, a myth, but when the elders found your sword ... things changed. They sent the lunar after you, and now I have you. Fate, at last." She laughed then, but not a girl's laugh, a woman's, rich and full. She came closer.

Ami thought through her next move. Blast her out of the way and fly for the door, but then what? Up the stairs to get Raven, through the window hatch in the roof—perhaps, if she were outrunning a normal adversary—but if there was one thing Ami was certain of, it was that this girl was not normal. She was a killer, and she was powerful.

"At first I dismissed the thought, but after a short examination of the blade I realised it must be you." She pointed, her finger long, her nail a spike directed at her heart. Her face was no longer that of Sofia-Maria, but of a terrible apparition.

If Ami was going to make a move, it had to be now.

"The Assassin Princess, filled with the power of the Sentries."

"You know of the Sentries?"

Her laugh filled the tomb and the earth trembled in response. Then she burst into flames, the dress disappearing in noxious smoke of white and red, illuminating the dead, sorry bodies. A golden armlet shone as dark hair flew a sharp wind.

The woman reached for her.

Ami pushed all of her power from her palms, but it was too late. *She* had her.

Her laugh was at last terrifying, a hoarse whisper against her cheek.

Chapter Six

The fire kindled and caught.

Sparking and spitting it danced a waltz of embers that winked out in the long dark chimney, finally breaching the keep and quilting the sky a tepid grey. Soon the library was a woodland cave of comfort, the leather-bound spines and old musty pages warming.

Silence stretched.

"What do we do now?" Florence asked, a bell in the crackling quiet. "Will she come through and speak?"

Hero shook his head. "We must be still in meditation. She'll find us."

Florence sank to her knees and joined him at the large hearth, enchanted by the dancing flames. So deep and alive they were, mysterious ribbons clinging to blackened wood. Her heated skin tightened and her eyes began to tire as the soft crackle and spit lulled her into a kind of half-sleep; and then came the smell of grass, wood and flower.

Time slipped away, as did the rest of the library, the books and shelves seeming to just fall from sight—and still she knelt there next to Hero, even when great pines and oaks rose up tall and thick around her, roots and branches alike growing wild and encroaching, breaking from the ground. Layers shifted and walls moved, opening a space that hadn't been there—and then from behind the fire came a shrouded figure in silhouette, stepping out and eclipsing its radiance. Her long, dark hair fell across her shoulders as she lowered her hood.

"Ami."

A short time ago the mere sight of the *stranger-girl* would have caused her fight, fright and flight—but she was no longer the enemy, if she ever truly was. She was the shadow of a girl, the shadow of a princess who'd been misled and used. This girl was their guide and a connection to Ami, to the Mortrus Lands, and to the mysteries that still hid within both.

All three rose as one, no longer hiding behind the flames. There were no secrets now.

"Greetings, Hero of the Guard. It's been too long."

Hero bowed his head, his eyes filled with a fear and adoration that Florence had only seen from him when in Ami's presence.

"Ami. I seek your help. Did Raven commune with you?"

"He did, and is with Ami now," she said, a wry smile on her face. "I led him to her."

"Is she safe?"

The girl paused and looked at Florence, as if noticing her for the first time, her eyes flints, impassive. "She is not safe, no." Her gaze returned to Hero. "And it's good you've come, for she'll need you now. Both of you."

"Where is she?" Hero asked.

"She is—" Her words were lost as a deep rumble passed beneath them, shaking the ground, the tall pines swaying in their shadowed gloom. Hero and Florence clustered for balance, even as the tremor lost its vigour and all returned to an unsettled calm. The girl continued. "She's in another layer that is neither yours nor hers. I sent Raven to aid her, though you would've had her come to you. Her need is greater and yet is the same."

"You mean these things are happening in other layers, too?" Florence asked.

"Yes, *next-girl*, these events are occurring throughout all the layers. I'm not the source of all knowledge, but I am connected to this place, to the true Ami, to the power that we all share. I feel the quakes as you've felt them, through the boundaries and walls that separate place from place."

"And the creatures that Florence has seen?" Hero asked.

Ami nodded. "They're from elsewhere, from an infinite number of layers. I know little of them, but I know that they're opening; slowly crumbling."

Silence gathered and the woods darkened further, the place heavy with dormant power. The birds felt it, the small and hidden animals, and Florence felt it also. It called to her, to Florina.

"I need to find her," Hero said. "Please send us to her if you can. If she's in danger and needs us then we need to go to her. Now."

"Yes, Hero of the Guard, you must."

A tune lifted on a breeze, an absentminded hum of an old tribal song lost long ago; it was Ami's song, a lullaby that took Florence away to a far flung shore, a slip of a beach, a cliff so lonely, the woman so young, so dead, so long ago now ...

She felt Hero's grip in hers as the layer slipped from beneath them, throwing them forward and into the fire. Only for a moment were the flames the world, the universe entire, before all changed again and they were cast down upon the earth.

It was dusk, and the silhouettes of trees snatched back and forth in a frightful wind against a sky rent with lightning; a cold torrential rain poured down, and for a moment Florence was disorientated and unable to grasp her bearings as she crawled through wet mud and grass.

Where am I? Where am I?

"Hero!" she called.

"I'm here," he said, a little way in front. He'd already gained his footing, and was now the shadow-on-shadow that bent close to her. She clung to him and he pulled her to her feet. Another boom and flicker revealed his rough-cut jaw and dark eyes in stark relief. "Are you alright?"

"Yes," she said. "Where are we? Where'd she go?" Soaked to the bone and shivering cold, Florence scanned the darkness, her unicorn eyes seeing through the tangle of limbs to a clearer path a few steps away. She pulled on Hero's robes, leading him toward it, breaking out of the treeline and into the storm.

There, beneath an open cut of bursting black cloud, they crossed a mud path, their boots sinking and sliding until they reached the verge opposite, where the long grass whipped wildly at their legs. Another black wood lay beyond, but it was the shadowed structure that seemed to hang within its grasp that drew Florence. A leaning white apparition, creaking and shifting, it seemed alive in the whooping wind, and something more. *Powerful.*

She pointed toward it and Hero nodded, pulling her to its steps, ducking into the creaking shelter. As they approached its empty doorway, Florence imagined it a black mouth lifting and lowering in the wind. *Laughing at us.*

"Hero, I'm not sure," she said, her unicorn heart trembling, yet the wind lost its teeth within, and the rain lost its bite, and when safely beneath the wooden porch, they were at least sheltered.

They peered out into the darkness.

The world they'd entered was a misted land of rain and wood, the shack the only port of call to be seen. Nature's fury battered the rickety canopy above them and a couple of times the shack lifted in the wind, throwing them forward and into the railing that creaked in objection with each hold. It was then she saw him.

A man was seated to their right. A black shadow, looking toward them. She grabbed for Hero's shoulder.

"What is it?" he said, reaching for his sword.

But the man had already gone.

"There was someone there. He was—he was there," she said, but there was no man, only the movement and groan of old, tousled limbs.

Hero shook his head.

"Tricks of the night—" he started, but was interrupted by a thump and a stomp that was louder than either the thunder or the wind. It came from the wood.

Florence held to Hero. "I—"

"Shh," he whispered, taking her arms and leading her deeper into the shack and through the doorway.

Laughing.

A triple fork above struck bellies of clouds unseen and the ground trembled and settled, the thumps louder, closer, now a suck, slurp and slide. From their right, Florence found a shape in the rain, bigger than a man or beast, eyes of light sparking.

Her own power sparked within, the unicorn magic wanting, needing the release, the change she was denying it; deeper still they backed in, the storm hidden in a veil of shadow—and the footfalls stopped. Florence calmed herself, her grip on Hero remaining firm as the shack lifted and laughed.

Laughing at us.

"This place is not normal," she said, touching the hilt of her sword. "It's full of power, like the Mortrus Lands, and perhaps ..." Through a doorway to her left, she saw branches, faint pastels of green leaves against the dark arms of trees. Flashes showed empty, desolate rooms, rotted floors and nothing more.

"Do you feel the power here?" Hero asked.

"Do you not?" she asked, shivering with the cold. "You once had the power in you. Surely you felt it, too?"

"It could've been the storm," he said.

"You know it's not."

They'd travelled further now, only small steps, the darkness complete on all sides.

"You think this place is a portal, don't you?"

Florence looked back to the doorway, feeling the shadow, the man, his eyes on her—and the other, waiting just outside.

"Yes—maybe, possibly." She shivered again. Hero's hand lay against hers, and she put all her effort into holding back the urge to change. She needed to be the warrior now, not the unicorn.

A branch snapped to her left making her jump—*some warrior*—and her grasp tightened on Hero.

They were now at the end of the hallway, and in the dim light that seemed to seep from the very walls and beams, they were able to see remains of a fallen staircase. The rubble was strewn at their feet, rotted, powdered; above, nothing could be seen of the upper floor at all.

"If there is a portal here," Hero whispered, "and we assume Ami and Raven took it, then we can follow." He reached out to touch the steps, but faltered. "Reach out with the power. Touch it with me."

"What good would that do?"

"A thought only, but perhaps the steps used to go ... somewhere else?"

She nodded, hating the feeling of this alien power crawling over her. It was in the air, in the walls. It was outside in the rain, too, but oh so powerful here. Nevertheless, she grasped his hand. A white light came and flourished, covering Hero's hand to his wrist, the grasp a union. They reached out together to touch the last remaining step, the white light too bright, a licking flame against their palms.

Just as the shack itself had seemed a ghost, a luminous apparition, the wooden steps became an ethereal sheen. The air above wavered and blossomed white, shaping further steps that shadowed the first. Otherworldly, they were there and not-there, glittering with the power, the gentle magic.

The storm raged on regardless and the shack lifted once more, impaled upon trees.

"What should we do? Climb them?" she asked.

Hero nodded. "And quickly, before they disappear."

Even as she took her hand away, the image began to fade a little, though she kept a firm grasp on Hero.

"Ready?" he asked, the ground quaking beneath, thunder taking his words. She nodded, and together they climbed the short rise to the third step, the last solid one remaining. "If I fall on my face—"

They felt the change happen much as it had before. The walls and the floor, the very steps themselves, began to solidify into something more substantial. Stone replaced wood as the two merged, light and dark shifting places, shadows shrinking to grow and pale into smooth grey.

The next step was of chiselled stone, wooden rafters revealing carved granite and chipped plaster as it changed, the temperature dropping dramatically.

And then they were there, completely in the *other*.

The last steps were easy and led into a large open space, the walls and floor rough, and the room empty; a single window welcomed them in a path of pooled moonlight, soft and silver, shadowing a few remaining runnels of rain that slipped down the panes.

Florence reached for the latch and threw the window open.

The salt-heavy smell of the sea filled the chamber, together with the fresh scent of a night, post-storm. Shadows of grey and black covered the ground below, and she could make out large, rounded shapes, stark in the lunar light; a few trees littered the cliff edge that fell into the sea, roots gnarled and reaching to point across the infinite ocean expanse, the beauty of the nightscape broken only by the shattered moon on rippled waves.

Hero joined her and leaned out.

"Almost a lighthouse," he murmured, before slipping back inside, squeezing water from his robes. Florence did the same.

"We were right about the portal," she said, shivering and returning to the top of the steps, stone the whole way and unbroken.

"Do you think that if we walked down we would return to the other layer?"

"No, I think not." He placed his foot upon the top step. "There is only one way to find out." Leaving her on the upper floor, Hero descended, reaching the bottom step, whole and complete, beckoning her down. "The place is quite empty."

With caution, Florence followed down into a hallway that reminded her much of a mausoleum. At the far end, Hero gave the stone door a mighty tug and it opened out into the night, the mystical moon clear and bright.

The wind caressed her skin with a cool hand.

"This is quite strange," Hero said, walking around the small plot of land. "The two places are connected, and in their own ways, quite similar, yet where there were woods there is now sea, where there was a shack, now there is a tower of stone."

"The Sentries split the world apart. The portals they created joined them." Florence looked down at the boulders, their smooth surfaces curious and deliberate. "There was a storm here, too, but it has passed. The sky still flickers. It's all connected." Partly to keep warm, she jogged to the side of the tower and peered round. "If Ami came through here, where is she?"

Hero joined her and started up the climb, following a worn and muddy path.

"There must be a settlement over there," he said, pointing to where the dark sky was lit ever so slightly brighter in the near distance. "She'll be there with Raven, I'm sure of it. We best set off now while the night remains."

"Yes, we don't want to be seen," she grasped her sword, "and I best stay as a woman for now."

"You'll be able to run free again soon, Florina," he whispered, "but for now, yes, as a woman." He smiled and touched her chin lightly before turning to the climb.

Florence hesitated for a moment, looking out across the ocean and all she could see of it. A strange ocean of another land, it seemed to go on forever. She was dedicated to Hero and Legacy, but she still missed home—her true home—the Solancra Forest. There, her never ending love would stay with her once lost heart, Talos, the only unicorn *sans* horn. He would never leave Solancra now, not for anything, not even for her. The moon told her that she would return to him, that she would retire from her newfound duties—just not yet.

With a small sigh she followed Hero, who'd already climbed a little way ahead, stopping only as a glimmer of something shiny caught her eye. Reaching down into the long grass beside the path she grasped it, wet and heavy, and held it up to the light. It was a golden chess piece. *Strange.*

A whistle, and Hero waved to her from the climb. Pushing the totem into her robes, Florence waved back and scrambled up the path to catch up.

RAVEN WOKE WITH A START, turning so sudden and swift that his feet became tangled. He'd been dreaming of the Mortrus Lands, the dark blue light, black, dead trunks—he kicked and fell, hitting the floor hard, knocking his eyes wide. Dust rose from the floor, the clouds *huffing* soft billows with each breath as he allowed the panic to wash away, to flow from him and into the house he now remembered; he quietened his mind. A flit of a memory, in a room with the Guards of Legacy, cross-legged and quiet, breathing slowly and hearing, seeing the blessed peace fall like a veil. Other images and memories came to him. Ami leaving him with the beautiful girl. She'd come close. Stroked his skin. He'd fallen to the bed beneath her touch, beneath her gaze. It'd been romantic and perfect, her lips to his a magic untold, unfelt—then darkness.

A cold ocean churned in his guts as the poisoned memories bled through.

Now everything felt damp, old and unused, the air holding a pungent perfume he'd been blind to before, a sense he'd been tricked out of.

Pulling the cord that swung at his shoulder, Raven opened the roof hatch, flooding the once dark room with moonlight of a dusky silver-grey. It allowed him to see, if only partially, certain subtleties he'd missed before. The room he'd thought so cosy was truthfully forlorn and in decay. The beds, the straw, the floor, all mouldered in disuse and neglect.

"Ami?" he called. "Princess?" But no reply came, his voice settling in the dust and cold air. The ocean could be heard some distance away through the open roof, but there appeared to be no one else present. No one in the house.

Ami had been right to be wary, and Raven had been taken in by the girl's charm, her witchcraft; but there were better times for self-pity. If he had truly become separated from his princess, there was no telling what could have happened to her. *At least I'm still alive.*

Ami.

Edging his way through the room, Raven found the stairs. The moonlight tapered out three steps down, leaving all else shrouded in shadow. The house creaked, a half-flash from the hatch, a storm moving on.

"Princess Ami?" he called again, but it was useless, he was sure. With no sword he felt naked, with no Ami he felt alone. He listened as the wind caught the side of the house and howled in the gaps and gullies.

There had been a candle and a tinderbox. He looked around for it now and spied the stump of wax on a small bureaux. The wick had been burned to extinction, but he thought he could save it if he dug a little. He pushed his nail in and fished the wick out while looking for the tinderbox. It was there, sitting on the other side. He took it and lit a flame to the stump, giving just enough light to see by.

Returning to the stairs he was soon back on the ground floor.

Walls lit a subtle orange, as did the door to the cellar that stood open.

"Ami? Are you down there?" The smell that responded churned the cold in his guts to a tepid froth. He knew it well, had smelt death before, dealt death before. Holding his sleeve to his nose, he ventured down.

The slope took him by surprise, the stone becoming earth, the stench stronger still. He gagged. "Ami!"

Rounding the corner, he bent down low.

The flame almost snuffed with his cry, the candle almost dropping as he backed into the wall, illuminating the shadow and gloom, and the dull, dead eyes.

They stared at him from beneath the massacre of bodies.

Raven fell to his knees and voided through his fingers, the splatter falling short of a woman's face—*Ami's face*—maggots crawling—

On his knees, he crept forward. He had to know, had to make sure. Closer now, much too close, and Raven saw that she wasn't Ami, and a sick relief passed through him—*but what of the others?*

"Ami?" he whispered, now to himself as he bent low across another upturned head. A man, not Ami. The third was beyond, and Raven set to the task, sinking down, down into himself. He felt the dead beneath him as flies rose and landed repeatedly on his face and hands. He waved them away but drew back as he gagged again, holding his breath yet still smelling the blood, the meat ...

The face of a boy watched him and Raven felt waves of relief, disgust and sorrow.

Quickly he backed out, focussed on retreat, focussed on Ami—*not here, not dead. Three only. A woman, a man, a boy. Not Ami.*

Reaching the sloped exit he grabbed the wall for support, his fingers coming away black and sooty. Breathing heavily, he brought his hand up to the candle and took a closer look.

"Burnt," he whispered. However, he could no longer stand it, and with a fast flight back up to the ground floor he broke through into the hallway, and then out into the street, his stomach emptying, his breaths gasps and whoops.

A family of three, dead, slaughtered recently. The girl *housesitting.* She knew, she was part of it, perhaps had done it. She. *She.*

Wiping his mouth with a bloody sleeve, Raven looked back into the house once more, the small portrait of the family, the toys, the plates ...

"Why?" He needed to find Ami.

Stumbling, his legs weak, Raven continued out into the empty street. Leaving was easy, but where was he to go in this strange land? The street sloped down and round, houses lifeless, the night deathly silent, his footsteps echoing. *To the palace?*

He held onto the side of a house and pressed himself flat against it, shimmying down to the ground. A mist kissed his flesh, cooling the fever there, his hand running through his hair, soaked in sweat and blood. In his other hand he still grasped the candle, the flame gone. He threw it away and covered his face with both hands.

He'd faced death before, but perhaps not so close, so personal, so putrid and foul. Even Kane's death, his late friend and fellow Guard, had been in battle. Smooth, quick, not painless, but accepted. The carnage he'd just seen? *A woman, a man, a boy.* His eyes filled with tears that he pushed away quickly with the heels of his palms.

"No," he whispered, "no, not here, not now."

Raven got up and looked down the street. The tower of the palace was visible, a silhouette against the night sky, stars peeking through, unfamiliar and out of place.

With as much courage as he had conviction, Raven pushed on.

FROM A WINDOW WITHIN a room in darkness, Jonus peered down at the rain soaked street. The bridge connecting him to it was but a shadow in moonlight and he could see the water of the river far below. It had flowed once, but was now all but still and dead. He knew what lay beneath.

His thoughts had been musing on Madam Romany and the sword of power. He'd also thought much about their failed attempt to capture the girl. She, too, was powerful.

He stroked his beard.

The lunar had never failed before in its tasks, but whom should he blame? The girl, or Mattus? Mattus had never failed before, none of them had, yet things were changing. Madam Romany's focus had shifted to the sword and the girl, and he knew where she had gone. He'd been watching. It was over now though, yet still there was movement in the street below, a lone figure limping.

"Breaking curfew? More strangeness." He curled his hand around his eye and let the magic enhance his sight. The street came closer and became lighter in the dark. "The *stranger-man*. How apt. And you are alone and injured? My, my, what could have happened?"

Jonus would let him pass, let him find his way to the bridge and let him cross it. Then he would make his move.

He stroked his beard and turned away.

Chapter Seven

The dancing scarlet fire that held her captive haunted the sparse room, while the open gallery teased her views of liberty she couldn't gain: the sprawling town upon the hill, the high-walled courtyard of red and white—charming, gothic, lacking only a smattering of snowflake to make a Christmas card scene; though no matter how picturesque, it was a gaol all the same.

The strange woman stood at her side, her ember eyes burning bright against her smooth *café au lait* skin. Ami's sword was in her grasp, the blade laid across her palm, her long, elegant fingers caressing the folded steel.

If she could have, she would've made a grab for it and jumped from the open gallery to the courtyard, bounding up to the tall walls, and over, escaping into the valley—but her power was muted by the fire that crawled her skin and licked her body. She was a slave to it, and could not speak or move, but only breathe and blink and watch the woman pace. This she did sporadically, stopping for stretches, the silence spinning with a statue's smile. Then she would resume once more, swinging the blade to and fro.

Time passed, much time, before a single word was spoken.

"You may speak."

Her voice was that of the girl, though she seemed more the woman. *A predator.*

Ami swallowed and coughed, feeling her throat work and fail and work again.

"Who ... are you?"

"Oh, and I expected so much more than that."

"You're not a house-sitter."

"No, no I'm not a house-sitter," she laughed. "I am, shall we say, the *Alpha* and *Omega*. I am the beginning, I am the end."

"You aren't God."

"Aren't I?" The woman smiled. "And what would a little girl like you know about gods?" Her expression hardened for a moment, then dropped to placidity. "Now, my turn. Who are *you*?"

Ami said nothing though the woman continued to glare, her red eyes fading to a dark brown. She looked as if an Egyptian queen, Cleopatra maybe, or her sister, Arsinoe.

"Shall I tell you who you are?" she asked, glancing now outside. "Shall I tell you of rumour and prophesy? Of heresy?" Holding the blade to the night, the woman pointed to the symbol at its base. "Do you know what this is?"

Ami remained silent, her mind reeling with images of Raven, of Legacy, of Hero, of the woman, her white dress catching the firelight, bleeding against her chest. Where was Raven? The bodies ... the family ... the house ... the blood—

"Is this your sword?" she asked, pointing it to the stars. A surge of white light gathered at her wrist and travelled the steel. It flashed a deep red, turning to violet, then green and silver. "It holds power, great power, but I've never seen a weapon like this before, and with the symbol ..."

She lowered the blade and leant against the wall, a breeze stirring her long dark hair, her armlet *chinking* softly against the stone.

"There was talk of a girl," she whispered, "a young woman who'd one day come. She'd have the power of the Sentries. I never believed it, never thought it. Any that were caught with it on their lips were removed, punished, their words destroyed for all time. I am the beginning and the end, and you are the Assassin Princess once foretold." She moved in front of her, reaching through the flames to caress her cheek. Ami could smell the sweet spice of her skin. It smelt of forgotten fruits, forgotten lands. There was a tingle, a strange sensation soon withdrawn. "Not a myth but real. You are real, are you not? Yes, flesh and blood, just a girl, a girl with a powerful sword."

The fire dropped suddenly, freeing her.

"You haven't any power, have you, not really? You aren't anything special."

At these words, Ami felt *Dangerous* flex inside. "I am the Assassin Princess." She made a grab for the sword, pushing her power, letting it flow—but her flamed grip dampened on the other, and the sword remained firmly in the woman's iron grasp. For all her might, she couldn't prise it away. She was only a girl after all, only Ami, and the smooth skin of the hand beneath hers was immovable.

"If this is the great Assassin Princess," the woman mocked, turning away, "I can see I have nothing to fear."

Ami closed her eyes and searched desperately for *Dangerous*, rushing across the lush green to the marble and stone—but those were only memories. *Dangerous* wasn't there.

At the gallery, arms raised high and sword in hand, the woman gave a flourish and thrust toward the town. Immediately the world began to shake, throwing Ami off balance. A storm brewed from nowhere and rain lashed the lands, a gale rising to topple and flatten, to tear and destroy as the lithe woman shimmered in white flares of fire, scoring the night with missiles of light. They arced a thousand miles and fell out of sight.

"I have to find a way to this blade," she murmured. "I have to break its secrets."

A cry floated up through the storm then, a call from beyond her prison.

"Ami!—"

Raven.

She looked out into the night and called out to him over the thunder; but the only reply that came was a caress of misted rain, and she dared not approach the gallery.

91

The woman sighed and turned to Ami, moonlight striking a crescent upon her cheek as the last of the flamed power left her, the storm continuing on.

"Your *Raven* is not important. I'm not even sure that *you* are that special."

"Who are you?" she asked, hearing no more from the land below; Raven's calls had fallen silent.

"I am Romany," she said, "ruler of Darkscape, goddess of this land. You should use these last few moments of life to tell me of the blade. But you begin to bore me already." She turned the sword in her hand. "This is your sword? You did not steal it?"

"It's mine."

Romany became still again, too still, a mime, a caricature. After a while of waiting, life returned. "Perhaps, then, not useless. How was this blade made? Where was it made?" She flicked it expertly through the air and Ami flinched as its tip landed against her skin, the steel resting across her arm. It shimmered with violet flames that ran to the tip and winked out. "Curious." She smiled down at the sword and then at Ami. "The power within it responds to you."

Raven is alive, but for how long?

The sword was close; if she could just grab it—but *Dangerous* was no closer, and Ami felt only the girl. *Just a girl, just Ami.* She focussed on Romany.

"Why are you so interested in my sword? How do you know of me?" she asked, but the woman had turned her back on her to inspect the blade in the moonlight, the storm now finished.

"This is not metal, but some other material, yes?"

Ami said nothing.

"You think I do not have ways or dragging every last thought from your mind? I could strip secrets from you as easily as I could flay the flesh from your bones." She paused. "I would rather you share with me your tales though, I think, for there may be some gems that prove useful."

Dangerous. A glimmer, a bloom in the barren.

"I will not be used," she said, but she had to think quickly. Her life, Raven's life and possibly many more lives depended upon her next few words. She had to be smart. "However, I am not adverse to talking, if you wish."

Romany considered her and caressed the blade as her dark eyes burned. Finally she nodded. "I shall call The Order and have them prepare a room where we may talk. In the meantime?" The column of flame flew around her once more, and Ami was caught.

Romany left the room.

HERO DROPPED TO THE ground, Florence steadying his landing.

All was black and shadow against the wall, the thoroughfare in front a long cobbled stretch of moonlight cutting through the town. There were no lit windows, no glow of a warmed hearth, and the only sound to be heard was the ragged puff of their own breath, a faint steam rising, curling and disappearing into darkness.

The light of life they'd followed still hung low and distant, beyond the streets, over the cusp of the hill itself.

"It feels wrong here," Florence said, stepping forward. "I can feel the fear."

"So it's not deserted then?"

She shook her head. "No. Far from it. I can hear whispers, though no words. There and there." She pointed to the closest houses, squinting. "They're hiding. All of them. There are so many of them ..."

"Is Ami among them? Raven?"

"I—" Florence shook her head. "I can't tell. I don't know. It's possible."

"But not likely. Not Ami, not hiding." His eyes scouted the road ahead as far as he could see. There were many side streets, narrow alleys breaching close-knit structures, but no movement beneath the eaves—a scurry of a cat maybe, the snuffle of a rat in the gutter—but nothing more than that. There was not a voice to be heard, their own whispers too loud.

Looking through a nearby window and cupping his hands against the cold glass, Hero saw very little: a chair and a table, an empty room, too dark to discern. He turned back and looked to the stars, unfamiliar and magnificent. Legacy had never seemed so far away, so distant. Even when he'd travelled beyond the Madorus Lands and to the broken islands off its coast, he had not felt as far from his home as he did now; now his home was in a different reality, a different layer of existence. But Ami was here.

A single star shot across the expanse, its long tail fading. A second appeared, and then a third, and as Hero watched, clouds gathered from nowhere and a storm quickened the skies. Thunder crashed and lightning licked, the wind a sudden gale that whipped their robes and snatched their hoods, all within the blink of an eye.

Hero pulled Florence to shelter beneath the doorway of a crooked house, while grey spectres glimmered behind windowpanes—the petrified and hidden, reticent ghosts thought missing.

The townsfolk.

The star-shots increased, seen through the bellies of swirling clouds; they did not peter out nor disappear, but instead arced downward, a thousand flaming arrows heading right for them. They fell with a hard rain, filling the black street with smoke, steam and mist, giant stars exploding over and over.

The thoroughfare was soon alight with a chicane of flame, running a hell's path across the hilltop.

"We have to run for it," Florence cried over the din. "We can't stay here, it's not safe."

A star hit a building to the right, firing stone missiles over their heads.

Hero agreed, and taking Florence by the hand, ran into the anarchy, dodging all he could.

RAVEN HAD WALKED QUITE some way down the hill, his eyes misting, staring up at the palace, his arms and legs aching. He was sick, for sure, sweating and shuddering. That girl, that dark haired girl—what had she *done* to him? It'd been a struggle not to trip on the cobbles or give up completely and lean against a house and sleep, but the urgency to find Ami was too strong; and besides, all that lurked behind his lids were the dead, and they accused him of much, of running away, of being a coward.

A woman, a man, a boy.

In a feverish stupor, he found himself at the foot of the bridge, exhausted and on the verge of collapse.

That's when he saw her.

Standing at the far side of the bridge, Ami whispered into the wind, her dark hair flying as she beckoned him forward.

"Ami? I thought I'd lost you. Ami!" he shouted, moaning as he made his way toward her, limping and tripping upon the creaking wooden path.

A sudden storm had broken out above, and as the rain fell he tightened his grip on the rail, the elements fighting against him. White flashes flew from the palace and landed somewhere behind in booms and fizzles.

"Ami!"

He was closing the distance, though each step cut his spine with ice. *She's wrong.* The wind pushed against him, then with him, swirling around and twisting his robes. *She's wrong.* Checking his footing, he looked up at her, now only a few strides away.

A shadow crossed her face and panic rose like bile in Raven's throat.

She *was* wrong. Somehow, something.

Perhaps it was the way her hair fell upon her shoulders, or how her eyes remained immoveable, like a picture, like a mask.

"Ami?"

Her smile dropped.

"You're—you're not—"

With a twirl in the dark, the wind whipped Ami away, and in her place stood an old man, his long grey beard flying about his chest, his eyes silvery and flashing with amusement as he laughed a low, dark croak, cutting through the storm.

"You're right. I'm not," he said, raising his arm and pointing at him, a bright bud of light pulsing at his finger's tip.

Raven turned to run but the bud of light flicked the distance between them and caught his back, winding tight around him, binding his body. It was fire, burning through his robes to his skin.

"Ami! Ami!" he cried, panicked and immobile. Then he was lifted from the ground, the old man against him, his face changing and morphing into that of a black serpent, its forked tongue lashing out between sharpened teeth against Raven's cheek. Hands were claws, grabbing at him and scoring his skin as it pushed and played with its prey.

Raven couldn't breathe, couldn't scream, and was thrown across the bridge and through the railings to teeter on the edge; the man/beast held tight to him though, keeping him there to hover above black waters—and now Raven *knew* why they were black. Now it was obvious. The tar-like substance bubbled, waiting impatiently, hungry for him.

He gave one last cry into the night, but the vines of corrupted power that bound him now penetrated his open mouth and clogged his throat.

"Thanks for dropping by," the serpent grated, and pushed him from the edge into the water.

HERO HEARD A CRY IN the night, and there was no question in his mind as to who the voice belonged to.

Raven.

"He's in trouble," Florence said.

"Raven! We're coming!" Hero cried, and together the two of them ran down the sloping street, ducking and diving through the star fall.

Upon the horizon a tower emerged, immense in size and lit like a beacon, while at its base a square courtyard surrounded it, all haloed in an eerie light. It was from the tower that the stars came, shooting high up to fall.

They saw Raven at the bottom of the hill, struggling upon a bridge with a second figure in embrace, a grey-white apparition, burning and steaming in the pouring rain.

"I can save him," Florence said, pulling her sword from its scabbard. "Follow me."

Hero nodded as she rippled in her own white flame and transformed into the pure white unicorn, galloping ahead and leaping from the street to the bridge.

Raven had already fallen, and Florina dived into the black water after him; but by the time Hero had caught up, the attacker had disappeared. Booms and crashes continued yet seemed far away as he walked across the bridge, sword raised, looking everywhere for the man or beast that had attacked. Light hid within darkness, shifting the balance; and somewhere in that darkness, someone laughed.

He knelt at the bank and peered into the water's depths.

Raven and Florina were nowhere to be seen.

Above him, the star-shots were fading, leaving only the storm and the sporadic ground quakes, though they too were lessening. He concentrated, listening for Florina and Raven, for the attacker somewhere in the mist. Wrapped inside the wind, the same low laugh crowed again. Hero turned his blade, his sword at the ready.

But then, in a flourish of splashing whinnies, Florina emerged from the water, tearing up the muddy bank with Raven slung over her neck. He was unconscious, and both of them were coated in the foul, black sludge of the river.

"Quickly, Hero," she panted, "we have to go. There is power everywhere, and it's strong and it's wrong. Hero, we need to run, now."

Making sure Raven was secure, Hero jumped up behind him, and then they were off, Florina breaking into a gallop away from the palace.

Where were they going to go? *Where is Ami?* He looked over his shoulder, the palace disappearing around the curve of the bank, its lights dimming.

Raven stirred.

"Hush, Brother, I have you now. Stay still until we are safe."

"Ami," he whispered, and then nothing more.

The passing night called out to Hero, animals unseen, chirps and screams, creaks and rustles—but he closed his eyes to it all, and lay over Raven, keeping his brother close, keeping them both close.

IN HER SOLITUDE, ALONE in the cavernous room, Ami searched once more for *Dangerous*. With the woman far from her, she found she was able to connect to her power.

Her eyes were closed, her breathing steady, and in no time at all her feet had found the grass again, her boots crushing prints into the short, kempt blades as she strode to the white platform, the incomplete arches rising high, the columns tall against a clear blue. The steps were few, and her shadow-self waited at the top, casually leaning against a pillar.

She ignored the trees behind, the entrance to the Mortrus Lands, and paid no mind to the low building to the left, though she did eye the stone walkway with its arched portals. The rosebush still grew to its edge, always in bloom, a sign of her power, a sign of her true nature. Ami longed to finger one of those petals now, but she had sought *Dangerous*, and *Dangerous* waited.

"Why did I lose my power?" she asked, the double of herself dressed as she was, the Assassin Princess attire of dress and boots—a killer style.

"You didn't, it's only been muted. Your power is still within you, a part of you. You can never lose it entirely."

"But it went away. You went away. I couldn't find you."

Her double shook her head and sighed. "She is a Sentry and she is powerful, but you are just as powerful. Believe in yourself and you will find your power when you need it; I will always be here." She touched Ami's chest above her heart. "I know you want to go in all guns blazing, but to stop her you must relent and listen. Talk to her. Then you'll find her weakness. But remember: do not give her more than you can afford, for your weakness is her power also."

Ami shook her head. "I don't understand. Who *is* she?"

"Talk with her. I will be here when you need me."

Her eyes opened to the dark room and the flickering red flame that still bound her. Though the storm had passed, she could still feel the rain in the breeze, cold and welcome against her heat-weathered skin. She thought of Raven, cursing herself for whatever had happened to him. *I should have helped him.* But of course, she couldn't, but perhaps she could find him now at least with the return of her powers. She closed her eyes again, but this time felt forward with her mind, out of the gallery and across the courtyard, the moonlight lighting the way as she peeked over the wall and allowed the power to feel out time. The storm restarted, or more precisely rewound, the strobes and flares flying from the land and back into the sky, soaring above her head. On the bridge below she watched a scuffle in reverse, too fast and quickly over.

Everything stopped.

Concentrating, remembering the sound of Raven's cry, Ami let the scene replay.

There she saw herself, though it wasn't her—a projection, a man made to look a monster, made to look like her. Disguises fell and Raven was caught, his trust won then quickly betrayed. Someone came though, and as Raven fell a white flash followed; a unicorn.

Next-girl? Florina?

Hero.

Raven had been saved and Hero had ridden away with him, but the monster-man that'd been her, had disappeared. With the storm gone Ami was able to project further. She'd never done this before, never left her body with such freedom outside of communing with *Dangerous*, and the world was hers to explore. The lightened sky was a lonely sight, the moon spreading its ethereal coolness upon wet streets, buildings short and tall, a dark town at rest. The stars were strange to her, making shapes and constellations both familiar and yet changed. She heard and saw much without meaning to, sensing the stirrings of others within the palace, and even the muted mutterings of those hidden in the houses, frightened and comforted only by each other—yet until the door opened behind her, she'd not heard the woman returning.

Her presence was a tumour on her senses, a dark mass entering her aura. She stood too close and it prickled like static upon her arms. Ami left the nightscape and returned in a rush, her eyelids opening to the dark eyes of the other, Romany.

"Come, Assassin Princess, we shall withdraw to a more comfortable setting." The flames extinguished, and Ami shuddered with the release, her relaxed muscles re-tensing. She fought her want for immediate flight and set her mind on *Dangerous,* her words running through her mind: *Talk with her. I will be here when you need me.*

The woman took her hand and Ami's power exploded inside her. It was as if every good feeling she'd ever had had been pushed into one, liquid metal beneath her skin, reigniting *Dangerous* in her heart and mind. Flowers bloomed behind her eyes and fireworks exploded until finally—always finally—blood spilled. Nothing Adam had ever given her had felt this way, and looking up at the woman now, Ami wasn't sure she'd meant to give anything at all. Romany's grasp was firm, her eyes sparked flints.

Raven was safe. Hero was here, and Ami was being pulled like a ragdoll.

"Where are we going?" she asked, but the woman gave no answer, pushing her through the double doors. Here there was a wide corridor laid with a thick red carpet, the walls covered with an intricate painted pattern, vivid colours, brushstrokes on plaster. Red threads connected with gold, making images of plants and vines such as Ami had seen climbing cottages and walls, ruins of castles and abbeys. They turned with the corridor, turn after turn, always left, always silent, sloping upward each time; a teacher leading a student, a parent leading a child, a guard leading a prisoner—Ami felt like all.

Romany's face was stolid, her expression fixed and blank, the hushed whisper of her dress the only sound. *Hush. Hush.* Sconces held torches high up and out of reach, bringing the woman's serpent armlet to life, its eye winking. Ami didn't like it.

The final turn revealed a dimly lit room through another set of doors, and despite herself, Ami felt comforted by the sight and smell. It was a library, immense in size and stacked floor to ceiling with books. Spines and covers of all kinds, many colours, different sizes. It was a jungle of knowledge. She could taste the tang of their musty pages and it made her think of home, back before Legacy, back before her power, back when she used to enter a library and browse the sections far removed from the mill of people; she used to imagine it was her own library, her own collection where she could spend her entire day reading, drawing, painting and creating.

In the centre of the room was a large marble hearth, a blazing fire within. A low table sat in front, guarded by two leather settees set opposite one another.

Romany let go of her hand and seated herself, indicating for Ami to do the same. Ami touched down on the very edge, her hands folding in her lap.

Out of the shadows came two of the robed elders who'd taken Raven and herself prisoner. They stood in waiting, thin hands stroking beards.

"Where is Jonus?" Romany asked.

The first man bowed. "Madam Romany, I shall fetch him for you."

"No," she said, "I do not wish to be disturbed. Find him, let him know that I've noted his absence. That is all."

The man bowed again and continued on out with the other. The second man locked eyes with Ami briefly before shutting the doors, and she wondered if it had been he who had attacked Raven. Then they were alone.

Ami shrank back into the sofa, weary and *en guard*. Was this woman aware of the power that now infected her every vein? That her own touch had revived that which she'd herself suppressed?

Romany's power was static between them—it almost crackled.

The woman placed the sword down against the hearth, her expression impassive, giving nothing away. Ami was sure her own told her whole story ... though perhaps not. If it had, the woman would surely not be wasting time on courtesy and comfort. The library was pleasant, caught in orange flickers and warmth. Disarming.

The crackle of the fire filled the silence between them.

Ami stared into the flames. They weren't the same flames that Adam had set in a similar grate, ones that turned to green and showed images of the past; they were just flames, hot on her skin, relaxing to watch.

Finally, with a sigh, Romany spoke, her soft lips parting to flash white teeth.

"I want your story. I want you to tell me everything about yourself, including how you obtained the sword."

"Why does it matter?"

"It matters." The fire licked at the woman's face, shifting the crescent of darkness, shifting the brilliance of light. "In turn I shall tell you of myself, if you wish to know."

"Are you the one causing the layers to shake?" Ami asked, and to her surprise the woman smirked.

"Yes and no. Is that why you are here? To talk of tremors and shakes? We cannot start like this." Her accent had become more pronounced, her voice remaining calm. Ami could have placed it in that moment, perhaps she could've guessed—something Eastern—but then the inclination slipped from her mind as the woman went on. "We must start with the story, the story from the beginning, for all reasons and all answers shall come from the story.

When we read a book, such as one from my collection here, we do not look at it and then ask of another how the middle sections ends. No. We shall start at the beginning."

"Then you start," Ami said, "and you tell me your story."

Romany's eyes touched on her, feather-light. "Okay, I shall tell you, I shall tell you my story so that you know, but once I have done, you are to tell me all of you. A decision shall be made, but only then. A decision that can only be sounded when all cards are shown."

Ami sat back, part of her mind chasing Raven through the dark, wishing she were with him, with her Hero; the rest remained focussed on Romany as she leaned forward into the light.

"Millions of years ago, there was a disaster that ripped the world apart; but for millions of years before that, there was us."

MATTUS CLOSED THE DOORS, but not without a further look back. The familiarity swept over him once more and he almost buckled. Trubus was there to catch him, but he shook him off. "I do not need your assistance, Brother."

"If you are about to faint again—"

"I did not faint the first time," he snapped. "It was—" But he didn't wish to say, didn't wish to confide. This was something that would frighten his brothers, and they would not understand. It could not be explained, though if there were reason behind it then the reason lay with her, with the girl.

He left the doors and walked away, Trubus hurrying to keep up.

"Where is Jonus? Madam Romany is not best pleased with his absence. She called on he before I. Where is he?"

Mattus did not answer, though he knew where Jonus had been. He'd found him playing with the man, had seen him. But Jonus had made matters worse, for the man had been spirited away by some unknowns—more strangers.

He pushed through a set of doors and continued on down a stairwell, no longer caring if Trubus followed. His mind was filled with the girl, images of the girl, images that haunted each corner of his mind. He would try to sleep, he would try to rest, but if she invaded his very dreams, what was he to do?

Slipping into his cell, he knelt by his bed in the pitch dark and prayed to the moon. He prayed that Madam Romany would give him worth, that she would have use for him, and that he would serve her well.

Part Two: Romany

Chapter Eight

A mber sparks burst from the dying log as if from a dragon, giving its last breath to the fireplace before finally collapsing, a used carcass burning still.

Carefully, the woman placed a new log upon the old; a dry snap of a broken thing, and the wood was lost, taken and consumed. The room brightened, and in that moment, all reflected with perfect clarity within the deep wells of her eyes, filled to the brim—a sheen, a shine, a glimpse of a tear ... gone.

"Millions of years. Yes, a long time ago, before such things as dinosaurs, and before the sea finally took back the land; back when all continents were as one, together for a brief union, and even then, back further still. There is no date I can give you in any calendar that you'd understand, and no way to explain how long ago I am talking of and how it doesn't even matter. Everything has changed, you see? Everything ... changed."

Ami listened in silence as the flames continued their obscene dance, the sacrifice slowly blackening.

They were dancing, too, the woman and she, she was sure.

"We were the *original* civilisation, the Sentries of Celestial. We ruled the lands as men do today, though we were more peaceful than men have ever been, more intelligent—too intelligent perhaps. Men existed, though were not much more than grunting apes. They lived outside the city in the forests and were of little concern. The city of Celestial though? How can I possibly explain?" She smiled. "It was our home, my home, a great city spanning almost the earth entire. I can see it now, the great white pillars of marble, the many steps of the tall council buildings; fountains flowing with sparkling water, tasting of fruits unknown and unmade; crowded markets, bustling trade, and the wide avenues that birthed scores of orchards for all to pick from and enjoy. There were many millions of us, all happy, each and every one. I never saw an unhappy person in all my time there, not truly unhappy. The sun would rise each day and crest the rooftops and buildings, setting a white fire on every stone surface, giving all that was green and brown life and growth. We had many meadows spanning hundreds of miles in all directions, home to woodland and lakes, and all animals that dwelt within each. Clear rivers connected the lakes and cut through the city to join the main branch, eventually leading to a faraway sea I'd never even seen, so vast was our world. And at night our land shone with white flamed lanterns below, and the brightest stars above. Perhaps the stars themselves saw our city as one of their own, a burning beacon misplaced from the cosmos. I don't know.

"As far as we knew, and as far as I have ever known, we were the beginnings of all that surrounded us, for who else but ourselves would have created such perfect beings? We were our own parents, our own history, spontaneous existence from eternal infinity ... a self-serving assumption to be sure, but who could say it was not so? We knew nothing of a *time before*. We were forever—or so we believed. In the end, it was that very belief that led to our ultimate demise."

Romany looked now to Ami, though she seemed not to see her at all. Her eyes had darkened and were now portals into memory of a long ago land.

"I was born and raised within the centre of the city, the capital of all governance within Celestial, and spent my youth with others my age, playing and creating, learning always. Upon reaching maturity I was tutored as a Creator, as my father had been before me, a position of great value. Others and I were tasked with the creation and recreation of life within the city, the wind of change and colour, such was the purpose of a Creator. I was to learn to master the powers that we all possessed, tame them, shape them, and with them learn to erect buildings from the ground, complete and functional—and of course, beautiful—and to level parts of the city no longer popular, putting them to better use. All of this was done with the power of mind and energy, magic.

"Though there was no death, and therefore no end, there *was* boredom and the need for change, and so the Creators were there to keep Celestial fresh. Inspiration was gained from imagination, though I also pulled from the wild forests outside of the city where the subspecies lived. I would visit them often, stepping quietly and quickly from the city, down the perimeter steps into the dark and unknown. I loved the feel of the branches as they scratched and groped, the cold earth beneath my bare feet, moist and strange, so much different from within the walls. I found all the inspiration I needed underneath the canopy of overlapping limbs.

"The smells were rich and I would close my eyes and practice, testing the scents and painting them as colours in my mind, and then off I'd go to explore, losing myself between the trunks for hours. I'd walk the slippery slopes of riverbanks where the ground disappeared, squelching through the mud to watch the shadowfish in dark water, and then on my hands and knees climb the fallen trees to reach a nest and spy on the feeding birds, their chirps so vital. I'd seek out the men who hid in hovels and rock caves, committing them to memory to bring back later as carvings within trees, their ape-faces exact in detail.

"I'd return filthy, the mud my paint, my mind brimming with all I'd seen. And then to work, to the courtyards of temples and council buildings, taking the drab stone surfaces in hand, and moulding them between my fingers into new life, new exciting, colourful things; vines, flowers, grasses; the brightest greens, blood red petals, sunrise golden leaves, scattered together in an explosion of life. The rose was a flower I'd found in the deepest and darkest realms of the outside, and the poppy had been lazing in the sun on the very outskirts of Celestial. I brought them all inside the walls. Ponds sprung up from grey, dry floors, and I squeezed the power within my hands tightly to create the golden fishes that swam there. It was a vocation and a passion. It was what I was."

Her eyes flickered in the firelight, and Ami watched her words play out in her mind like so many pictures, the pages of history. A cloud was coming though, she could see it, a swell of grey confusion. It shimmered on the edge of naivety, hidden by the shadow of surety. It was where the story was headed.

"The earth was a much different place millions of years ago, and so were the skies, the universe entire. We knew of planets and stars, systems and galaxies, more perhaps than any will ever know again. Our Scholars of Solitude studied the planets from their ivory towers, fine tuning their scopes and lenses, watching for hours, days at a time, the thirteen planets of the solar system, all in perfect alignment. They were irresistible to their curious minds, all laid out among the stars like a welcome path, whispering to them, teasing them in the night. *Come, know us.* Can you imagine? Perhaps you cannot see."

Romany sighed, folding her hands over and over. Ami saw the trepidation of the memories, almost felt sorry for her, for what was to come. She listened intently. "We were powerful, masters and creators of everything there was, all we could touch, taste, reach out to—but we could not reach out to the stars, and over time, the whisper became a voice, the timbre darkening in that one obsession. It became a thought that rippled through the scholars and out into the people. Celestial was no longer enough. We must have it all, for were we not Sentries? Creators?

"Soon everyone had caught the infection and a new fever was born within us, the voice a shout from the bell tower at midnight for crowds to gather for meeting and discussion. Eyes were drawn to the wonder of the tiny specks of flickering light, the small coloured spheres, and the shouts turned to actions, the magic that'd been a way of life to us becoming invention, industrious thought spreading like wildfire; everyone seemed to have an idea.

"Perhaps they should be brought? Lassoed and winched into an orbit? Or maybe a catapult of such power that half the city could be thrown in an instant to the unknown place? Roads were built, sloping to the skies, ending in nowhere as ideas changed. A stone ark was made, massive in size and ornate in design, big enough to take the entire population of Celestial. Upon its grand launch, hundreds were tasked with a joining of power to lift the giant boat swiftly into the night. We all watched as the white shape disappeared from view, and we all waited many days for its return. It never did. More plans were made instead, and while some took to flying, the power propelling them fast and long until they rose too high and froze, dropping from the sky, others thought of more subtle means, more scientific and mathematical.

"The earth was suddenly too small, too much a prison for our people. It was a virus we all caught, one that we had never encountered before. Why? Perhaps it was just our time to flounder ... though I still cannot truly believe that."

Ami was caught, the library no longer there as her eyes filled with the amber and gold of sunlight falling upon the figure of a woman, her hair a yellow fire as she leant against a doorway.

"One fine day, when all still seemed as it had, a friend appeared at the door of a temple I had been working in. I had just finished its new garden and was readying to leave.

"'Romany, come, all are being summoned,' she said, all too quickly and then was gone—I never saw her again. That memory stays with me most painfully; she, standing there in the doorway, the smile on her face like that of a child, pure innocence. I can no longer remember her name. We were but children, really." Romany shook her head and wiped at tears Ami couldn't see, composed herself and continued, bristling as if from the cold. The fire beside them burst orange embers that winked out into lapping tongues.

"I followed her through the doorway of the temple and out into the street. Immediately she was lost to me in a crowd, a mass of bodies moving as one and filling the wide avenue. From my last hold of the railing before being swept away, I caught sight of other streets emptying into my own, the throng heaving beyond the furthest buildings at the edge of view and filtering out into one of the large meadows I'd helped create at the centre of the city.

"I was taken, pressed between bodies both strange and familiar, my feet hardly touching the ground. It was hard to breathe. All was noise, chatter and talk, fearful, apprehensive and excited, a bubbling buzz. I caught few words, but those heard ignited the fever—this was an event, *the* event. *They'd done it.*

"We erupted as a cork from a bottle, spilling out across the lush green. Statues leaned over in greeting, empty marble eyes rolling, pale grey stone wings flapping in panic—I edged around them, stepping through flower beds and fighting hedge and shrub; the people, there were so many Sentries. It was an electric gathering, a festival brought together in a moment only.

"Spinning, I finally found an order and my place, close to the front, joining men, women and children, all encircling the centrepiece of our attentions: A marble and stone platform, rising up from the ground, an empty archway within, then another, and then a third; columns accompanied the arches coming to a canopy that sheltered all, settled upon the top. It was usual architecture, yet strangely foreboding, standing without structure, a lonesome gateway to nowhere. It made me shudder to look at it, though I didn't know why. This was not the same as the ark or the roads to the sky, nor a catapult or lasso. In its simplicity, its smooth and simple lines of marble, it spoke silently of power and thought. I cannot fully express, and maybe I alone felt it. It was bright white, but it felt like darkness.

"Eventually the crowds settled as a speaker with amplified voice took to the stage.

"'Fellow beings,' the speaker said, 'we have finally surpassed ourselves in all previous knowledge and ability. We, Sentries, are truly the creationists of the universe, for we, together and alone, have found the secret to bridging the mighty gap between the worlds.' He pointed up to the blue sky where, faint against the glare of the sun, outlines of each of the twelve other planets could be seen. Two were very much larger than the rest, and one of those was circled by ghostly rings. 'We are truly great, truly powerful, and finally we may continue to carry our wisdom from this place and onward.' All was applause and rapture. The speaker continued. 'We shall travel the planets, we shall extend Celestial through this gateway, and we shall do this right now.' He rejoined a group of robed men, the scholars who'd gathered close, eyeing their efforts smugly. I was hypnotised by this marvel of our intellect, of our power and superiority over all things. We all were."

Romany sneered, her beautiful and impassioned face a sudden contortion in the flames. Ami saw a shadow there that seemed bigger than the woman, as if it covered her and owned her, a parasite over a hollow shell. And then it passed, and the flames took her eyes once more.

"The scholars, each in turn, presented their power as if an offering to a temple, the worship of a new god—and why not call this god Progress by name? For that's what it was, what it was meant to be. Soon the power of each had combined to create the symbol of the Sentries. It floated in the air like a mist, rising from upturned faces and twitching fingers, all too keen, all too confident. Trails of power connected the crowd as willing Sentries gave themselves to it, feeding it as they'd done before. It was expected, it was why they were gathered, to power the crossing. Now many more joined—I joined—in intimate contact of body and soul, each Sentry just a puddle in the pool. The ghostly shape contracted and descended on the gateway. Now only a palm-width of glorious white across, it settled upon the surface of nothing and spread to fill the archway, shaped as the figure '8'. It glowed and shimmered, turning silver and then crystal glass.

"Then came the first shudder, a rumbling beneath us. The city shivered and Sentries grasped at one another, frightened perhaps for the first time. I looked about, hearing the crunch of buildings as they shifted and cracked. The air was thick with fear, the unsettled crowd now beginning to panic; chaos ensued. There were so many of us that more than half of us fell beneath the other, thousands of us scattering and scampering *en masse*. I was shunted back and forth, pushed front and centre until I was almost face to face with the strange arches and the symbol of the infinite. It was then that the world broke.

"There was a tinkling sound as the symbol cracked like a mirror from side to side, and then a terrible ripping that filled the whole world and silenced one and all. All eyes were on the archway.

"Then there was a scream, a scream that started with one and was echoed then by a hundred, a thousand. My hands clapped over my ears as the earth itself joined the one, high-pitched note—then there was no more symbol, no more crack. The figure '8' shattered, revealing a yawning mouth of darkness that sucked a howling gale through it. The world around us began to shatter, the meadow so many crystal fragments, a billion icicles falling under foot; buildings toppled and the trees of the woodland fell as holes were torn in reality, blue light flittering all around. The air was sucked from our lungs and blown out into the cosmos, and we were flying, here, there, hitting bodies of all those gathered, the entire population of existence. Stone, wood, animal alike, thrown, tossed—chaos I cannot truly convey." Yet Ami saw it, the utter destruction, confusion and panic. How quickly it had all happened. She would have been terrified. Then the terror multiplied by thousands, hundreds of thousands, as all minds connected for one universal '?' that hung above a chasm of nothing. "There was one of me, and then three, each facing the other, screaming in terror as the sky broke and the world just ceased to be. Now it wasn't buildings that fell but reality itself, shivering, splitting, the power of each Sentry exposed and exploited, exploding from each in desperation. The three of me were birds and trees, flowers flying from my own outstretched hand, petals disappearing into a void; then there was six of me and I saw ghosts of everything, saw everything from everywhere. I saw the world entire from a great height where the stars themselves had changed or departed, and the earth—now in a million pieces—reflected a million of me a million times.

"Then I fell and kept falling, though I remained somehow on the meadow, alone and yet surrounded. Then I was many, I was all, and the surrounding bodies that weren't there were all me. Words cannot describe." She gave a brief smile, her finger stroking the symbol upon the sword. "The world divided at that point, as did I, as did all, and through empty eyes I saw that all had been reduced to dust, remade ... remade infinite.

"I was thrown in all directions and scattered, knowing only that my final fall snapped branches and trunks, landing me on the earth with such force that a crater formed. I was cast out. Cast out."

Ami shifted in her seat, hearing the last words repeated as a whisper in her mind. *Cast out.* The light in the room seemed to dim with the emotion, with the silence of the moment.

"Confusion became order, and an eternity of darkness awaited. I was naked and cold, and the cold calmed me, comforted me like a blanket. I had never known death, yet the concept occurred to me then, in that time; the end of everything, the end of life, the incomplete and sudden stop."

Ami shivered and rubbed her arms lightly. The fire was burning hot, yet she felt the lonely cold the woman described. The innocence had been broken, shattered. She had a small idea of the shock, as her own life had been broken and remade—but this was much, much different.

Romany caressed the symbols upon the blade and hilt of the sword, her touch thoughtful, her eyes filled with a venomous heat. She pulled her hand away.

"Everything I had ever known was now different, and when I opened my eyes to the darkness, I knew I was different, too. My body had changed. I cannot truly tell you how, but only that it was not the same, as if it was missing something, though all limbs were accounted for. I had a power still, though I also felt the absence of power, and when I looked around me properly, I knew I truly lacked company. I was alone.

"The darkness was not complete though, but only a night, and I had fallen beneath the boughs of a large tree. The ground was earthy, and small animals crawled over my skin. I brushed them off and felt the change in myself again, how familiar it felt, yet how different at the same time. Pulling myself up from the ground I ventured from my crater, through the trees and out into a clearing.

"All around me were hills in the dead of night; hills, valleys, patches of woodland. There was a moon, a glowing orb of brilliance that I'd never seen before, and it shone pale upon the land, showing enough to be able to say for certain that I recognised none of it, that I was no longer in Celestial. Everything had changed."

She sat back then and stared at Ami, her hands placed within her lap. "That is who I am, where I am from."

"But, what happened next?" Ami asked.

"Perhaps you would like to start your own story now, Assassin Princess? Who are you, and where do you come from?"

Knowledge is power, true power. Do not give her more than you can afford.

Ami began.

THEY'D COME TO A STOP beneath a canopy of trees, and there, shaded from the moonlight and the lightening sky, they'd set up camp. A small peak between low-laying branches showed the palace tower, and before them, the side-rise of the hill and all its silent homes, cut at its base by the still, dead river.

Hero lifted Raven from Florina's back and lay him on the grass, pulling his hood from his head and smoothing his hair, remembering all too well the death of Kane, their brother in the Guard, their friend. He'd failed to save him ... but this was not then. Raven was weak, but alive, his breathing little more than coughs grating against his throat. Florina lowered her muzzle and pushed him onto his side where coughs became fluid barks, and a lungful of black water left him. Once rid, Raven seemed to settle and slipped back into sleep.

Hero looked to Florina, but she'd already trotted into the foliage, emerging a moment later the fresh young woman once more. Her hair fell in streams down her shoulders and she flicked it, kneeling now beside them, slowly moving Raven to his back.

"Is there anything you can do for him?" he asked, watching pale shadows slip across her face, the sky beyond the shade shifting clouds against the rising sun and paling moon.

"I'm not sure. See here?" She ran her fingers across Raven's skin. They came away oily and dark. "There's something in the water, something unnatural. Have you noticed it doesn't flow?"

Hero nodded, giving a glance to the silent stream.

"Whatever this stuff is, it sucked him under. I struggled to grasp him. It wasn't pleasant." She undid the front of his robes and pulled them open, stroking over his chest. "Dry here. I think he'll be okay."

A wind travelled down the side of the hill and crossed the river, blowing through the branches, howling light and low, a whisper of warning. Hero stood to face it, surveying the land. All was quiet now, but for the wind, the creak of wood, the movement of life in the dark disturbed. The rise of the sun, slow but close, gave him a sense of hope. It was barely enough to tinge a sea-bearing cloud violet-grey, but it was enough. The night had been too long.

"He was calling out for Ami," Florence said, bringing him back. "Perhaps he'd found her, or maybe re-found her?"

"Perhaps." Hero knelt back down, using his own robe to wipe the oil from Raven's skin, a thin layer of jelly. "Can you feel anything? Anything wrong with Raven?"

"I feel nothing wrong, just exhaustion." She paused, looking down at him. His face had slackened, relaxed. "You don't think ... Would she have deserted him?"

"No," Hero said. "Why would she do that?"

"It wouldn't be the first time. We don't really know her, Hero."

"Do I really know you?"

She sighed. "You're being defensive. Listen. You know what happened to her, the twisted power Adam gave her. It's never going to go away. She'll always be on the knife-edge of dangerous."

"Her heart is pure—"

"I have no doubt of that," Florence continued, "but it's a heart that's been corrupted before, and could be corrupted again. Wherever she is, she wasn't with Raven, she didn't come to his aid. If we hadn't have been there, then he'd be dead now. This is on her, this—"

"Silence," Hero whispered. "If it is on her, then it's on me, too. I sent him to find her instead of going myself. But instead of blaming blindly, let's put our efforts into finding Ami and the cause of the storms, the disruption between the layers. Raven is alive. Let us be thankful for that."

Florence remained silent, her eyes dropping to Raven, her hand on his cheek. Hero walked to the edge of their scant shelter, looking once more to the sky. Eventually, she joined him.

"This place is unstable, this whole town, this whole world. What I saw within the Solancra and Planrus forests, what I saw coming from the ground before the Mortrus Lands was terrifying. It's all linked, and Ami's absence is a bad omen."

His hand gripped the hilt of his sword, a habit he lapsed into more and more. "We need to be cautious of this, of these events and of the magic deep within Ami."

Florence knelt back down to Raven's side and began loosening his scabbard. "He's lost his sword."

Hero looked over and frowned. "Lost? He wouldn't have lost it. A Guard isn't careless. Taken perhaps?" A thought occurred to him then. "What if Ami's sword had been taken? What if Ami has been taken also?"

"She's too strong, too powerful to be jumped by rogues or thieves."

Hero pointed back to the palace. "I have no doubt. She wasn't taken by thieves, but that man that attacked Raven?" Hero paced, his heavy boots crushing the brambles that reached to snag him. He looked to the tower, tall and dark against the now pale grey, rubbing at his stubbled chin. "They would discard Raven, but they would keep Ami. For her and her sword. She must be inside."

"How do we know it hasn't been Ami the whole time? All that power, the falling stars?"

"I don't want to think that of her. No. The Shadow Princess—"

"*Is* Ami. We must consider it."

Hero looked down at Raven, knowing that if he were awake, he'd help to fill in the blanks. His eyes fell then on something that poked from beneath his robes. It was small, barely discernible in shadow, a sharp corner crossing his chest. He knelt and plucked the object.

"What is that?" Florence asked.

"It's a small book." He scanned the cover but it was blank. Flicking through the pages revealed text too small to read. He adjusted his stance to the light, but it was no use. "The writing is so tiny."

"He will have been carrying it for a reason." Florence took the book from him and scanned it quickly, stopping upon a random page. There, between the lines, was a hand drawn picture. "So much detail on such a small scale. Someone had fantastic eyesight. I'll keep it safe."

She slipped it into her robes.

"I wonder what Raven was doing with it?"

"We can't know until he's recovered," she said, touching her hand upon the man's forehead. There was a light glow beneath her palm, a white light of warmth. "He needs a little more time. He's been through a lot."

As the first full ray of sun filtered through the branches, it touched Raven's robes, stained scarlet.

Oh, Ami, he thought, *I hope it's not your blood.*

HE'D BEEN INTERRUPTED, and the man lived.

Something that shouldn't have happened, couldn't have happened, happened. A creature had appeared, full of power, full of magic. A unicorn. The existence of magical horned horses was absurd, and yet tonight he'd seen one. The bumbling man that had arrived with it was nothing, but ..."Where did the unicorn come from?"

He looked down from the window and across the town. The men and unicorn had fled long ago, and the sun now began to rise over the hill. It touched his skin, warming it. Trubus told him only moments ago of Madam Romany's warning—but something bigger was happening here. She was not angry. If she were, she would've found him herself and punished him. She was slipping, but not through carelessness. No, to think her careless would be a mistake. She was powerful, wise, a goddess; but all had changed with the capture of the girl, of the sword. Instead he felt ..."Neglected," he whispered to no one.

He turned now, leaving the room and walking through the torch-lit corridors toward the library. He would take her sustenance to show his regrets for not being on hand, he would offer apology and tell her the truth, that he was dealing with the male stranger that had attempted to cross the bridge after curfew. But should he tell her of the startling discovery of a unicorn within the land?

His pace quickened, his heart thumping inside his narrow, old chest. What was truly going on? Madam Romany was a goddess, no question of that, and yet she'd been releasing her rain of power more and more frequently, causing the earth to tremble, and it was getting worse. *He* was awake.

Things were changing too fast.

Jonus poured wine into two goblets and placed them on a silver tray, taking them the short journey to the library. His approach was cautious as he looked about him constantly; no one was around. The library doors were shut, sealed against him, against them, The Order, the only other occupants of the palace.

He placed his ear against the seal and listened.

"... left the Mortrus Lands. Adam had gone, and I was free once more."

"The Mortrus Lands, do they still exist? Is the power still—wait."

Jonus jumped back from the doors, but not quick enough to abate the suspicion upon Madam Romany's face as she appeared at the jamb, her eyes burning red.

The goblets toppled, and wine spilt as pain wracked his wretched body. He felt his age suddenly, felt all the years crushing him from all sides. His bones were breaking, splinters of ice pressing through his skin. His sight failed him.

The doors slammed shut against a goblet that spun across the floor. The pain left soon afterward, replaced by cold wine against his cheek that stained his beard red.

Bones mended within him, knitting back together as they always did. His chest puffed as the muscles strengthened, but Jonus remained on the floor. Even when he heard the patter of feet, he did not rise. His breath returned in short, sharp gasps, and the voices of his brothers surrounded him, but however much he blinked, Jonus could no longer see.

Chapter Nine

The doors swung shut, the latch snapping as Romany took to her seat once more. Her dress whispered as she crossed her legs, the anger exhibited only moments ago lost within the smooth contours of expression. It would've been easier to believe that nothing had happened, that the distant sound of shuffling and rasped voices beyond the doors weren't there. But Ami had glimpsed the emptiness beyond the beauty, and whether caused by abandonment or power, Ami could only wonder. What she was now sure of was that Romany was a monster. She'd almost failed to fear her as her memories gave voice to secrets she'd shared with no one else; now, though, she remembered her shadow's warnings and understood their meaning.

The woman leant forward to stroke the blade, one arm resting on her knee, her chin cupped in her palm—her eyes were an Egyptian dark, a soft shield hiding cruelty and malice. What she'd just seen unpicked woven words, and yet despite herself, Ami felt the spell begin to take hold once more. Her thoughts strayed to Adam and how easily she'd fallen beneath his shadow, and she vowed not to let the same happen here.

"You have told me much," Romany said, "but you have yet to tell me of this blade. I've seen weapons, but this is marked as Sentry; there were no such blades in our ancient land." Her eyes fell on Ami. "So, it was passed to you through your brother, and before him, your father, and his father before him, but from where did it come from?"

Ami hadn't thought it wise to speak of the power of the sword or its origins, for it was the one thing that she was so desperate to know. *Play the game,* she thought, *dance the dance.*

Time passed.

How long had they been there, how long had she listened, spoken? Hours could have been days, or perhaps only minutes and not yet an hour? It was not so easy to say. There were no windows that she could see, no way to tell the time of day. Perhaps it was midday? Or the next evening? Hunger had not arrived, thirst had not come calling, and the human need to defecate and urinate had disappeared entirely. The wood cracked and fizzled in the fireplace, the smell of old leather and warm pages comforting in the quiet. It was all calculated, all a setup, though she'd been slow to realise it. The library, the fire, all subtle magic to lure and to lull her; a soft interrogation.

Battle lines were being drawn here, and so Ami kept her silence, letting time tick by in flame-licked snaps and pops.

After a moment, Romany relented and her gaze returned to the fire. Her dress whispered again as she uncrossed and re-crossed her legs. "Very well," she said, "tit for tat. I will tell you more. It may yet illuminate.

"The land remained dark, with no sunrise nor sunset, only a moon that lit the path my feet might travel; and travel they did. I walked a desolate place for a time unknown, mounting each hill and crossing each stream. All sentient life seemed extinct. There were no birds, no deer, no horses; there were no fish in any water; there were no men or Sentries. I continued to look for any sign of my people nevertheless, for what else was I to do?

"I was the same, yet different, my flesh changed from what it had been; yet I was whole and alive, eternal still. Perhaps a hundred years had passed, or thousands more since my expulsion? Too long a time to travel alone in a dark world, rarely sleeping and forever searching. Occasionally, very occasionally, I'd spy a flash of light in the distance, a strange flickering against shadowed land—but were I to investigate, I found only scorched, burned earth and nothing more. Ground lightning, I told myself, and over time I learned to ignore such strangeness. Perhaps I was losing my mind? Who wouldn't, walking the earth alone for an eternity?"

Ami saw her words play out, a figure alone on a flat and endless meadow, the moon bleaching the rippling grass a silver sea; her hair whipped long and wild around her as she walked in no direction with no end in sight. Not a single tree stood by for comfort, not a single rise or rock, fall or gulley, yet she moved onward still. It was desperate and dark and chilling.

"There were times I would settle in once place for a while and sit, thinking of a life many lifetimes gone, of the friends I'd had, of my father, though I barely recall him now. I'd think of the humans I'd petted, and of how they'd brought offerings to me, their simple minds barely beyond savagery. I missed them all. I missed everything, and I'd let the memories fill me, imagining a reunion, perhaps over the next hill, within the next forest, where they'd all be waiting for me—would be happy to see me. I'd be home again ...

"My journeys were always in hope, from woodland to field, to mountainous climb, from each lake and pool to every cave within the deep, dank earth. Each dropped apple, rotting in the dark, could be a meal just finished and left by a traveller; fallen branches were a den abandoned, and I was always a step behind reconciliation. I'd arrive back at the same, familiar hills over and over, unsure whether I'd walked a circle, or travelled the earth entire; and the ghosts of Celestial walked and talked with me always, shadow on shadow, whisper on wind. They told me of their struggle and surprise, how if I were swift I'd catch up and find them gathered."

All became quiet as the final log died, and Romany reached into the hearth, creating three more from nothing but air. She lowered them into the flames and the dance resumed with a spit and lick and spark.

Ami watched the feast.

"It was in a woodland that I happened upon an object, an object that brought me both happiness and devastation. I'd been climbing a steep bank, my hands and feet bare, rough with callouses from healing wounds that reopened constantly on the rocks. It was a hard climb, and though I'd fallen more than once, I eventually made it to the top and to a mighty forest there. Looking out over the edge I could clearly see where the earth had shattered and fallen, having eventually grown over with grass, vines and brush to start afresh. I saw roots from the most ancient trees hanging grey-green and white against the lit slopes of the abyss, and I still pondered them as the wind rose, bringing with it the first light smattering of rain. It had rained so seldom that the very feel of it on my skin frightened me, and so I slipped between the trunks of the trees and entered the oaken forest. The shelter of the interwoven branches kept the rain out, though far above I heard the hushed sound of the mighty fall. The moon was also lost to me, and so I made my way between the trees mostly by touch, feeling my path ahead and listening to the muted chatter of the hidden limbs. They spoke, I was sure, tittering and ticking as they talked of me. My powerful sight saw only that which was in front, so thick was the darkness. My footing slipped more than once and as the ground gave way to a sharp decline, I quickly lost my balance. I tripped, slipped, and tumbled, stopping suddenly against a hard column of stone at the bottom of the slope. Dazed, I lay with my head propped upon its cold surface, staring up into the dark.

"Eventually my wits returned and I touched it, sliding my hand across it.

"I needed to see it.

"Raising my arm I sent power shooting upward to divide the trees, showering moonlight and soft water upon my upturned face, and down upon the stone. Smooth it was, curved and taller than myself. This wasn't shadow, but it was a ghost. A white stone column, a discarded relic, lodged at an angle and thrust between two trunks. My eyes and hands followed its course, and I climbed upon it as if a horse, shuffling up its shaft until I reached the broken top. It hung over a previously unseen chasm, a fall into darkness where there were no trees, only black rock and coal."

Romany paused, ever more the girl. "It was horrific. Soul destroying."

"Why?" Ami asked, a small whisper.

"After thousands upon thousands of years alone, I had created my own Celestial in my mind, an uninterrupted future from living shards of memory. Now I could touch a *true* shard of memory, a shard that shattered all illusions. It was a part of Celestial, it was a part of my home without a doubt—and they were all gone, everyone. My fantasies were nothing, the shadows only absence of light, of life. I was alone, and Celestial, each and every living being I'd known since time had begun ... gone.

"I'd found the first proof of end. Of death.

"It had been made, sculpted with hands, heart and soul, power and magic. It was real and I could touch it, and touch it I did, first stoking it, then slapping it, then thrusting my fists against it so hard that I bled. All that time alone, desperately desolate, and here from nowhere was proof of my isolation. There *had* been a civilisation, there *had* been a grand city ... had been. Gone."

Ami closed her eyes and felt the pain of the awakening. She saw Romany there, her fists pounding the stone, blood spattering black in silver light and shade; she looked down on her as if hovering above the trees, seeing the whole silent forest, hearing only her sobs.

"I spent a long time at the column, pondering and thinking, hurting and healing, looking around for other finds, a wall perhaps, or a single slab of marble. I dug deep into the earth, ripping skin from bone, and used the power to fell trees to look beneath them. Nothing. I found nothing. I stayed, thinking that if I left for even a moment, the column would vanish, sealing my madness. I knew that if that were to happen, I would scream and scream and scream and never be able to cease.

"My grief had immobilised me, but it had done nothing so dire to the world around me, and things began to change.

"It started light, a subtle rumble beneath me, a feeling so slight that I was able to lay upon the column and ignore it almost entirely, but then it grew stronger and I became cold with fear. I sat up, alert suddenly, for what if this world was to shatter as Celestial had done? Would I be lost twice over, or cease as all other life had done? The mighty earth was cracking, a sound that marked the end of everything. The empty void of *after-infinite* had followed me, had come finally, licking its darkest lips and gnashing its teeth. It snapped its jaws and the land split, the earth beneath my legs parting in such a terrific way that I had to scramble to keep hold of the column—but the column was moving also, heaved up and out of the ground by shifting banks. I clung on for as long as I could, clods of mud and rock falling as land rose above and fell. And there gaped the chasm of *after-infinite,* an awesome mouth of yellow-orange, burning spittle. The column upended and fell toward it, and in sheer panic I let go, gripping instead to the trunk of a tree. The last of my old world shot downward like an arrow into a burst of steam, lava and roiling white water. It disappeared, and I'd found purchase at the end of the earth.

"But the land hadn't finished, and the gap widened still, the tree I clung to falling—I had to climb as land folded back upon itself, releasing the earth's fiery blood which shot into the air. More came, spluttering and bubbling, all smoke, steam and cascading vapour, rising and consuming all, an inferno. Blinded by the fire in eternal darkness, boiled and seared by the insurmountable heat, deafened by the roar of end upon end, I fell."

"What happened to you?" Ami asked.

Romany startled, as if she'd forgotten she was there. "You are so interested? What is the secret of this sword?"

"There is no secret."

"Where was it made? What power does it possess?"

Ami remained silent.

Romany reached out and grasped the blade, a flare of red fire running the steel. She gripped it tight, her fingers bleeding as it cut into her, yet still it would not yield as another power pushed back, the flames joined by flickers and sparks of purple and green; then they ceased and disappeared, leaving only steel threaded with lines of blood.

She released it and leaned back. "I need the power within," she whispered.

"You can't have it," Ami whispered back. Her own power had tightly coiled within, though to what end she wasn't sure. The woman was too strong, she knew that, could feel it. She couldn't defeat her, and so she let the power settle, watching with mild disgust as Romany licked the blood from her fingers like a cat, the wounds fading with each grotesque lap.

"I can almost taste the power. The Assassin Princess, a sword of Celestial ..."

She seemed frozen then, the eerie statue once more, her gaze locked in space, her face slack and lifeless. It was as if she'd left her body, leaving nothing more than an empty shell in her place. Never, during this whole time, had Ami felt horror as she now did, watching as Romany's wounds leaked, dark liquid staining, the tap of blood spotting the shadowed floor.

Minutes went by.

Ami shuffled forward, looking with wonder at her vacant stare. Her sword was only a reach away, yet even if she had it, could she escape the palace before Romany could react? She imagined the strike of a snake, the elegant but powerful hands wrapping around her throat and snapping her neck in a second. What were her chances? She raised her hand and tested her power, feeling the crystal-formed-steel shift, seeing it tilt ever so slightly. Then Romany was back, her eyes fluttering, tiny muscles animating dead flesh across bones and sinew.

Ami lowered her hand, though the woman gave no sign she'd noticed.

"So," she said, "you will not tell me? I will know in time, I assure you. I shall either hear it from you, or force it from the sword. But perhaps we *should* continue with my tale until *he* is ready."

He. Ami frowned. *He.*

The woman stood now and strode past her, disappearing into the shadow of the stacks only to reappear in a blaze of light as a window was uncovered. Ami winced. The glare lessened and for a moment she glimpsed the pretty girl who the woman had once been, her skin a light bronze against the panes, her hair shining like falls of chocolate silk that she pushed back behind her shoulders. A princess, a queen, looking now from a great height on a fortified stead. The shutters were folded back from the windows and the library was fully lit for the first time, dust falling, rising, flying in secret shafts before vanishing. It was a cell of hidden knowledge laid bare, as was the woman, all menace veiled behind the façade of beauty and youth.

"It was the start of something more terrifying than I could ever explain," she said, thoughtfully touching the glass. Ami slid against the back of the sofa to listen, curling her feet beneath her. The heat of the fire warmed her legs and back; she felt sleepy. "It was the beginnings of a new world, though I'd never truly known the old one. I'd been thrown into a river of lava and steam, burning, burning, burning, my flesh slipping from my bones—and then I was discarded, thrown, and landed face down in the thicket of what remained of the vast forest. A bloody mess, a horror I'm sure, I stood final witness to the end of times, the earth splitting, the fiery blood of nature shooting high into the dark, smoke-filled sky. The chasm had divided into two, and with one half risen, the other sunk, taking water and earth alike deep into the depths. It swallowed all I could see; it didn't stop there. My body healed in hours as the world around me changed. Skin and bone rejuvenated. I moved on, watching the rapid rise of an ocean where there had once been land. *An ocean,* the first I'd even seen. It was vast and I watched it form as I walked the edge of the new cliff. Soon nothing was left of where I'd been, the terrain having changed for good, for always. Mountains were formed, broken and reformed, and in time I scrambled up them to higher ground, the sea continuing to rise, reclaiming the cliff and the ancient trees.

"What had been seabed was now land, flourishing in growth and colours I'd never known, the old lands a horizon, slipping further and further away. I went higher and higher, beating the rising water, watching as a mysterious glow filled the sky, the earth showing its first glimpse of sunlight since the split of the layers.

"I'd have to explore it all over again—and so I did—I as naked and as wild as the new world around me.

"The first desert took me by surprise, and without death, the agony of thirst and hunger burned. The first winter took me with cruel fingers and led me to freeze in ice and snow for a whole season, with no shelter or warmth to be found. I was but a dream, wandering and wondering and existing, though I never forgot Celestial.

"My familiar green came again, night and day the only break in an infinite existence. Valleys opened their grand mouths presenting fruit, flowers, streams and falls. I ventured deep, climbing down jagged slopes, slipping into pools and lakes where I bathed. All around were wild and dangerous animals hunting, razor teeth, fur covered tigers and bears; reptiles shared the waters and marshes, while creatures far bigger stalked and roamed above the tallest oaks and pines.

"I fashioned myself a shelter within a high up cave, using the power to protect myself from harm—I was lost, enveloped by a new life I didn't understand. I was alone, and I was scared.

"I spent many an eon within that valley, watching it flatten and wear away, watching even the largest of the predators fall and die before the waters claimed all again, and I moved on.

"Yet, no matter how far I travelled, I felt Celestial following me. Funny, I thought, that only upon the realisation that all I'd know had truly gone, did I finally realise that it was still all around me. Not the same as the column, a relic, no, but what was so different, really? The sun rose and crested the tallest mountain peak, besting its height and glory and flooding the land with golden light that brought each colour and shape to life. Indeed, more than this, I became engrossed in the detail of life itself, chasing the butterflies as they soared and dipped, crouching to watch four-legged beasts run in herds and jump ravines. Hadn't this been my world also, outside of Celestial's walls? And when the sun set, and thick mists rose from the rivers, did the stars, however different, not shine the same as always?

"It was in the night that I still caught flickers and flashes in the periphery of sight, the ground lightning I'd seen before. I felt the power in them each time, and each time I turned too late ... all but the last time at least. Out there." Romany pointed beyond the window pane, then slowly turned back to Ami. She retook her seat, glancing at the sword against the hearth, saying nothing more of it. Her focus wandered, and Ami thought that perhaps she would blank out again, but her attentions returned with a smile. A grimace.

"I had come at last to a cliff that hung above a raging sea, a lush and fertile land pre-dawn. To step out of the treeline was to meet a ferocious wind, cut with salt and spite, and though I'd tread many a water's edge, never could I recall such a slap of nature's wrath. The woodland around, green and alive as it was, reminded me of long ago times, of stepping from Celestial and into the wild woods beyond—and for good reason, for what did I find here but bipeds, a community of men?

"I was careful and curious, and having spied the animal-skin covered hunters, followed them in stealth back to their dwelling. In a gulley was a river, and to each side were huts of wood and mud. I watched them, camouflaged and as dark as any shadow. You cannot understand. None can. At first I hated them, and then I envied them, yearned for their company, these strange creatures who were so alike and dislike those long ago savages. All this time in contemplation, I moved not an inch. Yet finally I turned, set on leaving, set on bitter rejection, so long alone, and now? Such a revelation.

"Then I saw a flicker at sunrise, a flash so close. It came from the cliff edge. Through the thicket, cresting a hill, the white flashes lit a path for the sun and burned my eyes. Soon I found myself scrambling from the gulley and back toward the sea, slipping silently away from the sleeping men, women and children. It was ground lightning, power left by my own kin, I was certain. It called to me, connected with me, and now fixated on the white light, I climbed the land both hard and wet, clawing the ground on all fours, descending at a run on two. I darted between tree and beneath branch and jumped the rocks, the sea wind catching me, scratching with dark claws from shadows unseen.

"Then I was there, and from the first, knew I'd been right."

"What did you see?" Ami asked.

"It was a hole in the earth, a well, filled with light and encircled by stones. The men had enshrined it, recognising it as powerful magic, and had written meaningless symbols either side, scattering small, carven statues—they didn't matter. What mattered was that it was a link, a link to Celestial. Just looking down into it, bending against a trunk, gave me knowledge as if reading a note left long ago. I gained a little understanding of what had happened to the land I'd once lived in and loved in, and what it was I'd found. This well of white lighting was a portal, and I was suddenly sure of this as if it'd been whispered into my heart. Yet after millions of years alone, I was unsure of almost everything else. What did it all mean? Where did it lead, and why had it been left there? I got to my knees and peered into it, into the bright light of my people. I felt its power even more so now, and my own peaked and reached out toward it. It felt like *home.* I put my hand into the well, sending a spark high into the air, and as I touched the light I saw patterns in my mind, fragments of lands and beings, fingers of light and magic streaming into me. I saw myself reflected in mirrors, so many mirrors, stretching so far back into obscure darkness."

Ami's heart leapt as she remembered her own three mirrors, the three versions of herself she'd chosen from, finally choosing *Dangerous.*

"I moved closer to look deeper, to enter the light and travel back to Celestial—but something was not right, was in fact terribly wrong. Each mirror of myself was as lost as I was, as changed as I was. I saw no Celestial; and then I understood the terrible truth, the knowledge passing through the power in disjointed fragments. I looked toward the land that would later become this very town. I looked all around me, into the night and to the sunrise that had quickly risen beyond the ocean, that had broken and lay a fiery line across the furthest horizon. I looked back into the well, my hand submerged, and finally realised: It wasn't just *like* Celestial, the stars, the trees, the animals, old and new, it *was* Celestial. Every part of it. The split within the fabric of reality that had started at the meadow had been the fragmentation of our world, a fragmentation that had reformed into *this.* It was all Celestial. It was none of it Celestial.

"The well of power was a portal, but not for passage. It was a link, a string holding fragments together. I also knew now why I was changed, for the power had given this knowledge to me, too." She stood up and looked at Ami. "You said that the Sentries of the

Mortrus Lands joined with the land, with the forest, in a bid to continue to survive, to be ... more whole."

Ami nodded. "Yes."

"Somehow, I had joined with a human. It was the only thing that made sense, I suppose. It was why I survived. We were immortal, as I still am. We could not die, but we could not live. We were thrown from ourselves, and as Sentries merged with your Mortrus Lands, I merged with a different living thing. A human. As I look down at myself now, I see what I hadn't seen in all of my lonely years. I look human." She strode to the window and back to the door, returning again in agitation. Golden sunlight reflected in bright sparkles against her armlet, and Ami mused over its serpent form. "What you see of me now is not how a Sentry once looked, though what my appearance was then has faded from memory." Her eyes wandered to the sword. "I stood from that place and walked back to the edge of the cliff, taking all the wind had to give. I watched the sun rise fully, the yellow orb still a stranger to me, yet the most perfect sight. Its colours scattered on waves, bled over ripples. I thought to the tribe of men behind me, and decided on how I might live. It was time to leave Celestial behind and start again, new and powerful like the sun. That put an end to my lonely existence, and from that moment I was to learn who I truly was. I took control of the tribe and the land, and built upon the site of their *sacred well,* protecting my heritage. Now the hill holds a town, this very palace on the site of their wooden and mud huts. I found a life, a purpose, and as their goddess I am all powerful. Reborn, I've ruled this place for thousands of years.

"I returned, however, to the well of power again and again through the centuries, and the portal still remains. There is much to say on what the portal connects to, where the strings split and tie—but there's nothing I can tell you that you don't already know." She stood finally by the fire and extinguished the last of the dying flames, cooling the logs with her breath, the once glowing red wood now iced and frozen. "Portals have been opened, left open, closed, used, misused, through all of the layers," she said, still eying the sword, "each ground lightning an example, and your Mortrus Lands, too, where Sentries once tried to reform Celestial. I, myself, have attempted ... is that how you came to be here?" Ami remained quiet, watching the woman flirt with the sword, the powerful metal she couldn't master. "It doesn't matter." She sighed, her fingers once more tracing the symbol. "You are here, and now you know how all came to be as it is."

"That doesn't explain the tremors, the quakes," Ami whispered. "You've only recalled the past. Why does the earth tremor?"

Romany flicked the blade into the air with the tip of her finger and caught the hilt, slicing the sharp, curved steel of the katana at Ami's chest. Ami remained poised, though the power within her boiled and writhed, *Dangerous* roiling for a fight. The tip found and grazed her skin. A flourish of power followed, purple and green flames running the edge. Romany gasped with delight, her eyes taunting Ami's restraint. She spun the blade and angled it back to her heart.

"Of course, much more has happened since that time, you're right," she said, watching the coloured magic join with Ami and slip beneath her skin. Her hair sparked and fizzled, purple stars falling. "Yes, you're the key to this secret power. It answers to you, and you alone."

"What you're doing is hurting people," Ami said. "It's ripping layers apart—"

"You think I don't know what I do? Ah, but you don't know what I do, what I discovered, what I—"

She stopped and pulled back the sword, her face dropping, her expression vacant.

This is your chance. Taking great care, Ami stood from the seat and stepped backward. The blade had dropped to the woman's side, its tip touching the rug. Could she pluck it from her while she was in stasis? It was now or never.

Dropping to her knees, Ami snatched the blade from her, throwing herself clear as a slack arm rose to stop her, fingers snapping and clamping on nothing. She was almost at the window, only a jump away from smashing through the glass, a free fall to the ground below—then something struck her and sent her sprawling. She hit the floor, rising only to meet a wall of burning red brick. It surrounded them both, enclosing them, the library gone, the sunshine and blue sky of escape cut off.

Romany's fists crawled with black fire.

Ami raised her sword, but with a simple flick, the woman sent the deathly black flame out like a whip. It caught her wrist and snapped it with an audible *clack,* and the sword dropped to the ground. Ami screamed an echo around the burning chamber.

"That was very rude." Romany seethed red anger, her hands turning to talons, snatching and scratching the air in front of her. She opened her mouth to a yawn of black light that released a long forked tongue, licking and lashing. Ami dodged its thrust forward, her shoulders burning as she fell back against the wall. Cradling her hand, she made a grab for her fallen sword that now lay in the space between them, but the black fire whipped her again, snapping her other wrist as the first. The pain was unbearable, and she hated hearing her own screams echoed back.

The thing that had been a woman laughed. She was no longer beautiful, but a she-devil, flame and fury, her hair a fan around her head, the ends prickling with red sparks; her eyes were the colour of molten iron, and her grin was straight from hell. She breathed death and rot, the air becoming steel grey and silver with it. Ami couldn't breathe, and the fire wall contracted around them.

Dangerous.

There was nothing she could do.

"Show me its power," Romany cried, the poisonous air gathering, coiling in the shape of a snake, its eyes a blaze of red. "Release the sword to me, and you will live."

Dangerous.

Ami closed her eyes, letting the power within flow down her arms, mending her broken wrists. She felt the snake slither, its black body careening around her ankles, round her legs—but in her mind she was there, the white steps before her. She jumped them two at a time, swiftly crossing the white stone. There were the arches, broken and incomplete, and knelt at their base, the girl she needed. Ami threw herself down upon her, merging with her, power filling her entire body. Adam's twisted green fire bled from her skin, consuming the snake and turning it to smoke. It fell from her and dispersed as Ami turned to face Romany, her eyes wide and shot with green fire that lashed out at her adversary, sending her sprawling through the burning wall.

The apparition shattered, leaving only the library—all smoke and magic—and Romany on her back, with Ami standing over her.

She glared, her eyes wide and hateful as she got to her feet.

"Oh—I was wrong all along, wasn't I? You are not the key." She pulled at her dress, flicking her hair, her returned beauty a mask that Ami saw through. She circled, Ami backing up to the window, the sword still between them, burning with the light of day. "You aren't the key. You are the source. Oh, I—I need to keep you."

She turned then and fled the room, the twin doors a quick flutter, slamming shut behind her.

Ami was left alone, confused and reeling. She picked the sword up and turned to the window, swinging it at the glass.

THE SLEEP HE'D GOTTEN had been short, and as he'd feared, his thoughts and dreams were filled with the girl: the moment the lunar had hung above her, the moment he saw her face fully, he was haunted.

Mattus had woken in a full-bodied sweat, panting, the pungent aroma of an old man's weak bladder stained into sheets that were wrapped tight and cold around him. Feeling heavy he stumbled to his water closet to finish up, his head bowed against the stone. Wetting his hands in the water jug, he spread them across his face, wrinkles flattening beneath his fingers, his beard catching between them. Ah, it had been so long since he'd felt his skin taut and smooth, so long within the service of Madam Romany that he could think of nothing before her. Too many lifetimes he'd existed past his limit, as had each member of The Order, and there were days he truly felt it, days where the power refused to regenerate his old muscles.

The old man's head throbbed. He stepped to the window and threw the latch, letting in the brisk morning air. He knew what he had to do, and his eyes betrayed his plans as they searched beneath the waning moon, beyond the steep climb and toward the temple. The girl had come from there, had come *through* there. In his mind he saw a blue light between black trees—

Gathering himself and wrapping up warm, Mattus slipped out of the palace before the sun could rise, leaving by a side door and hurrying to the bridge. There was no one to see him, and it was just as well, for he was breaking the curfew Madam Romany had set upon the town; but the feeling within him, the sense of *knowing* the girl, was too overwhelming. It was all he could think about. Perhaps he'd gain nothing by visiting the temple, but he had to try.

The bridge was slippery from the earlier rainfall, and looking to his right he saw where the struggle had been, where the man had escaped Jonus's ruse. They all knew about it, had spoken of Jonus more and more frequently. The bank was broken in the dark, the black sludge still slipping back into the water. He shuddered. Best not to dwell on the water.

The climb up the street was done without a single look back, the clipping sounds of his staff against the cobbles too loud in the quiet town, where no one watched, yet eyes were everywhere. And it was so cold!

He shuffled on.

Reaching the summit, Mattus came to the town walls. The sky was lighter, the battlements above like black teeth against the grey, empty of any guards or soldiers now; but soon the morning would come. He had to hurry. Closing his eyes Mattus breathed deeply, imagining himself a bird upon a breeze, wings outstretched and light, so light he floated, floated ... Eyes open, he watched the ramparts sail beneath him, the woodland on a fast approach. He touched down on a black trail where neither moon nor rising sun ruled. There was a time, way back, when the town had been all forest, deep and dense to the very cliff edge. It was a time long ago, before there were more than twenty men, women and children living off of the river, a time before *she'd* come. A time before *he'd* come. A distant, hazy memory, more a thought or a dream once had, and best left alone.

Continuing on through, he listened to the trees talk, the tall pines clicking softly to one another. The conversation encircled him and he stopped for a moment to listen. Did they judge him? Some of the trees were at least related to those he'd first known—would they recognise him? The past was confused. He walked on, and soon the woods gave way to the grassy hill, mud-torn and hard to traverse, though the lightened sky helped his footing. He reached the top and was greeted with the broken golden rise of the sun across water. It was still a thin strip, shadowed by a night fast departing, though it would soon be full and following him. Make hast!

A flash, and he saw the girl again, looking up at him with eyes that were so familiar. His own fell upon the temple, and sighing heavy to the sea breeze, Mattus descended, his staff sinking into the ground.

It took little time, and soon he was at the entrance. The door moved for him as he waved his hand, and he slunk into the cold shadow where rooms broke from the corridor, left and right, and his skin prickled with the immense power. It was all around, seeping from the very walls, charged in the floor, vibrating with every step. He ignored each diversion, focussing only on the staircase that spiralled up to the level above.

"She came here," he whispered, "she passed through ... but how, and from where?" Leaning his staff against the wall, holding to its shaft, he let himself down to his knees and placed his hands on the first stair. It was hot, burning. "I mean no harm," he crooned, "just show me, where did she come from? Why does she invade my mind?" His eyes closed and he saw her face once more, backlit in blue—dark trees, green flame.

The ground began to shake, and his staff fell, clattering to the stone floor. Mattus reached for the walls, then grabbed the steps more firmly, but the tremor did not calm.

"Dear me," he cried, feeling for balance, losing his bearings, "what have I done? I didn't want to—I only wanted to—" Mattus was thrown down with his staff, dust falling and scattering over his body. "Why do I see her?" he cried.

The quake stopped, leaving a vacuum that echoed silent and loud. Then came the steps from behind him, all too familiar.

"Why are you here?" she hissed. "How *dare* you leave the palace at all, let alone come here?"

"Please, Madam, I'm having visions. I'm consumed with her, I'm—"

"Talking too much," Romany said, now standing over him. He saw her face, changed so from the placid and regal goddess. Now her features had skewed with uncontrollable hatred. "You dare to come here."

"Please, Madam Romany, I sought only to know, to understand why I'm—"

"Let me have those thoughts."

Mattus was pulled up to face her, her ancient beauty awesome and terrible, her eyes, gleaming red, her lips wide in a grin. His bladder gave in as she ran her hand through the few strands of hair upon his head and gripped his skull. She was inside, claws scratching through his mind, talons of power ploughing his thoughts, every doubt he'd ever had, every memory he'd ever cherished, and of course, thoughts of the girl. Her dark hair, her dark eyes flaring green, her voice—images of people and places he'd never seen, the girl with the sword of power.

Romany dropped him to the ground and looked away as he moaned, the pain throbbing, bursting from his skull. His nose bled. Nothing made sense, nothing in his life, his very, very long life. Mud lay at the bottom of a goblet, stirred and murky, no wine, no water.

Madam Romany made to leave, but not before grabbing his foot and pulling him out of the temple, flinging him against one of the rounded stones.

"Tell me now," she screamed, her voice a boom against the sound of the sea, "tell me everything, or I swear I shall rip you to shreds to find the truth."

"I don't know anything," he managed, but even if true, she didn't care. Madam Romany's hand swiped down against his face and ripped the flesh from his bone, scoring him. Blood flowed and he spluttered and sunk, his hand flapping at where his cheek had been. "Wah, waa." He couldn't speak. He tried again, frantic, the pain; he had to explain. "Way-t-t. Iya olee noo Iya noo err."

"You know her?" she said, her teeth clenched as she towered above. "How do you know her? Has she been here before?"

"Iya doo-t-t noo, Iya sare, Maam Oma-ee." He spoke the truth, though his words came forth as meaningless babble. It felt as though his face was on fire, the pain too much to even scream through, while his heart pounded, a constant slam in his skull.

She spat her breath and grabbed his head once more, wracking his body with spasms of pain. Was he drooling? He couldn't see—things were fading. Blinking out. She was inside him again, scratching and clawing. Murmurs and noises rumbled through him and he began to retreat into his mind to a distant place, a memory once held of a castle. The darkness would soon take him. Would the power heal him this time?

With a jolt, his eyes flashed open on rolling waves, sparkles of sunlight, ripples of magic. She'd found something, and he saw it also. It was a faded memory, hazy, seen through dark, murky glass, off colour and bleak. A pool in the dark, and upon that water the image of a girl, a brush held in one hand, her focus upon a canvas out of sight.

"There she is," Romany said, her voice crowing. "You have seen her, but not here, no. She has not been here. You have been *there*."

He was released and the world swam in a million colours. Romany's hand lay against his face as his skin spun back together like wool. He was alive, though perhaps death would have been a comfort.

The grey returned, and the black took him.

Chapter Ten

The dawn wounded the night's horizon with her first spoke of unruly red, and within minutes it'd bled across the ocean's tide, spilling upon the cliff and over the land. There, it filtered between houses, across rooftops and through windows, and permeated the deepest woodland groves, rousing birds to sing in chorus, stirring all from their rest and weary sleeps. And among the creatures of the wild, curled beneath a copse of trees, were three strangers, one of which dreamed heavily of dark things from other realms.

It was within one of these realms that Hero had first heard the footsteps behind him, and thought them treacherous, for they hid within the echo of his own and followed his progress along the muddy trail he'd trekked before, up toward the castle high upon the mountain peak—not the Castle of Legacy though, no. This castle was scorched and scarred and dead.

There was a storm that seethed above it, a storm that gave birth to pregnant clouds obscenely swollen, bleeding flares of dark, blood red.

Yet even the storm did not hide the presence of the other just behind him, the other that got closer and closer still.

He knew if he turned it would be Adam before him, a white faced phantom in black with lips of blubber, stretching a horrific grin too wide—but even as he thought to look anyway, to confront the darkness of the man, all faded in the flicker of lids.

Rising at the sound of *his* approach, Hero drew his sword.

The villain was fast, a man of earth and mud that swept past him. Jumping back he turned to attack, only to find his swing halted, his hand stayed by a strong grip on his wrist.

"A fawn, Brother," a voice wheezed, and looking down he saw Raven holding him. He turned back to his fleeting foe, only this time seeing the earthen coat of dark brown above four legs, eyes big and fearful. The fawn watched him for only a moment, then ran crashing into the wood, disappearing from view.

All around, the land held its breath, as if waiting for the sigh of the wind, and when it finally came it brought with it the faint voices of men from the town. They were rowdy and in good cheer, and though the words were lost in the drop to the riverside, the sound reminded Hero much of the air over Legacy, a people divided for thirty years of nights, united again each morn. This was such a place.

Raven's hand dropped from his arm as Florence crawled forward on all fours and stretched like a cat. Her blonde hair was dishevelled, and Hero had mind enough to find the look attractive, when Raven began to laugh.

"What's funny?" Florence asked, but Raven only waved her away and sighed.

"A fawn ..." Then his face grew grave. "Ami? Where's Ami? Where are we?"

"Hush now, Brother," Hero said, placing his hand on his chest. "You had a bad time of it last night and have only now come round. Be easy with yourself, we'll explain all."

"But Ami—"

"We don't know where she is," Florence said, taking his hand and helping him to sit. "She wasn't with you."

"I saw her on the—no, it wasn't her, it was something ... Ami was gone when I woke." Raven's voice broke and he began coughing a hoarse bark. Hero rummaged in his robes for a flask and handed it to him, and after struggling with the cap, he drank the water down in greedy gulps.

"When you woke? Raven, you'll have to tell us what happened from when I sent you to find Ami. We know only that you didn't return. Since then things have gotten worse. We consulted with the Shadow Princess and came to find you. She said Ami was in danger."

"If she is not here, then she is," he paused, looking around and squinting through the trees, "and so are we. There is a woman, a girl, a woman—I don't know what she is—but I think she is the cause of all of this."

"Go on," Hero said. "Tell us everything, from the start."

After a few more swigs of water, Raven began, starting with his visit to the ruins, his meeting with the Shadow Ami, and then his arrival at the shack. Hero and Florence nodded as he spoke, remembering the strange power that'd emanated from it and how it'd been a portal. Part way through, Florence uttered a gasp and slipped her hand from her robes.

"I didn't mean to hide it, I simply forgot," she said, frowning and handing a small object over to Hero. He hesitated before taking it, a small, golden chess piece. "I found it just as we were leaving the tower. I thought it might've been important, but with everything that's happened ..."

Hero eyed it with suspicion and wonder before placing it down in the gravel between them. "Strange." He looked back to Raven. "Please continue."

With a raspy whisper, he talked of their battle at the river, their confrontation in the street, and their sanctuary within the dark house of Sofia-Maria. He drank more from the flask, continuing with a darker tone as he told them of the events, the girl's trick, Ami's disappearance and the unfortunate family.

"I couldn't stay. I had to get out."

"I understand," Hero said. "Go on."

"Well that's when I saw her on the bridge. I made my way down the street and she was there, except it wasn't her. And ... the river ... the river ..."

Florence stroked and held his hand. "It's okay, Raven, it can't hurt you."

"It didn't," he said, turning to look her in the eyes. "It didn't hurt me, but I saw things in there. The water's dead." His eyes strayed to the still, black surface only meters away. "It's full of death." A low gurgle was followed by a sudden lurch to his side where Raven voided his already empty stomach. Hero turned to look at the water, seeing nothing, but expecting anything. It was too still, reflecting none of the light, and if he were to skim a stone across it, he'd bet it wouldn't make a single ripple.

Florence pulled on her robes and offered them to Raven as he turned back, but he held his hand out and wiped his mouth with his own.

"You took the book," he said, pointing to where a corner was exposed against her breast.

Florence looked down and plucked the small volume. "Yes, we found it on you when we tended to you. I was only keeping it safe." She raised her eyebrows and offered it back to him, but he gestured to the rook and she placed it next to it.

"What do you mean about the river?" Hero asked, inspecting the objects.

"I don't know, but somehow I saw it, all of it. It's deep, so very deep and ... full of the dead." He coughed hard, his voice rough as he wiped his spittle. "Rotten corpses, hundreds of them. It's not water there, at least not now. I don't know what it is."

"It's not natural," Florence said. "I can sense that. I didn't see what you saw, but I sure felt it."

"Did that thing not follow us?" Raven asked.

"The thing was a man, and he vanished."

Looking up to the town, Hero could just about make out a line of horse-drawn carts. They'd pulled up behind a tall building and were unloading stacks of crates. He imagined them to be loaves of freshly baked bread and thought that if he wished it enough, he'd be able to smell the rich aroma over the salty sea breeze that came through the branches. "Is it safe to walk through the town?"

"We'd be noticed," Raven said. "Ami and I were spotted straight away as strangers. We were told so by the bookshop owner, the man who gave us that." He pointed to the small book.

"What is it?" Florence asked, touching the cover and opening it up. "The text is too small to make out."

"No, you see, it was bigger, but too big to carry, so Princess Ami made it smaller, you know, with her power." He frowned, his head cocked. "But as for what it is? I don't really know. It holds a *history* of Ami, the Assassin Princess."

Hero raised his eyebrows.

"Seriously," Raven continued, "and there's more. It tells of the Mortrus Lands, and mentions the Sentries."

"Can you make it bigger, Floren—?" Hero broke off as the world rocked violently, throwing them to the ground. The book and rook danced in the dirt, and Hero scooped them up just before the earth split between them, the bank cracking in a crescent leaving a dark, narrow fissure across the woodland floor. The shaking stopped, and from the gap came a rumbling roar.

FOR A MOMENT, JONUS saw the entire room, and then it was gone. Darkness returned all too soon. "It's no use," he growled, throwing their hands from his own and standing, tottering on his feet. "It won't work without all of us present. Where the hell is Mattus?"

"As we've already told you," Franus said, "we don't know. He's not in his chamber and he didn't join us to break his fast. You know, you were there."

"Though I couldn't see what I was eating."

"There is no need to be grumpy—"

"No need to be, what?" he screamed, his voice echoing back at him, increasing the throbbing in his head.

"—with us, Jonus." Franus sighed, flicking his beard. "It's of your own doing that Madam Romany punished you."

"Just shut up, you—"

"Do not take it out on us," Sanus added. "She has known for some time of your doubt. So have we all."

"And I suppose it was you that told her, was it?"

"Jonus." Franus lay his hand upon his shoulder, though it was shrugged off. "Be reasonable. You were listening in to her private talks. You thought you would not be noticed."

"She knows all," Trubus piped.

"No she doesn't," Jonus spat, sitting back down again. The floor was cold, but at least it was stable—for now. The tremors had been violent, and were becoming more frequent. "She doesn't know about the girl, that's why she talks to her. She doesn't know about the sword, which is why she has the girl."

He turned his head in the direction of the light, hoping for just a simple shade of grey, a sense that it was only temporary. He detected none, only the cold morning and the smell of the sea.

"You speak too loudly," Franus said, standing. "Perhaps you need time to think."

"Time to think ... what else am I to do?"

He heard the brothers filter from the room. They were obstinate, but ultimately correct. His thoughts and feelings of Romany were becoming more evident, more vocal. Her crown had slipped in his eyes, and had continued to do so since the girl had become her focus. But of course she would know he was listening at the doors! He'd been stupid.

Were they still in there? Since the sun had risen he'd not heard her voice, nor sensed the girl anywhere in the palace. What did they have to talk about?

Knowing he was most definitely alone, scorning Mattus in the back of his mind—for if he had joined their circle, he might have had sight again—Jonus stood and felt around the walls, intent on heading for the library once more. He would pass, that was all, and see if the doors were shut by touch alone. She could not punish him for lingering now that he couldn't see, surely?

WIPING THE SWEAT FROM her brow, Ami leant the katana against the wall and wrung the pain from her hand. Her grip had been tight and her skin was now red and patterned from the hilt, but she hadn't given in. She'd slashed at the window again and again, one-handed, two-handed—she'd brought together all the power she could muster to try to break through, even to slice through the layers as she'd been able to do in Legacy—she drained her body until she could no longer stand—but it was no use. Romany hadn't left her an escape. She couldn't break the window no matter how much she tried, and slicing a layer resulted only in her sword getting stuck in mid-air, eventually falling to the floor of its own accord. She touched the cold glass panes with her fingertips and looked down into the valley, her eyes following the river as it cut back inland, its black line winding round to the right where it turned out of sight.

Above and beyond, the town had woken, and cleaning her breath from the glass, Ami focussed in on a family walking the thoroughfare, baskets in hand. The smallest of them, a boy, kept tripping and was constantly being righted by his sister or mother. She watched them until they'd crested the top of the hill and disappeared from view, then turned back to the room and to the double doors.

Of course, these were locked, and with a single swing of her sword she found the same resistance.

Reluctantly, she sat back down upon the two-seater and lay the sword across her lap, defeated. "What good are you?" she asked, looking down at the blade, and as if in answer it shone a gentle purple ripple from guard to tip. "You can't smash glass or cut through the layers, at least not in this room."

Sheathing the sword, she stood up and began wandering between the stacks, wracking her brains for a means of escape, but instead found herself browsing, her fingers dragging across the leather spines and covers, bringing to mind the strange man from the bookshop and the book he'd given her, the book Raven held.

Raven.

She pushed away the guilt. It wasn't helping.

The room was much larger than she'd first realised, the shelves leading her into shadow and dust. There was a globe to her left, though it held no map—strange—and more chairs were arranged here and there, small tables standing with unlit oil lamps upon them. Empty sconces adorned the walls, and there appeared to be no more windows, the light becoming weaker the further back she went. Once she'd reached the far wall there was only just enough to see by.

Many of the volumes in dark leather had writing upon their spines in gold, the lettering only symbols, alien words to her; she gave up trying to decipher them. Others were bound in blue and light brown, but were too high up for her to reach. Lower shelves held thick black books with titles such as *Děitereich*, *La Centee*, *Føxe da Na Katąŕl*. *Where did they come from?* Then a few more with distinctive red spines: *Dragø Maġ̈ï*, *Dragø Katra*, *Dragø Hişt*. Below these titles though, embossed in silver, was a symbol she recognised.

∞

Gently she pulled one of the red volumes, careful to avoid the storm cloud of fluff and dust, and opened the cover to the title page.

A STEP INTO DARKSCAPE

Dragø Katra

∞

She flicked through the pages, seeing mostly words and symbols that meant nothing to her. The occasional picture swept by, and she turned back to look at one.

It was hand drawn and a little faded, but most certainly something she recognised. It was a dragon perched upon a rock, its claws sharp talons, its wings webbed struts of scaled bone, spanning the width of the page. The illustrator had talent, and Ami could almost believe it to be real. Below the rock it perched upon was a mass of intricate black lines, organised and tightly drawn, though it seemed a maze of madness, a labyrinth with no solution. The detail continued round, making the border of the page.

Without thinking, Ami carried the book open in her arms into the light, studying the picture. There was something distinct and familiar about the mess of design, but her eyes wouldn't let her see it. Instead, she turned the pages until she came across another picture. This one was a close up of an eye, the pupil a large slit. Once more, scribbles made a border around the page. Now though she could make out the pattern. With her eyes fixed on the eye, the shapes became clear in her periphery.

Bodies.

Ami turned back to the previous page, the dragon upon the rock, and concentrated upon the long neck, the armoured body. And yes! Within the mass beneath the rock, within the border, she saw the shapes of hundreds, thousands of human bodies, fitting together as if a puzzle. The limbs, the necks and heads, the torsos of the absolute and undeniable dead.

There was a noise, a scraping against a wall, against wood, against the door.

Ami snapped the book shut and snagged her sword.

JONUS HEARD NOTHING but his own careful steps along the corridor, his hands a whisper along the wall. There were no shelves of murals, no hangings to catch, only the stone and the painted pattern that ran it as it had always done; then the wall ended and he felt the double doors, the room beyond silent.

With his hands against the doors, he listened intently, using the power within him to feel beyond wood and stone. There was a presence, but it was not Romany. *Perhaps the girl?*

His hand rested on the brass ring that latched the door, knocking it as he fumbled to turn it. There was a click, a release, and the door swung inward.

Air shifted, and someone moved close by. Jonus could smell her, an enticing sweetness somewhere in the black. There! A bright white flash—then pain down his spine as something hit him from behind. His old body collapsed too easily and he hit the floor face first. "Argh!" More pain erupted throughout, sending white sparks behind his eyes.

Even so, and despite the pain, he didn't move from the ground. There was the unmistakable sound of singing metal through the air, and at the nape of his neck a cold blade came to rest, its edge sharp and dangerous as it pushed aside his white, scraggly hair.

"Who are you?" she asked, the stranger in the dark. *The girl.*

"I'm Jonus," he said, "and I'm a brother of The Order."

"What is The Order?"

"The Order of Lunar. We are six." He was loathed to speak too freely. "I am but one. You have already met a few of us."

"Met is hardly the word I would use. You cower and tremble."

"I'm old."

"You're scared. Stand up."

The blade left his neck and his bearings scattered. Which way did he fall? Where did he face? Pushing up with his arms he managed to his knees, then to one leg, then to the other, holding his arms out to nothing.

He felt her behind him; but then a new sense emerged, something quite fantastic.

A fiery white body, a burning silhouette of the girl appeared. She waved white arms in his face, holding the sword he'd given to Romany.

"I can see you," he said. "At least, you burn with power." He reached out, but the girl moved the sword again to his neck.

"I wouldn't touch me if I were you. I need to get out of here. Show me the way."

"I—I am not sure I can," he said. All around was darkness except for the girl. He wanted to reach out to touch her, an anchor in a sightless landscape.

"You can, if you know what's good for you. Where are the rest of your *brothers?*"

"I don't know ..." He shifted his head left and right, the blade staying with him, a cool fire, the pressure increasing.

"You're not being much help. What's wrong with you, you're acting as if you're—"

"Blind?" Jonus chuckled, despite himself. "Recently, yes. Yet I can see you, or at least, your power."

"My power?"

"You're like Madam Romany? I didn't know."

"I'm nothing like her," she spat, though he sensed her hesitation. Her shape moved around him and leaned away, possibly to look from the door to the hallway. "If you're blind, how did you make it in here? You're the one that came during the night, aren't you?"

"I am. I know this palace very well, having been here for so long." He paused, daring to raise his hand to his own face. There was no reflection of light from her power. It didn't illuminate. "She punished me for overhearing—"

"Yet you came back for more? Why?"

"Why are you here, in the library on your own? Why has she kept you?"

"I tried to get out, but—"

"It is protected, the whole palace is. You could not escape. But still, she—" Jonus felt a heavy guilt in his stomach. He was speaking ill of his goddess, and after so many years of service, far more than he dared to count, it was finally hard to do ...

"I don't know what she wants of me, but she isn't going to get it. Now, I need a way out of here before she comes back. You're staying with me, so unless you want to be a little more dead than blind, I suggest you lead me the hell out of here."

Jonus bowed to her fire, mesmerised. A luminous being she was, full to the brim of power that burned so brightly. How bright did Madam Romany burn?

He sighed. His choices were limited, and half hoping they'd get away with it, Jonus agreed. Either Romany would catch them, or not, but this was too *different* to miss. Things were changing. The girl. The Assassin Princess foretold.

He nodded in her general direction. "Okay," he said. "I'll take you to the Lunar Room."

"I want a way out."

"And you'll find it, but we must hurry. Take my arm and I'll lead you."

"Why do I need to take your arm?"

He coughed, feeling very humble, a sentiment alien to him. "I do not wish to fall down if I misstep."

She paused, bending through the door once more, and then back to him, a cool touch of a hand on his arm. "Okay, then you lead and I'll keep you upright, but one false move and—you get the picture?"

"Death would be a sweet release," he said, "but, I do not wish to face it just yet. I get *the picture*, I assure you." He felt her tug on him and he walked, passing between the doors and out into the corridor.

THERE WAS A SILENCE so sudden that the whole world paused; birds misplaced their songs, and the many morning motions of the town were muted—just for a moment—before the wind sighed again and moved to tickle the leaves, to tease the world to life.

The three had held their breath but now exhaled with the wind, each feeling the fear of the others, though only Raven worded it so exactly.

"There's something down there."

In answer, a sudden rush of heat escaped through the cracked crust carrying with it a strong smell of sulphur and flame. They scrambled away from the edge to a chorus of squawking and wild flapping as birds fled their homes and perches.

"Hero, I think we should leave," Florence said, slowly backing away and dropping to her hands and knees. A cool white fire caught across her body, and she grew larger, changing form in a luminous sparkling light. Her proud horn lit a crystal staff, and she bowed to them as Florina. "If what's down there is anything like the others?"

Hero nodded, groping for Raven's arm, pulling him away from the fissure. It had split a grin across the woodland floor, and a faint orange glow now pulsed from its depths.

Quickly mounting Florina, Hero making secure the trinkets of gold and paper within his robes, they set out at a gallop, leaping the river in a single bound to land upon the opposing bank.

They rode the rugged hillside and passed beneath the outer wall, continuing on up into town.

It was a busy morning it seemed, and the townsfolk were out in force, causing Florina to pause for a moment at the opening to the thoroughfare as a procession of folk and fillies passed, being led by reign and rider toward the market square, perhaps for a quick sale. Other folks scrambled and squeeze through, and with much caw and comment, they slipped in behind the line of dapple greys.

Hero had hoped to blend in, but the townsfolk were all too quick to scupper their ruse, for fingers began to point and whispers began to churn of the sparkling horn that adorned the *white-one's* head. Florina turned off the main thoroughfare before the curious became a mob, and disappeared into the shadow of a narrow alleyway that nestled between a tavern and tannery.

They dismounted there, away from eyes and ears, their only company the rats and rubbish, broken boxes and rotting foods.

Florina shifted shape again back to the girl, and Hero rushed to the corner to peer back down the hillside, scouting out their camp.

He saw it easily, now a line of fire in dark green. Smoke billowed and wafted away from the town, and if none had been looking, he doubted that anyone would have noticed at all; though it was not the only place to have been wounded. Four or five more cracks were visible, each burning across the land.

"Okay, that certainly woke me up," Raven said.

"They knew we didn't belong and have obviously never seen a unicorn before," Hero said, shaking his head. "It hadn't crossed my mind. From now on, Florence, it's best you remain in your current form."

Florence nodded, straightening her robes. "Agreed."

"What I don't understand is what's causing these quakes?"

"Ami." Florence looked up. "Perhaps—"

"We can't assume that this has anything to do with her," Hero said. He turned to Raven. "Did she seem wrong to you, ready to destroy the world?"

"No," Raven shook his head, "but there were moments that I wasn't quite sure."

"Explain."

Raven shifted, kicking his feet and rubbing his hands across the blood stains on his robes. "There were moments that, if she wanted to, she could have. I thought I saw a glimmer that she might—"

"But she didn't," Hero said.

"No, she didn't."

"Then maybe—"

Hero turned on Florence, his voice a low whisper. "I know you have never seen eye to eye with the princess, but I will not allow you to accuse her of death and destruction every chance you get." He released his hand from his sword, realising that he'd had it in his grasp. A moment passed and he let his breath out between his teeth. "I understand you have cause, as we all do, but there is another player in this game and we already know she possesses secrets—the men around her certainly possess a power. This place is important and we need to focus on unravelling the mystery."

"I understand," Florence said, raising her chin to Hero, "and I apologise. You are right, of course."

"Where do we start?" Raven asked.

"Perhaps we should have a closer look at this book." Hero pulled the small volume out of his robes. "We need a place we can be alone."

MATTUS WAS VERY UNWELL. It seemed that the street cobbles pushed toward him with each step, catching his feet and tripping him to the ground. Sometimes he grabbed a wall, and other times the shoulders, necks and bodies of men and women who pushed him back, yelling at him, sometimes spitting. One man in particular took much offence to his wild gropes, setting two or three others on him—it hardly made a difference; bruised and bloody, his body began to slowly repair. His cheek though felt as ice. The flesh was new, tender, and already infected. There was this smell ... Mattus was sure it was rotting.

He'd woken at the cliff's edge, alone and cold, his limbs feeling their age as he pulled himself up on the stone. Romany had let him live and let him go, but he didn't feel any the less punished.

He now spied himself in the glass of a tailor's window and stopped. The owner grimaced at him beyond the stands of jackets and shirts, pants and jerkins, but Mattus paid no mind. It was his own reflection he looked at, taken aback. He was unrecognisable. His skin was ash grey, marred by the dirt, blood and mud of the ground on which he'd lain. The wrinkles in his skin had deepened, and his eyes were bloodshot and mostly closed, swollen. But it was his jaw that had truly changed. It had been repaired, for there was no longer a four-fingered slash, but the bones had shattered and left him disfigured, crushed and repaired with all the grace of a fist fight. His cheek was deeply infected, black and bubbling with swollen blisters of yellow puss. He went to touch it but pulled back with a hiss. Why had Madam Romany left him like this? He cried out a yelp, sounding even to himself like a wounded pup.

He would not let the tears come though, no. He blinked them away as he sheltered his eyes from the sun. He'd been left alive for a reason, and no matter the reason, perhaps he could regain the favour he'd lost. The girl's face entered his mind again, though this time he pushed her away with hatred and disgust. It was her fault that this had happened to him, his fall from grace. It was her fault. Where did he know her from? A flash of a pool, a brush ... but the answer wouldn't come. Had Romany found out?

"I never meant to be disloyal," he murmured, watching a cart roll by, its load of piled up crates roped together and creaking. He covered his ears, the sound hurting him. "I never meant to be, I—"

For a moment he wasn't sure what he was seeing, only that it was wrong. He rubbed his sore eyes and leant against the window, much to the tailor's distress, and peered round the corner. There, he squinted into the shadowed alleyway looking to the far end between old Mister Farlan's tannery and The Cock and Snout. A strange gathering was taking place of two men and a horse. As he watched, the white horse shivered and broke into a sparkling white glow that changed quickly into the shape and form of a woman. There'd been a horn that had formed a sword, and the white mane was now the unruly hair of a girl, dirty blonde against fair skin and grubby robes.

Mattus watched the two men talk with the woman, the sight of them breeding surprising hatred. Madam Romany would want to hear of this, would want to know of this for sure. It was a secret meeting, a definite plot, darker magic than she'd like. If he'd have been in better shape, the power within would have served to enhance his senses, but he was hardly in any shape at all, and he could hear almost nothing. Instead he watched, keeping his eyes on them as long as he could, committing them to memory. Agreeing on something, they headed in his direction.

Mattus stood and stepped from the alley as the tailor began banging on the window, shooing him away. The three strangers walked by without seeing him at all, so invisible and irrelevant he'd become. He brought together all of his strength, all of his reserve, all of his hate and anger and loyalty to a goddess who'd become his eternity, and pushed back through the throng of townsfolk to follow them. Wherever they were headed, he would go.

ROMANY HAD WATCHED the old man from the top window of the temple, stumbling and clawing his way back up the hill. If she'd have been a lesser being she'd have spat upon him, for he was worth no more than that. However, his was a life still worth keeping, if only to complete the circle. What was coming would require great sacrifice. Better them than she.

She pulled back inside and closed the window, latching it in place. The empty room behind her was cool and dark, a place of worship and sanctuary, for she had made it so. From the first moment she'd discovered the portal beneath the ground, she'd known that she could use it. This was the land to stay in, the place to create, to build.

There were more terrifying things in the world of layers than there had ever been as a whole, and soon they'd all know it.

With a cruel laugh, Romany left the temple.

Chapter Eleven

"Open this one," said the blind man, giving the door in front of them a firm kick. "You'll need to pull hard. It sticks."

Ami did as he said, hooking her hand into the iron ring and twisting it to lift the latch. With a firm yank the door creaked open, letting in the light from a second passage that sloped at a slight angle. The same familiar red carpet ran its floor, and to one side were arched windows that looked out upon Darkscape, the high sun casting dark arms and fingers across the sprawl.

To Ami the town looked like an insect squatting on a mound, its tapered legs gripping to the once green climbs, while beyond the ocean shone true-blue to the horizon, rough waves of folded silk rippling across the expanse. She felt a twinge of loneliness looking out at it and so suddenly wanted to be home.

Jonus kept his hand against the inside wall, his fingers tracing the contours as they reached the end of the walkway, and there turned right to enter another. Three more windows lined the outside giving view to the wild woods behind the palace, but the greens and browns, rich reds and seasoned yellows were soon gone as they continued their descent, and were replaced with turrets and walls and empty windows into empty rooms.

They'd met no others so far, and the palace, though quite beautiful, was desolate of warmth. There were no sounds, no people, no servants or maids, no soldiers or guards, none other than the five men who were presently absent. It seemed to all intents and purposes a lonely vault, a spectacle of sovereignty for vanity's sake, shared with no one. Form without substance. And where was Romany? Her flight from the library had been too sudden, the battle left open with the outcome undecided, and she'd carelessly left Ami alone to find her own escape. And then what of her emancipator? His dead eyes focussed on her every so often, only to fall back to nothing.

She didn't trust him.

There was nothing to suggest that he led her to any better fate than if she'd have stayed in the library.

A spiral stairwell took them to the base of the palace and out into a great hall, so large and richly decorated that it almost took Ami's breath away. There were carvings of painted faces barely seen, leaning from shadows and draped in coloured cloths and shawls; other statues stood off to the side between paintings and murals, looking grand and obscene, like Greek or Roman gods of old.

Ami wished she could study them, sketch them, commit their faces to memory, and wondered who they'd been in life—if anyone. Perhaps Romany had carved the marble with her mind, trying to capture those ghosts of so long ago who'd walked by her side, who'd once been her kin? It was likely, she thought, for each shape and face held a familiar look and feel. One face caught her attention in particular, a stone woman stepping out from the flat shadow of the furthest wall. She was tall, as tall as the room, her hair falling almost to the floor, covering her modesty—her mouth formed a perfect 'o', and her eyes were wide, as if she'd been caught in a moment of fear or surprise. Opposite her, at the far end of the hall, was an empty throne where Romany might sit alone, staring at the fearful statue who was undoubtedly herself.

Would she sit there for long, staring at a memory frozen? Would she cry? Ami didn't know, and Jonus soon pulled her through into another room, large and plain.

They didn't linger and instead took a sharp right and headed into a third, an airy cavern that looked out across the courtyard fronting the palace.

This was more spectacular than the first, and Ami twirled across the floor looking at everything. There, on the wall, was a mural of

Romany playing host to six indulgent men on their knees; and on another, depictions of rivers in motion, trickling softly over rocks and pebbles, all tawdry, splashed and imperious, each image divided by an iron grate, covering an alcove.

Beneath her feet was a single mosaic that stretched the entire floor and featured seven moons in gold and pale yellow; six were smaller, only two feet in width, while the seventh was much larger and dominated the centre of the room. From each of them, Ami felt the remnants of power.

Stepping up to the gallery now, she peered out across the courtyard, spying an empty stable block made of stone and wood, a smithy maybe, a tannery, all empty and open, not quite in ruin; a path crossed in the centre—perhaps originally to quarter gardens that were now only grass—and encompassing all were massive red brick walls littered with windows and guttered out candles.

Here was her way out.

"I can feel the sun, the air. I know where I stand. Yet I cannot see." Jonus turned, his brow furrowing. "I can see you though, powerful girl. I could've shown you the main doors and let Madam Romany catch you, but no, Jonus is being nice to the powerful stranger."

"So you think she won't catch me jumping out into the courtyard?"

With a wheezy laugh, Jonus carefully backed up against the wall. "I didn't bring you here to this sacred room for you to jump into the courtyard. See the shape in the centre? I may be blind, but my memory is sound. It's right in front of you. It's a lunar, and this is the Lunar Room, the room of The Order. It is where we come to join, to be as one, to be powerful."

Ami shifted her weight, knowing Romany couldn't have meant to leave her this long. She'd be back. They needed to hurry. "How does that help my escape?"

He pushed away from the wall, choosing his path toward her with care. "When we were brought into the service of Madam Romany, all those many years ago, we were each given a gift of magic. Each of us received a little; only a little. Only with the six of us joined can we really use it to its fullest. We form a circle, here, around the lunar," he indicated the white orb on the floor and pointed to the six smaller orbs, "then we raise the lunar power from the centre—"

"The ball of light that chased us—"

"—an immense power at our disposal—at Madam Romany's bidding."

"I can't see how—"

"You are very powerful," he crooned, a man used to giving flattery. "You wouldn't need six old men ... just the one, to guide you."

"I can use this to escape?" She pointed to the orb. Jonus nodded. It was just a circle, a pattern on the floor, nothing special. She stepped to its centre. "I can't see how."

"That's why you need me," he said, pausing. "Take me with you."

There was a disturbance, the sound of voices hurrying quickly through corridors. Ami looked out across the courtyard seeing shapes passing windows on the far side of the palace.

"They're coming. The others," Jonus whispered. "They've seen us. Take me, or take your chances."

"If I am so powerful in comparison, why should I fear them?"

"They can call Madam Romany in an instant. Wouldn't be much of escape if you were caught." His smile twisted the furrows in his face.

"Okay, tell me how," she said.

"First, take my hand." He held out his white, thin arm, his fingers spindly claws. The voices were closer now, and re-gripping her sword in one hand, she placed her other in his. The old man's grasp was surprisingly strong and she felt a flutter of power within him. "Now," he said, stepping into the circle with her, "push the power within you into the lunar, feel it gather and fill like wine into a goblet. See it ripen in your mind."

Ami closed her eyes and envisioned his words, placing the tip of her sword at the centre of the circle. Power descended the blade and entered the floor, radiant behind her eyelids.

"That's it," he said. "Oh, how exciting to see another do it, to see your power fill it. Now, look out of the courtyard and think of where you mean to go."

Ami thought of the parts of the town she'd passed through, but only one place stuck in her mind. She thought of the river and the bookshop, but it was no use. The destination was set.

"Once ready, thrust your power into the lunar and let it take you there." Ami opened her eyes to calls of *Jonus* echoing toward them. The power gathered beneath her, the orb pulsing white and fast. "Yes! You're almost ready!"

A moment later and they were rising up upon the surface of an emerging orb, the room filling with cries as the old wizards clambered into the room.

Ami thrust her blade down, piercing the lunar, and in a rush of light and power they were swallowed, all sound and sight sucked down with a final *pop*.

Everything vanished and merged, all the colours phasing into a single shade of white. The sensation was odd and Ami felt as if her whole body had been pinched. Air rushed by, a roar in her ears, the close presence of the other disconcerting. She was joined with Jonus and felt his malice and old sickness within his heart.

Then the world phased back in streaks of colour: sapphire, gold and emerald green shapes defining, becoming ordered.

Ami hit the ground, dizzy, trees spinning and turning with sky and earth, while Jonus landed beside her. He'd tried to stand but had fallen, disorientated and mumbling.

She was sick, cold, the wet grass against her skin her only respite and safe harbour as her head throbbed behind her eyes. She remained on the ground with little strength and listened to the echoing footfalls that stopped in front of her.

AT FIRST THERE WAS only the darkness and the familiar cold, damp stone, the crude steps shorn from the rock so many moons ago; then an unsettled grunt, a shift of scales across jagged rock so close. Romany felt *him* through the walls.

He's hungry, oh so very hungry.

But she was interrupted.

Her armlet burned against her skin and lit a fiery golden light, the serpent tightening its grip. It was the call of The Order.

The girl.

She grabbed it and immediately flew into flame, up above the deep, forgotten cavern and now a shooting star, a devil's tear burning across the sky over Darkscape.

Her fall blazed a trail of red as she descended upon the palace and flew across the courtyard, through the gallery and to the lunar, her body remade in crimson light, trapped once more within the confines of flesh. Such a limited form.

Around her were her servants, four of them at least, knelt as best as old men could, eyes averted. Two spheres remained empty.

"What is it?" she whispered, eyeing each in turn. Their eyes touched her, too rheumy, too old, too stupid. They were quite past their usefulness now, yet something had happened in her absence, and she'd been called. *The girl.* "Where is she?"

"Madam," Franus started, "we came too late. Jonus, it was Jonus. We saw him with the girl."

"By the time we arrived," Trubus said, "she was gone."

"Took him," added Laous.

"Just took him?" Romany asked, her eyebrows raising. "Just took him? Tell me how she managed to escape not only the library, but the palace?" Her voice was low, a hiss they knew well. They cowered, always cowered; sad old men, flicking their beards in terror.

"Well, we don't know for sure," Sanus whispered.

"It was Jonus," Franus said, stepping forward toward her. "He must had freed her from the library, brought her here, told her how to escape."

"Silence," Romany commanded, and the men fell quiet. "Mattus has betrayal in his heart and mind and must not be allowed within the circle. He is not important. Jonus though? I have seen deceit growing within him for a while now. His blindness was a punishment, but perhaps not punishment enough? He's chosen to flee with the Assassin Princess."

"The Assassin Princess, Madam?" Franus frowned.

"I have heard the name before," Sanus said, "but it's from a text that was banned, an old story from long ago written and—"

"She is the girl?" Trubus whispered, stroking his beard. "The text is true?"

Romany lifted her hand and Trubus was thrown to the floor, his head cracking on the stone. "There will be no talk of such things."

Slowly, Romany allowed herself to leave her mind, her power searching the town, the land, the sea—but it wasn't enough. She'd been careless, foolish, thinking her palace a fortress against a living legend. A legend that would end soon. She was *the one,* and she must have her.

"What will you do?" Franus asked, gently shaking Trubus, bringing him round. There was a cut on his head that was bleeding badly. It would heal.

"I shall have to hasten my plans," she said, coming together once more.

She took hold of Franus.

He dared not move.

It was the look on his face that surprised Romany, the utter horror that he'd been too vain to expect. He screamed as his skin blistered and burst, his blood a torrent down his cheeks. The two men still standing made no move to help—very wise—and only watched as their brother fell to the floor beside Trubus.

Franus let out a single groan, but Romany had already left, tearing out of the room and into the hall beyond.

They were fools, old fools, their never-ending and everlasting faith a failing farce. Who were they to talk of such things to her? Had she not made her domination clear hundreds of years before? Trubus would rise, as would Franus, but they might remember now to watch their words, for as each moment passed, their usefulness became less. She no longer needed six, and Jonus and Mattus were no longer necessary; as fortune would have it, the prophecy of so long ago was to her advantage, and far from being her ending.

She entered the Solar Room and looked out over the courtyard. Mattus had somehow *been* with her, had seen it all. *Questions, too many questions.* She needed answers before the end, before *he* finally arose.

Raising her arms into the air she let out a scream and the sky darkened. A clap of thunder answered her call, heralding the gathering clouds that swirled dark over the town. A rain fell from on high, tears of a million years, a sadness that wept all the way to the sea; and there a gale lifted waves to wash the sores and soothe the hurts, to sweep away so much as it always had. Let the land cry for its lost world; let the ocean rise and fall. It was Romany, last of the Sentries, who now commanded the power and the fear of creation and destruction.

As if a lightning rod in the eye of the storm, Romany released her power onto the town. It rolled from her and flew through the sky.

The flares once more fell to the land, the streets, and fed the hungry one. Her people screamed as one. Her armlet flared, her body the shining torch of an angry goddess. She was hurt, despair and power.

The ground shook with *his* awakening.

With as much flourish as she'd landed, Romany flew into the air and out of the gallery, soaring high and scoring the sky, leaving a fire-trail of sparks that fell from her essence, continuing to feed *him* as she shifted form into that of a burning phoenix to scour the hills, the land, the skies. She'd find the girl, and she'd take all she had; and then she'd kill her.

She flew low, chasing her ants, looking for her runaway princess.

RAVEN LED THE WAY, though he wasn't entirely sure himself where they were going. The streets were now heaving, crowded with people swarming in every direction. Bearded and burly men in faded cloth and hardened leather staggered forward with axes and tankards; women with headscarves herded children this way and that. Dogs barked, and more than once he was sure he'd seen a pig or two scampering between legs. Everything looked different from when he'd first seen it, stalls and shops in full swing, buildings barely seen through a haze of steam and smoke as things were cooked, heated, made and unmade. To his left a blacksmith worked on an object that looked remarkably like a hat stand, while his apprentice—a small boy of no more than ten—heated a broadsword and readied his hammers. A butcher was next, hung meats covered in salts and spices, and then a baker, the inviting smells of hot bread, sugared buns and fruited cakes. In front and beyond lay the market square dense with stalls of fruit and vegetables, cheeses, corn, wheat, and other such grains. Other traders crammed for space, carpenters and wine sellers, tailors and even a few scribes, though those seemed smaller stalls, lonely outposts of the few and far between.

Each leaning structure seemed familiar, and with every wrong step and about turn, the three gained new looks and stares, attention they could've done without. An old man sitting outside a tavern gave them a growl over his tankard, while even the heather-women kept their distance. They could tell a stranger in the crowd, that was for sure, though Raven had no idea how. They weren't dressed too dissimilar, with dirt covered robes and unshaven faces. Perhaps it was the lack of leather or iron rings on their belts? Either way, they managed to avoid hostilities, though a few drunkards had been up for a fight, spilling ale and rolling their fists—they'd given way to them, Hero whispering apologies for unknown offences.

For what seemed a simple town, there now seemed to be too many streets and turns. Alleys dark and dank led them to unexplored lanes, and those led to deserted areas where wooden huts rotted in the warm air. Eventually though, Raven led them right, onto the broad thoroughfare they'd started out on the day before. The battle for trade continued still, and it was sweet relief to finally leave the bustling bazaar behind, their feet striking the now familiar cobbles in the lesser crowded end of town. Raven averted his eyes when they passed the house that'd been the horror, and headed down the hill.

The bookshop was open, though there was no sign out front this morning, and no sign of life through the windows. Hero and Florence huddled behind him as he entered, the reek of dust, dried ink and old leather overwhelming.

"Hello?" he called out. "Britanus?" There was no answer, no noise, only the muffled far away sounds of the morning trade and a gentle creaking of old wood breathing.

Hero looked around and checked the shadows before pulling the small book out, laying it on the table beside a barely lit candle, the wavering flame dancing in a lake of wax. He flicked through the pages.

"Can you make it bigger?"

"I can try," Florence said, taking the book in her hands. Raven watched her carefully, his skin tingling as her eyes flashed and grew a steady white. Deep within them he saw the flicker of tiny flames, and as her hands clasped the leather cover, a light pulsed through her fingers.

The book began to grow, and a moment later filled the table.

"There, all done," she said, pushing her hair back behind her ear, a wry smile on her lips. "Now, what's inside?"

Hero gazed around the shop before taking hold of the heavy volume and opening it to the first page.

Raven stopped him, his hand over Hero's. "No, wait. Not on the first page. Try opening it randomly."

"Why?"

"It seemed to work last time."

Hero nodded, letting the cover fall back into position. He ran his fingers against the pages, stopping to gently tease them again. The book fell open on a double page of text and images. The first depicted a woman, dark of skin and gently curved, sketched in small lines of ink. She wore an armlet of a snake on her upper arm.

"Romany," Hero read, scanning his finger across the heading, "the goddess of the moon."

MATTUS SCAMPERED AND fell forward into a stack of crates, the smattered smells and rotten juices carrying with him as he was hauled up and pushed on. It'd been hard going to keep upright as he was shunted and shoved, a lone fish swimming against the flow of the river, fin flapping back and forth to no end. Somehow though, he'd managed to keep them in view, a glimpse of a cloak, the distinct grey wool in a sea of faded colours. The girl's blonde hair alone was unusual enough to pick out and pursue. Limping, his face blown and leaking, he leaned against a wall, watching the strangers gather at a doorway. He knew the shop, though he'd never entered, the library within the palace holding all the knowledge he'd ever needed.

The stranger girl who'd changed from a mythical creature weighed heavy on his thoughts, the visions, the memories that weren't his at all flickering through his mind. The girl with her long brown hair, her sword raised high, her eyes of colour; the blue light between black trunks, looking, searching, and the horses with horns, magic horns ... Was he replaying things he'd witnessed? His mind was tortured.

Either way, Romany would ask him back and would put his body back together, he was sure, for a prize such as this ...

The three entered through the doorway and Mattus wondered if he could peer through the window. He moved forward, but was shaken quite suddenly and violently to the ground as a thunderous quake began. His cry of pain was lost beneath the screams of a whole town as Romany's power fell from the sky once more. Everything darkened, and with ruined lips stretched in what should have been a smile, he whispered a chant as the rain poured down.

"It is she. It is she." He leaned to one side and found the shop through the rising ground mist, a single dying candle hosting a huddle of shadowed figures.

Mattus crawled toward the door as a phoenix cried out above the din.

"LOOK OUTSIDE," FLORENCE said, her eyes having strayed to the window and the darkening sky beyond. The scant remnants of blue were rapidly turning a bruised purple-grey to black. "It's changing so fast."

Beneath them, the ground gave another tremor, and Florence grabbed hold of Raven as Hero held to the table. Around them books fell and juddered from their places, pages fluttering to the floor, whilst outside the sky gave a terrifying rip, followed by a sudden torrent of rainfall and star-shots.

"What's happening out there?" Raven asked.

"The stars are falling again," Florence whispered.

"I think I may have something," Hero said, bringing their attention back to the table. "Listen." The others gathered round as he drew the candle near and brought it up to the opened page. "Here is an account of the Moon Goddess, Romany, starting with the night the sky fell." He looked to Raven and Florence both, before returning to the page. "I am but a man, a man who has borne witness to the coming of the creature known as Romany, the Moon Goddess. Our village was peaceful and simple, and though we cared little for the history of our beginnings, we cared much for the future of our kin; we were happy. We worshipped the Well and gave thanks to it, knowing we were connected to the afterlife through it.

"Unbeknownst to us, on a night now long ago, a creature who looked a beautiful woman found us. We woke to an almighty scream and a furious fire that filled the night sky and fell down upon the land. Many of our homes burned. Luckily we were few enough that most of us escaped the fall; and so, frightened and confused, we headed to the Well to appease the gods who would have us destroyed."

Hero scanned the page with his finger as Raven and Florence listened.

"The woman was the source, the cause. She was angry, and many of our men fell defending our people. She threw us to the ground and ripped us apart with little effort. It was a red field upon the cliff, our blood dripping to the sea. Only few survived. I was one who did.

"I threw myself to my home and burrowed deep underground, working tirelessly for hours to dig an earthen shelter to hide in. All too soon my hut above ground was destroyed, and yet I remained hidden and untouched beneath with my works and my writings."

Hero shifted the book closer. "It continues ..."

"When I awoke it was to a day unlike any other, where rainbows of the most vivid colours arced across the skies, and the dead of our village were piled high at the cliff's edge beyond the Well. I crawled up from my hole to witness the beauty and blood, and wept. Wept with every step.

"The woman was there pronouncing herself a goddess of the moon to all alive who'd gathered, and from that moment we were in her power. Miracles she showed us then as she created trees, fruit and water, causing a spring to rise from the very earth; and without a single touch, the body pile slipped and fell to the sea.

"What were we to do? Most of the survivors took her at her word and worshipped her, and when she claimed the Well as her own, they worshipped her with an ever growing fever. Work began immediately to build a temple of wood and stone around the Well. It had only one entrance, and it faced the open sea.

"I was there at the beginning, and I witnessed the six gather, and how they clung to her simple robes, how they reached to touch her skin, only to be kicked to the ground, their faces pushed to the dirt. They grovelled for her love and power. Something sheened in them, shined in their eyes, and a gift of magic was given for worship.

"Nevertheless, a new day had dawned, and every day after has been in service to the goddess. Many die, many live, many serve and worship, and a few, like me, keep their own council. I know her as a monster, a creature. She is not one of us."

Hero looked to the opposing page and the drawing there. It was of a crude tower, only slightly resembling that which they'd travelled through.

"This is a new section," he said, "starting much later, by the sound of it."

"Yes," came a voice. Blades were drawn, and Raven clawed his empty scabbard as a small man emerged from the shadows. "It continues much later, but please," he gestured, smiling a little, "go on. You read it so well, after all, and time is of the essence I think."

His eyes darted to the window.

"This is Britanus," Raven whispered.

Hero nodded and the man bowed in return. "Please," he said again, "do continue."

Hero studied the man. He was small and shrew-like, his eyes flashing in the flicker of the candle. Was he friend or foe? How could they know?

He looked back to the page.

"The Temple Tower," he said, clearing his throat. A goblet had appeared by his hand, though he'd not noticed it arrive, yet looking around he found they all had one. He grasped it and sipped. Fresh, clean water. Uncomplicated. He continued. "The Well has been sealed within a tower of worship, and work has begun to build a palace for Romany over the water—these are all things physical.

"But I have more to say on other matters.

"I am a witness to these events and yet I alone seem to have retained my faculties, or so it would appear. That is not to say I have not been affected by the goddess, Romany—for I have, in many ways. I've been gifted with sustainability, though it is hard to truly explain how or why or when ... especially when. I now eat little and less often, and I hardly need to drink at all, though I still need both to survive. I can run and swim, leap and walk with much more vigour and longevity than ever before. I see further, hear better, sleep well and feel more alive since my awakening. Yet she has taken over the village and enslaved us, and I shall continue to keep a record of this. And something further troubles me still. We visit the Temple

Tower every day when the moon rises high over the sea, and we settle there within. The cover is removed from the sacred Well and we pray and worship within its light. This has been the same since Romany appeared to us, and I have faithfully attended as each of us have; yet the closer I am to the sacred Well the more I feel that I'm not myself. Memories come to me that are not mine and I witness events I know nothing of. I cannot make sense of these images. I see a girl, a girl with dark hair and eyes that flash curious colours. I see her with a sword, and I see a woodland bleak—and I am angry. I see white, horned horses and hooded men. I see blue light between black trees.

"When it happens I want to scream and run, yet I feel I'd never outrun the alien imagery, and at times I visit the temple hoping to gleam even more. I shall write down what I see, and keep it with my other writings, hidden and safe, a chronicle of the strange and unusual."

Hero stopped and looked around him.

"Princess Ami?" Raven puzzled. "How? If this was—"

"How indeed?" Britanus rocked back and forth on his heels. "Perhaps a little more? I'm sure you all enjoy long and exciting, epic tales?"

"This Romany, this goddess—"

"Oh, she is no goddess," he said, shaking his head, "but please, go on. It gets better."

Hero took his goblet and looked to the window where the storm was letting up, the sky brightening a little, a blue hint through grey.

He knew they needed to hear more, but there was something curious about the small man that made him wary.

A bird screamed somewhere far away, and Hero continued to read.

Chapter Twelve

"Wake up girl, for heaven's sake."
Even in the darkness there was a smell of sweet pine, the scent of a recent rainfall, the feel of cold, wet grass beneath her cheek. Also in the darkness was *her* voice, the old cracked voice she'd heard before, disembodied and floating, demanding. There were other things in the darkness though, things that hid behind shadows and refused to reveal themselves, shades of black on black that were separate and yet one and the same. Ami's head spun at the thought, her mind building a maze of black walls dividing darkness from darkness, and from behind each a voice whispered beneath a breeze. *Hero,* one called; *Raven,* said the other; yet neither voice were the same as the one that called to her now, the one that seemed so close. She turned a corner of the maze, finding only the same darkness there and there and—

"Open your eyes, girl. Have you forgotten how to see? Golly."

Light fluttered like a moth against a flame, and the darkness fled, the maze undone, blurry shapes becoming solid as colours fazed and faded with each blink. There, up ahead and coming into focus, was the wooden shack, bleached wood creaking, moaning; and even closer were the trees, filtering daylight and swaying in a gentle dream; and also, closer still, were two seated figures ...

Her sword lay beside her and Ami scooped it into her grasp quickly.

"Oh, stop movin' about," the same voice crowed. "You've been crawlin' around in your sleep an gone an hurt you-self."

Ami tried to stand and settled on a swaying stoop instead, her blade pointed down at an old woman, seated in her rocker.

"Call me Grammy, that's what you should call me. Even though we ain't kin." Struggling up from her seat, the old woman slid her cane into the mud and anchored herself steady, her blind eyes staring. "I'm blind as a bat, yet I see you just fine, girl. You blaze hotta than a sun. Hell, I saw you walkin' down that road t'other night as if you were on fire, blazing like you do! I can't see cack all else, but I see you, alright. Lucky you got away before you were given over to *him*."

"Him?" Ami motioned to the only other body present, the blind old man, Jonus, tied up and leant against a tree.

"No. We'll get to him," Grammy said, working her way slowly toward her. Ami moved to help, but the woman waved her away. "You look after your own stability," she murmured. "You been rocking back and forth the whole time. 'Haps you should be in the chair?"

Ami grasped a low hanging branch, her back to the shack. She felt its power, its call. The blade in her hand vibrated to its tune.

"Who are you?" she asked.

Grammy gave a sharp laugh. "You don't know? You don't know nothin' then, girl." She hit her cane between two trees and stepped up to Ami. "You don't know nothin' ... yet."

The old woman was surprisingly strong and sure as she took her hand and lifted it, releasing a bolt of white power that passed between them. Her cracked calluses dug into her flesh and set her skin a tingling. The hairs on her arms stood on end as purple, green and white sparks fell to the ground like a November treat. All aches and pains from the fall disappeared, grazes on her bare knees rapidly healing; and then the light finally faded, and the woman dropped her hand.

"There you are," Grammy said, stepping back. "I can see the breaks in your colour have changed, the wounds healin' nicely." Ami looked down, the torn flesh now only red smudges across her skin. She brushed at them. "Right as the rain, for sure."

All around them the trees began to chatter as a hollow breeze shifted through the leaves.

A new day had taken hold that had washed away an unsettled night, and all was clean and fresh; though just beneath the polished surface, Ami felt the thrum of power behind her, the town, the palace, the woman so close, just beyond the veneer.

She turned back to the shack and fumbled for the totem she knew she no longer carried, the chess piece she'd lost somewhere.

"What you searchin' for?"

"I need to go back," she said. "My friends, they're back there, they're—"

"They're safe, for now."

Ami stopped rummaging. "How do you know?"

"Laws, I swear, if you don' stop askin' silly questions I'm gonna take this cane and rap it across your skull, girl." She chuckled, though her old, lined face looked less than amused. Her white hair was tied tight behind her head, an unsympathetic school mistress.

Ami looked away from her and closed her eyes, feeling out through the darkness for the light that filled a clearing and fell upon a ruin. Quick stepping across the green, she headed for the columns and arches that stood tall upon their white stone and marble base. Short blades bent underfoot as she sprung up, stopping before the triple arch.

Then she saw it, so suddenly that she was amazed she'd ever missed it.

Her eyes opened to the wood, the track, the swaying shack, and to the ruins of her mind and Romany's memory—a meadow of green, of columns and arches. *They'd gathered in their thousands to watch their own ending.* Like a jigsaw, the pieces began to fall into place. So obvious ...

"That's it, girl, I see you're gettin' it now. Your colours are a-changin.'"

"What colours?" Ami asked, her own voice vague and far away as she watched again the fabric of reality crack, the memories of another.

"In the dark I see you clearly. You're surrounded, girl, all the time, by so many colours. Your aura, some would call it. I think the word colours is jus' fine."

Ami heard the words but continued to watch the beings crowd across the meadow, not quite people but *beings* wrapped in logic and form. They shimmered an almost luminous silver, and then were ripped and formless. "Some became as horses, some became as trees ..."

"And some as men, and some as women." Grammy paced a circle, her cane leaving boreholes like woodworm in the earth. "She hoped in that singular moment of panic to escape and run to the woods. Several parts of her made it. Thousands of parts did not." The timbre of her voice changed. "Certainly she merged with a woman, though she didn't know it for the longest time. Ages passed, ages past. Of course, by the time she stopped her wanderin', found a place and a people? The loneliness had killed off who she may have once become, and instead she became what she became."

Ami fondled her sword and caressed the smooth metal, tracing the symbol of infinity.

"The tunnels, the portals, all put in place by fragmented Sentries tryin' to pull the world together again. That's what the portals are." Grammy spat the last word and turned to the shack. "They presented in different ways, sure, the different layers settlin' all different from one'nother. In that layer it was a hole in the ground. In another it was hollowed out trees where Sentries merged. In this layer? One of those places is here, a wooden shack, overgrown and broken. It's broken for a *reason*. The whole place is alive with the power. You feelin' it, girl?"

Ami looked through the doors of the shack, the broken staircase barely visible at the end.

Jonus stirred.

"The portal in that other place, where she is, is not stable, and is no more than a frayed rope. Romany, she pulled on it, tried to pull herself in—only it threw her out! She thought herself rejected, cast out from her lands she still believed to be out there. Course, now she knows different. We told her straight."

We. Ami let it slide.

"She built the temple around it," Ami said.

"Yes, to secure it, to enslave a people. Still she tried to enter it, time and time again, even when she figured she was the only one—course, she was wrong about that, too."

"You are a Sentry, aren't you?"

Grammy smiled, but shook her head.

"No, girl. I used to be, once. I used to be part of one, the one that you've just been havin' dealin's with." Her blind, white eyes found her, her eyebrows lifting. "I was part of the one you call Romany. One of many and but a slice, a sliver of a Sentry." There was no resemblance between them, yet how could she doubt it? Ami had watched the splitting of Romany over and over again in the given memory, and if the land had split, and the people had split, too, then there weren't just infinite layers of the world, but infinite layers of all living things, people, animal ... Sentries.

"Impossible," Jonus slurred.

The old woman held up her cane, the tip a glowing ember of white fire. "Don't be so sure, beardy." The ember flashed and flourished, a star exploding. Jonus squirmed against his bonds.

"You can see him, too?" Ami looked between them as the cane lowered and she leant down on it heavily.

"No, but the power within me can. I trust in it, for I have lived my entire, long existence blind. I see only through the power."

"Romany wanted to return to Celestial, and we told her that wasn't possible. She tried to pull the layers together herself, at great cost. She wished to recreate the lost realm of her youth." Grammy walked slowly back to her strangely placed rocker, and climbed down into it, sighing as she did. "But what she found instead was something much deeper and darker. A new way, a new weapon."

"The sword? But I have it here."

"Was she concerned with the sword?" Grammy chuckled, rocking gently. "No, girl, she was on the wrong track there. Powerful, yes, but only a second-hand relic of a Sentry's true power. No, the weapon she found is blacker than anything in these tame layers. Of course, the greatest weapon she's been gifted with has been yourself."

Ami blinked. "But she hasn't got me."

"You'll have to go back for your friends, and then she'll have you," Grammy said. "And though you won't give yourself willingly, and mustn't, she'll find you and use you. You see, you're the child of the power itself. You were bred by the power, a human-Sentry. With Romany a Sentry-human, you are her equal. Your powers combined would accomplish everything she's been trying to do alone for the last few thousand or so years."

A squirrel ran a path between two trees, jumping a gnarled root before leaping to a trunk. It scrambled up, pausing only to re-grip the large acorn within its mouth, and then disappeared into the branches. Ami watched it, listening to all the sounds around her. She could neither hear nor see anything of Darkscape or Romany here, though it was only a dream-span away. But she couldn't mistake the pull from the strange shack. It was a magnet for her, and it was hungry for her.

"What does she want?" Ami asked.

Grammy rocked harder, tapping her cane against the mud underfoot. "To break the barriers between the layers; to smash the walls that divide unlimited worlds. She wishes to recreate Celestial, and she means to knock down all the walls to do it."

The cracks in the earth Raven had described; the quakes beneath. The layers were splitting.

"But, how am I meant to stop her? By leaving my friends there?" She turned in a circle, pointing to the shack. "Should I just leave them there and never return? Why don't you stop her? Why aren't you her match?"

"She will achieve her goal in time, even without you." Grammy continued to rock, nodding. "And I am only a guardian of a portal. I am old and used, and a *thinner slice,* if you like. I ain't her equal." She stopped her rocker and climbed back up with revived vigour. "You have to go, Princess Ami of Legacy. You must go. You must lead her back to that which remains, the only thing that remains, of our dead world. Only there can she be defeated. She mustn't be allowed to break the layers."

"What is the weapon? The dark one you mentioned? Who is *him?*" Ami thought of Adam.

A laugh broke out behind her as Jonus choked and spluttered. "The darkness is an old, old creature. She will raise it, as it rose before. She will raise it, for the goddess is powerful." His laugh grated on Ami, and she turned without thinking, her sword extended and armed with sparks of jaded fire.

"Not so powerful," she hissed under her breath, "for she needed you."

A lick and a blast, and Jonus fell slack against the trunk.

"HERO, I THINK—" RAVEN pushed his face against the glass, looking out into the street where a moment ago he was sure he'd seen something, someone. He cupped his hands, feeling Florence nudge in next to him to join his vigil.

"I see him," she said, and a moment later had pulled the door open, letting in a brisk blast of frigid air. Raven followed with Hero at his flank, and beneath the cover of mist, rain and shadow, the three of them charged out into the street.

The man lay as if a grey heap of rags, swamped and soaked and barely moving, his groans only whispers. A skeletal hand, barely visible, poked from beneath a sleeve, old fingers grasping at nothing. Hero had squatted down and uncovered his face, which was badly bruised and bleeding.

"We need to get him inside," he said. Raven and Florence nodded, setting to the task immediately.

"Don't bring him in here," the book man's voice called out from inside, but they paid him no heed as they lifted up the sodden vagrant and dragged him between them back into the dry, the door slamming shut behind. "He can't be in here." A whisper.

The man's robes fell open, mud splattered, smelling of stale urine and rot. He'd obviously been beaten, and by the slow rasps of breath from his chest, it was obvious that he was not long for this world.

Hero brought the candle close as the other two lay him out on the table. "He's in quite a state. Do you have blankets?" But Britanus was nowhere to be seen. "Never mind then." He removed his own robe, handing it to Florence—leaving him in only plain undergarments—and stripped the wet clothes from the old man, throwing them to the floor. "Put my robe around him to keep him warm."

As she did, the man murmured something, his lips barely parted. Raven listened intently, yet couldn't make it out. What was left of his face broke into a gargoyle's grin, baring all his teeth.

"Don't try to speak," Florence said, rubbing down his arms, pushing the robes to his chin. His beard was matted and she stroked it out of the way.

Raven looked him up and down. "I'm sure this is one of the men who took Ami and I. They chained us up."

"He has power," Florence said, "only a little, but enough to be wary of." Hero nodded and placed his goblet against the man's lips, wetting them and allowing a sip to slip between them. "We can clean him up, but his wounds are too severe. I might harm him if I tried to heal him."

"He should die." A whisper from the darkness, from Britanus, hidden and watching. "He is not good ..."

"We're not going to let him die," Hero said, "and we'll not harm him either."

"He will call her ..."

"Let him!" he growled.

The old man's eyes fluttered, the lids bulbous and thick with bruises and dried blood.

"Read the book." Whispers in the shadows. "So much more, in the book."

The book lay open still on the table, pushed to the side and forgotten for the moment. The page showed a sketch of six men gathered around a circle. It was titled *The Order of Lunar*, and while Florence wet a cloth to wipe across the man's forehead, and Hero inspected his festering cheek, Raven pulled it toward him, looking up into the darker shades of the shop. A slow creak of movement, the small man hidden, afraid.

"That's it. You need to know," he said.

Raven bent over the text and squinted at the first few words.

"I said I witnessed the gathering of the six, but I didn't know until this moment that I was one of them." He looked up from the page.

"Go on," Hero said.

Raven continued, the low candle flame sending eerie shadows across the old paper.

"It is a strange magic I must speak of," he said, "and I must be careful to place events down in an order, for I've seen the future and the past, and the Assassin Princess."

ROMANY FLEW WITH FIERY wing and feather, the freedom of flight transcendent as she focussed her keen and powerful sight on the ground below. Her search had already taken her far from the settlement, out across the wild forests, and to the barren meadows beyond; flying lower she'd circled back, skimming the tops of trees and cresting hills, soaring to the cliff point and then out across the sea. The girl had to be found, and that Romany, Goddess Sentry, could not find her stoked her fury. It should have been simple, yet her own power failed her, perhaps for the first time.

The temple sat like a beacon at the land's end, the hidden well a tempting stop for a princess of power. She pushed her mind and penetrated the walls, looking through to the upper levels, searching but finding nothing.

A bolt of pain struck her white and grey behind her eyes, and suddenly her wings crumpled and she fell—the ocean blue with waves, so wild, all a blur—and there was the girl, filling the water, dark brown and dangerous. Beyond, a decrepit wooden hovel stood far back amongst the trees. Wherever she was, she was *there*, and *there* was not *here*. There was movement to the side, a frail hand, a cane raised—*her!*

She hit the water hard, rising up in steam and fury, her squawk a scream too loud through the land. Now the tower was far below, a mocking pike ready to impale her if she dared fall again. She flew higher, the land now a forked mass beneath misted cloud.

The girl was no longer here in this layer, she was sure. The hand, the cane ... *her!* Rain shimmered through her red-flamed feathers, and she felt a creature from the depths of the underworld. Was that so far from the truth now? Folding her fire behind, Romany dipped into a dive toward the hazy mass of land, a wet green haven, scarred by her black town. She screamed, watching the ground come closer. Where the girl had gone, she could not go. Where the girl had gone, she didn't know, could never know. She felt the presence now that she'd only briefly seen—knew it and hated it, hated it—somehow *needed* it.

All but a few people had taken refuge in their homes and the streets were clear, though cluttered with burning market stalls and broken stores. A lone horse trundled down the hill pulling an empty cart behind it. As she let up, her wings opened to buffer a gentle soar close to the street and she saw the broken figure crawl. *Mattus.*

Banking to the left, Romany touched down and settled upon a roof, her bird reforming in light and power to the body of a woman, her dress falling to her ankles, her feet rising high in gold and black heels. She was a feline predator, perfect in balance, her hair long and dark down her back, her eyes lilted and powerful, tinted a blood-red.

She scanned the street for the crumpled body and saw through the rain that three others had rushed to his aid. They'd appeared from a shop doorway, one of them the man she'd left upon a bed with a kiss. "Friends of the Assassin Princess," she whispered, her voice golden and pure. "You will return for friends, won't you, Princess?" She smiled, thinking of how she'd drag the girl into the lunar, gathering her order around her, and drain the power from her. The layers she could not bridge would shatter, and *he* would rise. It'd been her plan for some time, so many years, and yet long ago writings proclaimed another the victor against her. "I'll be victorious though," she said to the rain, and jumped to the ground, her heels landing with a *clack* against the cobbles. She stroked her hands through her hair, dark silk, powerful, and with steady, even steps, took a walk.

"ARE YOU SURE THIS IS what I'm meant to do?" Ami asked, though she needn't have. Did she want to leave her friends in the hands of Romany? Did she want to leave Raven, Hero?

"You don't think another thing about it," Grammy said, pushing her toward the porch. Her hand touched the railing and a spark of power shot like static. "You just go and do what you need to do."

"And what do I need to do?"

Grammy laughed, a rough bark that seemed too deep, too worn. "Well, just like I said. Take her to that which remains of our home. You know where that is, don'cha girl? Come now. And don't let her break those layers!"

There was to be no discussion. The old woman pushed her firmly up the steps and to the door.

"Now, girl. Go on."

"But I lost the piece, the chess piece." The stairs within were dull and in shadow, incomplete like the archways within the ruins. *Yes, the ruins.* "It was the way I got through."

Grammy stopped pushing and stood still, her dead eyes scooting in their sockets from left to right, left to right. "What chess piece?"

"I found it," she said, "there, beside the stair. In the rubble."

"Those stairs were destroyed so that none could return by them from the other side, nor leave their layer by force." Her words were slow, white eyes *tick-tocking* back and forth. "*Her* especially. We saw to that! You can travel through from this side though, the same way your friends got through, yes." She nodded. "No chess piece needed, though if you found one and lost it? It would be wise to re-find it, and quick, before Romany does. Girl, you must succeed in stopping her. Defeat her on her own ground, yes."

"Okay," Ami said, feeling overwhelmed. "I'll try." It was all up to her to save the world, each and every infinite layer of it. She wondered if this was how things were meant to be, if this was what the fates, or God, or the power itself had planned for her? She'd never asked for it, but it was hers, her responsibility, and if not hers, who else was powerful enough to stop her? *Dangerous* was with her, her mirrored self, her *own* self. She looked over at Jonus, out cold, her power having hit him hard.

"What is going to happen to him?"

Grammy tapped her cane against the steps and shook her head. "Oh, don't you worry about him. I'll deal with him, put him right, keep him safe. He might still be of use." A smile played her lips over rubbery gums. "Go on now, girl, before you miss your chance. Climb the steps."

Ami looked once more into the darkness and with a deep breath, her sword before her, stepped through into the shack.

Already it was as if she were in a different world, the whole place lifting and swinging freely upon many branches. The boards creaked as she walked forward, passing each of the dark doorways to her left and right, the woman's cane tapping far away trees, murmuring words unheard.

She focussed forward toward the steps, crippled and disused.

What had the Sentries truly achieved with their network of portals? They hadn't succeeded—from what she could tell—and yet these wise, old, magical beings of the first age of life thought they could simply anchor on and yank. Would it have seemed so simple a task for them? After all, Romany had told her of their creations, their imaginings become a reality, all coming so easily to them. The Sentries of the Mortrus Lands *had* used the portals to travel through, but the Sentries had ultimately failed to leave, merging with the trees and the animals to stay alive, falling into routines that had eventually shaped the very fabric of Legacy, and the rest of the world. Why had they failed so drastically? Had the Sentries simply overreached, or was it just their time to die out? Either way, Romany was a slice of Sentry who wasn't going to die out.

She had to end her.

A year ago Ami had known nothing of these things, had been only a girl, creative and imaginative, but just a girl, and the prospect of saving the entire world, shouldering that burden, seemed far removed from *any* reality. Things had changed though. She had changed, and for better or worse, she'd become the Assassin Princess of a place where magic and power were her tools, the price paid by birthright. *You can do this,* she thought as she stood amongst the shards and rubble of the fallen stairs, *you can do this—save the world, beat a powerful immortal, rescue your friends ... rescue Hero—all in a day's work.*

She looked to the remaining steps and began to climb, though her foot hung in mid-air as the moment hung in time. *This is it, fall or climb.* She stepped forward, closing her eyes, pushing a gut full of power down into the spiralled steps. Her boot set down on solid stone, and with her next step she ascended another. She smiled and took the last step up, opening her eyes to a barren room.

Rain fell heavy against a window at the far end, while a storm flickered and grumbled far off and out to sea. Approaching it, Ami looked out, her breath misting the glass. Below, the water formed rivulets that flowed to the edge to fall, and there to join the somewhat subdued waves upon the rocks.

"Okay," she whispered, "let's go find them."

Her boots scraped and echoed as she turned and crossed the room, down the now solid stone stairwell, and out into the grey day.

Her dress soaked through in the downpour immediately, and she began to wish that she'd snagged another robe from somewhere.

Ami stopped, slapping her hand to her face. "Ami, sometimes you can be so dumb; powerful princess my arse." She laughed as she raised her sword and brought to mind clothing superheroes wore in graphic novels, in those she would create herself. She saw black leather, covering her top-to-toe, a choker around her neck, her hair braided in a rope down the centre of her back, and in an instant the change was complete. The rain bounced and trickled off of her new outfit, only falling cold upon her face.

Breaking into a run, she was soon riding over the first rise and racing down toward the woodland that sat between the cliff and town, trees passing in a dark blur as the mud kicked from her heels—and then the path opened to the great fortified wall, rising black beneath a mottled grey, the moon or the sun hiding a ghostly shape far, far above.

Ami didn't slow her approach but leapt from the ground to the top of the wall, stopping only to listen to the footsteps that echoed loud from the streets below. Unlike before, the wall was deserted, the town guards long gone and not replaced. She swallowed her breath and paced the inner battlements, looking over, her hands slipping on the wet, moss-covered crenulations. Even from so far up and away, each step was clear, each click of heel against the ground deliberate. She was near.

Romany.

HERO TENDED TO THE wounds that he could, though there weren't many he felt safe touching. Skin festered, rotted and bled. The old man had been cursed for sure, damned most probably—yet he smiled, mumbled of nothing between cracked lips. He was delirious.

"Time tricks us all, eventually," Raven read, "and no more so when it is unnaturally long; but here is what happened.

"The six were chosen, haphazard though it seemed, and I was one of them. I had already started my chronicle, writing of her arrival and her conquer, of the Well, the flashing and flickering white power held within, and of the temple that had been erected. I'd also written of the girl I'd seen, the visions, the blue light between black trunks; I'd written all I could remember from those alien memories of her.

"The goddess baptised us as we knelt in the light of a full moon, and each of us took her blessing, accepting the power she bestowed upon us, our minds merged with her own, our memories and thoughts becoming as one; for a moment, we were inexplicably joined. Terrible pain came to us as her palm touched our faces, her fingers talons, digging into our skulls.

"And so when my turn came, I tried to hold back the things I'd seen, the location and content of my journals, my doubt of her and the insurrection of my heart. But she saw these things and her anger became more than I could describe. I was thrown into the air, her hand still upon my body, tearing at me, ripping me apart, and in the light of that full moon I was—"

"—*split in two.*"

Raven stopped reading as all looked round, for the last few words had been spoken in unison. Two other voices had joined his: Britanus and the old man.

"What? I don't understand," Florence said.

"Keep reading." Hero motioned, and the two men spoke together.

"*Through her anger and her spite, her hate and her power, her jealousy that there could be another—that I could have known of another—I was ripped apart.*"

Raven's eyes fell back to the page, his finger scanning, his voice picking up the flow. "*I* landed far away, winded and wounded but alive still, my body tingling with white sparkles. But when I looked back to the cliff, another man had taken my place, another me ..."

"*She seemed to forget me quickly, if she was even aware I'd been made of her wrath, and I was able to squirrel away my writings. I—*"

"—continued to write, and in time forgot who I'd been," the three men finished.

"She is here," the old man chanted, his eyes opened fully, his dry, bleeding lips a grin. "Oh, she is here, Madam Romany."

Hero looked up to see a dark figure at the doorway.

"Swords," he shouted, though he knew it was already too late. The door flew in and the woman entered.

"I'm so glad we could all be here together," she said, stepping inside. Behind her the rain ceased and the grey clouds lifted to reveal a luminous full moon, turning all to silver.

Her smile was dark, her eyes a flaming red.

Chapter Thirteen

The breeze whistled through the empty streets, hollow and low, the call of a lonely creature wishing for an ear to hear it, waiting for a face to feel it, a mouth to breathe it. It reached out to Ami, bringing with it the last of the rain to kiss her cold cheeks and caress her face, before dying upon the ground.

The storm was over.

She looked up from the shadows to the canvas of stars, and to the full moon that'd appeared; a large silver disc, familiar in every way. Upon its surface, men had walked and jumped, had planted flags and spoken the words: *This is one small step for man, one giant leap for mankind.* But not here. Now it looked down upon a different world, a world where a vengeful being used power and magic to play at being a god. If she were to see a rocket launch, would Romany tremble at such awesome power? Would it be witchcraft? Power and loneliness were the only things she'd ever known, after all.

These, and many more questions, Ami saw in the moon; and she longed for home. It came on her quite suddenly, though little by little, the weight of her duty to such strange worlds had pressed in upon her. *Only six months?* That's how long it had been, though it felt a lifetime ago that she'd left her work room within her high-rise flat, leaving her former life behind, truly, for the first time. A broken window, a shattered door, her art work just left upon the walls. Until the moment the strange bird had tapped upon the window, until the moment her life had changed forever and always, she'd been happy. Life had been plodding along, and she'd had dreams and ambitions.

The moon above had kept its singular eye upon her in every layer, and had been watching over her the night she'd first fallen in love, when she'd gazed upon it, misty from her window, one hand on her heart and the other upon her beau. It'd been there to watch her dance by herself across a darkened beach, and when a group of them had played games by the sea.

Everything had changed now from those simpler times, and she'd had to adapt. Fantasies of stories and dreams had become a harsh reality, and if she wasn't careful, people she now cared for would lose their lives beneath the same moon, and the happy memory of its silent sentry would be tainted in blood.

She looked down with a sigh to the path it had painted across the uneven cobbles, leading her to an open door. Within, lit by a single flickering flame, was the destiny and the future of the next human adventure, for her own fate now linked directly to every living thing.

She listened to the voices inside. Romany was speaking.

"—the Assassin's friends here to save her, though why you gather in such a place, I cannot fathom." There was a low rumble of words from Hero, and Ami felt a flutter patter within her chest. It'd been too long, she realised, and she'd missed him. "What I want with her? Such impertinence for one who should be on his knees to me!" There was a cry of pain and Ami tightened her grip on her sword. She wanted to charge in swinging, but she couldn't, not like that. It would be the death of everyone. Her hand in memory closed tight around a red-petal rose, forcing the thorns into her skin. The remembered sting sharpened her resolve. *Calm.* If she ran in now, Romany would turn on her. She'd have no need of the others. She'd kill them. Right now they were alive because she remained hidden. "I'll take you as fodder. Don't worry, you'll be useful. I'll—What?" A low grumble, another male, though she heard nothing of his words.

Ami shifted closer, her back flat against the side of a house, its old plaster flaking white and falling across her shoulders. She brushed it off, glimpsing a window to the side where a slim slither of light filtered through its frosted panes, betraying three huddled figures within. A face turned, eyes wide, and then the flame was doused.

"I find it hard to believe," Romany continued, "and yet, perhaps you too have your uses."

The door slammed shut.

Ami stepped out into the street, the silver path before her broken by her shadow, cutting a fine figure of soft curves and braided hair against the stone. She didn't want to spend too long in the open for she was certain she was being watched; a quick glance down the street revealed further flamed auras barely hidden behind curtain and glass—and so, stepping quickly to the doorway, Ami lifted her katana to the night and pushed her power to its tip. It sparked just the once, and the steel blushed white before lengthening and stretching, sneaking up the wall beyond the door, latching somewhere at the edge of the shadowy roof. She gave the sword a swift tug, and holding to the handle tight was drawn hurriedly up the side of the building. At the top she let go and landed on all fours upon the soft, dark thatch.

With her sword clasped beneath her arm, Ami crawled like a cat across the straw, making her way over the roof in silence.

She heard nothing from below and worried for Hero.

The building reached quite far back from the street and it took her longer than she'd have liked to get to the far side, but once there she dropped easily into the dark alley below. It was dirty and wretched, but she held a crouch low to the ground, surveying for movement and threat; but she was alone.

A light mist swirled around her feet as she walked to the door set flush against the back of the building. It stood slightly ajar as if she were expected.

"WHAT DO YOU WANT WITH Princess Ami?"

The disrobed man stepped forward, brandishing his sword toward her like a child with a stick. It would have been amusing, had it not been so insulting.

Romany lifted her arm and the sword flew a flame, burning red hot in his hand.

"What I want with her? Such impertinence for one who should be on his knees to me!" The man dropped the sword and screamed in pain as she clenched her fist tight. His insides were in her grasp, each slippery length of intestine wrapped twice around her fingers; it gave her a moment's amusement to watch him squirm. His neck strained, tendons pulling like wires as he growled between his teeth—a vicious animal trapped. It bored her.

"Let him go, please," Raven pleaded, the man she'd seduced so easily. "You don't have to do this."

"Bored," she whispered, throwing her hand out to him. He fell to his knees beside the other, crumpled like a wilted flower, its petals fight-worn and dying. "I'll take you as fodder. Don't worry you'll be useful, I'll—What?"

Mattus had turned to face her—oh, what a horror. The necrosis had spread far and wide, rotting the old man from the outside in. White bone protruded now, clear of the black flapping flesh, and his exposed neck was bruised purple, angry red welts boiling through the surface of his skin. His nose was almost non-existent, as if someone had come along and chewed it from his face; yet he had strength enough to right himself and speak to her.

"You don't want to—" he coughed, wheezed, and held his throat to continue, "—harm the girl. She is special, something ... unique."

"What could be so unique about this stranger, this girl, dear Mattus?" A smell wafted from him, that of over-ripe fruit and rotting meats. Puss drained from his jaw as he struggled to talk. She stepped toward him. "Tell me, dear one?" She stroked his beard, clumps of hair falling at her touch. He was coming apart.

"She's a unicorn," he managed, his eyes closing as he swallowed hard. "A unicorn who turns into a girl. I've seen it."

Romany looked sharply down at the slumped girl, barely stirring against her companions. "I find it hard to believe, and yet, perhaps you too have your uses." There had been unicorns buried deep in his mind. Unicorns, magical, powerful. "Let me see what you've seen." With reluctance, but no hesitation, Romany placed her hand against his face, letting their minds touch.

His eyes opened wide.

A wind rose up around them, swinging the door shut, coming from nowhere and everywhere at once. She saw the girl, a wood, a unicorn without a horn. And now she grasped the old man's head in both her hands, intent on pulling all she could from him.

"Noo," his voice barely a breath, "please, Mada—am—"

Romany closed her eyes as the images flooded in. She didn't hear the crack of his skull, though her fingers passed beneath the bone to sink into his brain, scratching and clawing. Her eyelids fluttered, his mind emptying into hers.

A unicorn yes. She saw one upon the beach, its horn sheathed in black, a booted foot breaking the crystal; she saw it charging forward with only a stump. She saw the girl doubled and lethal, head to foot, two flaming torches of power. How was this possible? *She was witnessing a battle, a battle Mattus had seen. A book, a quill running across its pages, a fever upon the hand as it sketched and wrote of the memories surfaced—and yes, memories they were.*

A blood curdling scream broke the bond and Mattus's lifeless body dropped to the floor beside the others. Romany searched the darkness. "Reveal yourself!" she shouted, lifting her hands above her head and gathering to her a white light between them. It was a fiery sun that spun and broke open to flood all with a splintered light. A second of muted illumination chased the shadows, preceding a low hum, and then the blast. It was an ear-splitting *boom* that tore the walls from the lower floor, blowing the back of the building clean out, scattering plaster, brick and stone; book pages shredded as dust and debris rose in a white cloud, to pass quickly into the night. It happened fast, the wound fresh and clean, clear and dark.

Those by her feet had taken cover as screams howled out through the night in fear. She paid them no mind, for in that instant, as the now three sided hovel settled and bowed, and the night displayed the infinite heavens through the empty space remaining, she *felt* her presence.

"Come out and play, Princess." Romany stepped forward into the rubble, her heels crushing all to dust.

MOVEMENT, A WHISPERED step, a shift in shade so subtle; there was someone else just inside. Ami raised her sword and pushed the door open, revealing the dim profile of a man leant against a wall. He turned to her, surprised, his grey eyes silver discs, mirroring her double in the moonlight.

"You," Britanus gasped, "but you should not have come b—ba—oh—" His words hung in the air unfinished as he raised his hands to his ears as if listening to a faraway sound. A moan escaped his pursed lips, a moan that quickly became a wail. His jaw fell open and strained, dislodging with an audible *click*. Ami rushed forward to catch him as he collapsed, his bloodshot eyes haemorrhaging within.

"Reveal yourself!" A voice, *her* voice.

"Inside," the man croaked, pointing through an inner doorway, "quick."

A light consumed the rooms then, illuminating all a lightning-white. In that moment, everything was visible, from the shelves and dusty stacks of books, to the mouse-holes carved so masterfully through the walls; each shadow that'd hidden had been dispersed, every sin brought into the open. Something was happening, something very bad. She dragged him and pushed him toward the doorway as a low thrum buzzed, a thrum that became a drone like a thousand bees—and then without warning, a sudden *boom.*

Ami dived through just in time as the walls behind tore apart. Stone steps rose to meet her as she tumbled into darkness and landed face first upon the earthen floor where sound was now a single note hiding the thud of her racing heart. It was the cry of her neck, twisted and hurt, the taste of the blood in her mouth, her tongue bitten and swollen; it was the ringing from the blast that had happened a moment ago, so far, far away. She looked up across the short blades of grass to the sunlit platform of stone and marble to see the welcome smile of her shadow-self, standing between arches and columns.

"How did I get here?" she asked, making her way toward the steps, shaking out her bruises and hurts. She knew her lips had moved, but the single note carried over all and made her deaf and mute. Shadow Ami crossed the distance, meeting her at the steps, and lay her hands against her face in greeting. The touch was intimate and allowed her to speak directly to her thoughts.

"You are always here."

"Is this only in my mind?"

"Yes, and no," the other said. *"Does this place really exist? You have been here, but how can you say it's not in* my *mind? Our minds are linked. You can always come here."*

Ami smiled, her body healing fast, her hearing slowly returning. Bird song and a rustled breeze ... she looked around, finding the stone walkway as it'd always been, connecting the low building behind her to the castle tower in front. The roses grew still, ever-reds, the petals peeling perfectly to the ground and flipping, dancing.

"You have to go back," the other said. *"You know you do."*

"How can I defeat her? Do you know?"

"*Yes,*" she said, nodding her head, "*and it won't be easy, but you can do it. Believe in yourself, always. Play to your strengths. She is old, inflexible. Adapt, overcome.*"

Before Ami could speak, her feet were taken from her and she was dragged backward into dark forest, branches now dead fingers searching and scratching, a woodland where blue light filtered through black trunks, where she could scream and run and never, ever leave. The green of the clearing was long gone, the blue sky replaced with shadow and deceit, all shades of black and blue, and then, finally, just black.

Ami opened her eyes.

All was dark and dust and ash, a magical scattering of stars the only light, seen through the doorway above.

Her sword lay across her chest, and gripping it tight in her hand, she rolled over on the cold floor to look for Britanus.

Was he dead?

She was still scanning the dark and empty ground for a corpse when Romany blacked out the stars.

"THE SCRIBBLER. ALL this time I never knew you were here, keeping low. I know it's you, filthy scribbler." She pushed his face to one side, then the other with the heel of her shoe. He was alive, which is more than she could say for Mattus. Not that it mattered. "You were hiding." She sighed. "You were hiding."

Romany stepped over him and looked up at the moon whose light bathed her a stark white, her skin iridescent, her hair as black as onyx. It had always been her constant companion and had showed almost no change in all of eternity. They were similar in many ways, the lunar and she, infinite, forever, unchanging, created from everything and yet ultimately desolate and barren. Still, it was a force for change, just as she; it commanded the tides as she could, invoking mood and passion as she did. She meditated on it now, thinking of all she'd learned and all she'd ever known. Mythology had begun to work its way into reality, and possibility opened the way for probability. A unicorn, a creature she'd never mused on, never thought about or seen, a story known, yet a nursery rhyme she'd never heard. And it was here. She'd seen the memories of one who'd witnessed a horn being broken, though how *he'd* seen it she didn't know. What was the Assassin Princess without her unicorn sword? For that is surely what it was.

She was nearby, felt like a breath of wind kissing her skin, goose-flesh rising and settling as she idly touched her armlet.

Romany scanned the debris. The blast had taken out more than the back of the one building, but also the houses behind it, too. Roofs were collapsed or collapsing, sagging and settling, creaking and snapping. Straw thatch scattered brick-strewn alleys. But the princess didn't hide behind the carnage. No, she was closer than that.

To her right was a darkened doorway, the wall around it cracked but mostly unharmed. The scribbler lay barely breathing at its threshold. With a swift kick to his side, Romany sent him through the doorway and down the shadowed steps, his cries hushed whimpers she cared nothing for. How could she not have known that the scribbler of falsehoods still lived within her lands? How could she have been so blind? He hit the ground below with a faraway thud, falling into darkness; and at that moment, Romany became certain.

She's down there.

She turned her attentions to the front of the building that held its structure with ragged pillars, a vague wooden arch bowing and splintering. Books were spread everywhere, torn, ripped pages amongst skins of gouged and ruined leather, and in the centre of the chaos were the three strangers who barely moved beneath a layer of plaster and dirt. Mattus lay dead, broken and rotting, and to his side was the girl—the unicorn. She moved closer to them, rounding the desk where the flamed candle swayed its final dance, almost done. Beside it was a large volume, now dusted in a light shower of dirt. She wiped it clean, revealing a sketch that slid in and out of shadow. She studied it for a moment.

"The splitting of a man? Well, what an interesting read." The candle tipped over with a wave of her hand and kindled against the pages. Fire flourished and ravaged quickly and efficiently, consuming all and leaving nothing but smouldering, historic ash. "There are no words to describe ... just, no words ..."

"You would burn it," the man said, stirring against the girl, sitting himself with his back to the door. "You would burn a history that paints you as a conquering monster."

"Does it?" Romany blew upon the pages, the cinders rising and falling in golden embers. "I never much trusted books. They tell lies."

"What have you done to Princess Ami?" he demanded, trying to rise to his feet. "Where is she?"

"Sit down," she said, and the man fell back to the floor. "I have done nothing to your *princess* yet. However, she is due a visit I think. She was a guest of mine, yet rudely departed before I had chance to tell her what happened *next*. Ah, but does it matter? Truly? Surely the stories of the past are not nearly as interesting as those yet to be told?"

"She will destroy you," he whispered, so small and pathetic; a weakling man. He leant against the door using all his strength to remain upright, while the brave Raven conserved his, his head bowed, his breathing steady as he listened. The girl was motionless. So much power, and yet not a single flicker?

"No," she said, looking off into the night behind the shattered window. "I don't think she will." With her mind focussed, Romany travelled now into the earth, into the layers of basalt beneath the land and the sea. She reached so far down that she could feel the cracks in reality scoring her skin; and behind them *he* lay in wait, hungry, angry. He stirred in the dark place beyond and below, and the ground shivered once more.

TIME WAS GETTING SHORT, and Ami knew the longer she stayed hidden, the more certain the danger to Hero, Raven and Florence. The woman's shadow had fled, leaving the dark mass of Britanus's broken body at the foot of the steps. She watched his crumpled chest hitch and release in short sharp breaths, while above, Romany's words trailed off and faded. Somehow, Ami was sure that her face would be hanging slack from her bones, void of all life, her dark eyes dry and staring as a corpse stares, into the beyond of nothing.

These were stolen moments, but to do what?

She stayed where she was, listening for the woman to come back, to make a move, but all was still. Down the street she heard crying, sobbing, while further out across the town mothers cradled children with words of comfort, to the fearful, to the sick, to the scared. All around were the creaks and groans of a building sighing its last, getting ready for the final fall, and the subtle scuttle of mice tracing the edges of the moonlight, rats scavenging dry boxes stacked against the walls; *no food here but us,* she thought, lowering her sword.

Faint cracks had crept soundlessly across the stone floor like the subtle web of a silent spider. She traced them, jumping at the grated whisper:

"Princess," voiced between laboured breaths, "come now."

With a quick look to the empty doorway, Ami scooted over to the man, carefully rolling him over to face her. Oh, what a mess. There was nothing that could describe the pulp that had once been lips and cheeks. Only his eyes seemed truly alive, now a bright blue, the source of their own light. Ami cradled him against her as the world trembled, the hairline cracks beneath them widening into fiery cuts. They gaped in grins, breaking the whole into mini islands of dark stone. She was surprised the floor hadn't caved in beneath them, but somehow it'd held.

"*Come now, Princess,*" a voice mocked from above, a shadow leaning black between the stars, murk and moonlight. She'd awoken. "You know, I don't have to come down there to destroy you. You know that." Ami felt the power of those words, could almost see them slip down each step in turn, dripping foul like oil spilt. She saw the burning eyes of deep red fury, though they failed to find her in the darkness. "I need you though, and I think you know that, too, so I want you to follow me to the palace. And you will, for I'm sure you wouldn't leave your *friends* to the fate of so many before them."

Hero. Raven. Florence.

Her instincts told her to lay low, yet her heart told her to leap, but before she could decide on either action, the rest of the building exploded. Walls that had remained were blown apart in the blast, collapsing the doorway and sealing it with brick rubble and fallen beams. Further sounds were muted and unimportant as Ami uttered a single sobbed word.

"Hero ..." A whisper, the loudest cry through the cloud of dust now settling.

"He's alive," Britanus said, though his voice hadn't come from beneath her, but instead from all around. It was disembodied, too close, like the coming of a storm. Above them a wind howled through the fallen rubble, yet none lived beneath it, she was sure, just as she was sure that Romany was gone.

She took a breath. "How do you know?"

"I know," he said, and with surprising strength peeled himself from beneath her and rolled onto his side, his half-dead and useless body slumping to the ground.

Now that the moonlight had been extinguished, the cellar lit a dim orange glow from the cracks and chasms that spanned the floor. By their light, Ami watched Britanus pull himself across it, anchoring his fingers into each gap until he lay across the largest. He looked back over his shoulder, his eyes burning blue.

"Come, please."

Giving a glance to the only exit now closed, she shuffled over to him and looked down into the warm-lighted abyss; the back of her neck prickled as a strange sense of power touched her. It was familiar and yet alien, emanating from the colour of the light as though it were something tangible she could touch and feel in her hand, as though it were separate from the essence and visibility of light itself. Sparks of jade and purple dripped from the ends of her hair to fall within the cracks, disappearing with no ill effect. Ami brushed her hands through the loose strands to keep them back and out of the way.

"What is it?" she asked.

Britanus smiled, the blood on his face now dark lines that defined him.

"It is a split between the layers of this world," he whispered. "They appear quickly now because of the quakes. *He* is moving beneath us. But here, thrust your sword within."

"Who is *he*?"

The man shook his head, grimacing. "Show, not tell. You must ... understand."

He grasped her arm and guided the sword forward blade first. "Will *he* get me?"

"*He* is not here, at least, not yet. Trust me."

Ami wasn't keen on trusting anyone, yet there was something in his eyes, something familiar that pushed her doubts aside, at least for now. The blade entered the light, molten gold sliding across folded steel.

"Just watch," he said, and Ami did, her eyes fixed to the blade as she continued to lower it. The feeling from before was now stronger, and for no reason it brought to mind the song she'd sung, the Celtic melody from a long-ruined wedding—it was a note that resonated in memory and actuality, a single sound that was joined by a second and a third, the perfect chord that made her want to sing and dance, and mourn and fear. She clasped the sword all the harder, yet her grip loosened all the same. The chord resonated and travelled into her arm, and when it reached the rest of her body the air changed, the temperature rising rapidly. Her heart raced in her chest, her breath held tight for a moment and then released.

Everything had changed.

It was as if she'd been picked up in a second she'd missed, and set down in a different place, a different time. The stone was now a rug, white and warm, her leather garb changed for jeans, a tee, a dark, worn hoodie. There was no sword in her hand, no fissure in the ground, and no darkness. The taste of plaster, dust and destruction had dissipated beneath the spritely scent of citrus.

Her hands steadying her each side of her crouch, her eyes sweeping the room. Directly behind was a low coffee table, sporting a colourful array of fruit in a glass bowl, and beyond that, lounging at one end of a dark brown sofa was a man she recognised, though it took a moment to place him. She stood up very slowly, backing up against the chimneybreast, her hands raised in submission—yet he didn't seem to be looking at her at all. He looked instead at the mindless colours of a television screen that sat idling in the corner.

"Hi, do you—?" The man pushed his finger deep into his nostril, rooting deep, his eyes still fixed, chapped cheeks stretching to a smile. Ami frowned and waved her hand. Nothing.

A sudden waft of freshly baked bread sailed in through the door in the corner, and from somewhere deep in the house came the sound of a woman singing amid a clatter and clang of metal trays.

Ami took a step forward, the man taking no notice. Finding nothing of interest, his finger was removed and wiped against his top. Another step and she was round the table, facing a painted landscape that hung on the wall. The house was unmistakable in its watercolours, though painted much more idyllic than she herself had seen it. Currington House. She could see the stable block behind where her cabin would be, and *was* in fact, just a few steps away.

"Hello?" she tried again, but it was Britanus who answered her.

"He can't see you." She turned, but there was no one there. *"He can't hear you either, nor me."*

"What am I doing here?" she asked, edging back to the fireplace where the coals glowed their deep orange and red. "I don't understand."

"You are walking the layers through cracks that have fractured."

At that moment the door opened and a small woman walked in with a tray of food. Her apron was marred only slightly, though her weather-worn face showed signs of flour, dabbed as if a fragrance upon her cheek. Her lips were set in a practiced smile, and when she set the tray down on the table, Ami turned and made a beeline for the door. She heard the muttered thanks, the clatter of a spoon against porcelain, and ducked round the corner just in time before the woman swung back through, sauntering off toward the kitchen. She saw it at the end of the hall, the stainless steel worktops, the pots and pans hanging high on hooks.

"Am I dead?"

"You aren't truly there, but neither are you here," Britanus said.

Ami shook her head. "I'm a ghost." Another step found her walking the dirt track she'd followed to the shack. She spun, seeing Currington House just down the slope, the cabins dark shapes to the left. The evening had drawn in and the wind snuck cool across her skin, throwing her hair back behind her. Through a lit window in the house, she could see the man, Benjamin, scooping the soup from his

213

bowl and dunking a fresh chunk of torn bread. She turned, knowing she was to follow the trail into the trees. The sounds and smells were vital and riveting, yet even here she was not seen, not heard. A roaming badger snuffled the ground, unaware of her presence at all, while other evening prowlers stalked the shadows to either side; an owl cut her path, a wild flapping and hoot that sent Ami stumbling backward, reaching for her sword and finding only the front pocket of her hoodie.

Ahead and to the right she spied the old woman nodding silently in her rocker, and off to the side the bound and blind Jonus. Ami hoped to pass by, though she felt the same sensation as before pulsating from the shack, camouflaged and yet also luminous, a nuclear power station on overload.

Her tread was careless, a twig snapping beneath her foot.

"I *see* you," Jonus sniped, his whisper a cutting edge in the calm. "A light like yours can't hide, even between the fabric of worlds." He lunged forward, the cords of his thin, frail neck straining against his bonds.

Ami's heart raced. "What am I doing here?"

"A tour," the voice said. *"Touch the old man."*

The shack behind screamed, a thick limb bending low and lifting high, the old boards bowing as it shifted and settled. It spoke, it cried. Ami walked from the track and reached out to the old man, but Jonus threw his head to the side.

"Don't come near me, Assassin. Madam Romany will—"

"She's not here," Ami said, and gripping the blind man's robes she—

—knelt in the circle, the high sea wind blowing hard across the cliff's edge. It was Darkscape, though not as she'd known it; each next to her was as she was, frail and old, nearing the end of a life just starting. The Well of light seemed a lunar up ahead, a ground moon of the goddess, open to the night. And there she was, the goddess herself who'd killed almost everyone she'd known, the sanctity of life shattered for all time; many younger than she had died, had been throw to the river, flung to the sea, left to rot in the hot summer sun ... Now though was a sacred time, a time long promised, the sharing of the gift, the power. They were a group of six, the wisest among many, a human link to her most holy, and when the goddess placed her hand upon each head, they were to be given everlasting life. The gift of power was to be used in the settlement, in the places of worship where the old gods of the trees and the water had been discarded and burned. They were to be the priests of the people, the chosen. The goddess had explained that together they would be powerful, that together they could keep order amongst the people, though none would be so powerful alone. She hungered and lusted for this power as Madam Romany passed around the circle. She was next, and she bowed ready, her beard white and long.

Not she, but he. Jonus.

The goddess had rested her hands upon the head of another, one of the six, and from her mouth came a scream that pierced his mind like a shard. "Heresy!" she cried above the wind and the waves. "Who is this girl? Who is she?" The man was thrown through the night, Madam Romany's grip still tight around his skull, and though he screamed, his screams were nothing beneath the cries of the goddess, and he fell back to the circle, broken but alive. "He has been purged," she said simply, and moved on.

Romany had never known that her own demonic power had purged one man and created another.

Ami removed her hand from Jonus, letting it fall to her side.

"Stay out of my head," he spat, waking the old woman from her sleep, but Ami was already beneath the undergrowth, her journals so important they were clutched painfully to her collapsed chest. *She* would not have them. Now she knew what *she* truly was, having glimpsed her mind in that brief union. She hid them. They were important, the truth, and some day, she now knew, the Assassin Princess would come ... She would, she'd seen it, but now she—

Britanus.

—was at the edge of the cliff, hiding.

The temple at the point of the cliff looked out over all and had grown large over the Well, over time, over eons. That's how long it had been since he'd been split, and it had taken him a long time to come to terms with the truth of it, though reading back his own writing had helped. The other, the one split from him, had continued in ignorance much as Romany herself had. But he'd kept the journals safe all this time, hiding them in the ground or within the hollowed trunks of trees, and with each new decade a new hiding place was found. He wrote more, hid more, until his collection had become a small library, histories taken as fairy tales, and only by those who could in fact read. Sometimes it was necessary to rewrite, to transfer pages into volumes, and so with each new age the book-man became his own descendants, passing down the bookshop from book-man to book-man, the scribe, *the scribbler.*

It was as the town's scribe he watched the goddess slip through the humble dirt streets, stealing out of the town in secret to visit her newly finished temple. He watched her through a crack in the door as she crawled the stone floor and lifted the first stone stair to reveal the Well within. The flashing white light humbled him, and he had to stop himself from falling to his own kneels to pray to the moon—but no, that was not why he was there. He was to write, to chronicle, to record the secret truth of the monster behind the façade.

He watched her step into the light of the Well and saw her thrown across the temple, rejected from that which she claimed was hers; her return was as swift as her anger. He sketched out the woman, never changing, slender and dark, her eyes a furious red as she screamed and cursed, thrusting her arms into the light and crying out names he couldn't spell. The earth began to shake then, and the temple walls began to crack. Britanus retreated, tripping over his own robes and landing amid the large rounded stones, grave markers old and new. He clung to one as the land shifted and buckled under the sudden violence. It was terrifying and terrific, and half hidden between a falling tree, slanted and bowing across his sight, he saw Romany thrown through the stone wall of the temple.

And then ... something happened to the world.

Trees broke through the ground where there had been none, while the temple exploded into a high rise tower that shot up from nowhere, scattering stone into the sea like pebbles. Its shadow loomed tall and dark, Britanus cowering beneath. He stood, not knowing which way to turn, clinging to the fallen tree and watching the world around him change and change again.

"With my own eyes I watched the land—gulley, slope and hill—bulge and bend; a crunching sound put me to flight and I ran, my heart nearly exploding in my chest as I witnessed the change, the birth of a new land.

"Walls sprung up quite literally from the ground as if a rooted vegetable shoot, reaching to find the sun; buildings, tall and strong, the likes of which I'd never seen, sprouted up across the hillside, our small settlement dwarfed by towers and grand houses of leaded windows and thatched roofs. I fell to the ground, fearing for my life and sanity as the grass beneath me turned grey and hard, and broke as brittle blades that changed to rock and dirt. The sky disappeared into shadows as men and women alike crawled from the earth as if the dead arisen, and the now town sealed itself behind giant walls of grey flint. An alien town, merged with our own small valley in a matter of minutes.

By the time the quake had stopped I was too weak to move and so stayed where I was, knelt in a new street, watching a new town and its new people. I watched them panic. Two worlds had collided that day, and it had changed everything."

Ami was apart again, not the man whom she'd shadowed, but an observer from the outside. She followed Britanus through the streets to the newly finished palace, a gothic Court with a tower that rose to rival the highest hill.

Then the cold floor was beneath her once more, the light of a day replaced with the glow of orange; the man beside her was dying, croaking, his thoughts turning to laboured words that echoed above the rumblings above.

"She'd reached in, and in her efforts and vain reasoning had pulled one layer into another, breaking the boundaries between them."

"That's what she did?" Ami lifted her sword from the ground and kept it close. Pieces began to fit together, everything that had happened and all that was still happening. Whether deliberate or not, Romany had begun to destroy the walls between the layers of reality, and instead of fulfilling the purpose of the portals, to re-merge all layers into Celestial once more, she was creating a new whole from the many.

"Yes," he said, "and I've borne witness to it for all these years. Keeping my writings, showing them to others in secret over time, making your coming ... legend." Britanus broke into a fit of coughing and lay fully down upon the floor. She touched his face, a gentle flow of power leaving her to enter him, colouring him a purple hue. A peace passed across his face, and his eyes remained closed as she withdrew her hand, his lips moving still with grated breath. "The memories I cannot explain. I do not know, but you, Assassin Princess," his eyes opened, slits only, "you are the one who can match her."

"She means to use me."

"To increase her power, to increase *his*, for beneath the layer she crushed into this, lay a world darker than any before it, a land where men have never existed, and the monsters rule."

Ami stroked his cheek, healing all that she could, but she knew it wouldn't be enough. "Tell me. Is it a beast?"

A laugh escaped him, the croak of a man too old and wise. "Much, much worse. The layers of the world, they are not all as this, or others you've known." His finger raised and he pointed into the fissure, the light steadily pulsing. "Down there, not too far away, are demons."

Then it happened fast, too sudden. His hand opened like a flower, his fingers petals, loose and dead. His last breath blew at the dust and dirt, a small cloud falling into the unknown chasm.

She placed her hand against his neck to feel for a pulse, but there was nothing there. His legs were bones in raw meat, a pool of blood reaching far and wide. "No, not yet," she whispered, taking his head in her hands, her tears touching her cheeks in small kisses. "Don't die, please." Her hands were the paddles, her power the charge. Flashes of green and purple lit his thin skin, outlining his ancient skull.

Flashes of a wood, black trees and blue light. A wood she knew all too well.

Flashes of swords, parry and thrust, duck and roll.

A black lake of tar-like mist, six spheres above; white skin, red lips, emerald flashing eyes.

Then nothing.

She withdrew from the dead body and shuffled backward on her knees, finding the blood trailing after her, thick and sticky.

He hadn't died. None had killed him. Anyone who had been to the Mortrus Lands remained immortal ..."Unless they've gone through the portal," she murmured to the dark, her eyes fixed on Britanus. "Adam."

Part Three: Revelation

Chapter Fourteen

The gates opened wide for their triumphant return, and Hero, Raven and Kane re-entered the city amid cheering crowds. Everyone had turned out for them, a true celebration, for upon the back of Hero's horse rode the beautiful heir of Legacy, Princess Ami, daughter of the long-lost Lord Graeme. Dressed pretty in pink, the princess waved to her people, sending up an array of colours that popped and fizzed and painted the sky. The crowds cawed with delight, their number stretching far back up the mountainside, disappearing behind litters of sun-struck buildings that lined the winding road. And at the peak, rising from the vibrant festivities and thunderous applause was the castle, a large and welcome sight. It'd grown outward from the single keep, now a sprawling mass of adjoining towers and halls, its turrets and spires scoring low-slung clouds. Each window draped a banner of red, gold or blue, the silk fluttering and flying for their victory, the heir of Legacy at last restored. Trumpets sounded out, the throng parting for Lady Grace who welcomed them with open arms and a warm smile.

"Hero!" The nudge in his side awoke him, and all slipped into the darkness of a dream, already half-forgotten. "Hero, wake up."

The next nudge was more painful and he groaned, making a grab for the hand that poked him. Florence. "Stop jabbing me, damn it, I'm awake."

"About time," she whispered, urgent and low. "Raven? Are you there?"

"Yes," he replied, though from far away. Hero twisted round to try to find him, but the space was too tight, Florence pressing his side, a metal grate at his back. Both were more than uncomfortable. "Where the hell are we?"

"We're in a cell, I think," Florence said, her voice muffled by Hero's shoulder. "A very, very small cell."

"Me, too," he replied, his breath a rasp chased with a cough. "Captive. There are these bars ..."

Hero nodded. "Same here." He strained against the grate and looked out into the room beyond where walls were bathed in the pallid light of torches and showed painted images, barely glimpsed. Beyond was a wide gallery, open to the night. A silvery moon dashed upon a mosaic floor, illuminating seven orbs, six small and one large. They appeared to shimmer like a flame to water. He watched them for a time, seeing patterns dance around and around.

"I don't remember much, not after the bookshop," Florence said. "We were sitting on the floor and now we're here. Are we in the palace?"

"I think so." Hero eyed the mural of Romany and her followers, ghostly figures on the walls of a tomb. "I'm sure of it, in fact. Can you not use your power to—"

"Shh," she hushed, her finger visible against her lips, even in the gloom. "She might be listening. Ami's alive, I can feel it, and right now that's all we need to know. We're only the bait."

"I think I hear something," Raven whispered, and sure enough, echoed footfalls followed his words, a pair of double doors opening to the far left of them. In a momentary shaft of firelight and shadow came four men, hooded and cloaked, their tangled beards hanging low before their scrawny chests. With their eyes downcast, they filtered in to stand silently upon four of the six orbs, the last two remaining empty.

Hero reached out through the bars.

"Let us out! We mean you no harm."

"It's useless," Florence whispered, "save your breath. They aren't who we're here for."

"No, I guess not," he said, and pulled his arm back through as the light in the room fluttered and extinguished in a sudden eclipse of shadow.

Romany was on the gallery.

This was the goddess, terrible, powerful and beautiful, her dark hair sparking with bejewelled power as it spilt across her shoulders.

She glanced between Raven's alcove and their own, and Hero caught a glimpse of the sensual power that made men fall to their knees before her. He would never be such a man. Ami beat within his heart, as did his honour as a Guard; bowing to temptation was for other men.

The woman stepped forward and addressed Hero directly. "For too long I searched for a world that no longer lives. I know now that my Celestial is forever lost. But I am still a Creator, and I shall wipe this canvas clean. I shall make the fragments whole again."

Florence shuffled further into the alcove as Romany moved slowly forward, skirting the edge of the largest orb. She reached out toward them, a faint smile tainting her face as the torches reignited once more upon the walls.

"What do you mean to do?" Hero asked, but the woman gave no answer. The newly fired flames turned red, and the quakes increased, cracking stone. He braced himself and sheltered Florence behind him as the chamber filled with dust that fell from fractures. Raven's coughing became relentless and the old men stumbled to keep position, mumbling chants in haste. A crack chased a black line across the throats of the painted order, mosaic patterns scattering as tesserae were shaken loose to chip and smash upon the floor.

She was close, her hand near touching the iron bars.

"I've been feeding *him,* but he is truly hungry, and so when a near-Sentry wanders so willingly, parading a power so carelessly ..."

"You'll not take her," Hero growled.

Romany grasped the grate between them. "Ami will be along, but I meant the *unicorn.*"

Iron screamed as the grate was pulled free, and Hero felt a force push and hold him against the wall. "No!" he cried, but Romany had already seized Florence by her hair and dragged her out onto the floor. "Don't hurt her, I'll—"

"It's okay, Hero," Florence managed, her voice a gasp through gritted teeth as her long locks were wound around Romany's hand, a shadowy claw. The grate slammed back into place and Hero's paralysis was released.

Florence was jerked to her feet and pushed onto the surface of the large lunar, her sword lifted free and sent clattering between the murmuring men.

"You cannot leave," Romany said. "Strays sometimes come, strangers from far away, drawn as moths to a flame. They feed *him,* though hardly a morsel, but this one?" She circled the lunar, her heels clicking. "This one will *free him.*"

Hero cried out and threw himself to the metal once more, grasping his sword; but he could reach nothing and no one. *Still,* he could do nothing.

"She will stop you," Florence said, her defiance for Romany only. "She will find us and you will—"

"What's this I hear?" The woman tilted her head to the gallery, her hand cupped behind her ear. "I hear the approach of a lamb to the slaughter. She is coming."

Then with a quick whip of her hand, Romany sent a column of flame around Florence that surrounded her entirely, the red tongues crawling her body and licking her hair before hitting the stone ceiling above. She cried out and fell forward, suddenly a blur beneath a shower of white sparks. Florence, and then Florina, screamed, her discarded sword spinning and scuttling into the fray to merge at her forehead as a crystal horn. She emerged from the light tethered and caught.

"Here, before me, a mythical creature of power," Romany mocked, circling the event with glee, "a cousin of the Sentry and my kin." She went as if to touch her, stopping shy of crossing the circle's line, and then raised her arms, hands clasped above her head. Power gathered between her palms and crawled across her in tiny beads of light. They swirled and swirled into a ball of fire that outshone even the brightest of lights. Hero covered his eyes, Raven's nearby scream echoing his own, his sight burning behind tightened fingers.

"Come, Princess," she called, her voice a terrifying boom. "Come to me, now!"

THE LONGER SHE STARED down at the dead body, the more morbid she felt, yet Ami couldn't seem to pull away. There was little to no resemblance, and yet the familiarity had been there all along. *Adam.* Could it possibly be true? Back in the Mortrus Lands the situation had been grim, and her memories had gotten confused and tangled. Those that had disappeared through the portal had their lives renewed, or so it had been reckoned, yet they'd assumed Adam lost—they all had—and yet ...?

She took a deep breath, smelling the iron of Britanus's spilt blood, the dust and mould, the destruction above; in her mind she ran through the black woods again, seeing Adam-doubled and sent into the hollowed trees. She bent down and took the man's face in her hands, staring into his dead gaze.

"Adam," she whispered, closing his eyes with her thumbs and laying him back down. It was a gentle gesture, for one who'd hurt her and helped her in more than one life, yet as she moved off toward the steps, lit the colour of hell itself, she thought it at least kind. Adam and Britanus would now be at rest.

She took the steps slowly, watching her footing and kicking away loose stone fragments as she went. At the top she knelt, inspecting the space where the doorway had been, now just a hole blocked by wreckage. She could hear the wind barely breathing beyond, but little else. Letting the power gather inside her and swirl in the pit of her stomach, Ami sent it shivering through her muscles. It dripped from her in colours that lit the carnage in hues of green, the colour of Adam's spite and malice—the poison that would never leave her—and purples, violets and dark pinks of her own. She remained poised for a moment only, wondering what she would face on the other side, if anything at all, and then holding her breath, leapt upward.

The wood and stone were splinters and shards, yet they hardly touched her at all as she broke free and landed deftly upon a mound of collapsed debris. Pulverised brick and plaster rose in dust clouds while thatch burned and spread throughout the town, black smoke lifting only to hang low in the desolate streets. There were no longer any surrounding houses, none to the back or sides, or across the way; only empty spaces and burning rubble, the occasional pan or bottle, a bath or sink, cracked and blackened, a chair overturned, a table splintered; a window frame held a single pane of glass, a single spark of moonlight glinting from the smallest of cracks. It looked like a lonely star.

Ami hadn't felt the tears streaking her cheeks until she wiped them with the back of her hand, smudging blood and dirt, and hadn't recognised the anger that had risen within her until her jaw began to throb, her teeth clenching back a scream.

With weightless steps, the princess slipped down in an avalanche, tripping to the ash-strewn cobbles. A loose sob came with her breath and caught painfully in her chest. How many people had just been killed, in the houses across the way, in the ones to the left, to the right? Had she not heard the tears of a family once alive and now dead? Ami sniffed back the pain and wrung her eyes dry. Oh, what it was to feel such guilt and empathy, knowing she'd once been the cause, knowing now that she was the only remedy. She saw each body buried beneath as she'd seen those butchered before only a street away, or those massacred in memories and revisited thoughts. Romany needed to be stopped, and so she would face her, knowing she might lose. How was she going to save them, any of them?

In a fallen pile of rubble, Ami spotted what looked like a hand, black and misshapen, a charred book covering the owner's face. Pulling it aside revealed the horror of a ruined man. The stink repelled her, but she didn't pull back; something else had caught her eye there. Unburned and wrapped around the corpse was a robe of grey cloth. She was careful not to touch the body, but instead teased the garment from his arms, peeling it from his torso. It was ripped and filthy, nothing more than a rag now, but as she held it up in the moonlight, she surely recognised it.

"The Guard of Legacy." Something metal fell with a tinkle and landed on the man's chest. She scooped it up in an instant, her eyes flashing a cool purple.

The golden chess piece, the rook. Her way back.

She gave the dead man one more look, and then as if following his spirit, looked to the heavens to spy upon the stars. They didn't care, didn't mind at all, and would keep watching her, offering only their eternal beauty to remind her that not everything was always so bad.

A sea salt wind scratched her sore eyes, carrying with it a pinch of pine and chestnut, undoubtedly from the rain-fresh forests, and the smell of sulphur and smoke, woody and homely.

Leaving the body to the night, Ami let her feet lead on, and by the time she looked back, she'd already passed several houses and had in fact walked quite a ways from the site of the inferno.

The moon still paved the way for her, sloping back onto the thoroughfare and out into a smaller side street with no name. Here there were many houses cramped and clustered together, fighting for room in the narrow row, and with a swift turn toward them, she realised that she was still being watched.

Scared faces were hiding, barely concealed beneath light drapery; peeking, watching, tear-stained and shaking.

She stopped as she came level with a low paned window, giving out knee high to the street. Three grey faces peered out at her, fearful yet not in flight. Even though she knew she had to get to the palace, something whispered to her of an urgent diversion. Ami shivered and grasped the doorknob, turning it. The faces disappeared as the latch snapped, and gripping her sword tight at her waist, she entered.

She was met by a wall of heat, and though the air was tainted with the smell of smoked wood and ash, the stuffy closeness was welcome, reminiscent of winter nights spent in front of an open fire wearing only pyjamas and fluffy slippers; she could almost taste the hot chocolate, though she couldn't feel it in her grasp—her hands were frozen—but the sense of being wrapped in arms of soft flicker and crackle-spit was comforting. Danger had so far followed her, chased her and begged for her pursuit at every turn, yet she felt no danger here at all.

There was a thump and scurry in the dark as the shadows of three children scrambled for cover beneath an upturned sofa, its cushions spread over a complicated arrangement of brooms and wound wool. Sheets and quilts and pillows galore were piled and laid, stacked and barricaded around the room, and Ami was acutely aware that hard, solid objects had been stockpiled—missiles to be thrown, given half a chance.

She closed the door to the outside world and stepped further into the room to the edge of the soft fort, holding her hands out either side of her, feigning ignorance of their whereabouts.

"I don't know where you are, and you don't have to come out, but I'm not here to harm you. I'd only like to talk to you."

A brass missile flashed as it flew through the air at her head. She dodged and caught it, reflexes as sharp as ever. Opening her hand she saw it was a pig, polished and smooth, a carrot stuck half in its mouth, a large slot cut into its back. A piggy bank.

"That was a good shot," she said, weighing it heavy in her hand. Whispers followed, the soft light of the fire touching silhouettes, long hair splayed in a shake, a finger risen to another's lips. Ami stepped back to the door in retreat, placing the pig gently on a dresser.

Opposite the main door was a hallway that led to the back of the house, the kitchen furthest away at the end. The door was open but she saw no food, dirty plates or cups; she smelt no recent meal either. *What are they eating?*

Another missile launched, this one going wide, clattering against the wall. It knocked a hanging frame to the floor, a family portrait in oil, dad, mum and three children. She picked it up gingerly, studying it for a moment, wondering where mum and dad were, before returning it to its hook. She expected another object, but none came, and was able to straighten the painting before turning back, her eyes passing over the fort.

There'd been a time she'd built similar, back before creation and destruction, before Legacy, Hero and Romany. She would take over the living room and align cushions and sheets to hide beneath, waiting for her mum to come looking for her, to find her and join her deep within the imagined tent or cave, dungeon or palace.

Slowly, Ami dropped to her knees and threw her plait over her shoulder. The power aiding her sight showed her each shadowed body, each beating heart, and even each expelled breath. They were frightened, huddled, and if she were honest with herself, she was just as wary of them, the place, the diversion she was trusting instead of saving those she knew and cared for. Hero's face passed in front of her and she strained to push it away. No, something was here, and it was *Dangerous* who whispered to her, whispered into her soul. There was something she needed to learn here, but in order to do it, she must put the fearful at ease and set aside the urgency of Romany's challenge.

Another missile, off course, a lazy throw, a warning shot only.

Ami sat back. "May I come in?" she asked, still too brash. She softened her voice a little more, shrugging off the Assassin Princess. "I don't wish to intrude, but if you don't mind, I'd like to sit here ... and hide also."

"We're not hidi—" a girl's voice shouted in defiance before being shushed by an older boy.

Through the fabric of the curtain, Ami saw a rain of lights fall once more, the explosions muted fireworks, loud and scary, missing choruses of *oooos* and *ahhhs*. "I'm hiding from the falling stars," she whispered, lost for a moment in the flicker and flash behind the curtain. "Hiding from the woman." Further shuffles and snuffles, whispers in the dark. The closeness of the heat was stifling, but she liked it, and she pondered on her own words. "I'd like to rest here, away from—" The ground began to shake and the girls squealed. A cushion toppled from the fort, revealing the youngest girl cowering against a boy and a girl a few years older. She couldn't see their faces, but she could see them trembling. More cushions tumbled and a sheet slipped to show the skeleton structure beneath. Ami wished she could put the sheet back up and repair the fort for them, hide them deep in the cushions, under the sheets where they'd sleep soundly in the crook of the overturned sofa—but she was not one of them, only a usurper. Once she had what she wanted, she'd leave them, and they'd be on their own again. She was a liar, she realised, out for bigger things than comfort and castles of cushions. But she had to go through with it. The show must go on, and even if they didn't know or understand why, it was still for them, wasn't it? "—away from this." She reached forward and grabbed a cushion or two, burying her head into the nearest barricade. It was nice to close her eyes, ears and mind between the soft cushions. In them she could squeeze the bad from the world and hide—but she wasn't a child any longer. She looked up to the three, and they looked back at her, and then to the window. Good, she thought, more afraid of what's out there than me in here.

"When will it stop, Thomas?" the smaller girl cried, but the older boy only shook his head and squeezed her all the tighter.

"Soon, Jay," the other girl said, reaching over to her. "It won't last long. It never does."

"He'll get us!"

"No, no, Jay," said the boy. "It's just a story. There's nothing out there."

"Yes there is," Jay shrieked. "He's coming back."

"Shh."

Ami pushed forward beneath the sheet, getting a little closer. It occurred to her that Hero, Raven and Florence may be dying, dead already, yet she hid beneath pillows and sheets … but the feeling of *rightness* was stronger than ever. There was a missing part still to be told, and even now she felt it unravelling.

"It's night when it should be day," Jay moaned. "He's coming."

"No, see, it's already ending," the girl said, wiping her sister's tears away. "Already going," she said with a smile.

The tremors were indeed coming to an end, the lights disappearing. The sheet finally slipped to the ground covering Ami in the soft, white fabric. She shuffled out, feeling like a caterpillar getting its wriggle on, and when she peeked out from the end, she saw the small girl giggling at her.

"Looks like a ghost," she said, and though the other two didn't laugh in the same way, they were still amused by their sister. How quickly the tears dried, the fears forgotten.

Ami smiled, and remembering her precarious part, asked, "Has it stopped?"

Thomas nodded, looking out of the window. "For now, hopefully forever." He turned back to her, frowning. "Who are you, and why are you here?"

The guard back up, young Jay was swept into his arms, elder sister closing ranks behind.

"My name is Ami. I saw you at the window and I hoped you could tell me why the sky falls, and why everyone hides."

"It's not the sky falling," he scolded, though his expression was doubtful. "Isn't it obvious why we hide?"

"It's because of *him*," the small girl said.

"Who's *he?*" she asked.

"It's … It's nothing, really, a story."

"Not a story," Jay said, picking at her fingers with great interest. "It's troof."

"Shh," came again.

"It's just a story," Thomas said, his eyes flashing on Ami. "It's said that—"

"I'm going to take Jade upstairs," the elder girl said, her gaze shifting between them.

Thomas nodded and watched them leave before turning back to Ami. "It's said that when the night comes, the Dragø will rise … It's a whole story, but it's just childish stuff."

Ami shuffled, the name Dragø thumping in her mind. The books from the palace library, *Dragø Maġġï*, *Dragø Katra*, *Dragø Hiṣt*, all books relating to this thing.

"Sometimes," she said, carefully wrapped the sheet around her shoulders, "stories mean something deeper than they seem to on the surface."

"Maybe," he said, looking to the fire, "but it's a myth that's been around forever. It's only when the quakes happen that anyone talks about the Dragø."

"Tell me about them. I'm a stranger here."

He shook his head and looked back at her, orange tongues flashing in his eyes. "Yes, you are."

"I'm no threat, and everything out there," she said, pointing to the night, "scares me, but I may be able to stop it. All of it."

"You?"

Ami bit her lip and thought to the bookshop, to Britanus and the book he'd given her. He'd tried to make her legend ..."Have you ever heard of the Assassin Princess?"

Chapter Fifteen

Raven watched Romany through the bars. She stood magnificent and terrifying, her face framed by a halo she didn't deserve, the swollen power in her grasp lighting all the shadows and making them dance. Even the torches were shamed, their flames shivering in near extinction, in fear and awe. Raven was in awe, and in fear, but it was desperate fury that truly raged within him now. This woman was no longer the young girl he'd felt a fancy for in the darkened house, but a fierce creature, the evil goddess of the text.

Her call to Ami echoed around the chamber and fell heavy like iron, though no reply came.

Ami wasn't there.

The princess wasn't coming.

He remembered the day that he'd first heard the rumour, the whisper that had flown swiftly from mouth to ear, on the lips of every man, woman and child in Legacy: an heir was coming, the long lost heir of Legacy had been found. It was an excited murmur repeated in the streets, in taverns, in shops and parks, and most heavily in the bowels of the castle where the Guard made its base. A girl, they said. A daughter of Lord Graeme, they said. She doesn't know, they said; and within a day the castle was in a frenzy, speculating about this daughter of Legacy. When Hero pulled him into the silence of a small antechamber to ask that he help escort the princess back to the city, it had been with great trepidation and excitement that he'd taken to the task. He'd been commanded to choose one other, though Hero had known as well as he who he would choose, and despite all his cynicism, Kane had taken to the mission with almost as much vigour. The princess was coming, roll out the banners and drop the colours, the princess was coming, and Legacy would be at peace. It hadn't been that easy. And where was Princess Ami now?

He'd felt defeated, crawling from beneath the fallen building, feeling Ami near and close and yet seeing her do nothing to stop the woman. Perhaps it hadn't been safe to do so, perhaps she'd been unable to; perhaps witnessing Romany's malice had been too much to bear, cut too close to the bone; perhaps Adam's venom fought within her and she no longer cared for the ones who'd call her friend. Whatever the reason for her no show, the hope inside him had begun to wane, and when the stand was taken and Ami did not appear, Raven felt the last of his strength leave him. He was swept up, his body crushed against those of his captain and Florence, and it was with a mild sense of wonder that he'd watched the ground disappearing far, far beneath him. It was a dream of silence and colour, an orange flare rising then gone in a blur of streets and houses, a model set upon a dark mound.

But that was then, and this wasn't a dream ...

Raven searched for Florina's eyes, now in a blaze of red flame. In them he saw the sadness and acceptance within.

"Florence, no!"

His words were lost beneath Romany's scream as she lifted the sphere of power high above her head and hurled it to the orb at Florina's feet. It exploded, throwing him back against the stone alcove, his head splitting painfully, a wound that would surely be a bleed. Falling forward once more, Raven caught the bars and managed to hold himself up long enough to peer through the gaps into the pandemonium of lashing white light and pain.

The unicorn's baying screams were that of a horse and woman combined, Florina's body twisting, sinking into the turbulent stone, now the lunar force he'd met before. The four old men who'd gathered around suddenly burst into flame and crumpled to the ground, leaving Florina on her own at the centre.

He could do nothing but reach his arm through the bars, the heat of the flames burning his fingertips.

From the centre of the lunar Florina's power swelled and gathered, reaching up from the simple stones in a pulsing beacon; a moment later it shot from the gallery and into the night, rising high above the town in an arc before making a swift descent to the land.

Romany clapped her hands and laughed, her lithe figure dancing a shadow dance across the walls, heels clacking as she skipped. "Yes, yes, yes. At last—watch, just watch!"

Oh, where are you, Ami?

Florina screamed, sinking further, her horn sparking and sputtering, extinguishing flames. *Don't die,* he wished, her head just above the raging waters of fire and ice and light, *please don't.* He could do nothing to save her.

The ground shook as the ribbon of her power hit its target and the palace around them began to break up.

Raven fell, his prison painted scarlet, his wounds emptying. Before him the cold iron grappled for his grip, and Florina's last struggle became a blur.

THE BOY HAD KNOWN A little more than just the name, it'd seemed.

"And this was all written down? You read all of this?" The boy nodded.

It was a strange thing indeed to have her own experiences recited back to as if they'd happened long ago, in a land far, far away, but forgiving some details, marred or skewed, or events told mildly out of sequence, it'd been a pretty accurate account.

"It's a local legend," Thomas said, "only a story." Ami was pretty sure where the story had come from though. Adam had been central in everything that had happened. Somehow the memory of her had stayed with him in the shadows of his mind as he'd entered his new life, given to him by the Sentries, and then also in his dual-life, split by Romany. The difference in time she couldn't quite figure out, but she was at least certain that Britanus's alien memories had been Adam's.

The boy was looking at her with weary interest. "You think you're the Assassin Princess, don't you?"

She smiled. "What do you think?" Slowly, she slid her sword from her side and held it out to him, blade first.

"That doesn't prove anything," he scoffed. "You could have gotten that made—"

The blade ran a purple flame along its edge that danced and sparked, soon joined by a thread of green. The boy gasped, his eyes reflecting the eerie glow. The katana then pulsed and faded in shape and colour, growing smaller and tapered, morphing into the spiral crystal horn of the first unicorn killed, the prize forcibly taken, and the true founder of the land of Legacy.

"That's just not—" His words were barely a whisper beneath the soft fort of imagination. "That's just not possible. They're only stories."

"Some stories are just stories," she said, watching the crystal horn flicker and pulse with white, purple and green light. It was beautiful, the spiral peaking at a sharp tip, the base a jagged and broken legacy of man's ignorance and fear. "Other stories are true. I am the Assassin Princess. Your long ago legends are my recent past, and I'm sure I'm here to stop what's happening, to stop Romany, and to save my friends. She has them. So please, Thomas, tell me *your* story, the story of Dragø."

The horn glowed and lengthened, turning back into the katana it'd been. The power dimmed and the blade was steel, dull and in shadow once more. The boy now looked from it to her, eyes wide and scared, full of questions.

Outside something exploded, the window lighting bright behind the curtains, the house trembling with the shock. They both started, their breath catching as everything lit unnaturally bright and the townsfolk beyond their fort screamed and scampered for safety. Ripples of whatever had just hit were felt in the very floorboards, and as the quake took hold and increased, the house began to crumble. The picture she'd hung fell again, and upstairs the small girl screamed; shelves emptied of their knickknacks, the fort itself failing in their hour of need. Ami looked to Thomas who was poised to make a break for it, to run upstairs to protect his sisters; but she couldn't let him go. Pans knocked and clanged as plates smashed, and the fort finally fell. In a moment of indecision she grabbed him, lifting him to her by his nightshirt.

"Please," she said, her tone a loud whisper against the sound of cracking earth and stone, the land giving beneath the town. "Please. Tell me what you know. Tell me of the Dragø. What is it, and where is it? I am the Assassin Princess, and I'm meant to stop it." As the words left her mouth, they felt true, for why else was she here if not to stop the triumph of evil over good? She could think of no better quest.

He looked around, eyes frantic, his world falling down around his ears. She shook him, knowing her eyes now burned a fiery green. "Please. Tell me."

"IT'S SAID THAT THE goddess awoke him. Madam Romany had visited the Well and had prayed to her people, to her fellow gods, lost through time; but they refused to answer her, and so she'd gone to join them. They rejected her and threw her to the ocean where she stayed for seven days and seven nights, learning secrets that only the gods could learn. Upon her return she approached the Well once more, only this time to reach deep down into it. The goddess pulled hard and day turned into night. A town appeared as if grown from the ground, trees and people alike sprouting into life. The world shook for the first time and the small settlement flourished into a mighty town. There was a palace for the goddess and hills and rocks that had never been before. It was a gift, she'd said, a gift for Madam Romany. She claimed that the other gods had blessed her and had blessed us. However, something much more terrifying had also appeared. From the river that had once been the vein of life came a great quake that split banks, spilling the water. It had split so deep that it had opened to the realm of demons. The gods had said that Madam Romany could rule her new lands, but only if she could defeat the Dragø.

"The waters darkened and the people fled, the banks flooded and cracked; a roar sounded out, felt in the air for miles, and from beneath the valley rose a monster, clawing its way to the surface, its talons caked with dripping mud, its black scales slick with slime. Its body slithered as if a snake, yet its terrible wings were so large they blanked out the stars. Its teeth were deadly white, and they gnashed as it threw itself upon the town, destroying houses, killing all it came across. It's eyes, when opened, were fiery red, burning with hatred and hunger, and from its mouth came a breath of flame that reached far, sought life, and snatched at those who'd fled. It's screaming fodder begged and wailed, but one by one were silenced, and blackened, and discarded, the life drained from them as the Dragø fed. It slunk back to the waters, towing hundreds of the dead in its tail, the river bubbling black in its wake.

"Each night it returned, and each night it would reap.

"The town lay at its mercy. Buildings burned, and the hill was left scarred and pitted. Everyone was scared. They hid in their homes, barring the doors and windows with all they had, hiding in cellars, dug down deep into the earth, covering themselves and hoping to avoid the flaming red eyes, the prying claws, the sucking snorts of the demon.

"Madam Romany accepted the god's challenge though, for she was the only one who could drive it back to the realm it'd come from.

"She waited for it to arrive once more, rising from the river, its tail swiping and breaking the palace walls; she waited for it to snare its latest prey, to suck the life from their bodies, turning them black in its talons; she waited until it was spent and filled, ready to return—and then she faced it.

"The goddess overpowered it with her magic. Its tail was too slow to trip her, its claws too clumsy to clasp her or clip her, and as she wielded a whip of light and power, it released a roar of fire that took after her. But its flames parted as a diverging stream, leaving the goddess unharmed. She flew at it, sending streaks of lightning to strike its armoured body over and over, its black scales cracking and bursting from it, leaving a patch, bald and tender. There she attacked, driving the beast back, slow and full from its last meal.

"The demon retreated to the river, Madam Romany thrashing it from side to side, beating it back, the townsfolk cheering in her wake. With one last roar the beast turned to chomp its teeth, flaming the whole town before sinking back into the water.

"The goddess sealed the rift with her power, and there the creature sleeps, remaining dormant below our lands.

"That's why we hide when the sun goes down, why we shake when the earth does. Its *him*, the Dragø, turning to scratch in its sleep. That's why Jay screams the way she does. She's terrified that the story is true, that the Dragø is rising again and will kill us, leaving us dead and black like all the others." Thomas was in tears as he looked about, jumping as bricks fell from above in a sudden tumble.

Ami pulled him to her, throwing a glance out of the window and seeing what looked like a ribbon in the sky beyond the curtain.

There was no doubt in her mind that the story had truth, though the heroics of the *goddess* left a sour taste in her mouth.

Jay wailed for Thomas and he stumbled up, though Ami pulled him back down before he could leave.

"She's my sister, she needs me."

"I pray you'll keep them safe," she said, feigning a smile, "but not up high. Below, just like in the story. Find low ground, a bunker, a shelter." The sword in her hand lit between them, reminding him even through his panic of the possibilities before him. "Keep them safe, Tom, and thank you."

She let him go and watched him flee through the darkened house to his family, the building shifting, the walls crumbling. She hoped it had a basement, a cellar beneath, and she hoped it would be enough as it had been for her not so long before; but Ami couldn't stay. The time was now, and she headed across the room and out into the street.

The ribbon was a channel of power, cutting the sky in two, and she now knew where it led: to the Dragø, a beast from another layer, to be brought forward to end all layers.

The wet stones beneath her were coming loose, rising up as the land shook. She could hear the sea far away, wild and roiling, and there at the cliff point, somewhere beneath the tower, lay the all-powerful Sentry portal that connected those layers. Tracing the white ribbon of light across the sky she followed its arc and dip down beneath the street to a far off point of the river. She tracked its course back to the palace where Romany was waiting for her.

She needed Ami, and she was sure going to get her.

BIRDS TOOK FLIGHT WHEN the ground trembled, but Grammy stayed exactly where she was. There was no way she was going to let *him* decide her horizontals and verticals, no matter how menacing and big. No. She allowed all to pass, anchoring herself to an old trunk, waiting patiently for the man to come, as if waiting on a suitor.

A wind shifted leaves at her feet, and the quake eventually died.

"That's better," she said, and slowly took a few steps forward, hearing the crisp rustling, feeling the soft touch of the grass as she passed out onto the path.

And there he was, luminous in her darkness, seated exactly where he ought to be.

It'd been she who'd built the portal, along with all her counterparts throughout the layers, all but one of which were now lost to her, through time, through age, through the lack of want for any such ancient company who'd once been one's self; and the portal belonged to the two of them now.

Only with him did she sit, down at the small table, the plain little porch their shelter, its cracked wood and fields of corn a southern comfort. In fact, she'd been sitting down with him for at least a couple of hundreds of years, trading moves in an infinite battle of wits, the silver and gold pieces glinting in the never ending sunshine of the American South.

In the years gone before, they'd hardly been aware of the humans growing up around them, fruitfully multiplying; and now they were everywhere, smart and curious and adventurous. Camouflaged as it was, and as camouflaged as it remained, all it took was a little curiosity, a stray from the path and *bang,* someone with a little power would be hooked in and led into the portal.

All who ventured up to the shack eventually saw him, the other, and each move he made as he played her. They'd feel the power like a burning in their soul, lighting their fear, an insatiable curiosity drawing them like moths to a kindled candle.

Ami hadn't been the first to fall into the other place, but she may well be the last.

Colours bled across a normally sightless canvas, painting the outline of the dark shack—except now it was changing as she was, as everything was. In place of trees and grass came the shiver of golden corn, fields upon fields of it that stretched out into the far distance. The shack itself was rejuvenated, solid and whole, and upon the unbroken porch sat the other, beneath the gaze of the ever watchful sun.

Pops relaxed, shoulders falling as Grammy strode through the ears—never blind in this land—breathing deeply of the scented warm air. Earth, dried corn, and a hint of apples hung about, though no orchard could be easily spotted.

Pops was older than she in appearance, at least, that's the way she saw it. His short cropped hair was as white as cotton, and almost the same consistency, his face as dark and as wrinkled as a discarded and hardened prune. His eyes were sallow and sad, and watched her closely as she approached, his generous mouth breaking into a smile.

He stood, a southern gentleman, and gave her his hand as she climbed the porch, tapping her cane on the hollow wood.

"She's feeding him, ain't she?" he asked as she hauled up next to him, grabbing for a beam as the earth shook lightly beneath them.

She nodded, turning to find her seat at the board. Her eyes skimmed the positions of the pieces, checking for unchecked movement, checking she still had a chance to win, which she did. She lowered herself down slowly, her cane taking her ancient weight until she was fully seated. The porch groaned, the land jumping and shivering around.

"She's feeding it with something more than usual, ain't she?" He joined her, his eyes on her.

Grammy nodded, studying the board. "Yup. She caught herself a unicorn from another layer. A prize for her, to be sure, though she underestimates her kin."

The old man nodded, his fingers touching the golden piece in the shape of a horse. It had a horn also, though not as long or as sharp as the real thing. "That she does, and always will. Underestimates our girl, too."

"We should've stopped it all the last time."

"We weren't to know." His voice, deep, grizzled, sung an unapologetic song. "We reached out to her the first time when we glimpsed her. We arrived before her, that was the clincher. We gave her the power she ached for, the joining, the help; what did she do but squander it? She smashed two layers into one with more consequences than either of us could count. Careless. Then she raised the beast thinkin' she could control it, thinkin' herself all powerful. We gave it to her, and we took it away. It was right as right to do."

Grammy remembered the breaking of the stairs so that Romany could never again try to cross the layers or bring them together. Banned she was, hobbled and trapped in the one layer, never to taste the dream of Celestial again. Until ...

"Seems she didn't like that too much," Grammy said, contemplating her next move, even as the earth cracked around them, the fields parting for a fresh scar of zigged shadow. "Seems she's raising the beast anyway."

"That we should have destroyed."

"Is not ours to destroy," she said. "Was never ours, these other layers. On the meadow fate was sealed, our own doom certain. Anything that came from that disaster and lived deserves the right to."

"But now," Pops sighed, leaning on one arm, "we must try. All is to fall if she don't get the girl."

"It'll all work out."

THE LAST MEMORY JONUS had was that of the old woman, bending low over him and whispering in his ear words he could not recall.

Then had come the dreams in the dark, dreams that had terrified Jonus more than anything ever had, and he'd woken from them shaking, cold and scared.

But he was no longer in a wood.

There were no trees here, no birds or dry earth, and when Jonus rose up on his knees and reached out with his hands, all he felt was rough rock beneath and to the sides.

That's when his stomach filled with dread.

Was this the price for defying Romany?

Or her counterpart?

The old woman ... his Goddess ... one and the same? It seemed impossible, and yet ...

Jonus knew where he was.

Before him were crude stone steps that he'd felt out with his feet, and with his hands he'd traced the walls, finding no entrance he'd come through, and no hole to escape.

He made a step forward and stopped, arms and legs quivering, his voice sounding too old and too weak. "Anyone there?"

His words echoed and fell flat.

After a moment, a low roar answered him.

His heart pounded in his ears, blood thrumming through his neck as his throat clenched and clicked.

"Madam Romany?"

A sickly smell of sulphur stuck in his nostrils as he took a breath and stepped down. It was hot down here, but he continued on regardless, wiping his brow and turning a corner into the furnace—in Romany he had faith ... in Romany—

The clipped sound of claw and scale accompanied the grumble and eventual roar, and the searing heat that made him scream.

HERO THREW HIMSELF against the grate, calling out to Florina. He could no longer hear Raven's voice, but no longer heard his own either. The ribbon of power that arced from the gallery pulsed loud with a heavy hum—the only thing Hero *could* hear clearly was Romany's laughter as she ran to lean over the balustrade and look out upon the hillside.

Ami wasn't coming. Ami had not saved them, though he still kept his faith in her. Her face was now constantly on his mind, her deep brown eyes, her gentle touch. She'd sacrificed them so that Romany couldn't win, he was sure, but they hadn't counted on Florina ...

The tower shifted above with a crunch as the palace beneath began to break up, and Hero was thrown to the side. Something was below, and it was close to rising ... His blade would do him little good now, and neither would his courage and years of guarding Legacy, of fighting and protecting. Now, behind simple iron, he would watch the magical unicorn, his friend, fail and die as all others would—as he himself would.

Yet when he chanced a look at Florina, almost completely submerged in the pool of fire, he was certain he saw her eyes, wide and focussed, and locked to his. She no longer screamed or whinnied, but fought only to keep above the surface, and the harder Hero stared into the depths of her eyes, the more he felt that something was about to happen, something he had to be ready for. He kept his grip tight on his sword, willing himself to take action, though what action he was unsure of. Something was passing between them in that stare, and without forethought, Hero raised his sword between the bars and waited.

Florina blinked, and Hero took a deep breath.

AMI FLEW DOWN THE HILL past houses of watchful eyes, each with a Thomas and a Jade inside, filled with fear of Romany and fear of the Dragø. She watched as the palace shook with the land, the blazing ribbon rising from it powerful and destructive. The tower itself was tilting hard to the left, looking about ripe to fall like timbre.

Hero.

She stopped at the river's edge, the bridge before her, the black water shivering below, the moon barely reflected and shattered on its surface. Scooting to the very edge of the bank, Ami sheathed her sword before bending her knees and taking a breath. With a simple drop, she dived into the dead river.

Chapter Sixteen

He was in no doubt now as to the trouble he was in. Blind and confused, his old feet stumbled the last step as flames licked his toes, sending him hurtling back the way he'd come. He clawed against the crumbling stone, his nails digging deep—yet there was no leaving.

A movement, a great shifting.

Jonus knew what was there, what was just around the corner. He'd seen it before, had seen it burn, destroy and kill first hand; he'd seen it heave the screaming people into the river, now black and lifeless. And after, he'd read about it in the many texts of Dragø, written by a great master of the power from long, long ago. They'd talked of the Dragø's origins, the magic it held, and the deep, dark workings of its mind. None of it would help him now.

A roar burst forth so loud that it shattered his reason, and sent him running and screaming in any direction, anywhere at all. He hit the wall and rebounded back, landing on the floor, feeling broken and done, his aged body failing him once and for all; all trace of power was a rumour, a forgotten thought now caught in flame as fire snatched his robes and beard. *Fire burns cold,* he thought, his last as his fingers found the brand upon his forearm, the mark of infinity, before it burned from him completely. He called to his goddess.

Even as the fat burned from his immortal bones, Jonus had chance to see one last sight through his blind eyes, a figure of white flame, an apparition, a ghost.

THE RIVER ENVELOPED her like tar, sucking her down into its depths, and though her eyes were closed, some things wouldn't stay hidden behind thin skin lids. There was power here for sure, a current through the water that penetrated her in the darkest of ways. She saw without seeing, knew without knowing, and could hear the sound of a thousand silent cries. She opened her eyes to see for herself, seeing the tar disperse in clouds like paint from a brush in water, leaving dark sediment in murky shadow. Rocks jutted from the land on either side to meet her, an almost magnetic force passing between them, intent on pulling and tearing her this way and that. For a moment Ami was dragged too close and worried she'd dash her brains against them, but somehow managed to stay her course. Once in open water though, she gave in to the pull, letting it lead her to the source of the power.

The deeper waters were shadow and light that revealed irrefutable shapes of human decay, forms clumped and gathered as reef, black arms, hands, heads nodding and bobbing in a dull orange spill. They were so close and horrid: dead fingers, hooked and skeletal, clawing putrefied faces, skulls rising up from fossilised rock, the grinning jaws of laughing men.

Black bubbles fizzled like cola, rising to join the thick surface, the filth of the long dead.

The myth had truth, she was certain, for everywhere she looked she saw horror. But there was also light, a wash of orange licking the crags, picking out the gruesome in small cracks and runs—even below, deeper still, where the world was coming undone.

To Ami's left the land fell sharply, leaving a sheer wall split in the shape of a cross. The vertical was thin, the arms either side large enough for her to climb through, and against the powerful pull—and her better judgement—she thrust herself toward it, coursing against the current with only the power to propel her.

Ami peered inside.

Beyond was another layer drenched in autumn shades of yellows, reds and deep golden browns, where crisp fallen leaves littered the floor; a few birds hopped and chirped, eying her through the split in their world, cocking their feathered heads.

She pushed away, allowing the pull to take her once more, leading her a deadly path down into the blackest of deep-water chasms plagued with fine amber cracks, each one a shimmering moment, each another life and layer disturbed.

Ami dove deeper.

It was fascinating, seeing snippets of worlds, both dark and light: a roadway here, a snowstorm there; a busy street with faces, eyes, peering back in at her; and as the land to each side of her began to narrow, the cracks became wider, and Ami saw even more through them. Streets were cordoned off with coloured cones in one, people passing by with stride and step and worried looks as buildings crumbled and fell. Stories of stories, each different and played out, a live broadcast, multi-screened.

This was the disaster unfolding, the world already crumbling.

Moments passed and Ami swam deeper and deeper into the dark, thinking of the girl she'd been not so long ago, the one who wasn't a princess of myth and magic. Was she now responsible for the fate of the world, of the dimensions of reality? Was all of this really on her shoulders? But in truth, she knew that it didn't matter if it was her duty or responsibility, or even her fate. It's just ... she was the only one *there*.

Soon Ami found she'd reached an impasse and had swum as far as she could. To each side, the jagged rocks had come together, the gulch meeting at an uneven dome that rose from the ravine floor. Cracked into it's crown was a star-like hole, big enough for a person to climb through.

Ami withdrew her sword to look inside, the blade lighting a soft violet that dappled the water and illuminated within; and there she saw a lone, stone stairwell, shifting in shadow and *phased* somehow, blurry around the edges and a little out of focus.

This is the place.

As if she needed further confirmation, a roar echoed from inside, chasing her courage to the brink.

This is the place.

Ami breathed deeply of the dirty water.

This is it.

Dangerous.

For a moment she waited, staring in at the desolate rock, knowing that if she continued on, she might not come back out ... and with that in mind, Ami climbed the dome and slipped into the hole.

Her feet hit the dry ground, a stale smell lingering about of breath and faeces.

There was no water here, no chasm of cracks, only the stairwell and the rumbling grumble and snort of the beast; the star had gone, leaving only the dark.

The familiar sound of crackle and spit preceded a golden bloom, the narrow way ahead kissed in fiery colours. Embers floated up toward her and extinguished upon the cold steps, winking out.

With a shaking hand, Ami pushed her wet plait from her throat, sweeping stray hair from her forehead.

The Dragø.

With a heart full of trepidation, Ami took the first few steps down into the unknown.

SHE THOUGHT SHE'D SEEN her for just an instant, a slip of shadow across a rooftop, a slinking panther stalking the streets—or perhaps not. Even with her heightened senses, Romany would've had trouble spotting a solitary drunkard stumbling from a tavern, let alone a powerful princess playing the shadows; the dark hill swarmed with light and magic, fire and destruction, and there was no sign of the Assassin Princess. No, she was not coming, not coming to save her friends, not coming to face her. *Coward.*

From her vantage point, Romany watched the flares of power hit the town, the slopes, the streets and the buildings. She watched as fires broke out, the screams of a people she'd bred reaching across the distance. Some of them would die beneath rubble, while others would fall or burn, or hide beneath the ground and hope to sleep awake in dusty darkness. But most were for the Dragø, for when he rose he would be hungry and he would need to feed on the life he found.

Beside her the powerful ribbon rose from the palace and cut across the sky, slicing the stars in two. It arced before the moon and fell to a point behind the land, and there to the river, deep, deep down. It fed him, strengthened him for now, but the source was weakening, the unicorn struggling for life in the fire-water of the lunar. She turned to her now, seeing her change between forms, the girl and then the horse and back again; at least the screams had stopped, her ceaseless whinnying noise ... but if she weakened too quickly, the Dragø would not have strength enough to break free.

The first time the Dragø had been released was a terrible mistake, and when her other-selves denied her the help she needed—begged for even—Romany had been left with a rampaging demon. She'd battled him, fought him and had beaten him back with her power, and when he'd slunk back into the river, into the chasm from whence he'd come, she'd sealed him within the crack, in neither one layer nor the other. The beast had shaken her, frightened her even, for what creature, large or small, had ever threatened her as he'd done in all her long years? Her victory was stale, her ego over-stretched, and the rejection from her other-selves a taste so bitter she couldn't stomach it. They'd told her it wasn't time. *Not yet. Patience.*

Many years passed where she took the role of goddess once more, and the land and the people prospered in her keep, but though they worshipped her, they eventually forgot what had happened and had woven instead some myth, part fact, part fiction. The Order had borne witness, and preached of her greatness from the temples in the town, but the lonely rejection of her long sought-after people festered. *Not yet. Patience.* Patience? For what? What else *was* there for her but then and now? How many long years had she truly endured alone, with no origin and no home? Her very existence was a torment to her. She'd reached out to the last remaining broken glimmers of herself and they had chastised her and abandoned her. The layers were shut to her. They no longer spoke to her. She was alone, the long ago memories of a peaceful land now a torture of her waking dreams.

The sea breeze lifted her hair, the salty smell pungent, fresh and welcome, bringing her back to the here and now.

Beyond the white pyre and the writhing unicorn stood the darkened shadow of the man behind his grate. She smiled and laughed, seeing his sword held aloft through the bars. How gallant and brave, foolish and weak. She thought of flaying him alive with a wave of her hand, or perhaps simply throwing him from the gallery and being done with him—his Assassin Princess wasn't coming, her legend only rumour; in the end, just a girl. She walked toward him, her heels coming down easily across the already cracking floor, the tower above tilting dangerously over as the walls began to split, the land and palace alike crumbling atop a roiling demon.

The light shifted and her serpent armlet grew hot and white. She clasped it. One of the six called to her. Five of them were dead, four before her, harvested and used, all burned up; the sixth however had disappeared with the princess. She closed her eyes and sought to see, but beneath closed lids the fire in the room died to darkness and Jonus's dead eyes showed nothing. There were four other senses though, and the ear-splitting roar told her where he was. *How did you get there?* His chattering teeth sounded in her head, his water spilling between her legs. In the distant dark of no perspective, Romany saw a figure of white fire crouched. *Could it be ...?*

"No, no," she panted, and Romany returned from the cave, her eyes set on the girl. She was changing quickly, her muzzle flattening, her horn separating and falling to the floor. The light around her waned, the powerful ribbon that stemmed from her lessening to a milky-pale stripe across the heavens.

But she could not stay to watch. Turning on her heels she raised her arms for flight, red flame consuming her in a rush as she flew up and out, tracing the ribbon with a trail that turned across the face of the moon and plummeted into the river's chasm.

WITH ROMANY'S FIERY departure, Florina was fading fast, her mane falling into the orb's flames in long, lank strands.

"Florence?" Hero's voice sounded out above the departing thrum, the cavernous room slipping to its former red shadow as it beat back Florence's failing power.

"Now!" she yelled, and with her last effort she thrust herself up, hind legs kicking, human arms reaching out of the pool to grasp for her sword. His eyes met hers and a soft moan escaped her lips as the last of her magic shuddered from her and into the crystal-steel. She swung the blade toward Hero, and with his face mashed against the bars, he stretched out further until sword touched sword.

A single spark exploded from the union and Hero was thrown against the wall of his cell again, his head cracking stone. Scrambling back to the grate he saw that Florence had dropped and was slipping into the pool. His head spun as he tried to stand, a heavy warm flow snaking down the middle of his back. His knees gave and screamed as he fell to them, the pain exquisite.

His heart broke in two.

The roiling orb of turbulent power had solidified to stone once more, now marred with hairline cracks that webbed its surface; and half submerged, now only stone herself, Florence reached out for freedom. She had one arm raised, her sword pointing toward him, accusing him, while her expression had been set in chiselled pain, blonde hair carved and shaped, parted wild over plain, cold eyes.

"Florence ... Florina ..."

His sword laid against the bars, the metal glinting and sparkling with the last gift of Florina's unicorn magic. He grasped the hilt and welcomed the cool flourish that travelled his arm, seeping into his flesh, muscle and bone.

"Burn through," he whispered, hoping he could command it, the ceiling above continuing to fall all around. "Burn through. Raven? Are you still with me?" There was no answer. "Damn. Burn through." The sparkles began to race the blade and chase, now beads of light that blurred and stretched, joining into strobes, swimming faster still until the whole blade was alight with the white power of the unicorns. The grate began to heat, the black metal glowing red, hotter and hotter.

Hero backed up as far as he could into the small alcove, watching with mute terror as the grate bloomed a fierce orange, and then white, dripping molten metal to the floor. Soon the drips were dribbles, streams, and the bars fell away, leaving a lake of cooling silver. He jumped it and tripped, his strength having all but left him, but he couldn't stop. The blood flowed more freely at the back of his head, but he ignored it and turned to the cell to his left, grasping through bars to touch Raven. There was blood everywhere, the moonlight and red flame painting it black like treacle. He felt his neck, digging his fingers into his flesh to feel for a pulse. There was one, though barely a patter.

Slipping his charged sword between the bars, Hero touched Raven's shoulder, willing the power to heal. "Please work, please," he whispered, his prayer for a miracle as the cell walls split open, the world a constant vibration.

Raven gasped a breath, a wet sound that gargled in his throat. *Alive!* Hero spun around and turned to his emancipator as the gallery yawned and tore from the palace wall, falling down into the dark courtyard, leaving a jagged hole out into the dying world.

Florence was a statue, a gargoyle reaching from the floor. The large orb split and split again, cracking a seam around her chest. She was dead and cold and frozen in time, and would soon be dust. *No!* Hero placed the blade against hers, his balance precarious as the floors in the tower above began to collapse into those below. A seam of bright fire split the room in half, and with his feet planted either side of it, he aimed the sword at her heart.

ROMANY DIVED INTO THE river, a fiery phoenix joining the dying arc of power beneath the surface. She was not alone though, for the dead chased in her wake, reaching for her, their pleas and confusion always the same and written loudly upon each of their rotten faces. *Why did you do this? Why did you let him take us?* Each eye remaining in a socket burned into her, each grinning skull mocked—she ignored them, for the dead couldn't talk and were only dead in the end. Lonely years of wandering had taught her how to be cold, to forget and dismiss. When all you love turns to despair, when all the world changes and all you once knew disappears? That's when the dead have nothing more to say and give up on you, too.

The way ahead was lit by a world shattered, and Romany travelled the path she'd never forgotten, back to the place between the layers where the dark lands came together and the chasm closed. The portal, a dark star in the rock, seemed to wink at her as she approached, a dark marker to the limbo where the Dragø had now awoken, incubated within a basalt chamber, ready to break free.

She planted her heels either side, breathing the heavy water into her lungs, pushing it out in swirls of force. Flakes of the dead crossed her as she looked into the gateway that would take her to the Assassin Princess, who'd somehow found her way in. She would be the power he needed, the one last kick to break free. Romany's Celestial would be reborn.

Romany dropped down, stretching as power flushed red flames against her skin, settling as she hit the stone and stepped forward, one hand upon the cold rock, her eyes lighting her way in the dark.

Fire flourished to form a sword at her waist. She'd fight blade to blade if she had to, Sentry power against Sentry power, for the princess was undeniably powerful, and more cunning than she'd first realised. She drew it now, crouching to enter the Dragø's domain.

Chapter Seventeen

For a moment all was darkness. And then came the fire.

Ami threw herself back against the rock wall, covering her eyes as the cavernous space ignited in a flourish of fierce flames. The air crackled and burned all around, and through splayed fingers she was able to see the outline of a terrifying beast, painted in shades of amber and orange. With a sudden raucous retch, the fire was extinguished, and the central plume lessened and disappeared altogether, leaving the cavern in darkness once more.

But not complete darkness, for a lone glow of fading colour collapsed a distance away. Ami shivered at the sight, a blushing case of bones, a ribcage still shifting, stretching out in black rock dust and gravel. In the post-burn air, Ami heard a single finger tap a grasp upon a stone before falling to stir no more.

That's when the creature moved.

Air shifted in the dark and Ami instinctively dropped to the ground as something large swung over her head, hitting the cavern wall with a thunderous crunch. Rock fell from above, the world shaking violently, bounding her across the gravel earth; she dared not whimper. By the time it'd stopped, there was blood in her mouth where she'd bitten her tongue. She healed quickly and swallowed the blood, staying still and small.

The creature turned, large scales chinking like armour, great talons gouging rock.

How was she meant to fight this thing? She couldn't see to guess its size, yet the heated air was close, and closer still with each movement. It must have almost filled the space entirely, for it moved too tightly, slowly circling as it searched for intrusion, as it looked through unseen eyes for her. Soon it would sniff her out, or light a blaze to reveal her. She had to do something. *But what?*

A pale light cupped the domed roof of rock then, quickly spreading to illuminate the cavern. It hadn't yet reached her when power burst down from it in a forked bolt, striking the revealed hulk of a creature across its plated back. Now she saw it in its entirety as it rose with a roar to deafen her. It was huge. A tower block tall, its long armoured body bent upward in an *S,* its skull cracking the jagged stalactites, breaking them off to fall beneath its feet. Blood red eyes flashed as its mouth filled with fire. It was a dragon for sure, black of scale and spiked in silver.

The power pooled again across the rock and struck the mighty beast, and Ami felt the gravity of her remit as it roared and clawed at ancient rock. She *must* stop it, for above ground nothing would be left standing. Its tail lifted and whipped toward her and she rolled away in time, her sword kept tight to her chest.

The light faded and darkness returned.

The dragon groaned a sorrowful sound and huffed, the smell of smoke and fire thick in the stale air. It was hard to breathe. Nevertheless, Ami slipped onto her side and climbed up into a crouch, facing the movements of the Dragø, listening with her eyes wide open. Her course of action was quite simple when she thought about it, however suicidal. She must strike.

The dome lit a third time and blossomed stark white, flickers chasing shadow across the deep crevasses of its scaled and sculpted head that lay in wait before her, its red eyes sparked and glinting, sharp teeth parting, ready to devour.

ROMANY WATCHED FROM the shadowy sidelines as the dragon filled the cavern with fire, the last of the unicorn's life force strengthening him from above. It was a sight to be in awe of, the massive demon thrashing and breaking through its prison, and beneath him the so-called Assassin Princess standing small and proud. This was the girl who was meant to be her rival, and perhaps it was vanity to think otherwise, but she would never be her equal.

Finally the unicorn's magic gave out and ceased, and with a wave of her hand Romany called off the dragon, its fire swallowed and snuffed.

All was darkness, silence, smoke and smoulder when Romany approached.

The girl had raised her sword, but Romany sent it skittering across the ground with another simple gesture. She was no match, just a girl, a silly little girl playing with a stolen magic.

"Stay back," the girl panted, her fists raised as if expecting a brawl.

"Oh no, I can't do that. You see, your unicorn is all used up and dead, and my pet here is so hungry." She smirked and swooped low to pick up the sword. She caressed it, but its light didn't shine for her. The blade was unblemished and sharp, the symbol clearly etched.

"Don't release it," Ami said. "There are other ways, there—"

"There *is* no other way." Her aura grew and burned a tall column, striking the dome as her cry echoed and fell. "Do you not think I have searched for an eternity?" she seethed, stepping toward her, skirting the black wings that rose and fell with the beast's breath.

"I have to stop you."

Romany laughed, raising the sword and pointing it at the little mouse of a girl. "You? I shall impale you upon your own sword and release the power from both. You'll die, and I'll ride the layers, burning the world upon the back of a beast."

She lunged forward.

AMI HAD ONLY A MOMENT to decide her next and possibly last move.

Romany thought herself all powerful, but that was her weakness. The truth was that she was a Sentry only in memory, for she was part human too, and they *were* equals in that.

Ami thought back to the first moments with Hero in the dark and mysterious Solancra Forest, to the ruins where she fought Adam in the shadows of her mind; she remembered the power within her and recalled the day she'd spent lost by the stream as a child, finding the magic that had led her the right path. Later it had guided her in her creativity and art, the lands she'd never known, lands that called for her ... She had a substance and grounding that Romany could never have. She had friends, a home, a love. She had something worth fighting for.

Romany charged with a scream, the sword up to her shoulder, aimed for her heart, and in her mad-red eyes Ami saw Grammy and Pops, gold and silver.

The ruins.

She grasped the chess piece hidden in her pocket.

The rook.

With the blade an inch from her chest, Ami clapped her hands upon its tip and stopped it dead. The power within her rose up in curling green ribbons and misted licks.

I can beat her.

"What is this?" Romany whispered, nudging and pushing at the blade. It would not budge, but instead began to change shape in Ami's hands, the metal moulding into a thick grip and pommel, becoming a sword of two handles; then the same in Romany's hands slimmed and sharpened, changing into a blade that cut deeply into her flesh.

The blood of the immortal spilt, and in a flash of white retaliation, Romany screamed, throwing Ami back against the rock.

"Burn her!"

At her command, the Dragø shifted, a black shadow falling over her. Ami raised her sword toward it, the blade colouring and pulsing, the beast's throat a fiery tunnel, ready to erupt. Then the fountain of flame released and fell heavy against the blade, arcing around its protective light.

When the flow weakened, Ami chanced a roll away from the red rocks into cooler shadow, crawling up into a crouch.

A threat hissed beneath the noise. "I'll kill you. I'll kill you."

Ami jumped through the fire, ducking the dragon's tail that swiped at her, swinging round to catch the beast as it careened in circles and shook the earth. The steel was small against the matte-black scales, but an evil green fire was already spinning around the blade, faster and faster, forming a dark crystal shard, finely tipped and infinitely sharp. Ami thrust into its armour and the beast roared, its body a thunderous mountain, the cave walls an avalanche of cascading rock that missed her by an inch. Dust and smoke blinded her as she twisted and turned, losing her bearings and balance.

Then Romany was at her back, driving a blade of red flame deep between her shoulders.

The venom was intense, the pain almost unbearable, her screams that of a banshee wailing in the dark. Black spots swam through her vision, each limb screaming ice and fire and steel, her blood running cold and rushing against cut bone and broken flesh to pour to an unknown ground, spilt so far away from home.

Ami weakened and Romany pushed deeper still, licks of power passing between them. She swooned in darkness and light, watching scenes flash before her eyes of Romany's Celestial, white stone and marble buildings, meadows of faultless green glade—

She fell to the ground, turning onto her side, seeing the silhouette of the great, black dragon above, its wings closing around her.

Romany twisted the blade.

"Die, Assassin," she cackled.

This was it, the end surely—but then she saw it. A single chance.

Her sword had skittered away from her when she'd fallen, but it still shone a tepid purple light that reflected on the underbelly of the beast. And there, she saw where the scales were worn away by time spent crawling the rock cavern. Scratched and broken, they were a captive's wound, offering no protection that she could see—but she was dying, surely there was no escaping it?

A memory scorched through her mind then, a remembering of her time spent in the Solancra Forest with the unicorns there. Talos had tried to teach her how to pass into the power, had practiced with her over and over, showing her how he was able to make himself as if a ghost, to jump rivers as a flash of light and gallop through solid trees and walls. He'd told her that she could do the same, though she never believed it at the time. But if she could do that, then—?

Could she become the power?

Even as the blade inside her deepened, piercing muscle, organs, scoring bone, she thought on it and concentrated all of her will and power to the task. She felt her body shudder, felt it fill with light and smoke as Talos's had done. She saw herself in her mind's eye fading as if a ghost, her flesh taking on a sheen of silver white. Her body was crushed against the rock, staked by the witch who'd once been a goddess, yet she no longer felt the pain, only elation.

Dangerous.

Ami shivered, feeling the change, feeling her body morph into something new. Something *magic*.

The dragon released its fire, but the flames slipped through her, warm but empty, while Romany's blade skimmed air and pierced rock.

She stood, luminous and wispy, swirling in colours of violet and green and white, blues and yellows, sparkling, her hair flowing over her shoulders, a white mane of power.

Romany spat curses, swiping through the mist and fog of a girl now transformed, her sword finding no purchase or flesh to pierce; her scream was a roar that rivalled the beast's as Ami stepped back and levelled her sword to her chest.

A blast of white fire sent Romany flying against the cavern wall, breaching the rock and exposing the layers. Turning, Ami pivoted her sword and buried it within the beast's worn belly. It roared once again, tearing round, its mighty tail and head smashing the cavern walls, widening the fissures, spilling the light of the layers as its tomb broke open. Fire consumed shadows as wings lifted and beat the walls, rock flying through Ami's body until her powerful form fell to the ground, solid once more.

"You bitch," Romany shouted above the fall and fire, "this is my world, my time. You shall *not* destroy what I create!" She rose, a fallen angel draped in dirt and blood, her beautiful face now a melted mask of fury and vengeance.

The Dragø whipped and swiped, teeth and claws grinding rock, the cracks now chasms, ever widening, the light of layers splashed across its mighty spikes and plates.

Ami recovered, dizzy, and spun to avoid her coming foe, rolling forward beneath the beast and between its legs. Sword in hand she thrust again into the wound, hoping to kill it, kill it dead!

This time though something felt different, for there was a pull on her power from above. Tendrils of light within her connected through the sword, and in her mind she saw a world of green that shuddered and cracked and fell to flame. She saw dragons taking flight, hundreds and thousands of them, disappearing into the sky.

Romany's hands found her throat and Ami was caught, fused to the sword, fused to the dragon as it lifted upward, wings and tail and flame-roaring head smashing the rock walls and roof, the cavern collapsing.

She couldn't let go, her power channelling and fluxing *into* it.

What had she done?

Golden light broke out a new sky above them, and through it Ami saw houses and streets, cars and people, throngs of people, tripping and running in fear as reality fractured around them, the layers slowly becoming one.

"I *shall* kill you, I *shall* end you." Romany's hands gripped and slipped at her throat in an attempt to find purchase, long nails raking skin and scoring bloody furrows in their wake; but Ami managed to wriggle free each time, turning her head this way and that.

Ami pulled back on her power, reversing the flow, not wanting to feed the dragon but to starve it; she pushed and pulled with all her might until she felt the creature's power flux back into her, channelling through her, the two powers colliding within the sword—

—and with an ear-splitting *boom* Ami and Romany were thrown to the ground as the dragon was set free, and the scenes buried deep within the forbidden sky began to overlap.

THE QUAKING HAD STOPPED some time before, and all had become quiet across the fields that stretched out beneath a solid white moon; the wind swept through the crops, a whisper that told cold secrets. It would've been a peaceful scene had it not been for the large fissures in the earth that cut the dark scape in two.

Grammy eyed them now from where she sat, their rough edges a web across the land. A faint orange light emanated from them. She brought her eyes back to the board and the game in hand, the creased brow of her opponent hovering over the pieces. His eyes were levelled to her queen.

Only a handful were still in play, the rest—all but the missing piece—were stacked neatly to either side of the chequered board, threatening to fall from the dented old table. Somewhere a bird squawked and flapped, though her tired eyes couldn't locate the source. Certainly not from nearby.

She frowned, finding her position weak. Her king was out of play, swiped off the board early on, though his still stood. It was the queens that worried her, for their glittering bodies of silver and gold stood too close together. Her knight was too far away, and the bishops were all gone.

Grammy grasped her fingers to the base of her silver rook.

"Nope," Pops said, though his lips barely moved. "Wouldn't be doin' that if I were you."

"Helping me is not part of the deal," she said, lifting the piece; then spying his knight she placed it back down.

"It's goin' to happen. There ain't two ways 'bout it."

She sighed, released her rook and stroked the metal queen. "I know. Just wish it were different. I've come to like her."

Pops grunted a laugh and raised his eyes from the board for the first time. "We'll soon know." He glanced toward the swaying, silver corn. It was all dead in the night. Skeleton corn. Dead. "Won't be long."

Grammy nodded, sighed once more, and then pushed her queen into stalemate. Small threads of light passed from one to the other as the pieces trembled and fell, rolling ceaselessly across the board.

Chapter Eighteen

There had been a moment.

The moment could not have lasted more than a second or two, and yet in that moment Hero had seen something of what she'd meant to do. Her eyes had sparkled within the white flame of the orb and he'd felt her reach out and touch him with faint images that floated beneath the surface of thought, half-remembered dreams that lingered. When the time had come, he'd known what to do.

Now though Hero acted on instinct alone.

The split beneath him filled with fire, setting alight his garments; it would be only seconds before he was consumed, and Raven along with him. The palace was ripping apart. With a quick thrust, his sword entered her chest, the steel scraping stone—or whatever she'd become—coming to a stop inches in. Then the breach widened. Hero leapt from the chasm, his skin singed raw and screaming as he slid, the floor tilting, the stone room splitting in two.

Everything was sideways on and upside down, the chamber now a puzzle set, raised and demolished, the pieces tearing from each other like bread. Fire licked slick tongues in all directions and nothing made sense except for the knowledge that he'd failed and everything was for nothing. *Ami,* he thought, *please forgive me.*

He slid, grasping and grappling for grip as stone turned to stars and the sky to fire.

Something snagged him, fingers curling tight around his wrist, and looking up Hero saw a face worn and marred, shadowed within drapes of wet hair. The sword was still within her chest, fluxing and spitting sparks of white flame.

"Come on," Florence shouted. "Climb."

Broken mosaic floor jutted to the right, and with a painful tug on her steely grip, he swung to it and clung on. The small squares were sharp and dug into his skin, the blood seeping from his body now in many different places—but he barely felt it. He pulled himself up, the world tumbling toward him in a rush of cold air, while below, pale-lit tree tops ran over scoops of land, cracked and laced with rivers of molten light. He crawled onward, regardless of the death that awaited him, the final fall, and held on to the girl, locking her in a tight embrace.

She was alive!

Raven crouched beside her and helped pull him onto the small ledge that remained.

The tower had broken just above them, the courtyard an inferno below, and they were now the tallest point of the palace—but not for long. The plinth shifted and tilted forward, breaking the small segment of wall from the stairwell, a chasm grinning, yawning, screaming in bright fiery light. Within that light, Hero saw faces peering through with arms beckoning. *Another layer, another world ripped open.*

He looked to Florence and Raven, soon to die—and in that moment came to a decision.

"Farewell, my friends," he shouted above the winds, and launched his weight against them both, toppling them back from the plinth and into the light. Arms reached out and grasped them ... and they were gone, just like that. "May you live on ..."

The chasm disappeared from view as the plinth gave beneath him, and both Hero and the palace fell into flames.

SUMMER BREATHS SCATTERED rose petals and Ami watched them fly the cotton-candy skies of late evening. They twirled and spun, blood tears spilt and briskly wiped.

She blinked and sighed. It was so beautiful, so tragic, each petal a life. Each one a love.

And so she turned to her side to let it be.

Pain didn't need to be watched to be known, didn't need to be known to exist; yet there were more petals on the ground, forgotten and lost. Some had blackened and curled, dried to a crisp. Others were so soft she could have reached out, could have … what, saved them? No. They'd already fallen, though they still held the scent of the living. But they were dead.

Across the grass the setting sun made a dial of the arches, their long shadows pointing to the black woods, and there the branches moved. Slowly. She watched them. They watched back.

"She won't come unless you bring her."

Ami sat up, looking around for her double. She couldn't see her. "Bring Romany?"

A giggle came from behind her and then finally the soft patter of small feet. "Back to that which remains, silly."

"Why?" Ami asked, turning in time to see the small blonde girl dance onto the walkway behind her. Grace. "I thought this was your place, our place?"

"It is," the girl sang, "but it's hers, too."

"Bring her here," the Shadow Princess said, somewhere out of sight. "Bring them all. They will come; they never truly left."

Summer breath kissed her cheek, a petal falling down and down to her throat where it cut.

Dangerous.

"Pitiful Princess."

Ami stared into the light, the black body of the dragon a silhouette, clambering. Above and to her left, Romany leered, her own sword at her neck.

She swallowed. "This won't bring back your home."

"It will create a new one," she sneered, "and with your death, the Dragø will be strong enough to rip through all the layers. Everything will be as one."

"But what if I could get it back for you? Your home?" Ami looked across the now shattered ground, lined with cracks where orange light peeked like lava, the layer about to collapse.

"You have no power, Princess." She laughed, drawing the sharp blade over her heart. "Now be still, this will only hurt a little."

The blade pierced her suddenly and all at once, the leather outfit splitting, her skin slitting, the sword cutting into bone and muscle, straight into her heart. The pain was torture, a sudden release of life from limb—yet still, her eyes were locked to the mighty dragon that spread its wings high above and roared into skies, lands, hills and meadows; into seas, cities, towns and deserts, its fire touching each and all.

She was dying, for immortal she was not.

Hero whispered sweet nothings into her ear ... as her mum wiped the soil from her. She swung back and forth and pushed ... and the higher she got the dizzier she felt ... and flying was a rush but the landing was ... Legacy and magic and unicorns and ... Hero loved her, she was sure, and she loved him ... Raven, dear Raven ... and the Mortrus Lands ... and Talos ... and art ... and the ruins ... and ...

Ami sought the eyes of the witch who killed her. "I'll take you back."

Romany twisted the blade with a grin while green-misted power lifted and swirled from Ami, her body convulsing, her hands reaching to the blade. When she grasped the unicorn steel, the power spun around it, faster and faster, growing and surrounding them both.

Ami smiled, seeing Romany falter. "I'll take you back."

"What is this? Why won't you die?" But even as she spoke, Ami felt her spirit soar, her body changing beneath the released power, morphing once more into light, into smoke and colour.

She reached out to the woman, her ghostly hands twisting tangles around her arms as the power entered the sword, its steel tip slipping through her non-corporeal body, penetrating the thin crust of ground beneath. It gave way in rush—and then they were falling.

Skies and lands spun and tumbled, they a part of each, and each a part of them, until finally the earth landed upon their backs and solidity returned.

Ami gasped and looked to her side.

Romany was beside her, laying in the grass, her head upon the white steps of the ruins. She looked peaceful, younger than she had before, Sofia-Maria perhaps, or maybe someone else entirely.

There were no cracks here, no marks of orange, though a tremor could be felt beneath the earth.

Ami stood, taking hold of her sword.

There was no sign of her shadow-self, the stone and marble empty, the walkway shadowed as the sun sloped off behind abnormal clouds. They were dark-bellied and oppressive, filling the air with the sweet smell of rain to come, and perhaps a storm.

Romany stirred, slowly pushing herself up onto her hands and knees. She didn't look half as dangerous here, though *here* wasn't quite *here* yet.

She'd have to call them.

Ami looked to the castle tower that overlooked the green, a monolith of mystery unexplored, its grey battlements a jagged black silhouette. *It was part of the city,* she thought, *a left-over afterthought.* It had always been there, had in fact been the place she'd emerged from when she'd entered the ruins the first time. Within its doorway were the mirrors of herself, her choice and strength, though she always thought them part of a dream more than a real place; but now she knew better, for elements remained, created by neither Grace nor herself, elements that were created by the Sentries.

... but it's hers, too.

"I'll kill you," Romany hissed, now turning about, her eyes darting the clearing, the dark woods and the arches—eyes lingering on the arches. *Does she recognise them?*

"You haven't though, have you?" she whispered. "And I don't think you can. Not here, not anywhere."

The woman spun on the spot, her red fire-blade emerging from her closed fist. "Where are we? Where's the Dragø? I'll—"

"Kill me?" Ami finished, stepping slowly up the steps to the columns, to the arches broken or unmade, or perhaps only unfinished, a vision incomplete. "You'd like to, but you can't."

"Why can't I?" Romany sneered, her steps stealthy as she followed her, her blade ready to strike again. "I'm the goddess here. I'm—"

"—already dead. Don't you know where you are? Don't you recognise it?"

Romany looked around, shaking her head, though there was hesitation, apprehension, her mouth opening and closing without a word.

Ami turned to the arches and lowered her sword, presenting it to the ground, placing its tip to the centre where it stood balanced by itself, perfect and still. She didn't know how she knew, but she knew it was right. *Dangerous* told her it was right. *They will come; they never truly left.* She backed away from it, allowing it to turn on the spot, a single solitary note singing, then another and another. It was a tune she herself had sung, as another being, as the double of herself; it was a tune she'd heard played at a tragic wedding. Romany looked like the bride somewhat, comprehension crossing her once innocent features, all things beginning to end. Her own sword had lowered as the Celtic tune carried across the green, vibrating each blade of grass as if they, too, had joined the song; then there were voices, somewhere far beyond the clearing and the platform, from the tangled forest, from the walkway, the spill of petals dancing with the sound.

"What is this?" Romany asked, walking the edges of stone while Ami's sword gently spun. The voices were far, far away, and yet were getting closer, ever so much closer. She stood aside and leant against a column, waiting and watching with muted awe as the arches began to grow, the sculpted and shorn stone stretching to join.

Clouds passed above with little breeze, the tapping of the dead branches marking the coming of the others as they stepped dim and vaporous from between the trunks. First there were a few, and then ten, twenty, a hundred and more; wispy white and pure power only, the ghosts marched toward them.

With each step taken the land stretched and changed, the small clearing blurring and becoming bigger. Romany dropped her sword, the blade bursting to flame and expiring. "How are you doing this?"

Ami remained quiet and watched her sword sparkle and spin, faster and faster, singing the notes that the Sentries sang, a haunting melody that called to them, all of them. *Bring them all.*

GRAMMY REACHED ACROSS the board and held onto his hand, gripping it as hard as she could. Pops gripped back. *A quiet and thoughtful man,* she thought, *such a shame to lose him.* Though of course, she wasn't losing him at all.

The stalemated queens juddered on their board and fell.

"Goodbye, old friend," she whispered into the man's ear.

"Goodbye, and hello, and welcome back again," he sang, a sweet old voice disappearing into the void.

THE FIRST SPITS OF rain tapped a beat to the bass line of thunder beneath the melody, the darkening blue sinking finally to a dusky lilac. These were no longer the ruins, if they ever were. Something was happening all around her that Ami neither planned nor expected. It was personal, and it was for Romany. Beyond the walkway against the coming dark emerged many shapes of white and rose. They were hazy at first, stretching far back into a land that had not been there before. Buildings, streets and trees were sketched out, branches overhanging monuments and fountains, a grand staircase rising from nothing to go nowhere. The castle tower was now far away, a pike of a distant land, the green a meadow that fringed a massive woodland, carved and kempt by a river. Statues of men and women littered the spaces, and colour began to bleed into the indistinct, as vivid yellows and reds hung as fruit from laden branches, from windows of on-looking buildings, flags and banners, rich greens, royal blues, and burned orange-shades to match the life-blood of the layers.

And she'd brought them all.

The forms of Sentries, millennia and millennia dead, gone, transformed, swarmed onto the meadow. Faces peered and watched, each clear and yet unclear. She felt them, the power emanating from them intensely. It made her want to run, it made her want to join them, it made her want to scream ...

Romany's aura fluxed red and white as she turned to Ami, the rain falling heavy across the forming landscape. Her wet hair spat and sparked, plastering and cupping her chiselled face, curling just below her jaw. *"They're all here. They're all here."* There were thousands clustered, hundreds of thousands, all advancing with the same melody on their lips, a chorale of merging white so bright that Ami had to shade her eyes.

Romany raised her arms to the sky and screamed while thunder broke overhead, the flash and burn of the storm's whip lashing down upon her face, tearing scores of deep lines into her skin which folded and greyed. Her Cleopatra beauty drew to a close in flanges of loose flesh, her eyes closing and reopening white-blind. "What is happening to me?" she whispered, all colour blanching from her long hair leaving it white. Her clothes remained unchanged, though the serpent fell from her arm and disappeared into nothing.

Romany turned on the spot, pirouetting as gracefully as a ballerina, yet far too quickly, her body a blur of white and red. Ami stepped forward and shielded the still spinning sword, fearing what might happen next, knowing only that the faces that flashed in the cyclone of power were of those who guided her. She had to trust in Grammy.

The woman who'd been Romany came to a stop and screamed, her hands tearing at her hair, her voice cracking and rasping until her scream died and fell into chorus with the bride's melody, rising above the howl of the wind and the slash of the cutting rain.

Ami readied to grasp the sword and summon her power, but the woman simply held her hand up and the singing stopped. Only the storm ignored the gesture, the downpour too loud on the stone.

Then she spoke.

"I've been lost, so lonely. I've done terrible things." Ami nodded, pulling her sodden hair back from her face. She thought of the stories she'd been told, the destruction she'd seen, the brutality of the woman. "I've brought hurt, pain and death."

"You have," she agreed, eying the ghostly forms who'd come to a stop at the base of the stone platform.

"I was less than myself and less than a human. It was not who I was ..." She flung her arm out to the gathered. "We were peaceful, only curious. Too curious." A murmur flittered around them in agreement. "But then it all went so wrong, and yet we lived on."

"Fragmented, split."

"Yes."

Behind her the blade sung her song, and beyond, somewhere further out in the shadows, she could hear her other self pick up the tune. Where was she and why did she hide? A whisper answered as if by her ear. *Don't trust them.* Flickers tickled the bellies of clouds as the rain fell hard and fast, a mist rising from the stone, across the sodden grass. Trees swayed and limbs bent, tall old oaks dancing with ash and pine. The Sentries were clustered, as she'd seen them in Romany's memory, as they'd been on the day of their end. *Don't trust them.* Ami pulled closer to the sword, fumbling in her pocket for the rook.

"The dragon is going to destroy the world because of you," she said.

Romany's skin smoothened, wrinkles shifting in faze, almost breathing. "I'd gone to the sacred well and had communed with the last two shards of my soul. I'd found them there, somehow, after so long ... and I found there'd been an ancient purpose, an attempt to merge the lands back together through the portals. Each flicker of power I'd seen had been an attempt I'd ignored. I convinced them, convinced myself, to try again. They agreed. Our power was linked and as one for the first time since our end, but when I pulled, something else happened. The power was great, so great that it moved the very layers of the world, and in an instant another had collided into my own. All things changed and the worlds merged, and the demon raged below. The Dragø found its way to the surface and devoured."

Ami watched her closely, her hair a witch's mop, her body shivering in the freezing rain. "But you let it roam."

"Yes, I was fascinated by its power, and when I fought it I realised how I could steal the power it thrived on and weaken it while strengthening myself. I trapped it at a point beneath the layers where the cracks between the two were the largest. I created the cave there and kept the Dragø, weak and unable to leave, just as I was unable to.

I could not cross the barrier, deemed too dangerous by my selves. The layers could not be breached by force. They abandoned me, told me *Not yet. Patience* ... and took the dream of my home away. Now I am with them both, here in this form.

"Over the years I plotted and planned, and when you arrived and I realised your true potential, I knew you were the sacrifice I needed. You, the Assassin Princess who are as Romany is, part human, part Sentry." She paused and looked around the darkened meadow, her eyes flashing white as they passed over her fallen people. "You created Celestial though as I never could, and soon all of this will be gone. The Dragø will collapse every layer, full of my malice, and stolen power. Only you can stop it now." She took a step forward, and with her came the mass of forms, shifting ever closer, a crowd looking to a stage. "You must end me. You above all have the power to do that." *Don't trust them,* the whisper said, and Ami thought she saw her shadow-self winding between the trees, crossing the walkway, now so far away. A petal fell with the pour, touching her hand and sliding to the ground. It swelled and twirled and was washed away somewhere else. "We three cannot live apart, for one is too dangerous. Sentry of new, stop us, destroy us, before it's too late."

"I don't know," Ami said, shaking her head, her hand stroking her leather clad thigh, her fingers twitching and ready to draw. "I don't want to kill you."

"You have to," the Romany-being said. "Please."

The souls began the song again, the melody that marked Ami's turn to darkness, heard even over the thunder and the roar of rain. Were they moving forward? Their faceless faces seemed to crawl beneath light, reminding Ami of late night horrors on TV, zombies rising, the dead feeding—and is that what they were? Their non-mouths moved, yet not with words in song, but in o's, hungry fish in a pond, needing, wanting ... *Don't trust them.* She looked back to the Romany-being, the merge of the three. Don't trust *them* out there, or ...?

"How would I kill you?" she asked.

"With your unicorn sword, of course." A smile and a sheen of red beneath her skin. *Who are you beneath?*

Don't trust them.

Them out there, or ...?

Them in her.

She'd brought them, out there, but who'd brought *those within her?*

"Pierce us, kill us, end our suffering." Three against one, she realised as Romany stepped ever closer, her own back touching the stone column that held the canopy above. Grammy, Pops, Romany; they were all the same, not just splinters of the same Sentry, but *all the same divided.* She'd been played, used, Adam's play all over again.

Dangerous.

Not this time.

"Okay," Ami said, and then whirled around, snagging the spinning blade.

The woman who was Romany thrice let loose a triumphant scream through a mouth too wide, her body bursting into red flame as she rushed toward the arches; but Ami jumped clear just in time, and flew high up above the crowd to see her foe fall between them, writhing and caught within the ancient stone like a fly to a web. Her screams and curses were perpetual and pointless, as her people moved forward.

Clouds split open with golden shafts of sunlight that illuminated the long dead city, and everywhere the light touched the streets buckled and the trees fell, the houses broke apart; all tumbled to dust and rubble, the horizon closing in around them all.

The Sentries were ghosts for sure, packed together and chained in power and essence. And they were hungry, hungry to be alive, greedy for the power they once had, a power now caught in their trap, their portal of destruction, their ultimate downfall.

They began to climb the steps as Romany flourished in sparks and glimmers and flames of power, all her hate and longing bursting from her in an inferno. Her face changed and revealed the truth, the jealous, the vengeful, the schemer, the powerful dead of long, long ago. Her screams and curses rang like a bell as the storm cleared completely, the sky returning to a blue, the land cracking and falling in chunks into chasms of nothing. It was a snow globe, its dome contracting, the meadow reshaping, the forest now just the black trees of no further, entrance to the dark, exit of sanctuary—only this was no sanctuary. Not anymore.

"Get away," she heard her cry as the white beings pushed in their hundreds, thousands, upon the white stone platform, all gathering and singing her fated song, reaching and grasping for the power long denied them, long dead to them. Moths to the flame, a power-hungry race, extinct in life and their worst in death.

The beings reached the arches and smothered and covered the screams of the self-styled goddess, before they too were consumed, the meadow now only green, the petals flying up, up, up, dancing the warm air.

"I'll kill you," she heard, a sigh only as the Sentries faded completely, leaving only broken stone, incomplete and silent.

"THEY THOUGHT THEMSELVES superior, and once they were, but every living thing has its time." Ami looked up to find dark brown eyes staring down at her, framed in the fall of a chocolate mane. She was as always, her constant strength, her choice, her mirror. *Dangerous.*

Ami had sat upon the steps after and had closed her eyes, covering them with her folded arms in her lap. With only the gentle breeze for company, the creak and rustle of tree and branch, Ami was able to imagine herself away, far away, back home perhaps and sitting on the back step of her house overlooking her own back garden. It'd not been small, or large, but had always been well tended. It was comforting to see herself there, her mum and dad close by, just out of sight. But there were no birds here to sing like there had been at home, no traffic passing a road away, no casual chatter from a couple walking. She wanted to cry, and did a little, and sat up straight to better see the Shadow Princess.

"The old woman was a liar," she whispered.

"She was as she had always been. That one being from long ago had been as every Sentry had been, too sure of their own righteousness; splintered, they weren't much different in the end." Shadow Ami sat beside her and looked out onto the green, her eyes flicking to the dark woods. "They could never accept that the end had come. If you'd have thrust your sword into the three of them combined, they would surely have overpowered you and stolen all the good, and the bad in you."

"To live again?"

"To continue, in some form," she said, and smiled. "But her people were also the same, jealous and greedy even in death. You called to them here to witness, and they hated what they saw in Romany, in a Sentry who would have power greater than theirs."

"What's happened to her?"

She shook her head. "That I don't know. But she has gone, and you need to stop the dragon. Romany can no longer control it, but it is still there right now, breaking through the layers. This has not ended yet." She stood and pulled Ami up with her, the connection between them a magic of purple light and sparking flame. She saw only spits of green, most having left her for Romany.

"But, how do I do that?"

The twin touched Ami's sword at her waist and smiled. "Go through the arch. Return." She pointed to the place Romany had been lost, where her own greedy people had devoured her, or taken her—had gone with her either way. The negative space between pulsed and seemed to swallow. "It's not ended yet. There is still time."

Ami followed her direction, thinking of the old woman and how she'd taken her at her word, thinking of her as Grace the elder, who'd been both a child guide and her mother. Trust was deadly, sentiment anaesthetising. *Adam, Grammy, Pops, Romany—how many more times must I be used before I learn?* Her power bristled, her skin swimming with light beneath the leather. *Never again.* The Shadow Princess stood behind her as she reached the arches and looked around at the peaceful place, the rainfall and storm gone as if never there, as were the Sentries. "This *is* Celestial, isn't it?"

"Yes. All that remains, a layer all on its own. It belongs to you now."

Ami pulled her sword and it flew aflame, the colour of lavender. "You cannot come with me?"

I am you, she whispered by her ear, and Ami stepped through, back into the cavern.

The temperature had dropped dramatically, her breath an icy mist as she stepped tentatively between the numerous cracks. Around her, rock had broken and fallen, the cavern now more a stone cage open to the sky, the light of the layers bleeding through in shafts and pools; above, the orange light swam a sea of overlapping landscapes that rippled into one another. There were mountains there that had scattered rock down upon towns, and men in simple animal skins that had wandered lost into streets and houses; fire spread from lava fount to forest to field, through suburbs and valleys, melting icebergs that swamped deserts; and in the centre, now only a flapping shadow, was the Dragø. Its roar cascaded down upon hundreds of layers, gargantuan wings seen in a thousand skies. Claws and tail swiped at planes that exploded and scattered, littering millions of lands and seas. *Soon the beast will feed*, she thought, *and the new Celestial will reign.*

And so, letting the power gather inside her, Ami raised her sword and pushed her body into light, the power lifting her up into the air in pursuit of the dragon.

She ascended quickly beyond the broken shell of rock and into an assortment of so many colours and shades; it was psychedelic, and Ami wasn't sure her senses could handle it. It was as if she were surrounded by seas of reflections, pools of all different sizes, each showing something different. Some pools were huge, those she'd seen from below easily enough, but others were tiny and flickering for space, each and all rippling into the greater ocean of orange light. She tried to focus on the dragon, the only singular and unique shadow above her, but her attention continued to stray to destruction and desolation, dark depths pierced through with strobe light, night and day, rain and dry, blood-spilt wars, cries and screams, all heard mutely from billions of puddles, pools and rivers of life. What did she look like to those who saw her? A shooting star perhaps, or a missile aimed for the beast? There were already many of those, each falling with the wrath of fire it'd loosed upon them. Without doubt it would do the same to her, given the chance—but she was no dumb missile.

In seconds she'd caught up with it and rolled to her side to dodge a swipe of its spiked tail, her sights set on its mighty scaled body. With a downward thrust of her sword she pierced the beast's black armour, digging deep into the flesh beneath; it roared, spitting fire in all directions as Ami flailed to the left and right and over, over again, holding fast to the grip—now solid once more—and knowing nothing of her next move. Could she drain its power and send it back down to the cave? Perhaps, but the cave had already gone, had sunk beneath too many layers, too many worlds.

A wind blew against her as she pulled herself up, a hissing sound like white noise in her ears. It was quickly followed by a loud *pop* that blew her backward and almost off of the dragon's back. Ami scrambled for hold on a raised plate across his spine, finding the view around her suddenly changed.

A single fiery rip scored the black sky above, while below lay a coastline of tall structures, ornate and mostly white, lit by an array of fires sprinkled throughout. She pulled her sword from the Dragø and clung to its back, looking down upon bulbous domes sitting upon white stone towers, walls of a palace adorned with turrets and spikes, and braziers lighting streets thronging with nightly comings and goings.

Somewhere she heard a voice in the wind, near and yet far away. *Something's coming.*

They soared down with a torrent of fire. Lives, hundreds of lives ... Ami turned from the blazing cull, too horrified to watch or listen. Instead she looked to the sky, to the mighty tear. It was gaping where they'd made their entrance, crumbling like stone and cutting the night, unfurling like an unzipped jacket. Soon the sides would peel apart and collapse into another world. How could she stop *this?*

They were swooping low, and with her eyes fixed to the thick black scales in front of her, she imagined Romany rising triumphant, a song on her lips and hate in her heart.

The matte black armour shone dull with the flame, and Ami slowly began working her way along, grabbing for the next plate, the whole row of them equally spaced, jaunting to one side and then the other. She found she could worm her way between them while still remaining steady, the only thought driving her, to pierce its massive head, the fiery orifice of evil. If she could reach it.

Souls were being harvested, but she wouldn't look, and instead concentrated on hooking her sword between the plates and pulling herself forward, one at a time. She slipped as it turned back toward the tear, catching herself steady on a spike as the mighty wings flapped.

Behind her, its tail was curled tight and she knew that clasped between the chinked scales would be the dead of that place, of that city.

It was too much to bear, and pulling up, Ami regained her footing and continued on.

More spikes rose from its skin, those that moved with its wings and met like knives to cut her path. She slashed at them as they came to meet, and felt the Dragø falter, roar, its foot reaching up to scratch at the irritant. Ami had to duck and hide behind one of the platelets, hearing the monstrous scrape of talon on scale. A moment later though normal flight resumed, and they were back on course for the great orange tear.

Ami forged ahead, clambering over the dragon's back. If she could get to the head before it reached the rip ... but the rip was so close now, and by the time she'd battled her way to its neck, they were already passing through it.

The terrain changed dramatically, the sea and the fiery land below replaced in a moment with a city street seen through the infected wound of reality's rip. She saw overturned cars and bodies left discarded in the wake of the layer's wrath, and had only a moment in which to make a jump.

The way ahead was a treacherous path across its narrower neck, its spine a series of smoothened humps and sharp bristles. Ami made a run for it, jumping and landing at the centre of its neck as the dragon loosed its flame, and with a *pop* they broke through into the world beyond.

Their entrance was an explosion of brick and tarmac as they smashed through the roadway and through the corner of a high rise building. Ami dropped and clung to its neck as they flew higher, talons clipping and tearing, the fire rushing beneath her with a roar.

Screams followed them into the air as the dragon's tail was lowered to collect the roasting dead, and when they swooped low, Ami dared a look up into the rip that had torn through the entire city. It stretched for miles in either direction, smaller cracks of orange surrounding the major bleed, other movements coming from it as *things* from other layers crawled and staggered and slunk through to invade, lost and scared and vengeful. Black creatures groaned and clawed their way across roads and scattered steel cable, crushing cars and bodies alike.

She didn't want to see anymore and turned away, back to her path. Only a short way to go, the climb to the head, and then ... She hoped it would be enough.

With a further earth-shattering roar, they sailed up into the air, preparing to return. Ami ran as the beast's head lowered, jumping and skipping, sliding smooth scale just as it rose up once more.

The rip in front pulsed, the layers waiting beyond all doomed, all condemned.

It was then that Ami knew what she meant to do, and with only two wings and a prayer, she raised her sword and jumped. The Dragø's skull was armoured in smaller scales, and as she touched down on them it flipped its head and loosed its fire. Ami spun in the air and landed upon the snout, two terrible red eyes, double her height, blazing with stolen power.

She turned from them and hunkered down, facing the fast approaching rip. Even as it shook its head and snapped its fierce jaws trying to shake her free, she held tight, letting her body slip into light; and then, a moment before they'd enter the seismic rip, Ami skipped forward and slashed the air in front of them, cutting into the layer.

With a *boom,* she was blown from the beast's nose and thrown backward, her hand finding grip on the spines of its neck, her sword finding purchase in the back of the dragon's skull—

—and suddenly there was no longer sound, only a constant whine that filled the world with a bad chord. Her eyes closed and refused to open, and for just a moment it seemed it might all be done.

SHE SAW A WORLD DESTROYED by fire, the change so sudden. Those who were flighty took caution in the air, while those who were curious stayed.

She saw the one who couldn't move, captured in the fast slowing waters of a river. Its captor had bound it there to study it through a looking glass, holding it there to poke and to prod, to sketch notes into his leather bound books. He was a man unknown, but Ami understood who he was. He was from the *other* layer, the one soon to be merged with Darkscape. A scholar, a magician, a professor? Did it matter? The dragon was caught in the river, and then the rapture came.

The man had gone and had not returned, but the binding spell still held the creature, and when the river turned to steam and the land became scorched and burned, when reality shifted at speed and without grace, it was still there, protected. It watched as others perished, their skin flayed. It was alone in a world of death.

The earth beneath collapsed and the beast slipped into it, emerging from another river in another place, its hunger renewed ...

Chapter Nineteen

The palace shredded in an eruption of lava that spewed its fount against the canvas of the night, painting the moon in blood before falling to chase Hero to the river; but the river was now a cut of amber ash and smoke that turned the world black with smog, leaving Hero blind as he fell.

Wind rushed in his ears, the journey seeming to last a lifetime, though he knew at any moment he would hit the ground or be lashed by fire, lanced by rock—it would all end soon—yet down and down he still fell, flailing and choked by death's inevitable grip.

The underbellies of lava-kissed clouds swirled and filled the heavens, eventually fading to blue, a new sky emerging behind a knit of branches.

He'd not landed, yet beneath him lay a cushion of soft reeds, perfumed by petal and flower, dry bark and grass, and to each side a cluster of trees that bowed low to make an arch above him. To his left was a pond where small beasties danced, skimmed and skidded across the lily-covered surface. *Perhaps I am dead after all,* he thought, though he felt alive enough, his aches and pains screaming in agreement as he grasped at the nearest old oak and pulled himself up, leaves skittering to the ground between long stalks and blades.

The view beyond was that of fields and meadows, reminding him of the Planrus Lands back home, the green and yellow grass quivering under a wind that swept across the prairie in waves. There were more clusters of trees scattered all the way to the horizon, yet no wood or forest to join them that Hero could see, though the land cantered and sloped in places, and could have hidden many a treasure within. Wild flowers sprouted the ground around the pond, fed by the still water. A beautiful land, though empty and unfamiliar. There was nothing of Darkscape here and nothing of Legacy. Nothing of Ami. *I've been swallowed by the layers.* Looking back up to the sky he saw the long orange gash he'd fallen through, a cut across the sun that stretched for miles in either direction. It looked sore and infected, its edges dark and red.

He stepped out from beneath the shade, shaking his sore limbs and massaging his taut neck, letting the wind touch him and soothe him, cooling his burnt skin. "It's the end of the world, Ami," he whispered, "the end of everything."

Not everything, a voice whispered somewhere within.

Ami?

That's when he heard the hooves, the gentle *thud-thud thud-thud* muted and close, heavy in the grass. He turned to listen, honing in on the direction and seeing a momentary flick of movement somewhere in the dip of land unseen. And again, the rise and fall of a rider upon a steed.

Hero grabbed for his sword and held it out, half turning to watch the skyward tear falter and flux, the centre beneath the sun dipping slightly as if torn flesh. His shoulder throbbed and the sword in his hand felt unnaturally heavy, yet he presented it ready and stood his ground.

The hooves slowed and the rider came into view, a girl with long blonde locks tossed and flying back from her face as she met the stronger wind. Wearing a simple dress of marred white, she carried no load and rode the white stallion without saddle, her bare feet swinging freely without stirrup.

She pulled up to his side, her fair pale face staring down at him.

"Lower your sword," she said.

Seeing no danger, Hero let his blade dip to the ground.

"Is that your doing?" she asked, pointing to the tear beyond the trees.

Hero shook his head. "No, my lady, it is not."

Her brow furrowed. "Who are you?"

"I am Hero of the Guard—"

"Of Legacy," she finished.

"Yes, but how did you know? Have we met?"

Somewhere far off, thunder rumbled. Clouds were gathering where there had been none only moments ago. Something was happening.

"I am sure we have not," the girl said, steadying her horse, "and yet you look familiar."

He thought that she looked familiar, too, though he was also sure he'd never set eyes on her before. She looked young, perhaps in her early twenties, yet her clear blue eyes bespoke wisdom and knowledge. He stared into them until she looked away, back to the tear.

"I am Infinity, of the Forlorn Forest. What is the meaning of this disturbance?"

Hero could only shrug and sigh. "Infinity, you say?"

"That is my given name." The thunder rolled closer, the white wisps of clouds now darkening and sailing for the tear. "Is it a passage to another world?" Her eyes fell on him again. "It is, isn't it? That is where you are from."

"Do you know this, or are you guessing? Do you know Romany?"

Her eyes widened. "No, I—I don't ..."

Time was running short. The tear was changing and looking more a scarred mouth, its lower lip bulging and pouting, rolling back into grin. *Isn't it funny? Isn't it? Laugh then,* it taunted.

It's her, the same voice whispered.

Ami?

Hero, heard above the brewing storm, felt beyond the wind.

Fields were falling to dusk swiftly as clouds teamed together to blot out the sun, leaving only the light of the mouth, a grotesque gargoyle laughing. The horse whickered, the girl holding lightly to its mane.

"Hero, I can hear voices in the dark," she said. "I must get back to my people."

"No, wait," he said. "Are you ... are you Ami?"

"I am Infinity," she said, sounding scared. Soon she would ride, but Hero needed answers.

He took hold of her hand. "Do you know of Ami, the Assassin Princess?" Thunder burst from clouds above them, scaring them both; she gripped his hand tight, and in that moment he felt the essence of something familiar, someone familiar, the feel of power passing between them. *The horse, the girl, the layers. Not Ami.* "Florence?"

The grin fell as the lip was cut, and drips of burning fire hit the ground and began a blaze. The layer was coming apart, and this world would soon be destroyed. He pulled her close to him.

"Florence? Florina? Is that you?"

She gasped, eyes wide and flashing. She gripped to him tightly. "That name. That name?"

It's her, the voice said, *infinity—the power never dies.* The voice was close now, and Hero thought he knew where. The drips of the leaking layer had already made a pyre taller than the trees, yet beyond it he could see a figure, barely there in silhouette, her arms raised and beckoning.

Hero, come.

Ami.

"Come, now," Hero said, holding onto the girl as she leaned too far from her horse. Her hands found his face and stroked soft against his growing beard.

"No, no, I cannot. I must go to my people. They need me. Hero ... I do not know how I know you, or how I know the name you give me." She pulled him toward her now, surprisingly strong. "But I know what you need; the voice is telling me. *She* is telling me."

Hero looked back to the pyre, the rip sliding down like a zip, a terrifying bridge of light emerging from the centre. Could he see buildings within? There were people, he was sure, some screaming, and between the chaos and the fire the shape of the Shadow Princess danced, a sweet melody he'd heard before trembling in the stormy air.

"Come with me," he urged, but the girl stayed stolid, her thighs tightly wrapped against her horse. "This world is about to die."

"You can stop it." She reached forward and placed her hand over his sword, the steel shining bright beneath her touch. The world lit a halo around them in a glorious white—but all too soon the girl grew tired and slumped, the power drained from her, captured in the sword. "Now you can stop it," she breathed. "Quickly, Hero."

Hero, come.

The thunder came again, rumbling and tumbling in the sky. The tear in the layer flashed and dropped, another world opening only a step away. The horse moved backward, its rider now fully seated.

"Go, Hero," she cried, before turning tail and galloping away into the darkness, down into the slope of the land hidden from view. He could not hear her hooves this time, the thunder too loud and monstrous.

"Good luck," he whispered, and turned to the fire beyond the trees. With only a quickened beat of his heart, Hero ran.

Out in the open he felt exposed, caught in the spotlight centre stage, seeing through the blur of other layers, other lands, mountains and ships, towers and turrets. *They're all there, each and every life ever lived.* And they were all going to die.

"Ami, please help," he panted, his approach to the fire swift.

Hero, come.

A flamed hand passed through the fire wall, a sword lit a purple green, and as the sky ripped across and consumed the entire world, he jumped forward, falling into the flames and landing in a cold, black earthen tunnel. Dust and earth sifted and fell between shafts of burning light, the entire tunnel under threat of collapse.

Hero ran, forward into the darkness his lungs burning, his feet hurting, while howls and shrieks of creatures unknown chased his steps, below, above and beside him, through thin crusts of reality that were quickly breaking away. The tunnel turned and opened to a chamber that echoed with rumbled thunder, and to his right a slope dragged upward, wet and sludgy; the air came fresher from there.

He followed it as rocks fell and the earth above collapsed into the hollow, his last leap throwing him clear out and into the night. But the night was dark and just as deadly.

Hero rolled and groped through wet mud and stone to right himself, crawling the bank to the crest of the rise. There, he looked down upon the tense scene, air pensive as just before a storm ...

An ear-splitting *boom* burst with a hollow thrum, and Hero watched through wide eyes as the wild greens and forests of Darkscape fell suddenly into the earth, smoke and flames rising along with the mighty roar of a beast.

Ami.

He thought of nothing and no one else in that moment as a dark creature blotted the burning sky, dark wings spreading dominance and shadow over everything. An ignited breath of noxious flame fanned out upon the town.

Oh, Ami.

Below the burning inferno, a mass exodus was taking place as hundreds of townsfolk made their way out of the woods and up the rise toward him; all muddy torsos and bloodied limbs, they drew close, chattering and sobbing, wailing and walking, evacuees headed for the sea.

The water was a welcome thought. Waves from another world where no fire could take hold ... They came in their masses, approaching and dividing, swarming either side of him and paying him no mind. Why should they? He was not their leader, just a stranger in the dirt.

The beast's wrath shook the earth as he spun and rose to follow the crowds, the townsfolk screaming as one, eyes frightened and flighty, scarves, blankets, furs and jerkins drawn closely over the elderly and the young. Those that cried did so in heavy sobs as they made their way to the cliff, and to the temple tower at its end.

Hero set his sights on the beast, whose wings flapped and flagged and rose and fell. There was no trace of Romany—unless she were the devil driving the creature—yet Ami? A faint green glow of light answered his fears and hopes.

He must go to her.

Fighting through bodies, Hero dragged himself down the other side of the slope and into the wood, now singed and fallen. The ground had opened up in an eerie light that low-lit snapped and bowing branches, trunks and splintered stumps. A sure path was marked only by the diminishing lines of fleeing shadows, but it wasn't hard to find his way to the town's outer wall, fallen rubble and stone, wood and iron. The fire was low here, and Hero was able to climb the mound easily, crawling through to the street beyond.

It was unrecognisable. Houses that had pressed tight against one another had fallen, fire consuming everything. Roofs were now devil's bonnets, stars hiding behind fanned and flickering tongues. The cobbles were stepping stones across the layer-light, and the dead were scattered all around; and reigning above all the plunder and squander, was the black dragon.

Hero broke into a run, his sword in his hand, Ami's name on his lips.

AMI STAGGERED TO HER feet as the dark dragon cast its fire upon the remains of the town, its huge form blundering, stomping on what remained of Romany's palace.

In her absence Darkscape had been destroyed by the breaking of the layers, and Ami could only hope that its people had time to get to safety, though she knew that many of them wouldn't have.

Hero ...

The night was alight with fire, and everything burned, yet Ami had one last job to do before she could consider anything else.

At the base of the dragon's neck, her sword still protruded, embedded in its skull and fluxing power. She would need to remount the beast and quickly, and so, with all the energy and power she could muster, the Princess of Legacy passed into light one final time.

All her senses heightened, like the cold nip of a winter's frost, the burns and scars and wounds she'd yet to register disappearing completely; she readied herself, standing upon air and light, remembering the unicorn's lessons, his words of magic and power. *You can be all, be anything, be power, be pure.* And pure she was, limbs and torso, a ghost of her own. Noises dimmed, and the world brightened, and Ami was the most powerful being alive.

Dangerous.

But someone was coming, someone near.

Ami spun to find the movement of a man between founts and flames.

Hero.

Blackened and bleeding, he held his sword aloft.

HERO HAD FLOWN DOWN the street, jumping cracks and gaps and dead bodies alike. In many places whole sections of the town had fallen and caved into the earth; all burned and the street was but a boulevard between fault lines of fire. *Fire.* So much of his life had involved fire, whether lightly touched to the wick of a lamp, or blazing across a riotous city, doused by barrels of brine on the backs of Guards. Fire called the Shadow Princess, while the power thrived like fire in almost every way. *A life of flame.* And now, having run the broken hill, climbed and mounted many a hurdle of brick and body, he stood in the midst of the largest and darkest creature he'd ever seen. And yes, there was fire! As tall and as wide as Legacy Castle, the black, winged monster strode through volcanic lakes and rivulets where there had been a palace, a river, trees and a town—and standing away from its mighty form, drenched in a white fireless-light, was his princess.

"Ami," he breathed, running the edge of a large crevasse in the earth that divided them. He held his sword up as she turned toward him.

"Stay back, Hero," she cried, and he followed her gaze, seeing Ami's sword in the dragon, a jade pin within its skull.

"Let me help!" Hero panted. "You are my princess, and I am your Guard. I'll not let you die here!"

"You'll not help by being killed," she said. "Go back to Legacy. Here." After a moment of searching, she retrieved the golden rook from her person and threw it to him. He caught it. "Take it to the temple, to the first step. Take Florence and Raven."

"They're gone. Florence to a layer where ... she may already be dead. Raven, too, though I don't know ..." He walked closer, slipping the totem into his garments. He pointed to the Dragø. "We're all that stands in this creature's way." *And we're all each other has got,* he didn't add. The dragon had already begun making its way past the burning town, readying its wings to take flight toward the sea, toward the people. "The townsfolk. It'll—"

"Kill them all," Ami finished, sighing a ruffled sigh before holding out her hand to him. "Come on then."

Hero reached across the dance of fire for Ami's ghostly hand, their fingers touching and sliding together in unison. He felt the magic there, the power that had made her almost translucent, and iridescent.

Suddenly, they were both flying up into the sky, curving an ascent across a summit of flames. As fearful as he was, Hero trusted Ami wholly, and kept his eyes wide open as they descended and landed heavy upon the town's hill, now hell's inferno. He had time enough to gasp a lungful of char and burn before they were off again, this time the leap taking them higher, through the thick smoke and ash, and down upon the dragon's back.

Hero's worn boots caught a scale as they landed, tripping him—but Ami held him steady.

"This is suicide," she said, "for you."

"Everyone is going to die, and besides, I have this," he touched his sword, "and you." His fingers stroked her wispy cheek, but fell as the beast crashed through blackened and burning trees, its talons tearing through layers beneath, cracks falling and opening like old sores, raging and bleeding—the world was hurting. He wondered, and not for the first time, how Legacy faired. Was it still there at all?

They held to the plates at the Dragø's back, eyes on the sword within its skull; the sight and sound of the people gathered at the cliff's edge came fast into view where they surrounded the temple. Hero felt the rook safe against his thigh. *In the temple,* he thought, *I use it at the temple step.* But he wasn't planning on leaving without her.

Clasping her hand, Hero readied himself for the leap to the beast's neck.

"We need to drive the blade down and kill it," she said. "Are you with me?"

"Always," he mouthed, his hand feeling the tight bond they'd formed months ago. "My princess."

Fire bellowed and arced across the fractured ground, while screams and cries rose from the thousands gathered by the sea; waves gunned the rocky coast and fire ripped through the land upon the rise—and between the two, the innocents sheltered against their tower of false hope.

The two launched hand in hand and landed upon the skull, Ami twisting to grab her sword, and Hero to plunge two-handed deep with his own. The dark green fire whipped them, slapping visions like memories into their minds: the lush land of colour and beauty of the lakes, the forests, the wooded mountainsides, and of course, the skies of the vast, clear air, far above the flight of birds. Wings spanned and unfurled, never casting a shadow upon the land far below. Only peace above, tranquillity, harmony, until ... the fall of the sky and the rise of the wizard—and who was to say which came first? Hero saw this and all that Ami had seen before.

His blade pierced the dragon's armour and released Florina's power, joining that of Ami's sword, now sunk hilt-deep.

A moment passed as the Dragø slowed and stopped just shy of the temple.

Then he fell, swift and sudden, a blast of power exploding and throwing them back, away and into the darkness that awaited them.

In that darkness, Hero heard the birdsong, and the bubble of a virgin stream.

Chapter Twenty

and there shall be light to follow the darkness, a voice said, ••• somewhere.

SHE WALKED THE SHORT cut grass, stepping lightly up to the raised platform, one booted foot placed upon the first white step; it was so beautiful. The roses bloomed and flourished, all fallen petals forgotten bar one that spun and lifted, blood red and pale pink against the sun. It dropped, touching the clear water stream that now ran beneath the walkway. From there it went with the flow, past her and beyond, into the black trees of elsewhere. She watched it for a while, wondering where it would go now, to which world, if any at all? Perhaps it would find its way to Romany, lost forever she thought, somewhere ... Perhaps she was still here, now part of this layer, this stranded part of a world gone. There was no way to know.

A giggle sounded, and Ami looked over to the arches to see the small girl who'd later be her mother, Grace, and beside her, smiling down at her, her shadow-self.

"Hello again," the girl sang out.

Ami waved but the girl was already dancing away, spinning barefoot off the side of the platform and onto the grass, following the river's course into the dark lands beyond.

"She cannot be away for long," her shadow said, her body the exact double of her own, down to the clothes, the ruined leather outfit, torn and ripped and bled on. "She'll be back."

"What of the dragon? And Hero?" *Hero, of course, Hero.* She looked about but saw no trace of him here.

"You did it," she said. "It has been done, and your man is with you."

"What about the layers?"

"Healing slowly. They have been badly wounded, and already some are crossing over to explore. It's inevitable. The damage has been done." She touched the columns, stroking them, inspecting them casually. "Boom."

Ami cocked her head, frowning. "Did you just say—"

"Boom," she said again, and as she did a clap of thunder echoed over the word. Ami jumped. *"Boom."* Her lips moved but the skies spoke, blue turning to grey, the sun blotting and hidden.

Boom.

The landscape changed and sunlight burned golden against flames that rose and settled across a wasteland of destruction. Everything was fuzzy, blurry, her hand coming away from her face red with blood. Her head pounded, and by the feel of it many bones were broken.

"Where the—how?" Ami wiped her eyes of the already drying, sticky wetness, the first clear thing seen, a white flare sailing through the sky followed quickly by another *boom.*

"Princess? Are you okay?"

Hero was beside her. She turned and fell into his arms. It felt natural, and she needed no explanation when he kissed the side of her head and ran his fingers through her hair, her plait undone and long gone. His voice soothed, close and gentle. "Look at this."

Had her eyes closed? She guessed they had, for when she opened them, all seemed too bright. They lay on the grass, what was left of it, staring across at the felled body of the Dragø. It seemed now just a dark mass of scales, burning in its own flame, its long neck stretching to the very cliff edge, the destroyed head mercifully hanging over to the sea. Dead lay in its path, but also many thousands of the living, crowding around in hushed chatter, watching the beastie burn. A scale popped and scared them, launching high into the sky before exploding, this time in purple-green.

Ooo's and *aaah's* rose beneath nervous giggles and chortles, reminding Ami of cold November nights around a bonfire. Sparks fell to the grass and disappeared between the still exposed cracks of layers, the orange light strong, but growing weaker with the coming dawn. Some cracks began to close as power shot up and fell between them—but others did not. Ami guessed it would take a long time; there was so much destruction.

"It's hers, Florina's." Hero sighed a shuddered breath.

"What is?"

"The power," he said, pointing vaguely as another *boom* tore the night and sparkled out across the sea. "It's all that's left of her magic. She gave it to me."

Ami turned in his grasp and looked into his eyes, seeing the sorrow there, watching a tear shiver and fall. They stayed like that for a time and watched the last of the power shoot and fall. Ami folded into Hero and when the time seemed right, they stood up and strode away from the burning dragon.

"Is she going to be alright?" a small girl asked as they passed the temple tower, away from the crowd.

He looked down to her, and then to Ami and smiled. "She will be."

The girl nodded and reached up to touch Ami's arm, but Ami could no longer see, think, or really walk on her own. All of a sudden she was just so tired. The girl let go and they continued on, Hero guiding her to a far edge of the cliff where no one was, where green shrubs still clung, hiding the fractured rock. There they sat and looked out to sea, out to the bloom of a new day at the end of the longest night.

HE REACHED FORWARD and kissed her lips, and she allowed it, smiling. "I've been wanting that for ... a while."

"Me, too," Hero admitted. "I was only ever frightened of what it would mean."

"But it feels right," she said, and he nodded.

They let a quiet moment pass, his arms around her.

SOMETIME LATER, THEY passed through the crowd, dirty and scared, hungry and lost, all clustered around the temple. What were they to do? Some asked this, and some just wept and watched the eventual rise of the sun as it crested whole and magnificent across the eternal sea. Ami had no answer for them. None at all.

Together they entered the strange temple, the rook in Hero's hand. Men and women knelt in rags facing the stair, the sacred well hidden beneath the last step down. They did not stir as Ami and Hero stepped up to their sacred altar and stood upon it.

He placed his hands around her waist.

"This might not work," she warned.

He made no reply, only took Ami's hand, the chess piece between them.

THE SHACK LOOKED THE same as before, though it didn't feel the same at all. There was no magic left; for whatever reason, the power had gone from the place. It was only old now, old and abandoned and cold.

Hero placed his hands on her shoulders and led her outside, and they walked together in silence, hands touching, almost too exhausted to hold. At some point the rook had disappeared, though by the time either of them had noticed they were already back at the cabins, and it could have dropped anywhere. Even Grammy's supposed brother seemed absent, and all the lights in the big house were off—if there had been cracks between the layers here, they'd healed fast and were no longer evident.

Soon they were in the cabin, and when the night came it was mild and uneventful. Ami introduced Hero to the shower, taking one herself after he'd finished, and by shrinking her sword to a covert pencil once more, she was able to sketch out for him a new set of robes, pulling them from the page into reality. They were the same plain robes the Guard always wore, but they were clean and warm.

The rest of the night was spent in each other's arms, and a few kisses in they fell into a sleep more sound than either of them had had in a very long while.

THE MORNING CAME AND went, and the afternoon had turned to early evening before they were ready to leave. Hero had showered again and dressed in his new robes, while Ami lingered by the cabin door, looking out on a world she knew too much about. The little path into the woods now looked neglected, and it seemed so long ago that she'd arrived. Something had led her here ... Romany? Grammy? The power itself? She shook her head.

Hero stood beside her, set to return to Legacy, while Ami herself had packed for home though she wasn't going home, not yet.

His eyes burned for her, and she wanted him badly.

"You should come with me," Hero whispered, coming close, his hands sneaking around her waist.

"I will," she said, "but not until I've found them." Hero had told her of Raven and Florence, and though poor Raven's fate was unknown, it seemed Florence had somehow changed with the power and become someone new—Infinity, another piece to a greater puzzle.

"You may never find them," he said. "I don't think Florence could have survived."

"I think there's more to her. She's been changed in so many ways—she's not like us. She's a unicorn."

"She's like you. I wish I could come with you."

"Your place is in Legacy. Keep a home for them to come home to."

"I hate parting from you," he confessed, reaching in for a tender kiss that she allowed. A second she would not, for a third would follow and then she'd never be able to let him go.

"I hate it, too," she said, stepping back, "but until we know their fate, I can never be happy, and neither could you." She pulled the pencil from her pocket, the shaft lengthening in purple strobes, sharpening to a blade.

Hero nodded, and stepped aside, allowing her a good swing.

With a circular motion, she cut into the ground, allowing the power to flow through as it sliced the layers and created her a portal to Legacy.

"Come soon," he said, and with a fleeting stroke of her cheek, he stepped in.

The rift sealed a moment later, and he was gone.

Her knees gave as she collapsed to the floor in tears, letting out her love and her sorrow, and everything in between.

AMI COLLECTED HER BELONGINGS and started up the long driveway, leaving the cabins, the house, and the shack behind. She'd left all the money she owed on the dresser.

Out onto the lone country road, her thoughts were with Hero, and sometimes Romany. She'd been so alone. She also thought of the Dragø and the wizard who'd sought to use him and study him.

Raven and Florence could be anywhere, true, but there *was* somewhere she could start looking. Deep in the dark mountains of Noxumbra, Adam had created a castle, a castle of dark and twisted things. In that castle Adam had sought their father, opening portals to numerous and unknown layers. Perhaps there was something there she could use? It was a start, and however dark a place, it remained part of her legacy.

Pausing her trek, Ami slipped the pencil from her pocket again and sketched a doorway in mid-air. It fell open, swirling white, purple and green.

"I'll see you soon, Hero," she whispered, and blew a kiss into the air, before stepping through into the rip, into the infinite unknown.

Acknowledgements

I'd like to thank my constant source of strength and love, my girlfriend, Emi, who sticks by me through thick and thin. Additional thanks must also go to my beta readers for taking the time to go through this book and provide valuable feedback.

Also by Blake Rivers

The Assassin Princess Novels
The Assassin Princess
A Step into Darkscape
The Assassin's Codaci

Watch for more at https://buxhall.uk/blakerivers.